DELTA

New York Times and *USA Today* Bestselling Author
Jasinda Wilder

Copyright © 2025 by Jasinda Wilder

DELTA

ISBN: 978-1-964892-99-3

All rights reserved. This book or any portion thereof may not be reproduced or used in any manner whatsoever without the express written permission of the author except for the use of brief quotations in a book review.

This is a work of fiction. Names, characters, businesses, places, events and incidents are either the products of the author's imagination or used in a fictitious manner. Any resemblance to actual persons, living or dead, or actual events is purely coincidental.

DELTA

1

ON HOLIDAY...SANS PARENTALS

My stomach does excited, nervous little flips as the enclosed cable car lift ascends to the peak of the Matterhorn. On my left, my younger brother Killian is obsessively—nervously—fidgeting with a zipper on his jacket. On my right, Cal—Uncle Val and Aunt Kyrie's son and my BFF/sister/cousin Rin's younger brother—seems perfectly at ease, absently tapping his snowboard against his unclipped boot.

We're on a solo skiing holiday in the Swiss Alps—solo meaning without our parents; we still have an embarrassing gaggle of bodyguards that follow us everywhere we go. For example, in this skycar with us are Roger, Albie, Gleason, Cutter, Zidane, and Kazinski—two guards for each of us; the men are kitted out with their own skis and cold weather gear, full visored helmets with built in comms, and probably an armory's worth of weapons...most of which are probably extraordinarily illegal in most of Europe. But they're with A1S, and we're the children of, respectively, Layla and Nicholas Harris and Valentine and Kyrie Roth. They can get away with it.

In the car behind ours is another group of guards who will spread out around us, skiing down ahead of us, fanning out behind us, and making the run down at our flanks. These, we won't see for the most part. They're geared to blend in, and we don't know what they look like, on purpose, so we can't give them away. Yes, we have personal bodyguards as well as undercover, plainclothes bodyguards we'll never see, unless shit hits the fan.

I fucking hate it.

Guards, guards, everywhere I go. Head to the ladies' room? A guard waits outside. Head to town for dinner and drinks? Guards in the lobby, guards outside, guards in the kitchen, guards at the back doors. Meet a guy at the club and go to a hotel to hook up? Yep, I'm followed to the hotel, my guards waiting a discreet distance down the hallway, watching the elevators, stairwells, and emergency exits.

And windows, for snipers.

I'm pretty sure there are snipers watching us from somewhere, too. Or a satellite. I don't know that for sure, but I suspect it.

You know how those hairs on the back of your neck stand up when you're being watched? I have that feeling *all the time*. It's as fucking awesome as you'd expect.

"Brynnie." Killian elbows me. "Are you sure about this? This isn't Vail. It's the fucking Matterhorn."

"I'm sure about it, Killy," I say, trying to sound nonchalant when I'm as nervous as he is. "If you're scared, don't go down. Ride the car back around and go chase ski bunnies in the lodge or something. I don't give a shit what you do."

Killian sighs in irritation. "God, you've been such a bitch since—" he cuts off with a wide-eyed glance at me, recognizing the danger he was about to put himself in. "It's a big damned mountain and I haven't been skiing in a couple years."

Cal reaches across me to whack Killian's knee with the back of his mittened hand. "You'll be fine, Killy. Stick with me."

Killian just lets out another sharp, short sigh, nodding. "I've got this." He's muttering to himself, but loudly enough that I can still make out his words. "I'm a badass. I can do this."

I suppress a snicker of laughter—if you have to tell yourself you're a badass, then you're not a badass. I don't mock him out loud though—he's right, I have been a bit of a bitch lately.

Or, if I'm being brutally honest with myself, a colossal, mega, ultra bitch. Super bitch. Bitch extraordinaire. Bitch-tastic. And it's not his fault, the poor guy. But he's my younger brother, so he tends to get the brunt of it more often than he deserves.

I mean, I've got my reasons, sure, but that's no excuse for how I've treated him.

I lean against him. "You'll be fine, Killy. You're a great skier. It's like riding a bike, I promise. Just go slow at first and stay to the sides until you get your legs under you again."

"Pizza, French fries, huh?" he says, laughing. "They don't have bunny hills in the Alps, I guess."

"Somehow I doubt it," I answer.

The skycar slows to a stop and lets us off. Cal is first off, pushing away from the loading zone with one foot still loose, getting out of the way so Killy and I can get clear. I join him and click into my skis, shove my hands into the oversized mittens, and grip my poles while Killian follows, doing the same.

We make our way to the mouth of the run, adjusting goggles, tugging hats and hoods in place, wiggling our hands in our gloves and mittens.

Cal pulls his balaclava up around his mouth. "See you losers at the bottom!"

He stomps his boot into the clip, hops to put his left foot forward, and carves down the slope.

"So much for sticking with me," Killian mutters. "Fuck-tard."

I nudge him, pulling my scarf up around my mouth and nose. "Go. I'll follow."

Roger and Albie, Cal's guards, are scrambling to catch up to their ward. Gleason and Zidane, my stalkers—I mean, guards—are close by, ready to go, as are Cutter and Kazinsky, my brother's.

Killian rolls his shoulders, lets out a breath. "Fuck this. Let's go, bitches!"

He launches himself down the slope with a jump and a push of his poles—*way* too fast.

"Goddammit! Killy! Slow the hell down!" I shout.

I glance at Cutter and Kazinsky. "Well?" I gesture after Killian. "Go get him! He breaks a leg, it's on you two."

They both respond with muffled "Yes ma'am's" and bolt down the mountain after my brother, who, despite his nerves, is blasting almost straight down, only kicking out to arrest his momentum here and there.

"Fuck," I mutter. "The little shit is gonna get himself paralyzed."

I totally ignore my guys and take off down the mountain after the boys at a more responsible pace, making long, lazy esses back and forth across the width of the run.

I breathe easier on the way down—with my guards behind me, this is as free as I'll get. I blast past a slower-moving couple, kick my heels out to carve right around a long curve, and then settle back on my heels, poles tucked, as I swish a short, shallow series of slaloms.

Faster.

Faster.

Put all the boiling emotions down in their box and just enjoy the ride—-it's a perfect day, cold and clear, sunny and crisp. For a few minutes, I can pretend everything is normal.

There are no guards watching my every move with hawkish intensity.

The parents don't freak out if I miss a check-in by five fucking minutes, even though I'm a legit grown-ass adult.

And most of all, in this brief, pleasant fantasy, Zero

is still alive, waiting for me at the bottom wearing that stupid hat he loved so much—the one that made him look like a six-foot-five, lanky, black-haired version of Pippi Longstocking.

Alas, the run to the bottom is over all too soon. I cut hard at the last second and skid to a stop by the boys, spraying them both with a fine cloud of snow.

Killian, who had just removed his helmet, brushes his hair out. "Nice, Brynnie, thanks."

"You're welcome," I tell him, grinning. "You made it down in one piece."

He grins. "Sure did. Forgot how fuckin' fun skiing is. You guys ready to head back up?"

Cal steps on the release of his board to free his feet, scoops it up under his arm. "Been ready. Let's fuckin' go, slowpokes!"

That's Cal for you—first on the skycar and first off; first down the hill, first to the big waves back home. He's a daredevil, an adrenaline junkie. He loves anything that's reckless, fast, dangerous, or otherwise borderline psychotic. Uncle Val and Auntie Key hate it, but he's always careful and hasn't had any major accidents, and he's been putting in a lot of hours with Uncle Val, taking Rinny's place as his right-hand man, now that Rinny and Apollo are busy running Valkyrie.

On the ride up the mountain, I find myself missing my best friend. In the past, this trip would have been a foursome—the big sisters and the younger brothers… the way it's always been from the day we were born.

But now she's married and pregnant, and busier than ever, especially since Valkyrie went into business with Hunter Hawkins. And god, I'm jealous of Rinny for getting to meet that man. Talk about *fine*—the man is sex on a stick. I swear to Holy Moses I'd sell an ovary for five fucking minutes alone with him. Alas, he's happily encumbered with some lucky-as-fuck Alaskan bitch. And please understand that I'm only calling her a bitch because I'm green with jealousy. I bet he fucks like a god.

I let out a sigh. I miss Zero so damn bad, some days. Most days. Every day. All day.

All night.

I miss his messy black hair. I miss his green eyes and the way they sparkled greedily when he slid down to bury his face between my thighs. I miss the way he kissed me—all tongue and teeth, as if he was trying to actually eat me. I miss the way he'd roll over the moment he was conscious and nuzzle me and try to kiss me with his nasty-ass morning breath.

I miss his laugh.

I miss his cock.

I miss the music of him.

Okay, that's enough. I allow myself five to ten minutes a day to wallow in missing him, and then I force all that sorrow and anger into a cage, lock it, and put the cage back down in the depths of myself.

Does it work? Not really. Does it help a little? Sort of.

Mostly, I'm just a mess.

My phone buzzes, which is deeply annoying, since it means I have to take off my glove, unzip my jacket, dig down into the cavernous interior pocket where I keep it, and haul it out.

It's a text from Teddy, Zero's mom: a photo of Zero and me from this day a year ago, when we were touring the Pacific Northwest of the US with his band; the photo is a selfie taken by Zero. We're side-stage in Portland, and he has his mandolin in his hand held across my front with his arm around my shoulders. We're grinning ear to ear, and so, so happy. So in love.

> TEDDY: *Miss you, darling. Don't be a stranger.*

I heart the photograph, but hesitate on what to say back. I love Teddy to bits. I was over the moon excited to have her as a mother-in-law. She taught me how to make lasagna. We spent several memorable evenings together getting wine-drunk and telling embarrassing stories about Zero. We're bound together by the grief of his loss, so suddenly and so senselessly—a car accident. No one's fault. Just a wet road, a patch of black ice, and a head-on collision with a cement truck. He was dead instantly.

That was nine months ago.

I'm having a grief baby, I guess.

And yes, I've been to therapy. All sorts of it. Mama and Dad flew in an A-lister-approved therapist from LA, and she spent a week with us in the Keys, helping me process my grief. I did horse therapy. EMDR. Ketamine. But at the end of the day, I think you just have to grieve and be sad and try to move on.

I've got the first two down; I'm still working on the moving on part.

Cal, Killy, and I spend the day skiing; Cal and I race a few times. He wins twice, and I win three times, although Killy says the last one was a tie. Bullshit—I won.

When even the seemingly-tireless Cal says he's ready to call it, we pile into one of the SUVs and let Roger drive us back to the hotel. We spend the late afternoon and early evening napping, snacking, and watching TV in our respective rooms in the penthouse suite. Around seven or so, we head down to the hotel restaurant and have a long dinner, during which we chat idly about nothing in particular.

After dinner, the boys head for the elevators. I'm antsy and restless and in need of distraction.

"You guys wanna hit a club or something?" I suggest.

"Nah," Cal says. "I'm beat. I plan on hitting the slopes early tomorrow."

"Same," Killian says. "And also, you shouldn't hit up any clubs either, Brynnie. Remember what happened last time?"

"That was *not* my fault. I was behaving myself."

He arches an eyebrow. "There's a photograph of you dancing on a bar. Wearing a skirt so short, I'm *still* traumatized after seeing the photograph once for five seconds."

"Okay, well first of all, fuck you," I say. "I don't dress for your approval so you can fuck all the way off. Second of all, that photo was taken out of context. There were like eight other girls dancing on the bar. It was a dance-off. Which I won, by the way. They just only published that picture of me."

"Gleason had to carry you inside," he answers. "Because you were obliterated."

Gleason, behind us, does his best to look invisible—good luck with that one, buddy—he's a six-foot-eight former NFL linebacker who can bench press entire Volkswagens. He and Uncle Thresh often have arm wrestling competitions, and he can give Thresh a real challenge, which says something, seeing as Uncle Thresh is the strongest human being I've ever met.

I look at Gleason. "Was I obliterated, Gleason?"

Gleason looks frightened. "Um. I believe you passed out that night, ma'am."

I glare at him. "Sellout."

"Sorry, ma'am."

"Whatever." I sigh, wave a hand. "Fine. Be lame-ass losers. Go to bed even though it's barely midnight and we're on fucking holiday, by ourselves, with no parents."

"Right, because these guys are definitely *not* reporting our every move back to the parentals," Cal says, jerking his thumb at the six massive humans forming a wall of Brooks Brothers-clad muscle between us and the hotel foyer.

I look at Gleason. "Are you?"

"Am I what, ma'am?" he asks, endeavoring to look innocent.

"Reporting back to our parents."

He shifts his monumental weight from one foot to the other. "Erm. In certain cases, yes. Every move, no."

"So, when I met up with that guy from the bar in Berlin…" I say, leading. "Did you report that?"

"No, ma'am. I knew where you were, and I did a brief look into your…date. But I did not say anything about it to your parents."

"You looked into him?" I ask.

"Yes, ma'am," he says. "Of course. I photograph and investigate everyone you spend time with."

"Wow. I didn't know that."

"You're not supposed to."

I hum thoughtfully. "And? What did you find out about Eric?"

Gleason grimaces. "Um, his name was actually Kai, and he was pretty vanilla. Studying biology at the university in Berlin. Engaged for six months, the year before you met him, but they broke it off somewhat amicably, according to his social media. Excellent credit rating, and no priors."

"Kai. Right." I smile, remembering. "We had fun. He did this thing where—"

"SHUT THE FUCK UP RIGHT NOW!" Killian shouts. "I do *not* want to fucking know a single detail about your sexcapades, *sis*."

I pinch his cheek, laughing. "You're so easy to rile up, Killy-Billy. Like I'd actually tell you anything? Gross. No."

He flicks up both middle fingers and shoves them in my face. "You're a walking catastrophe." He punches the call button. "And if you call me Killy-Billy again, I swear to god I'll put Nair in your shampoo."

Cal wraps an arm around Killian's shoulders. "Killy,

buddy, do you remember when you and Bryn got in that prank war?"

"Fuck you," Killian mumbles.

"Do you?"

"Yes, I remember," Killian grumbles.

Cal claps him on the bicep. "I'm just saying, man, I'd think twice about starting that shit up again. Better to just let her call you Killy-Billy. You refused to come out of your room for a month until your eyebrows grew back."

I can't suppress a snort of laughter. "That was awesome."

"Oh yeah? How awesome was that ghost pepper powder in your underwear?"

"My vagina still burns just thinking about that," I admit. "Fine. Truce. Besides, I was just fuckin' with you."

The elevator finally arrives and we all pile in—all nine of us. Gleason does his best to wedge himself into the corner in an attempt to take up less space, but there's only so much you can do to reduce your footprint when you're six-eight and weigh three hundred-plus pounds.

I head back to my room, waving to my guys before I close my door. And to clarify, "the boys" means Killy and Cal; "the guys" means Gleason and Zidane. Zidane is a mystery. Six-foot even and lean, he's got dark brown skin, a shaved head and long beard, and never, ever speaks unless spoken to, and only then to say "yes ma'am" or "no ma'am." Once, I actually got a whole five words out of him: "I don't think so, ma'am." Basically, he's a scary shadow, one of those guys that just exudes fuck-off vibes. Of my two guards, he's the one who'd do the bloody work, if called for. Not that Gleason is just for show—after an injury ended his NFL career, he pivoted to security and made a name for himself single-handedly fighting off a dozen armed attackers who were trying to kidnap his A-list actress client…who got the whole fight on video. And posted it on TikTok. Gleason is TikTok famous *and* can throw down with the best of them. *AND* he's scary as fuck, despite generally being a big sweet teddy bear of a man.

Alone in my room, I try to watch TV, but after flipping through all the channels at least four times and finding nothing, I turn it off. I'm not sleepy, despite a day spent skiing.

I need to do something.

How can I get out of this room and past Gleason and Zidane undetected so I can go clubbing by myself?

Fire alarm? Too big and too obvious.

I can't ask the boys to cover for me, because the little bitches will squeal on me.

The only real option is to go down to the hotel bar and hope I can slip away. I'll have to turn my phone off since it's tracked six ways to Sunday, and if it's on, Uncle Lear can pinpoint my location anywhere on the globe within seconds. I'll also have to be creative about my outfit.

I put on my favorite silver sequined miniskirt paired with a strappy, slinky, low-cut, iridescent midriff-baring top. I leave my hair down and keep my face makeup free, and then put on a baggy pair of sweats and matching hoodie—stolen from Killian because they're worn and soft and cozy. The hoodie, coincidentally, is voluminous enough to hide the strappy silver wedge heels under it. Along with my clutch—which has my compact pink SIG Sauer 9mm, because I'm not a total idiot. Just mostly. I know, I know, guns are highly illegal in most of Europe, but I'm Bryn Harris, and people are fucking nuts. I may be foolishly ditching my bodyguards to go dance at a nightclub, but I'm not doing so unarmed. How will I get it past the club bouncers? Wait and see.

I grab my room keycard and clutch my phone in my hand as I leave the room, breezing past Gleason to the elevators. "I just need a nightcap, guys. I'm bored and can't sleep."

They follow me dutifully down to the bar and post up where they can see me and keep an eye on the bar and exits.

Now…we hope a distraction pops up.

I order a Moscow Mule from the dour old woman behind the bar and sip it, idly scrolling TikTok while surreptitiously watching the bar, looking for ways to create a distraction so I can get the fuck out of here and away from my babysitters.

My deliverance comes in the form of two groups of skiers—all bros who are all already drunk and are eyeing each other in a way that speaks of some kind of in-built cultural enmity I'm too American and too sheltered to know anything about.

Time to set things off. I let a guy from group A catch my eye and none-too-subtly eye-fuck him.

Let him buy me a drink.

Chat him up, flirty-flirty, *don't you wish you could see what I'm wearing under this baggy gray* sweatsuit.

I finish my drink and excuse myself to the little girls' room—a very real necessity since I'm on my third Moscow Mule and second glass of ice water.

When I head back, I act more tipsy than I am, and "mistakenly" join group B as if confused about who I was talking to.

More flirty-flirty.

Boy-toy from Group A is jealous and pissed off, and getting more so as I let the mark from group B get handsy.

Oh, yep, here he comes.

Words are exchanged.

Shoves are traded.

A punch is thrown.

Chaos ensues.

Here come Gleason and Zidane, on cue, ready to rescue li'l ol' Brynnie-Winnie from the big bad angry boys.

As if I needed rescuing from soft putz-fuckers like these tools.

But I digress.

In the chaos, I slip behind the bar, steal the bartender's security card from off of the register—she's hiding on the floor in a huddle, hands over her head. Which is, honestly, smart, because glassware has been thrown.

I toss a pint glass toward Zidane—it smashes behind him, and he and Gleason whirl to assess the threat.

I bolt through the scrum to the employees-only door, which is where the keycard comes into play.

Boom.

Almost free.

The hallway here is narrow and stacked with boxes of booze, plastic racks full of clean pint glasses, rocks glasses, and high balls.

Now I just have to find my way out of this maze of back hallways and outside.

It takes almost twenty minutes and a lot of wrong turns, but I eventually emerge into the cold night air, and hustle, shivering, away from the hotel to the nearest road. I use my phone to summon a car—thankfully, there's one around the corner and it arrives within a couple minutes.

I slide into the back seat, grateful for the piping hot interior.

"*Wohin?*" The driver is a middle-aged man of Middle Eastern heritage, speaking Arabic-accented German.

I name a nearby club, and he nods.

"*Sprichts du English?*" I ask.

He rolls one shoulder. "Little."

"If I pay you, will you stay near the club and wait for me for a couple of hours?" I ask.

"Wait? No ride other customer?"

"*Ja, bitte,*" I say, which is about the extent of my German.

He frowns at me in the mirror. Looks away, blinking—coming up with his number in his head. He holds up two fingers. "*Zwei hunnert.*"

I dig my purse out from beneath my hoodie and withdraw some cash from my wallet, showing him two hundred dollars. I give him a hundred-franc bill.

"The rest if you're still here in two hours," I tell him.

"Okay, *ja*. I wait." He takes the hundred and stuffs it in his hip pocket. "Two hour only. After, I go."

"Two hours," I agree. "*Danke*."

We pull up to the curb near the line, and he points to a parking lot down the road. "There. I wait."

I peel off the hoodie and sweatpants, switch my shoes, and fold the clothes into a pile on the seat. "See? I'll be back."

He just nods. "Two hour."

I step out of the four-door Audi sedan and hustle to the end of the line, which is, fortunately, short…seeing as I'll be a popsicle in about ten minutes out here in this brutally cold wind.

I reach the front of the line, and the burly bouncer juts his chin at my purse, flashlight at the ready. I open my purse, keeping my ID in hand, along with a pair of 100-franc bills.

The bouncer sees my ID first, and his eyes widen at my name—as the kids of very famous parents, I'm pretty well known by name, if not always by face. Plus, my social media presence is pretty big, if I do say so myself. Then he sees my gun.

I lean close and whisper to him. "You know who I am, and you know why I need that. It's for protection only, I promise."

The francs vanish into his meaty palm, and he

nods. "Don't get me fired," he mutters in English. "You won't like it if you do."

I smile sweetly at him. "I'm a perfect little angel."

He just snorts. "My daughter follows you on TikTok."

Unfortunately, that's really all that needs to be said. I'm…notorious, I guess, for shenanigans, getting into trouble, and being an all-around nuisance. Thus, the bodyguards—they're as much to prevent me from pulling stunts exactly like this to keep me safe.

I show him my powered-off phone. "Look, it's off. I just want to have fun…Kevin." I look way up at him. "Can I call you Kevin? You look like a Kevin." I bat my eyelashes at him.

He rolls his head. "Name's Jerry. Just…stay outta trouble, okay, Ms. Harris?"

I point at the black Audi visible down the road a way. "That's my driver. I'm paying him two hundred francs to wait two hours for me, and then I'm going back to my hotel. I promise."

He jerks his head at the club. "Go on." A big hand wraps around my wrist, and hard brown eyes fix on me. "No trouble."

I give him a saccharine smile and a cutesy little "who, me?" shrug. "Never."

I hurry inside out of the icy wind, rubbing my hands up and down my arms and then sticking my freezing fingers under my armpits.

Clicking on my heels down a low, dark, narrow hallway lit by a handful of neon signs, I descend a short set of stairs into the belly of the club. Dance music thuds and pounds, sending adrenaline and excitement surging into my veins. I'm dancing before I even hit the dance floor. I don't even need a drink, I just need this.

Sweaty bodies everywhere, the air so thick you can taste it, flesh against flesh, the rhythm pounding through you, abandoning yourself to the moment, to the music, to the palpable, unspoken unity of hundreds of people all moving to the same beat.

I dance my way through the crowd, pausing here and there to share a moment with a cute boy or two. I always move on; they're just boys.

Eventually, I find my way to a bar and order a vodka sprite and a glass of ice water, and ask the bartender for the time—I still have an hour.

Back into it.

More than a few boys try to keep my attention—sorry boys, Bryn's not on the prowl tonight. This is just for me.

Hands find my waist and a chest pushes against my back—I go with it for a few minutes, reach up and behind me to clutch a slick, sweaty neck. When his hands get handsy, I shrug out of his grip and vanish into the fray.

I wish I didn't have to count the minutes, I wish I could stay here all night. Just dance, drink, and forget everything.

I get another drink—thirty minutes left.

I don't want to cut it too close and miss my ride, as I know for a fact that the driver will bounce with my money and my clothes after two hours on the dot, so I decide to visit the bathroom before I make my exit.

I take care of my business and wash my hands. A pair of girls about my age are primping at the mirrors—one of them does a double-take.

"Are you Bryn Harris?"

I grin, shake her hand. "Hi, yeah."

"Can we take a selfie with you?"

I hesitate. "Okay, but you *cannot* post it until tomorrow. I don't want anyone to know where I am right now."

They agree, and we take the selfie…or ten. You know how it goes: you gotta take a dozen to get one good one. They each want a hug as well, and I'm finally exiting the bathroom. I'll never shake the imposter syndrome that comes from being famous—sort of—for nothing more than being my parents' kid. I mean, there've been big studio movies, indie films, streaming limited series, and even a short-lived weekly cable series based on Mom's and Dad's and Aunt Key's and Uncle Val's adventures before I was born. Shit, there's even talk about a limited series sequel being made about Rin's whole thing with Apollo.

I didn't do shit. I haven't done shit. I probably won't ever do shit to become famous. I'm just famous because of other people. Yet I have to pose for selfies with strangers in a club bathroom and then ask them not to post those selfsame selfies.

It's just a weird thing, and it's hard to know how to feel about it.

I leave the bathroom in a weird mood; the shine has rubbed off my little solo adventure. Time to head back to the hotel.

I hear a scuffle—the bathrooms in this club are located at the front of a long, dark hallway. At the end of the hallway is an illuminated exit sign casting a ghostly red glow on the silver of the emergency exit's crash-bar.

I peer, squinting; strobe lights flash from the dance floor, slicing stripes of sudden light, casting shadows—moving shadows.

A pair of large male figures wrestle with the smaller shape of a female. One has his hand around her mouth and is trying to subdue her arms, while the other struggles with her legs.

One of them barks something in a low growl, in a Slavic language of some sort. Or German? I don't know. A language I don't recognize, is the point. But to me, the tone of voice communicates a statement like, "Grab her legs, you idiot."

The other one responds with what I imagine to be: "I'm trying, asshole, she's very strong."

Fuck this shit.

Not on my watch, jackasses.

I creep down the hallway, pull my gun. Assume a nice solid Isosceles stance like I've been taught my whole life. Finger in the trigger guard but not on the trigger, yet.

"HEY!" I shout. "LET HER GO!"

In my mind, what will happen is very simple. I'll shout my challenge, and they'll see the gun and my imposing six-foot-tall frame and my adorable pink compact 9mm, and be so startled and afraid that they'll drop the girl and bolt out the exit, and I'll be a hero. The end. Cue the ticker tape parade. See my agent, Netflix.

The reality is a little different.

At my challenge, the ogre manhandling the girl's feet drops her kicking, writhing legs and stalks toward me, reaching behind his back.

Um, fuck.

Panic hits like a Mack truck, freezing me in place. Mom's words, Dad's words, Sasha's words, Uncle Duke's words all ring through my skull: "Never pull a gun on someone unless you're mentally prepared to pull the trigger and end a life. If you pull a gun and then freeze, you're fucked."

I've heard variations on that theme a billion times in my life. And I always thought to myself, "I won't freeze. Look who my parents are. Badassery runs in my veins."

Turns out I'm a coward. Or, at least, someone who freezes the first time the shit hits the fan.

The hulking ape-man is mere feet away from me, and I still have time to shoot. Or run. But my hand shakes. My finger simply will not curl around the trigger. The barrel wavers.

He's huge—six feet tall but broad as a barn, big-bellied, powerful, and good god almighty he stinks *so* fucking bad even from here. He laughs once, a cruel, amused bark.

He lashes out with a paw, knocking my gun aside, and then my gun is gone. His other hand swings around from the small of his back—at first, I think he has a pistol, but instead of shooting me, he jabs me in the side with it.

The sensation is unlike anything I've ever felt, and

I've been stung by jellyfish and broken bones. It's like a charley horse times infinity. Excruciating pain spears through my whole body, a hot, crackling, burning sensation radiating from my skin into my muscles and tendons. My whole body locks up. My teeth clench, and I go rigid. I can't scream, can't breathe. He catches me one-armed and lets me slump to the cold, sticky hallway floor. Barks something over his shoulder at his companion.

Something clatters across the concrete.

My skin burns, my muscles tingle, and I'm confused, disoriented. Conscious, but…scrambled.

He grabs the thing his partner passed to him—a syringe. He pulls the cap off with his teeth and jabs me in the arm, slowly depressing the plunger.

"Night-night, extra girl." His voice is low, cruel, and thickly accented.

Darkness swallows me.

My last thought is, *Well, fuck. This isn't good.*

2

A DEAL WITH THE DEVIL

THE RINGING OF MY MOBILE IS AN INSISTENT annoyance. For a while, I can tune it out. But it rings, rings, and rings, stops. Ring-ring-ring, stop. Ring-ring-ring, stop.

Three rings, a minute pause, three rings.

I fucking hate that pattern. The twat on the other end is a right fucking menace, a pretentious, self-absorbed, too-good-for-everyone pile of moldy goat shit, and a cocksucking turd with too much power and influence. I'd run my blade through his throat, given a half-chance. Too bad I fucking need him.

"Shouldn't you answer that?" This is the voice of my…companion. Shelly? Sheila? Sharon?

Something like that. Fuck if I know, and fuck if I care.

I grin down at her. "I will. When I'm ready. You just keep going, love. Ain't gonna suck itself."

I know, I know. I'm an arse. But I talked myself up to her flat after thirty minutes of conversation over a pint. And for further clarity, I led with, "Those pretty lips of yours would look lovely wrapped around my eight-inch cock."

So here we are. And they do. So she can't be bothered by me being an insensitive prick seeing as I didn't hide that from her.

And my god, she knows what she's about, this pretty little slag. Only thing I don't like is that her hair is too short to make for good handles, so I grab the back of her head and show her how I like it.

Gobble gobble, sweetheart.

She's eager to please, taking my nonverbal instructions without hesitation.

Ring-ring-ring—stop. Ring-ring-ring—stop. Ring-ring-ring—stop.

"Fuckin' cunt bastard," I mumble. "What's so fuckin' important?"

I reach for my mobile, which is just barely out of reach, and the girl on her knees is just about to the best bit of the process, so I'm not about to stop her now. Stretch a bit further. Got it.

Ring-ring-ring—

"The *fuck* you want, bastard?" I snarl. "I'm fuckin' busy."

The voice has a faint Italian accent—it's an educated, self-assured voice. A man who wields authority like a very large club—one with spikes. "Un-busy yourself, Rush. I have need of your services."

I hit the mute button, addressing the girl. "Faster,

sweetheart. I'm—ooof, yes, love, that's right. Just like that. Jesus, you've a real hoover of a mouth, haven't you?" Unmute. "What is it this time, you greedy wanker?"

"I need you in Germany. I have a shipment arriving and the men I've assigned to escort the merchandise are of…limited utility. There was a complication, and I do not trust them to handle it."

"Just a…" my eyes cross, and I have to hold back—I'm not about to blow my load while on the phone with this fuck. "I'll ring you back in a minute."

I thumb the end call button and toss the phone back onto the table.

I hunch over as I near my climax, and then bolt upright, holding her head in place. "Hold still, now."

She holds onto my ass cheeks as I fuck her face. Now, I may be a mean, selfish, insensitive bastard, but I'm not a complete prick. I'm careful. Gagging sounds make me gag. They put me off my game, you might say. So I'm not the sort of bloke who likes to deep-throat until they're yakking on the floor—not unless I know they can take it that way. Nah, mate. I'm good on that.

"Ah, fuck, fuck, that's good. I'm—oh, yeah. Ready, love? Oh, fuck. Fuck. Take it all, now."

"Mmmm!" she hums, eager and ready. Her gulp manages to sound surprised, but she's game and takes it all.

When I'm done, she sinks back on her heels, wiping at her mouth. Grinning up at me, she rises to her feet. "You weren't kidding about eight inches, were you?"

I brush my thumb down the corner of her mouth,

smirking at her. "I never joke about money, killing, and sex, sweetheart. Go lay on the bed and touch yourself. I've just got to call my mate back and then I'll eat you out till you see your ancestors."

She traipses naked out of the room, her lovely bits jiggling. I can see her on the bed from here—she flops onto her back and starts flicking her bean while I watch. It's a lovely show, I must say.

I ring him back—he answers on the first burble. "Don't ever hang up on me again, Rush."

"Fuck off, cunt. Where, when, and what's my take?" I pause for effect. "And the number had better start with a 2 and have at least five zeroes, you feel me?"

"Just head to Berlin and stand by. I expect them to fuck it up somehow, but I've no way of knowing where or how. I'll just have to update you as I can. As for when, you ought to know better, Rush. Yesterday would be good, last week would be better. As for your take? I've got a very specific number in mind."

"I'll bet you have," I mutter, half to myself. "And that would be what, then?"

"Two-hundred and seventy-six thousand, four-hundred and eighty-eight Euros. And…sixty-six cents."

I go stone still. If I didn't know better, I'd think my heart had stopped. "How the *fuck* do you know *that* number?"

His laugh is unkind and amused. "Have you forgotten who I am?"

Yeah, a bit, I guess. I don't say that though. It's not surprising that he knows that, but it's very, very bad for me. It means I *have* to do this job, no matter how distasteful I may find it.

"How many?" I ask, after a moment of thought.

"Two. Supposed to be one, but they managed to acquire an extra, somehow. Which is where you come in."

"I don't fuck with your human trafficking bullshit, you evil cunt. You know that."

"Then you'll find the money some other way."

Fuck.

FUCK!

I fight the urge to crush the mobile in my fist. "I really hate you."

"The list of people who hate me is very long and you're at the bottom of it, so pardon me if I'm not overly bothered."

"Fuck you. Make it an even three hundred-K, and I never do this shit for you again."

"Coercion, intimidation, assault, and murder, you have no problem with. But this you do?"

"I'll coerce, intimidate, assault, and murder other violent cunts who do bad shit. Innocent girls being turned into fucking sex slaves for you and your vile pile of depraved sickos? Yeah, nah. Fuck that very much, fuck you even more, you filthy fuckin' cunt."

"Must you use that word so much? It is supremely distasteful."

"You work with the Yanks too much. By which I mean fuck off, cunt."

"So vulgar." He sighs in annoyed disgust. "Three hundred thousand Euros, paid when I receive my merchandise—alive and…of use to my clients."

"Half now."

"Very well." My phone dings—I look at it, grinning when my bank account balance shows an increase of 150k. "There you are. Now. Finish with your little friend and be off. And expect the unexpected."

"Yeah, yeah. I'm no wet-behind-the-ears boot, you know."

"I'll expect an update in the next seventy-two hours."

"Sure, sure. Fuck off…*cunt*." I end the call, shut the device off, and swagger down the hallway.

She's about to go, arching off the bed with her fingers flying. I wait till she's right on the cusp, and then I knock her fingers away and take over with my mouth. I show her the promised good time—I always follow through on that promise, at least.

Behind the scenes, though, my mind is swirling with chaos. How did he know? No one knows. *No one.* Yet he does.

And I have no choice but to do this.

It's her last chance.

And I'm out of options.

We have a good time, me and…Shannon? Shenandoah? Something with an S-H. But really, my heart isn't in it.

So, the moment she falls asleep, I pull on my kit and leave her flat.

It's a long train ride to Berlin.

3

TRAIN RIDE FROM HELL; A COCKNEY SAVIOR

Ow.

Everything hurts.

Why does everything hurt?

My skin hurts. My muscles hurt. My head hurts. Even my hair hurts. Did I get wasted again? I don't remember…what do I remember?

Skiing with the boys in Switzerland. The bar, the fight, sneaking out. The driver. The club. Dancing. Going to the bathroom. The selfies with those girls.

The hallway.

A girl being kidnapped. Trying to stop it.

Getting tased or stun-gunned.

I crack one eye open: a window, through which I can see precisely nothing—it's night, and pitch black. But I do get the impression that I'm on a train.

Why am I on a train?

I hear something—a shuffle, a breath. Holding stone-still, I open my other eye; I feel wobbly, thick-headed, and sluggish.

Yes, I'm in a train compartment, and I'm not alone. There are two men and one woman. The men are asleep sitting up, heads nodding; They're both in their late thirties or early forties, pudgy and unfit but strong-looking, greasy, unshaven, unwashed—the men from the hallway. The compartment smells of body odor and old cigarette smoke clinging to clothes that haven't been washed or changed in who knows how long. They're both white men, and I remember thinking that they spoke a Slavic language or something, but I don't know for sure. I'm no polyglot like so many of my extended A1S family.

The girl—she's about my age, so a young woman rather than a girl—is white as well, with long, fine, straight blond hair, pale skin, a few freckles. She's curled up away from the man beside her, so I can't tell much about her other than, like me, she's dressed for the club in a tiny red miniskirt and a sheer black top with black tape in an X over her nipples. No shoes. No bag. Come to think of it, my bag is gone, too.

Which means I have no phone, no money, no ID. I'm dressed in a skanky little outfit with no shoes, I've been drugged, and I'm on a train going who knows where.

This is *not* good.

I really, really, *really* fucked up. The boys don't even know I'm gone. Neither do the guys. Or my parents.

They'll find out eventually, but it'll take Lear's expertise to track my movements.

I can't bank on being rescued at the last second by my family. I mean, they'll rescue me eventually. But in the meantime, anything could happen. And by anything, I mean rape and murder.

Plus side: I'm not bound. I wonder if I could just sneak out? And go where? I'm on a fucking train in the middle of nowhere at night. Barefoot. In a skanky little skirt.

The girl across from me shifts on the seat, moaning as she rouses to consciousness. Beside her, the man cracks an eye open, peers at her, and then closes the eye.

So, they're not sound asleep. Sneaking out likely wouldn't be an option anyway.

I close my eyes to the point that I can see through the hazy flutter of my eyelashes, considering my situation, what led to it, and what to do about it.

I've been at odd ends for a while. Killy has taken an interest in the family business, training with Dad's underlings in hand-to-hand combat, close quarters combat, room clearing, intelligence gathering, recon, off-grid operations, surveillance…everything he'll ever need to know to eventually take over Alpha One Security if and when Dad ever retires.

I've expressed interest, but Dad won't let me do any of the fun stuff. I mean, I've done all that stuff, too. I'm damn good at it. But he won't put me on any real missions. He wants me to work with Uncle Lear on computer operations.

I've done recon training, intel gathering and

processing, self-defense, off-grid stuff, room clearing, and firearms training. Top marks in all categories, according to Uncle Duke and Sasha.

"You're not ready, emotionally," Dad says.

The fuck does that mean?

And Killy is? Killian still thinks crop-dusting me is peak humor.

I want to learn how to be an A1S badass like everyone else I know, but I'm not emotionally ready? Sure.

Not that I'm bitter.

I wouldn't need fucking bodyguards that I have to sneak away from if they'd teach me what I need to know. Or rather, I *don't* need the bodyguards because I *do* know all that shit.

What, because I'm a fucking girl I can't be a badass? What about Auntie Cuddy? Or Mom? Mom is a certified badass.

That was circumstantial, she said. She told me she hoped I'd never need to learn the way she did.

Well, guess the fuck what, *Mom*? Here I am, up shit creek, alone, learning the way you did. Must be a family trait, like the curly hair and brown skin.

I recognize the burn of anger in my gut, and I'm cognizant that letting anger take over is a bad plan, so I let my eyes close all the way and try to release some of it.

The train sways as we round a long, sharp curve.

One of the men lets out a long, bubbly, wet-sounding fart, and a few moments later the compartment is choking with the godawful smell of it. The other man rouses, leans forward, and kicks his companion in the thigh, grumbling and cursing at him in whatever language they speak.

This starts an argument with lots of wild gesticulations, and both men end up on their feet, nose to nose, all but barking at each other. At any moment, I expect them to bust out their dicks and a ruler. Or maybe start throwing down—that'd be better. I could use the distraction to escape.

I sneak a glance at the other girl—like me, she's pretending to be asleep, but I see her eyes slitted, watching the men bickering.

After a while, their tempers cool and they each retreat to their side of the compartment, petulantly turning away from each other like scolded children.

The girl and I trade eye rolls: *Men*. Ugh.

The man next to the girl pulls out his phone, leaning against the window and scrolling idly. The man beside me seems content to just…sit there. Freak.

After perhaps ten or fifteen minutes of scrolling, the man opposite me rotates his phone to landscape, resting it on his thigh. I hear dialogue; obviously, I have no idea what's being said, but…god, how do I explain it? Even in a language I don't understand, it just sounds like bad acting. Lines being recited stiffly and woodenly.

And then…a female moan. A male grunt. A gag. Wet slurping sounds. Another gag. A male voice growling something that's probably a version of "oh yeah, baby, take it all."

The jackass is watching porn. Just, like, in public, volume up, no earbuds, with three other people mere feet away.

Dude, *really*?

The girl and I widen our eyes at each other in disbelief.

I want to laugh, but I don't dare.

He watches the whole video, and we're treated to every gag, slap, slurp, squelch, and scream. Ah yes, porn, the ASMR version. Lovely.

Things take a worrying turn, however, when the porn-watcher reaches into his pants and adjusts his junk…lengthily. Rhythmically.

The other man says something that sounds like "What the fuck, dude? For real?" Followed by a gesture at the door, as in, "Can't you do that in fucking bathroom?"

Grumbling, Porny McGee lumbers to his feet and shuffles toward the door; his hard-on bulges against his zipper, and he gives it a rub over his jeans.

And then, the nightmare begins.

He looks back at the girl on the bench. Speculative, greedy. Evil.

No, no, no.

My heat starts pounding in my chest, and I can see the girl's hand clenching into a trembling fist. A tear trickles down her nose.

The other man, still seated, sees what's happening and mutters something. Porny McGee gestures at the girl and then his dick.

Seated thug gestures at his face—it seems like a "you can't fuck up her face" sort of thing.

And then Porny McGee stomps back across the compartment, grabs the girl by the wrist and yanks her to her feet. She thrashes, starts to scream, and the man slugs her in the gut. Her eyes bug out, and she goes limp, gasping and gurgling, bile dribbling down her lips.

I lurch to my feet, unable to do nothing. The man beside me grabs me by the shoulder and shoves me back down to the bench; before I can so much as blink, the sharp, cold point of a pocketknife is pricking my throat.

"You sit, extra girl," he snarls at me. "Or you next."

The girl's eyes met mine, pleading, as the thug drags her from the compartment. Once in the swaying hallway, he drags her to her feet and slings an arm around her waist, hauling her against him, laughing as he paws her ass; to an onlooker, it would appear as if they're a couple who can't wait to get to the toilet so they can get it on.

Nausea curdles in my gut, but I don't dare even breathe. When he's satisfied I'm not going to try anything, my captor removes the knife from my throat, but doesn't put it away.

My throat burns, vomit boiling behind my teeth, rage and horror warring for dominance within me.

I'm next.

It's only a matter of time. This isn't an adventure. No one is going to save me.

What did Mom always tell me?

I'll never, ever beat any man pound for pound, strength for strength. I have to rely on my wits, courage, and ruthlessness, as well as my superior speed and reaction time.

Women are faster. Our reaction times are exponentially better than a man's. And when we have to, we can be far crueler and infinitely more vindictive than any man could ever dream of being.

I understand now, Mom.

I hesitated back in the club because I didn't know I had to kill him. I saw him as a human. A life. I didn't have the conviction that it was him or me.

Now, I do.

This isn't hot, mindless, reactive anger I'm feeling.

This is cold, calculating hate.

Thoughtful, methodical, brutal rage.

That man is going to die, and I'm going to kill him. And it's not going to be pretty or quick.

I wait for him to bring the girl back, and I think back to the self-defense lessons given to me by…well, a variety of people.

Uncle Duke taught me to throw a proper punch, and even let me break his nose so I'd know how it feels. It hurts your hand like a bitch, that's how it feels. And the crunch of cartilage under your knuckles is awful.

Auntie Cuddy taught me how to fight a much larger male: go for the soft spots and hit as hard as you can. Nuts, throat, eyeballs. No mercy. Keep hitting until they stop moving.

Mom taught me to use whatever's around me as a weapon.

Surreptitiously, I scan the compartment for possible weapons, but there's not much. I don't think much of my chances of disarming the fat fuck beside me, so that's out. No luggage. No, like, vases or encyclopedias or anything heavy.

There, on the floor under the opposite bench: a

discarded pencil. Now I just have to figure out how to get my hands on it without getting my throat cut open.

A few long, nauseating minutes later, the compartment door is yanked open, and the man hurls the girl inside. Her skirt is rumpled up around her hips. If she was wearing panties, they're gone. Her top is torn, and the nipple tape is gone. Her hair is rumpled. Her cheek is red and bruising. She's got ligature marks around her throat—fingerprints.

She's sobbing silently, and I get the impression that she was told to keep quiet. Slowly, in visible pain, she curls up in the corner of the bench as far to one side as she can get. Blood smears her thighs.

I'm shaking with rage.

I scramble off the bench, moving to comfort her. The man beside me allows it, laughing cruelly as his rapist friend sits beside him. They murmur to each other in low tones, chuckling. Probably sharing awful details.

I trip on purpose so my knees hit the floor, and I crawl across the compartment for the girl, wrapping one arm around her while fumbling under the bench for the pencil. I snag it with my middle and index fingers and tuck it inside the waistband of my skirt—the only hiding spot I can think of under the conditions.

"I'm so sorry, I'm so sorry," I whisper to the girl. "I couldn't stop him. I'm sorry."

Staring at nothing, the girl just weeps.

This just got a whole hell of a lot more real.

The men mutter to each other—Not-Raper glances at the girl and his eyes narrow in on her bruised cheek and purpling throat; he gestures at her and then at the man.

Cue another argument.

Raper gesture at me.

Oh no. No, no, no.

Not-Raper gives me a speculative look.

Shit.

I fight nauseated horror, fight to stay calm.

What did Mom say to do in a situation like this? Go along with it. Stay calm. Wait for the opportunity and take it. Don't hesitate. Better to take the opportunity and die trying than to let them get away with it. Cause as much pain as possible. But *wait for the right moment*. Use whatever you can. Do what you have to do. Put the nice parts of yourself in a box deep down inside and lock it away. Leave only the fury and the hate and the survivalist.

Survive at all costs; there's therapy for everything else.

He rises to his feet, knife blade tapping at his thigh. His eyes find mine—cruel, cold, lecherous. Yeah, this is about to happen.

He jerks his head at the door.

I just stare at him.

He grabs my hand and yanks me to my feet, wraps one arm around me and puts the knife blade in my ribs, hidden between our bodies and his fat fuck arm.

Out the door.

I can't swallow past the hot lump of horrified, terrified nausea. My heart hammers a mile a minute in my ears.

My hands shake.

The pencil is a cold rod wedged between my skirt and my belly, just above my vagina.

Wait. Not here. The hallway is exposed and too narrow. The knife point is wickedly sharp—I feel a drop of blood trickle down my skin.

The toilet is just down the hall at the end of the car. We reach it all too soon, and he yanks it open, shoves me in.

I stumble forward into the tiny space; he has to pull the knife away from me so he can fold his bulk into the space with me and close the door after us. Collapsing against the far wall, I'm not faking the breathless sob of terror that rips from my throat. Fumble at my skirt for the pencil—almost drop it in the open toilet.

Grip it so that the length of the pencil and the sharp point face up. Huddle against the wall, shivering, sobbing.

I hear a belt buckle jingle.

A hand paws at my belly, yanks at my top, pulling a tit free. A rough, vicious, clammy hand grasps greedily at me as he shifts behind me.

"Not fight, is over quick." His breath is hot on my ear, stinking of halitosis and garlic and onions and cigarettes.

I bet it's over quick, you fat fuck.

Can you even find your pathetic little dick?

I don't say it, but I think it.

Grip the pencil hard. Wait.

He tosses the knife into the little sink and presses a hand onto my back, pushing me down so I'm bent over.

Something hot and squishy nudges my ass cheek as he fumbles at my skirt. My underwear poses a problem—I think he assumed I either wasn't wearing any or they were a thong. Haha, nope. Full coverage bikini-cut. Not so easy to just pull aside.

Which provides me with my moment.

He grumbles in frustration as he hunts blindly for the gusset—the clumsy oaf couldn't find my pussy if you gave him a map and a flashlight.

About to vomit, I wait and wait as he tries to get the gusset aside. He finally manages it, and then has to use both hands—one to hold my panties aside and the other to grip his tiny, pathetic little dick.

You fucked up, my dude. And now you die.

I pull my hips forward, brace both hands against the wall, and then slam my ass backward into him as hard as I can. He flies backward in the tiny space, crashing against the door with a loud crunch. His pants are around his ankles, his sagging, fish-belly-white stomach sagging over his dick, which barely protrudes past his belly.

Yes, I'm fat-shaming the motherfucker *and* dick size-shaming him.

And now I'm about to fucking murder him.

I spin, teeth gritted and bared as I let out a low, teeth-clenched scream of rage.

Drive the pencil into his eyeball. Jelly squishes messily, but I refuse to stop. Push it deeper. Place my palm on the eraser and smash my fist onto the back of my hand as hard as I can. The pain of the pencil digging into my hand is a small price to pay for the way he twitches, gasping quietly, and starts slumping to the floor.

I let him go, staggering away as he twitches and goes still.

Holy fuck.

I killed him.

I vomit into the toilet.

His knife is in the sink. I grab it and then rinse my mouth out. Wash my hands.

Shaking like a leaf, I try not to look at the fat, ugly, half-naked, dead guy at my feet.

The dead guy I killed with a pencil.

At least I'm not raped?

I puke again.

Fuck, that was awful.

Way, way too close.

Now what? Eventually, the other guy is going to come looking. Can I stop the train? Find help? Do I go back for the girl?

Part of me says no. I'm only in this situation because I tried to help her. But…

Fuck.

I hold the knife in a shaky fist, creep out of the toilet, and close the door. It's night, so the hallway is empty, everyone is either sleeping or trying to.

I make my way toward the compartment, peek into the window. She's huddled where she was, staring at nothing, heedless of the tears tracking down her cheeks. On the bench opposite, the thug stares at her, absently fondling himself while smirking.

I've never understood how men get to a point

where the only way they can get off is rape. What happens to them that such a vile, violent, selfish, degrading, evil act becomes normal? Funny, even?

I'm starting to understand The Punisher.

Killian was into that comic for awhile, and he liked to sound off to me about it, so I'm pretty familiar with the character.

This motherfucker needs to die, slowly. And I'm feeling ready to oblige—Punisher-style.

Nice Bryn is in a cage. This version of me is…kinda scary, TBH.

I try to catch the girl's eye, but she's not seeing anything.

Fuck it.

I tap on the glass with the knife blade—Raper's eyes flick to me, widening when they see me grinning at him, his partner's knife in my hand.

I don't know what comes over me, but I yank my top up and flash him, use both hands to flip him off, and then take off running down the corridor.

I hear the door slam open and heavy footsteps lumbering behind me. I'm running toward the front of the train, slamming into one wall and then the other as the train sways side to side. I reach the end of the car too soon, slamming into it before I've fully slowed down, knocking the air out of my lungs.

The next few seconds stretch out like a slow-mo scene in a horror movie where the idiot heroine suddenly forgets how to door. Do I remember how to door? Yes, I do…after a split-second of blind panic. Sorry, horror movie heroines—I get it, now.

I stumble through the cold, rocking space between cars, the black rubber seal between the cars accordioning as the cars shift and sway. Through to the next car—another long hallway. Closed doors. People are sleeping in the compartments.

Glance back—he's not far behind me. What's my end game, here? Where am I going? Reach the front of the train, and then what? Jump off? Barefoot and half-naked?

Fuck that.

Filled with hate, rage, and a bloodthirsty need to watch this evil fuck bleed out at my feet like the last guy, I stop running. Grip the knife blade up, sharp edge up, lowering myself into a combat crouch.

With a cruel grin, he produces his own knife—a much bigger one.

Um.

Oops.

Still not running.

Uncle Duke's words ring in my head: everyone gets cut in a knife fight, so the only way to win is to either run away or be faster with the blade. But if you stay and fight, you're *going* to get cut. That's not a maybe.

Well, fuck it. There's nowhere to run and only so many places to hide.

He approaches, waving his knife at me with that sick little grin that suggests he'd probably fuck my body while I bleed out.

I watch him move, assessing him the way Duke taught me. He's holding the blade low, down near his belt buckle, blade pointing down from the bottom of his fist, because that's how they do it in the movies. His whole body is facing me, empty hand at his side. Yeah, this guy has zero clue.

Still dangerous, but he's no knife fighter.

Neither am I, but I was trained by some of the best warriors on the planet. I was taught to survive. Taught to use my wits.

I stand my ground and let him approach. His jiggly, porcine jowls are coated in sweat and stubble, cheeks red, huffing and puffing from chasing me all of fifty yards.

He shuffles to a halt a few feet away. "*Pange nuga käest. Tule vaikselt*."

"Yeah, fuck you too, fat-ass." I flip him off. "Come and fuckin' get me."

"Not need you, American bitch. You die, no one care."

I laugh at that. "You could not possibly be more wrong, dumbfuck. You have no idea who the fuck I am, do you? You kidnapped the wrong extra girl."

This makes him pause. "Who you are?"

"Ever hear of Nick Harris? Alpha One Security?"

"Everyone know him."

"He's my father."

"You lie."

"I might be, sure. But what if I'm not? Whoever you work for, they're *fucked*."

He just grins at this. "Him I work for, he is not scared of your papa. And *I* am not scared of *you*."

"Neither was your friend, and he's dead in the toilet with his pants around his ankles."

This gets him. "You lie."

"Yeah? Where is he, then? And how do I have his knife?" I wave the weapon. I twirl the knife in a come-here gesture. "Come on, fat ass. Come and get me. I'll cut you to pieces like the fat ugly fucking pig you are."

"Fuck you, American bitch."

Yeah, he's pissed. So I needle him a bit more, hoping anger makes him stupider, which it typically does with idiot men like this.

"Awww, is your sad little prick even gonna work, fat ass?" I mime jerking off with the knife. "I bet the only way you can get hard is by forcing yourself on innocent girls. You know why, *fat ass*? Because it's the only way anyone would *ever* fuck an ugly, stupid, sad, fat sack of shit like *you*. I bet you can't even pay for sex. I bet even the most blownout old hooker wouldn't take your money to let you fuck her."

Oooh boy, he's *big* mad, now.

"I will fucking *kill* you, bitch," he snarls. "But I will make you scream, first."

"You wish you could make me scream. I bet your fat, ugly mother screamed when she saw you the first time. Probably thought she'd given birth to a tumor, you're so fucking ugly."

Yeah, I'm resorting to your mama jokes. You try coming up with witty banter while a knife-wielding rapist tries to kill you.

And you know what's funny? It's the stupid joke about his mother that sets him off.

I would laugh at that, but he's charging me, yelling,

swinging that six-inch black folding knife up toward my gut.

Thank Jesus, Mary, Joseph, and all the saints for the hours of training with Uncle Duke, because the moment I see that knife-tip hurtling toward my belly, my training kicks in. It's not even conscious.

The start of his swing is low, which gives him good leverage and force, but leaves him off balance when I dance backward out of each. I slice my blade across his hand, bloodying his knuckles. He's tough, though, I'll give him that—he hisses in pain but keeps hold of his knife. He turns the upper cut swing into a lunging swipe; I twist out of the way, and the blade barely misses my tits, slicing along the front of my bicep. A sharp, hot line of pain blooms as the edge bites skin—it's shallow, nothing to worry about, just painful.

And it's a prime opportunity.

Twisted to the side, his arm is now parallel to my torso. I use Auntie Cuddy's self-defense training to wrap an arm around his elbow, twisting my body further while crushing his arm the wrong way against my hip. The joint snaps, and he screams, dropping the knife to cradle his broken elbow.

No mercy. No hesitation.

Again, it's instinct. Training is taking over. Dodge, break, stab. My blade whistles upward, digging under his ribcage on his left side just like Uncle Duke taught me.

I'm not sure this blade is long enough to reach his heart—there's a lot of pudge in the way. The tip scrapes over bone with a judder that sets my teeth on edge, like scraping your fork on a plate. I push harder. Deeper. His fat swallows the blade, and I keep pushing, putting my nose to his and letting him see the hate in my eyes.

I feel the moment I pierce his heart—there's resistance, and then a give, and then his eyes flare wide and his mouth falls open, and a soft gasp leaves his throat. He sags toward me, dark eyes going flat and vacant.

I stagger backward, letting him topple to the floor with a hard, wet smack. Blood pools under him, spreading in a dark ruby stain.

At that moment, the brakes squeal and I'm thrown backward as the train slows. I land on my ass and then smack my head against the floor. Dizzy, seeing stars, I scramble to my hands and knees, coming face to face with the sightless, vacant stare of the second man I've killed in less than five minutes.

I retch, but only a string of bile comes out.

I hear a scream back the other way; someone has found the corpse in the toilet.

I stagger to my feet and put distance between me and the corpse. Through to the next car, staggering, horror, nausea, and confusion swiftly taking the place of the rage that's fueled me so far.

I just killed two men.

"Fräulein? Entshuldigung? Bist du verletzt?"

I don't speak German either, but I know concern when I hear it. An older man, tall and thin with white hair and a neat goatee, stands in the doorway of his compartment, looking worried. He's quite literally wringing his hands.

"*Ihr arm… es blutet.*" He gestures at my…well, arm. That's the same, I guess.

I glance at it, and suddenly it stings and burns like a bitch. "Oh, shit, yeah, I guess I'm bleeding, huh?"

"English?"

"American."

"You are not wearing enough clothing for this weather, *fräulein*. It is winter." *Vearing…zis…vinter.*

"Tell me about it, dude." The train lurches forward, scuds a few hundred yards at a crawl, and then stops again. Outside, nothing but darkness. "Why are we stopped?" I ask.

"*Weiss nicht.* Is a train. Who knows?" He frowns at my bleeding arm. "You are in trouble?"

"Nothing I can't handle." Ha. Right. But I'm in shock, and I don't know this guy.

He's dressed in a tailored navy suit with a pale blue tie and pocket square; he removes his tie and pocket square, presses the pale blue swatch of silk against the cut, and then winds the tie around it several times, tugs it tight, and knots it. Next, he removes his suit coat and settles it on my shoulders.

"Here, *fräulein*. We will arrive to Berlin soon." He checks his wristwatch. "*Ja*, Berlin in eleven minutes, I think. Will you allow me to assist you when we arrive?"

I want to. But a worm of worry wriggles in my belly. This is a kind old man. And some unsettled instinct tells me this super fun adventure I've gotten myself into isn't over yet.

I clasp his hand in mine. "Thank you, sir. You're very kind. But you're right—I am in trouble." I glance past him; his wife is asleep in their compartment, her head resting against the window. She's a sweet little old lady. Someone's grandmother. "I won't involve you in it."

"But *fräulein*, I have friends—"

"I appreciate the offer, truly, but no, thank you." I gnaw on my lip. "Actually, do you have a cell phone I could borrow?"

He winces. "*Nein, es tut mir leid*. I do not own a mobile phone. My grandchildren think I am so crazy, *ja*? Who does not have a mobile phone in this day and age, hmm? But this way, they come to see me." He reaches into his hip pocket and pulls out a folded stack of euros, peels off several of the larger bills, and hands them to me—it looks like four or five hundred euros. "Please. Take this."

"I…I can't. It's too much."

The train lurches into motion again and this time keeps going, albeit rather slowly.

"*Nein, nein*. You must have some money, at least." He smiles at me with kindness in his blue eyes. "You are of age with my granddaughter, Anja. If it was she in your situation, I hope someone would help her as I help you."

"What's your name, sir?"

Another of those wonderfully kind grandpa smiles. "I am Gregor Mueller."

"Gregor Mueller, my name is Bryn Harris." I can't help but hug him. "I won't forget what you've done to help me, Mr. Mueller."

"*Nein, nein, es ist nichts, fräulein.*"

I pat his shoulders. "If anyone asks, you never met me. Okay? It's safer for you that way."

"This trouble you are in…"

"There will be police. Just…remember, you never saw me."

He frowns. "I shall remember. I hope you will be well."

"I'll be fine. I'm very resourceful. Thank you again, so much, Mr. Mueller."

Before I chicken out and take refuge in their compartment, I move forward toward the front of the train, if only to put more space between me and the dead men.

Nope, nope, nope—I put that out of my mind. I'll cry later.

When you're in the shit, baby girl, Mom used to tell me, *you do what you gotta do first. There'll be time to fall apart later. But when you're in the shit, there ain't no time for blubbering.*

She'd tell me this stuff all the time. Little lessons that I thought were so random and stupid. What did "in the shit" mean, anyway? I never understood. But I also never forgot. And now, I'm in the shit.

I remember, Mama. No time for blubbering. It's Badass Bryn time.

Exactly eleven minutes later, because this is Germany, after all, the train pulls into a station. The lights of Berlin are bright. The station is empty, the voice of the announcer echoing. I'm first off the train the moment it stops—the frigid winter air smacks me in the face like an icy fist, wrapping deathly cold fingers around my bare legs. Gregor's coat is suddenly much thinner than it had felt moments ago, as the wind knifes through it.

Worst of all, though, are my bare feet.

I catch a suspicious look from a conductor, but then he's distracted by a customer asking him a question, and I jog inside the station. It's warmer in here—as in, I won't freeze to death in a matter of minutes. There are shops galore where I could use Gregor's money to buy some clothing, but everything is closed.

Wait...hold on.

I slow to a walk as something occurs to me. I started out in Zermatt, Switzerland, on the border of Switzerland and Italy. Now I'm in Berlin, Germany. The two are...not close. My knowledge of European geography is, sadly, limited. I mean, c'mon. I'm a spoiled rich girl who grew up on a private island compound. I got a great education, but remembering geography seemed pointless.

How long was I unconscious?

A conductor passes, and I flag him. "Excuse me, sir?"

"*Ja, fräulein? Wie kann ich ihnen helfen?*"

"Um, do you speak English?"

His eyes betray a touch of annoyance, but his tone is polite and respectful. "Ja, a little."

"How far is it from Zermatt to here? Like, how long is the train ride?"

"Twelve hours, or something like this." *Some-sing like zis.*

"Oh. Wow. Okay. Thank you."

"My apologies, miss, but where are your shoes?"

I grimace. "I, um…lost them. Long story."

"Will you wait here, please?"

"Sure?"

He scurries off, returning a few minutes later with a pair of Ugg boots, the calf-height tan ones with the fuzzy insides. "Perhaps these will not fit, but it is better than no shoes in this cold, ja?"

I've been trying to pretend I'm not freezing my ass off, but the moment I slide my feet into the boots, a moan of relief shoots out of me unbidden. "Oh…my…god." I cover my face, embarrassingly close to crying from sheer relief. "Thank you, god, thank you so much. Where…where did you get them?"

"The lost and find. People lose things on the trains very much." He shrugs. "You will be frost bited without shoes."

"You're a lifesaver. Thank you."

He nods and continues on his way. People are so friendly and helpful around here. I guess there are good people in the world still, after all. Who knew?

The boots are too small, but far better than being barefoot. I hear a radio crackle somewhere and a voice murmur quietly. Shit—cops.

I put my arms through the sleeves of Gregor's coat and head for the exit, passing by no fewer than six uniformed officers; I guess my stunt got some attention.

I stuff my hands into the coat pockets, duck my head, and walk calmly out of the train station and into the cold of Berlin.

Twelve hours?

It was…two am? Around two in the morning when I encountered the kidnappers in Zermatt. So at some point along the way, I lost several hours. They must have kept me unconscious for a long time. The better to keep me cooperative, probably. They likely pretended we were their passed-out-drunk girlfriends. Who would question that?

So, now I'm alone in Berlin. I have shoes and some cash, but no phone, no ID, and I've killed two men. I couldn't say whether the cops will be looking for me, but I'm not eager to find out. I didn't do anything wrong—I defended myself. But I also know that in situations like this, it's best not to trust anyone. The first order of business is to find a phone and get ahold of my parents. Shit, even a computer cafe would work.

I'd just sort of walked away from the train station at random, putting distance between me and the police who will be looking for whoever killed the two men on the train.

I wonder what happened to the girl? I can't go back for her. I can't worry about her. I'm not a religious person, but I send up a generic prayer to whoever and whatever may or may not be up there—look after the poor girl. God knows she'll need help after what she went through.

What I almost went through.

Fuck—nope. Nope, nope, nope. Not thinking about that.

Focus, Brynnie. Where are you? Where are you going? What's your plan?

I stop walking and assess my surroundings. Behind me, the train station is a massive glass edifice. Directly ahead, a street. Beyond that, train tracks, another street, and a tall glass building. The area, otherwise, is wide open, designed for a lot of foot traffic.

A bus whooshes by.

A taxi.

Shit—a taxi! I need to get away from the train station. I have no idea who those bozos were working for, but I know for a solid fact they weren't operating alone. They snatched the girl easily—if I hadn't intervened, she would have just vanished without a trace. Those guys were just hired lackeys. "Him I work for, he is not afraid of your papa." Yeah, the boss is someone powerful, then, if that shitstain knew who my father is and felt confident saying his boss wasn't afraid of Nicholas Harris.

Everyone is afraid of Nicholas Harris. You'd be a fool not to be. So whoever the boss is, either he's a fool, or he's a big fucking problem.

Which means this ain't over. I mean, obviously. I'm still up shit creek without a paddle. But I can't assume there won't be anyone looking for me. Anyone bad, I mean. Hopefully, good people are looking for me, too.

I flag down a passing cab.

The driver eyes me in the mirror. "*Wohin?*"

"Um. I don't...I don't know. I need clothes and a cell phone."

"No English."

Shit.

I lean forward and point at the cell phone in the

holder suctioned to the windshield and then flash him one of the 100-euro bills. "Phone. Buy a phone."

"*Alles ist geschlossen.*"

That sounds like "Everything is closed" to me.

"Um. Food? Eat?" I mime eating.

"Ah. Okay. Ja. Ja. I know." He starts the meter and pulls away. Exhausted, I feel myself drowsing.

A few hours later, I've eaten a filling meal at a twenty-four-hour diner, which, conveniently, is located across the street from a place that sells mobile phones. I ate slowly, sipped coffee, and dozed off—the waitress seemed to recognize that I was in some sort of distress, because she let me sleep for quite a while, only rousing me when things started to pick up. I leave her a generous tip and head out into the cold—it's a crisp, clear, bitterly cold winter day in Berlin.

I cross the street at the intersection, making for the cell phone store. I'm halfway there when the hackles on the back of my neck raise. I try to be surreptitious about scanning my surroundings—there, behind me. Four men walking in a line abreast, taking up the whole sidewalk. They're dressed in brightly-colored ADIDAS track suits. Their jackets bulge with obvious shoulder-holstered handguns.

Fuck.

Their eyes are cold and hard, even from here, and fixed on me.

Fuck, fuck.

Panic ignites. I'm unarmed. I can't fight off four men, even if I did have a knife.

I try to stay calm, walking faster. Past the cell phone store. A pharmacy. A liquor store.

"Stop running, American girl."

How did they find me? How do they know I'm American?

Questions with no answers, and this certainly isn't the moment to waste time wondering.

Fuck it. I start running. A shout rings out.

"STOP!"

My brain is a runaway train, even in shit like this. For example, as I'm running, I'm wondering why anyone ever bothers yelling "STOP!" Like, what, they expect me to just…stop? Oh, sure, Mr. Murder Man, let me just stop and let you kidnap, rape, and murder me. Okay, buddy. Even cops do it. Why? It's so stupid. Yet, that's what my monkey brain does—always running on a million tracks at once, because ADHD is a harsh mistress.

I do not stop. I run faster.

Reach another intersection and turn left. My soles skid on an icy patch, and I land hard, cracking my elbow on the cement and skinning my knees. Ignore the pain and scramble to my feet, take off running…and smack face-first into a hard, warm, male chest.

"Whoa, whoa, whoa!" The voice is deep and rough, with a thick London accent. Young. Bold. Brash. Strong hands lift me to my feet. " What's all the fuss about, then, Gorgeous?"

The hands steady me on my feet, and I catch my first look at male perfection.

I'm six feet tall, so very few men can be said to tower over me—Uncle Duke and Uncle Thresh are about it. But this man…"tower" may be a stretch, but he's got to be six-four. Tall enough I have to look up at him.

But this guy.

This fuckin' guy. Where do I start?

Inhumanly perfect looking is a decent starting place.

His eyes. Not quite green, not quite gray, not quite brown—a changeable mixture of all of them. He smiles at me, and those eyes flash green. But…they're not *good* eyes. They're not *kind*. They're dangerous. They twinkle, but…it's a shiver-inducing twinkle.

His jawline is sculpted from marble. Hard, rugged, and craggy. Dusted with dark stubble. His hair is shaved on the sides, the top a messy tangle. A scar bisects his right eyebrow, disappearing into his hairline and denting the bridge of his nose.

He's wearing expensive, well-worn black jeans, well-cared-for combat boots—the kind professional operators wear. A tight maroon crew neck shirt wraps around a lean, hard torso, and a battered, scratched, beaten-to-hell leather jacket strains around massive arms. A variety of silver rings grace his knuckles.

Fuck, he's gorgeous. My heart skips a beat when those changeable eyes fix on me. It skips another beat when his lips—plump, pillowy, and expressive—curve in a cocky smirk.

"Jesus wept, you're a looker, ain'tcha? Proper

stunner." *Prop-ah stunn-ah.* That smirk. Fuck. It's a lethal weapon. My heart pitter-patters. "What you runnin' from, 'ey love?"

He's hard to understand, though, I've gotta be honest.

"HEY! You come, now." The men have caught up, huffing and puffing.

My…savior, maybe?…turns to address them. "Oi. You lot can fuck off."

"Is not concern you." The speaker, an older guy with salt and pepper hair and the ugliest face I've ever seen in my life, produces a gold-plated Desert Eagle .50-cal hand cannon from his shoulder holster. "Now is you fuck off, Brit boy."

"Oooh, look at that whoppin' big fuck-off gun you've got, mate. Put a big fuckin' 'ole in me, wouldn't it? An' Brit boy? You come up with that witty repartee yourself, bruv?"

Jesus, he sounds like he's got a mouthful of marbles. He seems totally unconcerned, though, which is reassuring, because I'm concerned. Very, *very* concerned.

"Girl. You come." The speaker gestures at me with his howitzer.

"How about no?" I answer, in a shitty but funny Austin Powers impression.

Funny to me, at least.

My Cockney savior snickers at my response, but doesn't take his attention off of the four men. "Look, mate. I've got a busy schedule, so me an' my new friend here are gonna scarper. You do what you like. But a word of warnin', yeah? I ain't the bloke you wanna fuck around with. Last chance. Fuck off." *Fuck around wiv.*

"Girl is ours. Run away or you die."

"Um, I'm no one's," I say. "Suck a dick, ass-face."

This gets me another amused snort. "Got on smart mouth on you, 'aven't you, love?" He looks at the four men with annoyance, as if they're flies buzzing around his head. "Fine. 'Ave it your way."

His hand flashes behind his back, blurs around front into a Weaver stance—BAM-BAM-BAM-BAM. The four shots are so close together they sound like one rolling peal of thunder, and all four of the track suit-wearing thugs rock backward in near-perfect unison, red holes weeping trickles of crimson at the centers of their T-boxes.

For a moment, I'm stunned silent. Then my usual running commentary emerges. "Fuck me." A pause. "That was…impressive." Not my wittiest commentary ever, but I'm not on my A-game at the moment. Sue me.

He grins at me, the picture of debonair cockiness. "Who are you, Gorgeous?"

"Bryn."

He takes my hand in his, brings it to his mouth, and kisses my knuckles without looking away from my eyes. "Rush, at your service."

4

A SMILE YOU'D KILL FOR

WELL, SHIT.

My not-so-wee little prick is rather intrigued by Bryn. Usually these girls who manage to get away are scared shitless, helpless little bambis.

This girl…is not.

She was impressed by my drop of the four fat fuckos. She didn't scream, didn't cower or cover her ears or act all squicked out by the buckets of blood currently sluicing down the kerb.

Also, she's fucking breathtaking.

Only a few inches shorter than my six-four, she's slender and willowy, but she's got some killer curves for all that. Her skirt barely covers her ass, leaving her mile-long legs bare, and fuck me, those legs. Strong, thick, smooth. The kind of legs you'd tear apart the earth to have wrapped around your waist all fucking night. If she's the extra, I wonder what the original merchandise is like.

According to the overblown twat I'm forced to work for, the unexpected did indeed occur, in that both of the girls vanished and both of the mules are dead. But I can't just come out and ask this girl if she's the original.

I mean, I could. But it would bodge up my plan. See, I hate this job. I mean, I really, *really* fucking hate it. I'm a shit human, okay? I drink too much, I use and objectify women, I murder people, and hand out beatings on the regular. But I do have a few little morals. Number one, I only kill people who either deserve it or are trying to murder me. Number two, sex is consensual. If you have to force it, you're no kind of man and I'll personally rip your fucking pathetic little knob off your pathetic little body with my bare fucking hands and shove it all the way down your gob. Number three, people are not objects to be bought and sold. Just about everything else is up for debate, and I'm damn good at debating.

But I'm up against an immovable force. I've no real choice. There's always a choice, people say. But people who say that are usually not the ones making the choice, are they? Nah, they're not. Sometimes, there really isn't a choice.

Case in point—this shit situation. Or, shit-uation, as it were. I've got to get this girl to Lyon, ASAP. If I don't, my world is over. I don't want to hand her over to him. I know what he's like. I know what happens to girls who end up in his clutches.

But there's just no fucking choice.

I could crack her across the noggin, but you're likely as not to scramble someone's brains doing that. It ain't as easy as they make it seem on the telly to give someone a whack *just* hard enough to knock 'em out but not so hard they end up a drooling cucumber. I don't have any sleepy drugs, and while I could get them and put her to sleep, I ain't a fucking chemist. Give her too much…drooling cucumber, or dead. Too little and she wakes up confused and panicky, and then I've got to subdue her or calm her somehow, and knowing my luck, she'd wake up while I'm doing 130 km/h on the motorway. And all in all, while I'm aware of the gruesome, horrible fate that awaits her after I turn her over to Satan's favorite minion, I'm not eager to traumatize her any more than I have to along the way.

Especially this girl.

Have I mentioned how fucking gorgeous she is?

The fucking hair, Jesus. A massive explosion of perfectly spiraled black curls, the kind I'm itching to dig my fingers into while she wraps those pretty, plump pink lips around my cock. I can almost feel it. And her eyes? To say they're brown is to lack imagination. They're not just brown, they're…dark chocolate, the 85% cacao kind that's got a hint of bitter to balance out the sweet. They're the color of rich dark soil in the summer sun. They're infinite pools, mesmerizing and hypnotic. Dangerous.

Right now, those not-just-brown eyes are searching me as if hoping to unearth my secrets. Which is when I realize I'm still holding her hand. And what a hand it is—tiny, soft, clever, quick. Her skin is magnificent. The exact shade of the kind of hot cocoa that comes out of those cheapo tins at the corner Tesco. I suppose that's not a sexy description, but it's accurate, and I happen to love that shit with an unhealthy zeal. Put this girl in a mug and I'll drink her all up.

I may just anyway.

I tuck my trusty old Browning Hi-Power back in my waistband and keep hold of her hand. Pull her into a walk. "Come on, then, love. Best get scarce, unless you feel like explaining them dead fucks to the Berlin police."

"Oh, no, nope. I'm good." She trots to catch up and then manages to match my stride without effort. "So your name is Rush?"

I wink at her. "That's me, yeah."

"Well, Rush, thank you for…" she waves at the bodies now well behind us. "That."

"Didn't seem like they wanted to have a pillow fight, and I don't think much of that sorta business."

She glowers. "No, they didn't want to have a pillow fight."

I look her over—skimpy little silver skirt clinging to her tight little ass, bare midriff, and swishy little rainbowy top cupping what seem to be a magnificent pair of tits. Over that, a man's suit jacket. On her feet, those furry boots girls like to wear, but they seem a bit too small.

"Interesting fashion choices," I note.

If looks were blades, I'd be carved up into pieces about now, the way she's glaring at me. "Yeah, well, when you get kidnapped out of a fucking nightclub, drugged, and hauled halfway across goddamned Europe, you do what you gotta fuckin do, okay?"

Fuck, I hate this.

"So, I feel like maybe you skipped a detail or two in that telling," I say.

"What, you want the graphic audio version?"

"The what now?"

"Graphic audio? Audiobooks, but instead of an actor narrating the text, it's actors and sound effects and everything. Like a movie, but audio only."

I give her a puzzled look. "That's a thing, is it?"

"Uh, yeah."

I narrow my eyes at her sarcastic tone. "Hey now, no reason to be sarcastic about it. For one, sarcasm is *my* thing. And for two, I ain't exactly had a lot of opportunity in my life to go around listening to books on tape."

"Books on tape," she echoes. "Don't you have a smartphone?"

"Yeah?"

"Let me see."

Ha, right. So you can call your parents or whatever? Not bloody likely.

She reads my hesitation. "Ohmygod, just open up your phone. I'm not gonna swipe through all your dick picks."

I open it and hand it to her, watching her over her shoulder. "I've never once taken a picture of my knob, thanks very much. Doesn't do it justice. Art is meant to be appreciated live and in person."

Her jaw drops open, but it's also part grin, part

shock. "You…wow. You think pretty highly of yourself, don't you?"

"I think accurately of myself." Sirens howl not far away. "Whatever you're gonna do, best do it quick. If you want to vanish, we can't stay on the street."

She hands me my phone. "Press play."

She's downloaded an app and, I assume, signed in using her login. I press the play button, and a woman's voice emits from the speakers.

"…His finger penetrated her slowly, filling her tight channel until her eyes crossed and her wails of ecstasy ricocheted off the cavern walls. Growling hungrily, Kraden wrapped his long, prehensile tail around her thigh, teasing upward—"

I stab the pause button when an awkwardly realistic female moan of sexual pleasure overlaps the narration. "Wait, wait, wait. His fuckin' *tail*? What in the actual fuck are you listenin' to? Monkey porn or some shit like that?"

She glares at me. "No, you fuck-bag, it's not *monkey porn*. And just because it has sex in it that doesn't mean it's *porn*. It's spicy romantasy, thank you very much. This is a series about a girl who gets magically transported to an alien realm where the males have prehensile tails and erogenous horns."

"Erogeh-what-now?"

"Erogenous. It means sensitive to sexual stimulation. Your upper thigh could be erogenous, but your nostrils, not so much."

I laugh. "Never had your nose twiddled? Missin' out on some fun, you are." I pause. "So, lemme get this straight." I wiggle my phone in her direction as I guide her down to the U-Bahn. "You could be sitting on a train with your headphones on, and you're listenin' to some girl get railed by a bloke with a tail and horns?"

She grins. "Hell yes. I do it all the time. Lay out on the beach next to my brother and my mom, listening to that. It's hot."

"Wouldn't it be…I dunno. Weird? Like, I'd think you'd get all bothered."

"Oh, I do. But I'm a girl, Rush. No boner to give away the fact that I'm turned on."

"Right, right, I guess there's that." I look at the app. "Are there other books on there? Ones that haven't got spicy tail-boys in it?"

She cackles. "Yes, Rush, there are. There's millions. Not all of them have the sound effects. Most audiobooks are just someone…well, I was gonna say reading, but it's more of a performance. They're actors. The good ones, at least."

"So, like…" I find the book on Roman history I've been slogging through on my Kindle app and show it to her. "I could find this, but someone reading it to me?"

She frowns thoughtfully, taking my phone again and tapping and swiping. "Yep. Here it is. It's got Whispersync, too, so it'll pick up where you left off, if you're reading and listening to the same book at different times."

"No fuckin' way. Are you for real?" I boggle at the price. "Thirty-four fucking pounds?"

"If you get a membership, it's a lot cheaper, assuming you actually use the subscription, though. But yeah, audiobooks can be expensive. Think about it, though: you have to pay the actors, and then you have to pay someone to do the actual recording, like the machines and such, and then a producer to cut and edit and mix…a lot goes into them."

"Fuck me, mate. Where *was* this all my life?" I buy the audiobook right then and there, pull my earbuds out of my jacket pocket, and thumb one in. And sure enough, the crisp, arch, high-brow British male reader picks up reading where I'd left off. "Fuck me," I mutter again. "That's my life changed."

She stares at me. "You really didn't know audiobooks were a thing?"

"No." It's all I'm willing to offer her.

We reach the ticketing kiosk and I buy us tickets with cash. A train arrives just then, and I guide her onto the train. So far, she seems willing to go along, almost not realizing what I'm doing. Best-case scenario here is she keeps on like this and there's no fuss about it. I'm starting to like this sexy brown goddess. Which could pose a problem. I don't want to have to do anything unpleasant.

Once we're seated, I put my earbuds away and settle back, hoping she'll leave the topic of my reading issue alone.

"So…you have a hard time reading?"

Fuck. The questions. Always women with the fucking questions.

"Yeah, you might say that."

She sits twisted in the seat, staring at me expectantly. Waiting for me to fill the silence.

I've withstood torture, all right? Needles under the fingernails, waterboarding, beatings, electric shocks. Wouldn't recommend it, but I survived it and didn't give them shit but name, rank, and serial number.

But this girl's silence is fucking unnerving.

"I'm dyslexic, alright?" I pick at a loose thread on the belt loop of my jeans.

"That book on Roman history looked *dense*."

"Yeah." More of that stupid, effective silence. "I didn't get much schooling. I'm trying to make up for it. And I like history. That all right with you?"

She smiles at me, and fuck me sideways, that smile lights up her face. It's the kind of smile you'd kill men for. And she's turning it on me. I don't much like how my gut flips about because of it, either. Or my clammy palms.

"I think that's great, Rush." She leans closer to me. "Can I tell you a secret?"

"Sure."

"I hate reading. But I love books. So, I listen to audiobooks."

"You hate reading but love books."

She nods. "Yup. My eyes cross after about thirty minutes, and then the lines start swimming all over the page, and I end up reading the same paragraph eighty-seven times. But I love stories. I love books. I just…I'm not great at reading."

I fiddle with the zipper of my jacket, watching a young fella trying to pickpocket an old woman. I catch his eye and shake my head. "Take what you've got and make it about a thousand times worse," I say. "The letters flip around and get all jumbled up, words jump around, it's all a fucking mess. Damned impossible, is what it is."

"Huh. I wonder if I have, like, a mild form of it." She sits in silence for roughly a minute. "So, where are we going?"

I gesture in the direction the train is going. "That way."

She rolls her eyes. "Wow. So helpful. So informative. Just absolutely brilliant conversation."

I'm mostly successful at hiding my grin of amusement. "Just getting away."

"From the cops?"

"Them too."

"Who else?"

I sigh. "Those blokes weren't just your run-of-the-mill troublemakers. They were career gangsters. They wanted you for a reason." I should know. I'll probably catch hell for killing them, but it's worth it to erase scum like them from the planet. "And that means there'll be more out there looking for you. Stunner like you'll fetch a high price in the right markets."

Her gaze snaps to mine, suspicious and wary, suddenly. "You sound like you're familiar with the market, Rush."

"Not as such, no. Not like you're thinking." Which is true. I make a point of not lying if I can help it. I'm a shit liar. What I'm good at is omitting the truth, or stretching it. But I almost never outright lie.

She doesn't answer for a moment or two. "Not sure how satisfactory that answer is, Rush."

I shrug. "Only answer you'll get, Gorgeous. It is what it is."

"I hate that stupid fucking phrase," she grumbles. "It doesn't mean anything."

I don't respond to that. The more I talk to this girl, the more I like her. Which is a bad thing. I *can't* like her.

We ride the U-Bahn to the opposite end of Berlin. I nudge her knee with mine when the doors swish open, and she precedes me out. I follow her with a hand on the small of her back—her body heat radiates through the thin material of the suit coat.

"Ain't cha cold, love?" I ask.

She shrugs. "I mean, yeah. It's fucking freezing and I'm not exactly dressed for the weather. Assholes."

"Who?"

"The turd-suckers who snatched me and the other girl."

"Turd-suckers. You've got a way with words, you have." We hit street level, and I guide her away from the intersection. I've no clue where we are, but it doesn't matter. This is just to keep her off-balance. And also, I'm genuinely trying to lose her pursuers. You'd think he'd lay off now he's got me on the situation, but I guess he doesn't trust me all the way. Smart man—I'd double-cross him in half a heartbeat. We pass a small breakfast cafe; an older couple exits just then, and the scent of hash browns and pancakes wafts out with them.

Bryn's stomach snarls noisily.

I laugh. "Hungry, hey?" I press her toward the door. "Come on. Let's get some food."

"Thank fuck. I'm starved."

5

THAT STUPID FUCKING SMIRK

I just can't get a firm read on Rush. He's charming, sexy, funny, and downright chatty one second, and then he's all broody and distant the next.

Not to mention how casually he dropped those four men. The display of skill, speed, and marksmanship is damn near unparalleled. You don't acquire that kind of godlike talent with a gun by going to the range a few times a week, nor by gallivanting around playing gangster, nor do you kill four men without so much as blinking unless you've done it so many times it really is nothing.

And then there's the tiny little fact that he's hot as *fuck*. Drool-worthy hot. Fan myself just looking at him, hot. The jawline? The stubble? The eyes? God, the eyes. Right now, he's pensive and broody as he devours his food—and it seems pensive means his eyes are more gray.

Let's talk about his arms, shall we? Because *damn*. His arms are pussy-killers. Mine is sitting up and taking notice, that's for sure. I mean, what is it about a man with big, sexy, strong arms wearing a long-sleeve Henley? It's fucking sinful. Arms should not be able to ripple *inside* the sleeves of his shirt. Yet, there they are, thicker than an overfed anaconda, rippling inside his sleeves with every movement.

I think there's actual drool at the corner of my lip. I bet he has at least sixty-eight abs, too.

Gah. Down girl, I internally yell at my vagina. *Get a grip.*

But how can anyone expect me to have a grip on my libido when he says things like "art is meant to be appreciated live and in person" in reference to his cock? Plus the exquisitely self-assured way he said it? He *knows* he's telling the unvarnished truth. Meaning, he has a giant, beautiful cock.

My libido has been on an extended hiatus. Even my usual spicy romantasy books haven't been able to revive the spark lately, and usually my spark is more like an out-of-control wildfire.

Shit, shit, shit. Wrong direction to take the train of thought, Bryn. Good job. Now you're thinking about Zero.

Libido...*dead*.

The food—hash browns slathered in ketchup, pancakes, sausage links, and cheesy scrambled eggs—is suddenly unpalatable.

Rush notices. "All right?"

I nod but say nothing.

"Wasn't born at night *or* last night, love. C'mon. Out with it." Maybe it's because I've talked to him more now, but I'm gradually finding it easier to understand him.

"No. It's…nevermind. I'm fine."

He nods, spearing a sausage with his fork and biting a huge chunk off the end, speaking after he's swallowed most of it. "A'right, then. I know better when a woman says she's fine, but you don't wanna talk about it and I ain't the one to push."

I expect him to push, despite what he said, but he doesn't. He just eats in silence—he ordered two full meals and has polished them both off in the time it's taken me to eat half of my one meal.

I force myself to go back to eating, pushing away thoughts of Zero. "You're really not going to ask?"

"I did. But when a woman says no, I listen. You wanna tell me what's got you giving me those sad puppy eyes, I'd like to hear it. But nah, I'm not gonna ask again."

"There were no sad puppy dog eyes."

He snorts sarcastically, gesturing at me with his fork. "There absolutely was. Big, deep, sad, brown puppy dog eyes. Tragical. Full of sorrow."

I sigh in disgust. "Jerk."

He laughs. "What? Why'm I a jerk? Just pointing out facts. And, I'll point out, showing concern by asking about it."

I sip coffee—which, by the way, is leaps and bounds better than the burned, watery swill you'd get in a similar establishment in the US. "Well, if there is sorrow, it's nothing I want to talk about."

"Fair enough. We've all got sorrow about somethin', haven't we?" His own gaze turns brownish-gray and distant, thinking about his own sorrow. His gaze snaps me to me, and for a second I catch a glimpse of raw, unbridled rage that steals my breath and sends a centipede of fear skittering down my spine.

It's there and gone so fast I almost doubt that I saw it, but the lingering fear is the reminder that I did, in fact, see it. And that I should be careful with the sexy, dangerous Mr. Rush.

"Is Rush your real name?" I ask.

"Yeah." He shrugs a lazy shoulder. "Only name I've ever had."

"It's not short for anything weird?"

This gets me a grin and a laugh, and the sheer beauty of the man when he laughs is almost scary. "Nah, love. What would it be short for?"

"Um," I start, spluttering laugh. "I don't know. Rush…an? Rush…icles?" As in *Russian* and *Rush-ick-leez*.

"Rushan, or Rushicles?" His shoulders shake with silent laughter. "Sweetheart, if you ever have kids, leave the naming to your husband."

Husband.

Zero would be my husband now if he were alive.

"Ah, fuck. I've stepped in shit, haven't I?" He peers at me carefully. "How'd he die, then? Your 'usband."

"Fiancé," I murmur, looking away and blinking hard. "Car accident barely two weeks before the wedding."

Rush covers my hand with one of his—he has

W-A-R tattooed across the knuckles of his index, middle, and ring fingers of his right hand, the letters oriented to be read by him rather than a viewer. "Fuck, sweetheart. I'm sorry. Losing someone like that…it rips your fuckin' heart out." He's utterly genuine. You can't fake the look of understanding in his eyes—which are greenish again.

I nod. "You?"

"Me what?"

"Who'd you lose?"

"Everyone." He shoots to his feet, tossing a stack of much-folded euros on the table. "Right back. Gotta have a wazz."

Well, I guess that's the end of that bit of sharing.

But…*everyone*?

I go back to the flash of anger I saw. I didn't get the impression that he was angry *at* me. More…*Because* of me. I can't pinpoint why I feel that way, but I do.

I toss back the last of my coffee while waiting for Rush to return from the bathroom. As he's passing the counter where the cash register is, he pauses, scenting the air. He gets the attention of the woman behind the counter, makes a request. A few moments later, he swaggers to the table with a lidded paper to-go cup from which he sips, looking pleased.

"C'mon, Bryn. That's us off." He takes a sip, his eyes fixed on me with a small, secretive smirk on his absurdly sensual mouth.

Outside, he pauses on the sidewalk, scanning our surroundings over the top of his paper cup. I follow his gaze, and see nothing—no one suspicious, nothing that sets my hackles on edge.

"This way," he murmurs, setting off in what seems to me to be a random direction.

"Do you know where we're going?" i ask.

He shrugs. "Nah. Just movin' around. Best get out of Berlin quick-like, though. I wasn't exactly subtle, y'know. Rozzer's'll be on us eventually if we don't get scarce."

"Sometimes I have no fucking clue what you're saying," I tell him, arching an eyebrow at him. "Like, what the fuck is *rozzers*?"

He snorts, sips, slurping and sighing happily. "Fuzz. Old Bill. Bobbies. Coppers."

I roll my eyes. "You can't just say 'the police'?" I point at his cup. "The coffee there was good, but not *that* good. You sound like you're about to come."

"Well, that's cuz it ain't coffee." he shrugs. "Never been a fan of the coppers, so nah, I ain't likely to be polite about what I calls 'em."

I take the cup from him and steal a sip, and it's… hot chocolate? As in, totally standard restaurant-grade cocoa powder. "Um. Okay. That's just hot chocolate."

"Nobody's asked you your opinion on it, 'ave they?" He takes it back from me with narrowed eyes.

"I'm not judging, Rush, I just…" I laugh. "Okay, well, sure. Fine. I'm judging you a little bit. I mean, I was under the impression that you were an adult."

"Yeah, yeah, har-har-har. I'm a grown adult who likes hot cocoa. Fuck off with your judge-y bullshit, *Bryn*." He sounds genuinely peeved.

I snort. "Sensitive about it, too."

"My mates used to take the piss outta me for it," he murmurs. "And yeah, I'm rather preferential to the bog-standard cheap shite. Right out of the tin with boiling water. None of those stupid, crunchy fake little marshmallows, neither. Rather a good mug of cocoa than coffee any day, and tea can fuck right off."

"An Englishman who hates tea?" I say, faking outrage. "What is this world coming to?"

He frowns at me. "Y'know, I've never once in my life thought of meself as an Englishman. A man from England, sure. Brit, yeah. Englishman? Never. Dunno why, neither." He glances at me sidelong. "You really can't understand me?"

"Sometimes yes, sometimes no. It's the slang, mostly." We're just sort of…strolling down the sidewalk, in no particular hurry. "I'm not an expert, mind you, but this has got to be the most casual getaway ever."

He grins. "This may surprise you, but I've not always operated on the right side of the law."

I clap a hand over my chest. "No! I'm shocked! *Shocked*, I tell you."

"Yeah, yeah, I know." A dangerous grin, wicked dimples, twinkling greenish-brown eyes. "Me? A crook? Nahhh. Point is, in my experience, it's the running around all panicky-like that gets you caught. Stay calm, act natural, and don't look like you've done nothin' wrong. Like as not you'll get away with it."

"But we're not just evading the police," I point out. "It's the people who kidnapped me that I'm more worried about. I didn't kill anyone." I wince. "Well, that's not exactly true. Maybe I should be worried about the cops, I guess."

He cocks an eyebrow at me. "It's not true that you didn't kill anyone? I think maybe you've left out the good bits of your story, love."

"How about you get me some real fucking clothes before I freeze my actual tits off and I'll tell you everything."

His gaze rakes over me, lingering blatantly on my cleavage—which, if I'm honest, feels nice. I don't have the biggest boobs in the world. They're not mosquito bites, but they're not Rin's monster knockers, either. So to have a hotter-than-sin bad boy like this guy checking out my rack? It just feels good.

"Be a real shame if a perfect pair like yours froze off," he says. "So then, we best find a shop, hadn't we?"

A taxi sidles past right then, and he flags it down. He speaks to the driver in rapid, excellent, Cockney-accented German.

"A perfect pair," I mutter, half to myself. "Flattery will get you everywhere."

"What, has someone told you otherwise?" he asks.

I shrug. "Not explicitly, no. I just know when it comes to men and boobs, bigger is better, and mine aren't exactly tipping the scales."

"See, love, that's where you're wrong. Are there men out there who have a fetish for women with beach balls stapled to their chest? Sure. And that's all good and well, live and let live, says I—like what you like and I'll do the same." He lets his gaze linger on my chest again, a smirk curving his lips when my nipples harden under his scrutiny. "But most of the blokes I know feel as I do."

"Which is?"

"A tit is a tit, no matter how small, and I love them all."

I frown. "But you used the word 'perfect.'"

"I did, yes. And I meant it. Because if I had a gun to my head and was told to say what I consider the perfect pair of tits, I'd say yours."

"I'm going to require an elaboration. Because I'm not sure I believe you."

"You're just fishing for compliments, now."

I gasp in mock outrage. "How dare you! I thought we had something, Rush. And then you go and point out the truth like a heartless *jerk*."

"Had me in the first half," he says, chuckling. "You really want me to explain? Or is this where playful banter gets my head done in when I take it too far?"

"Speaking from experience, are you?" I ask, laughing.

"Let's just say that, speaking from personal experience, I'd rather walk into a firefight unarmed than deal with a woman I've pissed off with jokes about her body."

"I don't know where to start with that statement, Rush."

"Don't start, then?" He laughs.

"I mean, you can't say something like that and then expect me not to ask questions."

He sighs. "Such as?"

"You've been in a firefight unarmed?"

"Oh yeah. That was a fun one."

I just stare at him expectantly.

"Fuck. Fine. Story time, is it?" He rubs his jaw. "My first tour in Afghanistan. Me and my unit were supposed to be working with one of your Yank SEAL teams to take out an H-V-T in the mountains."

"Sorry, sorry, but I have to ask. You weren't regular army, were you?"

He grins. "Nah, love. S-A-S."

"Figures. The way you dropped those four, yeah, I pegged you as an operator."

His gaze sharpens on mine. "Familiar, are you?"

"Let's just say yes, I'm familiar. You might say it's sort of a…family business."

"Shoulda known when you didn't go into hysterics."

"Hysterics are for later. I'm saving it. Right now, I need to be Badass Bryn."

"That's the spirit, innit?" He grins at me. "I've got questions, but we can get to them later. So, yeah. We had a hell of a hike into the mountains. Supposed to rendezvous with the Yanks at a specific location and time. Remember, this was my first deployment. I'd been in the military for a few years by then, but I hadn't seen combat yet. I got pulled into the S-A-S, trained up, assigned to a unit, and shipped out. Very first mission, we're totally fuckin' lost. Those mountains are no fuckin' joke, and that ain't a word of a lie. Brutal place, that is. Top of the world, can't breathe for shit, everything looks the same. You're always cold. Fuckin' miserable. Nothin' to eat but tinned rations. Might be T-M-I, but it's important to the story—I was all clogged up. Know what I mean? Pipes were plugged. So, I was off on my own, fightin' for my life. Cliff edge was a few feet away. I mean, one wrong move and I'm taking a thousand-foot tumble."

"I can't imagine that helps you relax your bowels," I say.

"Nah, not exactly. I'd set my rifle aside so I could balance. I was halfway to success, if you know what I mean. Had a loaf half-pinched off."

I make a disgusted face. "Yes, Rush, I knew what you meant. I was good with the euphemism. Don't need the details."

He just chuckles. "Well, of course, that's when the enemy decided to ambush us. Heard the gunfire start up, heard my mates shouting and what all, tryin' to find cover and figure out where the tangos were. Bullets were whipping over my head, and my mates were yelling for me, so I, y'know, shook off the halfsie and ran for my mates. Forgot my fuckin' rifle."

I can't help but laugh. "No! That's, like, rule number one. You never, ever, let your rifle out of your sight."

"I know, believe me. When I got to where my mates were taking cover, I got reamed out, and I mean all the fuckin' way. My C-O damn near killed me himself for that stunt. And of course, by the time I realized I'd forgotten it, we were taking fire too heavy to go back for it. So I had to plink at the bastards with my sidearm. I never did live that one down."

"You made it out okay, though, obviously."

"Yeah. The Yanks showed up and helped us sort the fuckers out proper-like. Our target'd done a runner by then, though, so it was all for nothing."

"And the whole jokes about a woman's body?"

He glares at me. "She asked if the dress she was wearing gave her a fat arse."

I snicker. "Oh, shit. You said something idiotic, didn't you?"

"I said no, the dress don't give you a fat arse because you already *have* a fat arse."

I splutter a laugh, covering my face with my hands. "And you live to tell about it?"

He turns his head to show me his left cheek, pointing at a thin scar on his left cheekbone. "Backhanded me and left me this with her ring."

"Ring?" I ask, eyebrow arched.

He rolls his eyes. "Not a wedding ring, no." He looks away, though, which seems to be hiding a guilty conscience.

I gape at him, mouth open. "You fucked a married woman!"

He rolls a shoulder, not looking at me. "She made the choice, didn't she? I wasn't married. Her marriage was her business."

"That's a bullshit excuse. If you knew she was married and you still fucked her, you're part of the problem, Rush."

He sighs. "In hindsight, it may have been an error in judgment, yes."

"Why? Because you got caught?" I ask, my tone droll and openly judgmental.

"I did get caught, yes. Not with the fat-arse girl, but someone else." He gives me a flat, annoyed, side-eye stare. "No, I'm not tellin' you the story of that one.

Wasn't my finest hour and it fucked my life up but permanent-like. Not somethin' I care to relive."

I shrug. "Alright, then. That's fair."

He pauses, eying me as if waiting. "What? That's it?"

"I don't play head games, Rush. If I want answers, you'll know. If you tell me you're not talking about it, I accept it, if only because you've afforded me that same consideration."

He nods. After a moment, he grins at me. "We got sidetracked, and I'd like to get back to discussing my favorite topic."

I blink at him. "What?"

"Tits. Specifically yours."

"I thought we'd covered that already," I say.

"You said you required elaboration on why I think yours are perfect." He meets my eyes, and then pointedly takes a nice, long gander at my chest again. "Still interested in that elaboration?"

I roll my eyes. "This feels like a setup to get me to show you my boobs."

"Is it workin'?" That stupid, fucking smirk.

"Nope."

"Shame. We can still talk about 'em though, can't we?"

I laugh. "I'm good."

Truth be told, I'd like to hear what he has to say. But I don't want to come off insecure or needy. I'm not insecure about my boobs, I swear. I mean, sure, when your BFF, who's basically your sister, has the biggest, most perfectly tear-drop shaped natural melons I've ever seen and I'm sporting these cute little grapefruits, yeah, there might be a bit of inferiority complex happening. Or maybe just a little jealousy.

Zero, when I confessed this to him during pillow talk one night, offered to buy me, and I quote, 'an upgrade.' Yeah, guess who slept on the couch that night? Was it a bit of an overly-sensitive reaction to an offer coming from a place of love? Yes. But I maintain that saying he'd get me implants would be an upgrade was insensitive. He admitted it the next day and apologized, and we never discussed it again. Because I don't want implants. Most of the time.

When Rush looks at me the way he does, with that lecherous little smirk, telling me my boobs are perfect? Yeah, that feels nice.

"You're thinkin' about it, aren't you?" Rush asks, and I realize he's been watching me carefully this whole time.

"Stop staring at me. It's creepy."

"Remember what I said? Art is meant to be appreciated. What's the point in you being so fuckin' stunnin' if I can't have a look at you?"

I roll my eyes at him, but my cheeks feel warm, and I can't bring myself to look at him. "You and the charm."

"You say that like it's a bad thing. I'm just callin' it like I see it."

At that moment, the driver pulls into the parking lot of a department store, right as an employee unlocks the doors.

Thirty minutes later, I'm properly dressed in a pair of jeans, thick wool socks, warm, comfortable boots, a decent sports bra, a long-sleeve white T-shirt, a thick fleece pullover, and a top-of-the-line shell jacket. Rush insisted on paying, and I let him—keeping the fact that I do have some cash stuffed in my bra to myself just seems prudent. He seems like a decent guy, and he did save my life, but I don't fully trust him just yet.

Girl's gotta have a few secrets, after all.

It feels amazing to be properly attired, finally. It's only when I huddle into the jacket as we exit the department store that I realize how cold I'd been—I think I'd sort of disassociated from my body, to be honest. I get that from Mom—she can just sort of…turn off her physical needs. And so can I, apparently. Because I'm shivering and chattering, now.

Rush notices. "You weren't acting cold at all when you were wearing a whole lot of not much, but now that I buy a thousand euros worth of warm kit, you're shiverin'?" He laughs. "You don't make no sense, love."

"I think I was in denial, actually. Or maybe just on the verge of hypothermia. I don't know." I look around—we're on the outskirts of Berlin, now, away from the bustle of downtown. "Now what?"

"We get out of Berlin. Maybe out of Germany altogether."

I consider my options.

Stay with Rush, trust him to help me to safety? What if he's not safe? He saved my life and killed four men doing it. He's bought me food and clothing, and while he's the very definition of rough around the edges, he seems like a decent sort. He's got secrets, and he's definitely no angel, but I don't get the sense that he's evil. That's option one—stick with Rush.

Option two? Go it alone. Find a train station and get a ticket for Zermatt. But without an ID, can I even get a ticket? Especially since I'd be crossing international borders from Germany to Switzerland. This feels risky and problematic. What if the kidnappers are still after me? I have to assume they are. I killed two of their men, and Rush killed four. It doesn't seem likely that they'd just let that go. I can't see myself capping dudes like Rush did. I mean, shit—I froze when I had the chance. I froze, and now look where I am. So yeah, this is probably not my best option.

Three…go to the authorities. Have Rush take me to the US Embassy and throw myself at their mercy. They'd send up a flare to my parents, metaphorically speaking, and I'd be home within hours. Knowing Dad, he'd land his Harrier on the front lawn of the embassy. But something about this niggles at me, too. I have to look hard at myself to figure out what it is. I don't trust the authorities. I guess I've grown up hearing stories about what Mom, Dad, Auntie Key, and Uncle Val went through, how authority figures are so often compromised by bad men with too much money and influence. What if I show up at the embassy and the motherfucker running the human trafficking ring that I'm messed up with has paid off someone in the embassy, and I end up right back in his clutches? There's no way to know either way, but the spectre of the "what if" makes me leery.

"Thinkin' deep thoughts over there, 'ey?" Rush's voice shakes me out of my thoughts.

"Oh, yeah, I guess so. Just trying to figure out my next steps. Where to go, what to do." I look at him. "It's hard to know who to trust. I don't know you, but you've been nice so far, and you did murder four men on my behalf. I was thinking I could go to the police or the embassy, but if these traffickers are bold enough to snatch girls right out of a nightclub, it feels like they're connected enough or powerful enough to feel like they can get away with it. And honestly, they did. They just didn't factor in me sticking my big nose into their business."

"Yeah, I don't think I'd trust the police or the embassy. Those sorts are easy enough to buy, and you're right. The blokes who were after you were gonna haul you right off the street in broad daylight. Speaks to what you said—they feel confident they can get away with it." He looks at me. "Maybe it's about time you filled in the gaps of what happened."

I regard him. "But that means my only choice is to trust you to keep me safe. I can handle myself to a degree, but..." I shrug, embarrassed to admit that I froze, especially to an elite operator like Rush.

"But what?"

"I froze," I mumble.

"Everyone freezes at some point," he says. "But if you've got the sand for the job, then it only happens once. You feel like a shit, y'know? Like, 'fuck, I fuckin' froze. I had one job, and I fuckin' froze.' Yeah nah, mate. You only freeze once." He shrugs. "That, or you die."

I cackle. "Wow, that's *so* comforting."

Once again, it seems like we're just aimlessly strolling. His head is on a swivel, though, and I can tell he's alert. But…where are we going? I get my answer a few minutes later when we reach a bus stop, and he sits on the bench to wait.

"C'mon. Ttell me about it." He nudges my leg with his; when I hesitate, he sighs. "Fine, how's about this? We'll trade. You tell me how you ended up in Berlin, and I'll tell you about the time I froze. And spoiler alert, I wasn't a rookie when it happened, neither."

I suppose it can't hurt, can it? There may be a few details I'll keep to myself—such as who my parents are, and my relationship to Auntie Key and Uncle Val—people get weird when they find out your found-family aunt and uncle are the richest human beings on the planet, or that your parents are…well, who my parents are.

But the rest is fair game.

And Rush is a surprisingly good listener.

Which is hot. But then, there's not much about him that *isn't* problematically, distractingly, absurdly sexy.

6

A DIFFERENT KIND OF RIDE

"...And then I literally ran into you," Bryn says, finishing her story.

We've taken the bus back across the city, and we're now waiting at a different stop for the bus that'll take us to the train station.

And I'm one conflicted motherfucker. On one hand, I'm legitimately impressed. It takes some big fat fuckin' stones to try and stop a kidnapping from happening. And to then have the presence of mind and self-control to stay calm and let a horrific situation play out like that? Letting some fat ugly old fuck almost rape you so you have the best shot at killin' him? Stones, mate. Big brass ones. Especially after seeing that poor girl dragged off like that, coming back all fucked up and traumatized, knowing you're next?

Rage burns in my belly. This is a shit situation. This girl is like no one I've ever met. She's not complained once. Not about the cold, not about walking for hours, not about a dirty city bus, not about anything. She ain't judging me, mostly—and some of my life choices deserve harsh judgment. I ain't no choir boy, and that's fact, innit? She's fucking goddamned exquisite. Breathtaking. Funny. Witty. And them two ain't the same, mind you. She's got a helluva sharp tongue, which is a turn-on for me. I like a girl who can keep up with me, keep me on my toes. I guess I feel…like she gets me. I mean, fuck, mate. The dyslexia bit? When most women find out I can barely read, they assume I'm stupid and uneducated. I ain't. I mean, my accent don't help none, either, but I ain't stupid and I ain't uneducated. It's just not been a formal education, you might say. Given my life and the way I grew up, it's a miracle I made it out of London and off the streets without getting sent down, let alone with any kind of education. The military made sure I got some learning, but once I was up for deployment, reading Hemingway and being up on my maths wasn't as much of a priority. I've had to make it a priority for myself. For *her*. So I can be someone she'd be proud of.

And she wouldn't be proud of what I'm doing now, would she? Tricking this fascinating, beautiful, intense woman into the hands of the very man she's running from?

Low, even for the likes of me.

But I haven't got a goddamn choice. I just haven't. Time's about up. I could take a deployment with an outfit like Wagner or Blackwater, but…the risk is high. I'd make the bank I need, but there's no guarantee I'd live to use the money. What other options do I have? Not a fuckin' one, that's what. I'm no grifter or con artist. Robbing banks won't do it. Extortion? Blackmail? I'd sell a fucking organ if it'd pay for the treatment she needs.

No. This is it. It just sucks a fat one that the target is so goddamned perfect in every way.

Why couldn't she be ugly or annoying? Like, one of those whiny slags who go on and on about their vegan cheeses and hot yoga and those fuckin' awful essential oils and shit. I shagged a girl like that, once. And I swear, even the fact that she had a great pair of tits and a mouth like a hoover was almost not enough to overcome how fucking annoying she was. Why couldn't Bryn be like that? It'd be at least a little easier to betray her like I'm going to. Not much, but some. Shit, no woman, no matter how awful or obnoxious, deserves the fate in store for Bryn.

I'm gonna have to harden myself, at some point. Let the massive arsehole I really am come out. Let her see my true colors.

She don't need to know the reason I'm doing it. It won't help. Won't make the betrayal any less bitter. Nah, best keep that to myself.

Would it be better to stop letting myself like her now? Just be a massive wanker to her until I turn her over to him?

Can I do it? I dunno.

I dunno if I can.

I push the thoughts aside and look at her. She's stopped shivering, finally. "You killed him with a pencil?"

She shrugs, nodding. "Did what I had to do."

"You've got sand, Bryn. Truly." I mean that, too.

She shrugs again. "If I hadn't frozen in the first place, none of it would have happened. That poor girl would be home. She wouldn't have gotten raped. I'd be back at the hotel with Killy and Cal. I just…" she sighs, shuddering. "I can't help but feel like it's my fault."

"Nah, love, nah. It ain't your fault." I can't help but wrap my arm around her slender shoulders; she resists for a moment and then leans into me, and rests her head on my shoulder. "It's not. Yeah, you froze. But if you've never shot someone before, it's a tough thing to do. It's hard to cross that Rubicon. You can't take it back."

She scrapes her fingers through her hair, sighing. "What does it say about me that I'm not, like, super upset and sick about the way I killed those men?"

"Not a damn thing, if you're askin' me," I tell her. "Some people just deserve death, and those two did. And aside from that, you did what you had to do to stay alive. No shame or guilt in that."

"I just feel like I should…*feel* something." She sighs, shaking her head and shrugging. "I mean, if I think about it too hard, I get icked out, but I don't feel bad. I don't feel guilty. Honestly, I wish I'd just shot them both back at the club."

"A pencil to the eye for your first kill is fuckin' wicked, Bryn. I served with blokes who struggled with that. It ain't easy. You're doin' brilliantly."

"Don't feel like it. I feel like there's something wrong with me."

I chuckle. "It's called having a moral compass, sweetheart."

"But I don't feel guilty."

"Exactly. Because you shouldn't. You didn't do nothin' wrong. You protected yourself. Or you could think of it as you took revenge for the girl who got raped. You killed a filthy fuckin' maggot who probably deserved a much slower and more painful death than what he got."

The bus arrives then, and we board, sitting near the back. She's close to me on these narrow seats. I feel her body heat. I'm hyper-aware of her. I can almost let myself believe this is real. That I'm really saving her. Helping her. That I'm the bloke it seems like she thinks I am.

The trip is short, and when she sees where we are as the bus trundles off, she sighs. "I just left this place."

"Well, this time, you'll be traveling with a ticket, and you'll not be drugged," I say. "So hopefully a bit different."

"Maybe." She looks at the soaring, imposing glass edifice of the Berlin Hauptbahnhof with doubt.

We reach the ticketing counter, and I pretend to think. "You know, I've got a friend who lives in Lyon. He's well-connected. He might be able to help you sort this out."

"I mean, really, I just want to get back to my family."

"Obviously, I don't know your family, but are you sure you want to bring this to them? My friend can sort this out, and you'll keep your family safe from it. These blokes ain't playin, love."

She doesn't answer right away, thinking. "I guess that makes sense. You don't know my family, though."

She shrugs. "I don't know. I don't know what to do. I brought this on myself. I snuck out."

I'm still not clear on why she had to sneak out to go to the club in the first place, but I suspect she left out a few details on purpose. Doesn't totally trust me. Smart girl.

I don't want her to trust me. I want her to get away from me. But I can't let her. I need her to trust me.

Fuck me, I hate this. I hate this fucking bastard for putting me in this situation. I hate the universe for putting me in this situation. I hate myself for putting me in this situation

But, I do what I must. For *her*. I'll just have to learn how to live with the guilt.

"My family would be pissed if they found out I didn't call them for help."

"Dunno what to say to that one. Never had family to care like that. Good on ya for having that."

Shit. Didn't mean to say that.

"No family, huh?"

"Nah."

Here she goes with the leading silence. I know what she's doing, but fuck me if I can't help but fill it.

"I'm an orphan. I was left at the door of a vicarage when I was only a few days old. No note, no clue who my mother was, nothing." I shrug. "Lived in orphanages and foster homes for the first few years, but I done a runner on 'em when it got hairy. Lived on the streets after that. Joined the army at seventeen, soon's they'd take me."

"When it got hairy?" she asks.

"Bah," I say, waving her off. "You got to know what that means, Bryn. I know for a fact the foster system in your country ain't any better than the English one. Worse, maybe."

"I've heard stories about it, yeah," she says. "Saw stuff on TV."

I snort. "What's on the telly ain't the half of it, love. Fuckin' awful, what it is. Taught me early to keep my own counsel, and how to take a hell of a beating." I see her mouth open and hold up a finger to stop her. "Nah-nah, don't. No sorrys. No, 'oh, how awful.' Shove all that shit back in your gob. Don't wanna hear it."

"Honestly, Rush, I can't relate. At all. Let's just say that my life, growing up, could not possibly have been any further from yours."

I laugh. "Yeah, love, I gathered that."

She frowns at me. "What's that mean?"

"Nothin'."

"No, tell me."

"People who grew up with everything have a…I dunno. A unique way of movin' through the world. A sort of…what is it? An assurance, I guess. Sort of the opposite of my type. I'm a cocky bastard, right? I know that. But I am because I've fuckin' *earned* it. I know who I am. I know what I can do. I know where I been and what I come out of. And it's made me strong. Your lot is different. Not better or worse, just different. You know your place in the world because you've never had to question it."

"Till now," she murmurs. "Definitely questioning it now."

"Fair enough, yeah." I gesture at her. "So. Where to?"

She sighs, looking at me. "Lyon. But…Rush?"

My heart hammers when she says my name like that. Soft. Hesitant. "Don't fuck me over. Please. Okay? I'm starting to like you, a little bit."

Fuck me.

You can't like me. I'm a bastard. I'm ruining your life. I'm fucking you over. Can't you see it? Can't you sense it?

All I say, though, is: "I've got you, love."

Not a lie. I do have her. Just…not how she thinks.

We board the train for Lyon forty-five minutes later.

Within ten minutes of leaving the station, she's nodding off.

Her head slowly tilts toward me. Rests on my shoulder. I don't like how this feels: right. Perfect. Good. Warm in my chest. Hot in my belly. Boiling in my balls. Just her—her scent, her warmth, her courage.

I hate myself for this. I think I always will.

The world is a cruel, unfair place. Some days, I wish I hadn't made it out of Afghanistan, or any of the other places I should've and could've died.

I let my arm curl around Bryn's shoulders protectively, and I close my eyes and I let myself pretend that we're a couple heading to Lyon for a holiday. Me and my girl.

I doze off.

When I bolt awake, Bryn's head is on my lap and

she's curled up in a tight little ball on the seat beside me. Fuck, this is bad. Too close. Too real. Too tempting.

Her eyes flutter, lift to mine. Soft brown like pools of melted chocolate. She's got a bit of drool at the corner of her lip.

I brush it away with my thumb, and her cheeks darken with a blush. The tips of her ears, too. Fuckin' adorable. Turns my heart to goo.

She slides upright, staying close to me. Pushed against me. Her tits are firm against my chest, her breath hot on my cheek, my chin.

No, girl, no. Bad plan. The face is a lie. The looks hide a black soul. Don't believe me.

I'm a horrible piece of shit, though.

I don't stop her.

Don't move.

I pull her closer. My hand slides down her back, rests on her waist. Glides to her hip. A soft breath leaves her plump lips when I palm her ass—and my god, what an ass. Taut as a drum, a nice big handful each spot, plump and juicy. Just perfect. Like the rest of her.

God, I'm a monster: I fucking kiss her.

Her mouth is warm and wet and soft and inviting; from the first touch of my lips to hers, I'm gone. My cock goes hard as a steel beam instantly, and when she lets out a quiet groan as my tongue traces across her lips, my cock throbs, twitches. She stretches against me, hands winding around my neck, fingers scraping against the shaved skin at the back of my head.

Bryn twists into me, pressing a thigh over my crotch, resting the weight of it on my hard, aching cock.

The friction and pressure are a tantalizing tease, ripping a soft snarl from me. I flex against her, driving myself against her leg, clawing my hand into the curve of her ass. And just like that, she's straddling me on the bench, both hands on the back of my head, cupping, fingers dimpling, nails softly scratching.

No one's ever held me like this while kissing me—so intimately, with such tender affection, as if…I don't know. It makes my heart pound and my stomach fall away and rise into my throat all at once, makes my hunger for her naked body ravenous and undeniable.

I shift her so she's straddling my thigh, pressing her center against my quad. Plunge my tongue into her mouth and devour her whimper, grab her ass in both of my hands and grind her against my leg. Her whimper becomes a groan, and she breaks the kiss, gasping as she rocks on my thigh, seeking the right combination of friction and pressure.

She removed her jacket and jumper when we settled into our compartment, so when her t-shirt rides up with her movement, it bares the skin at the small of her back. My hands find that sliver of warmth and seek more. Skate up her back, roaming from shoulders to small and back. Her jeans gap at the back as she leans into me, and my hands, without consulting me first, dive into the space between garment and body, finding her lush, firm flesh. I groan in wonder and delight at the way her ass fills my hands.

Her gasps are hoarse and quiet as she rocks against my leg; I press up against her movement, give her something to move against. Meet her rocking rhythm, helping her move with my hands on the bare flesh of her ass, her mouth slipping and sliding against mine with stuttering, gasping kisses.

Harder, faster.

Fuck, she's going to come.

My cock pulsates with arousal, aches, crushed and bent against the prison of my zipper. I'd do any manner of horrible things to have her hands wrapped around me, or better yet, that sweet, sassy, sarcastic mouth. I dare not even dream of having her ride me, having her pussy clamping down on me as we come together.

She rocks on my leg, her kisses going staccato, pausing as she loses focus on the kiss to zero in on her building climax.

"Rush," she murmurs, panting. "I…oh…oh god."

I bring my lips to her ear. "Let go for me, Beautiful. Show me what you've got."

She grinds on me desperately, clutching at my head. "I…I don't know if I can. Not like this."

"Sure you can, sweetheart."

"I…I need…" She trails off, whimpering.

"Need what? Tell me."

"More. I can't. Not like this."

"More what?" I nip at her earlobe, fit my hand against her belly; she sucks in, but there's no chance I'm getting my big hand into the narrow space between her belly and her fly.

"Rush," she breathes, rocking and grinding and rubbing, antsy and desperate. "Fuck."

"Not sure fucking is an option at the moment," I murmur. "Or I'd be buried inside you already."

She writhes harder, whimpering in frustration. With an almost feral growl, Bryn yanks her fly apart. "Please."

I wedge my hand under the elastic of her underwear, finding hot, wet, willing flesh. Her seam parts for my middle finger, and the hard little nub of her clit greets my touch; she gasps, jerks. Buries her face in the side of my neck, muffling a gasp, a whimper, a whine—each one more desperate than the last.

I explore her depths, slicking my finger into her channel. "Fuck, Bryn. You're so goddamned tight."

She writhes against my touch, mewling. God, she's desperate. Wild for a release. How long has it been for her? Way too long, I think. Time to rectify that.

I slip my finger, now drenched with her the essence of her need, against her clit. She muffles a cry against my neck, rocking against me. I circle her clit with the pad of my finger, barely touching the bundle of nerve-endings. Her gasps come short and quick, and shallow, as much moan as gasp. Her hips buck, writhe, twitch.

She's seconds from exploding.

I drive my finger inside her again, receiving a frustrated little snarl at the denial of her release. "Rush!"

God, the way she says my name is fucking intoxicating. Makes my cock harder than ever, which I recognize is ridiculous and possibly concerning.

"You want to come, do you?" I tease, curling my finger inside her sweet, hot, wet pussy.

"I *have* to," she whispers. "I fucking *need* it."

I slide my fingertip against her clit. "This?"

"Yes!"

I hold my finger still. "Take it, then, love. Fuck my finger the way you need it."

Arms tight around my neck, she growls against my throat as she grinds her clit against my finger, driving herself against my touch. "Fuck, fuck," she hisses. "So fucking close."

"I thought you needed to come," I tease. "Thought you were right there."

"I am," she snaps. "I need…oh—oh fuck. I need—"

"Tell me, Gorgeous. Tell me what you need to come for me."

She grabs my wrist and moves my hand in circles. "Faster. Make me come."

I bury my hand in her hair and yank her face away from my throat. "Eyes on mine, love."

Her limpid brown eyes are wide and deep and glistening and fraught. "Rush," she whines.

"Say please," I growl.

"Please," she begs, shameless and greedy. "Make me come, Rush. Please."

I push two fingers deep inside her clenching, pulsing pussy and fuck her with them, and my cock throbs at the wet squelch as my fingers drive through her clamping, squeezing channel. Fuck, I want to be inside her. Want it to be my cock instead of my fingers.

She grips my wrist with bruising strength. "Touch my clit, Rush. I'm there—I'm *right* there," she whispers, pleading. "Touch me, touch me, please-*fuck* touch me now, Rush."

Slick fingers smear against her clit, and she detonates instantly. A cry rips out of her throat, and I slam my mouth on hers to silence her, swirling my fingers against her as fast as I can, as fast as the awkward angle and limited space will allow. She writhes on me, thrashes, grinds, wailing into my mouth, pulling back with gritted teeth, head hanging, keening desperately as her orgasm leaves her shuddering and shaking.

I take her through her orgasm with slow circles, milking the last throes of climax until she drags my hand away, collapsing against me, panting raggedly.

After a minute or so of trying to catch her breath, she pulls away to look at me. "That was…unexpected." A grin. 'But amazing. Thank you."

I bark a surprised laugh. "You're *thanking* me? That was the hottest thing I've experienced in a long time. You're sexier when you come than you've any right to be." I brush a thumb over her cheeks. "You're fuckin' adorable when you blush."

The conductor strolls past at that moment, frowning at the sight of Bryn straddling my thigh. He raps on the glass with a foreknuckle, shaking his head.

Bryn giggles and slips off me, curling against my side in mortification, face buried against my arm.

He moves on, and we both burst into laughter.

I shift on the bench, trying to be subtle about adjusting myself.

Not subtle enough.

"Problem?" Bryn asks, her eyes locked on mine.

"Yes," I admit.

A sly smirk curves her lips. "Is it a *big* problem?"

"You're a bold one, aren't you?" I ask. I find her hand and guide it to my cock, slanted sideways in my trousers, trapped at painful angle. "*You* tell *me* how big a problem you have on your hands."

She cups my length, eyes widening. "Oh. *Oh* my. That is a *very* big problem."

I hold her gaze. "And what are you going to do about this very big problem? Hmm, lovely Bryn?"

She smirks. "I might have an idea."

"Do tell."

"Well, it's more show than tell, actually."

This is a bad idea. This whole thing. The mission. Her. Getting involved. Getting attached. Letting myself pretend. Touching her.

I slip my fingers, stained with her juices, into my mouth, suckling them, growling at the taste of her. "Sweet as sugar. God, I'd love to go down on you about now, Gorgeous. If only we had more privacy."

Her gaze goes heavy-lidded. "Don't fucking tease me, Rush."

"Who's teasin'? I'll eat your tight, wet little pussy for hours. Make you come so many times you'll beg to suck my cock just to have a break."

Her teeth snag her lower lip, need painting her features. "Who's begging?"

"You."

She flips open my trousers, lowers the zipper. Traces a fingertip over the bulge that springs to fill the opening. I twitch, hissing at the teasing touch.

"Conductor's gonna come back this way soon," I warn.

"Then you'd better behave yourself."

"Behave myself?" I ask.

She smirks, snagging her coat and throwing it over my lap. "Lean back."

She nudges me to lean against the side of the bench at an angle, as if I'm trying to find a comfortable position for napping. She wedges herself between my body and the bench-back, more on me than not, and now it seems as if we're just cuddling together, using her jacket as a makeshift blanket.

"Yes," she says, her smile eager and teasing. "fBehave yourself and I might see how I can…handle… your little problem."

"Who are you calling little, love?"

She tugs my underwear away from my belly, and my cock unfurls to spring upright, and then works my underwear down a bit. I lift my hips, and she shifts them down past my buttocks. My cock aches and strains beneath the warm weight of her shell jacket, and then her hand is smoothing over my belly, teasing past my rigid erection down my thigh, rubbing upward again, and back down my other thigh, avoiding where I need her touch most.

"Fuck," I growl. "Not nice to tease."

"There's a difference between teasing and playing," she murmurs, resting her chin on my chest, watching me as she smooths her touch all over my belly and thighs without ever directly touching my cock.

"And you're playing, are you?" I ask.

I shouldn't be doing this with her. I'm only ruining myself further. The way she sounded, coming for me? I'll not soon forget that. I'll fucking dream of it. Fantasize how tight her pussy is, how wet. The sugar of her juices linger on my tongue, and my cock throbs to have her grab it.

None of this is right.

I'm not supposed to want her like this. Need her.

I'm not supposed to crave her touch. But I fucking do, and I'm a weak man where beautiful women are concerned.

And fuck me if Bryn isn't the most beautiful woman I've ever met.

My usual cocky, demanding banter is absent at the moment, because all that's in my mind is need.

Especially when she slides her hand over my belly until my cock rests on the back of her hand. I bite down on my tongue involuntarily—coincidentally preventing me from uttering the plea that's on the tip of my tongue.

I can't stop my hips from lifting, my ass from flexing to push me upward against her hand.

A growl rattles my chest. "Bryn. *Fuck*."

"What was it you said to me?" she whispers against my ear, breath hot, words hotter. "Oh yeah. I don't think fucking is an option right now, or you'd be buried inside me."

Her hand slips away, back down my quad, drifting upward along the inner side of my other leg. There's a brief hesitation, and then she cups my balls in her palm—I grunt at the sudden touch, my cock pulsing.

"You'd be so fucking big inside me, Rush," she whispers. "I'd be so fucking tight. How long do you think you'd last?"

"I could fuck you for ages, Gorgeous." I swallow

hard, faking a casual, unconcerned tone that I in no way feel; I'm desperate for her to touch me.

"Ages?" She breathes. "I dunno. I think you're about to come right now, and I haven't even touched you yet."

"You wanna find out how long I'd last inside you?" I say. "Don't test me, love. I'll have you up against the glass if you're not careful."

"Oh? You're an exhibitionist, are you?"

She whips the jacket away, and now my cock is ramrod stiff in the air, bare and aching. She giggles at the sight of me, a sound of awed disbelief. "Rush, Jesus."

I grin at her. "What, sweetheart? See somethin' you like?"

Her gaze is rapt, hungry. "Fuck yes, I do." Reaching slowly, almost hesitantly, she finally, at long last, curls her fingers around my cock, and I can't even pretend to hold back a long, sighing groan of utter relief at her touch.

I reach for the jacket, but she keeps it out of reach, smirking at me. "Oh no. You want it? It's happening just like this."

She strokes me slowly, watching her hand slide down my length. I groan raggedly, clenching my muscles to keep from blowing already like a randy boy getting his first handy. She doesn't miss that, either.

"Holding back already, Rush? I thought you could fuck for ages?"

"Fuckin' witchcraft, I tell you," I mutter. "You've done something to me."

"Classic," she says, laughing, "blame it on the woman."

"Maybe there's just something about you," I say.

She twists her hand around the head of my cock, then plunges her touch down to my root, pulses there a few times, and then strokes my length again. "You do have beautiful cock, though," she says.

"It'd look even better in your mouth," I say, brushing my thumb over her lips.

"Would it, you think?"

"Only one way to find out."

She lowers her face to my thigh, resting her cheek on my quad while pumping my length. "Ask me very nicely, Rush."

"Suck my cock, Bryn." My voice is raw and ragged with need. "Please."

She grins up at me, caressing my cock faster, now. My hips move on their own, my ass flexing as my cock pulses. I ache, I throb, I—fuck, I'm nearly there.

"Fuck, woman. I said, please. What more d'you want from me?" I growl. "I'm not gonna come on my belly like a fourteen-year-old who's just had his first wank."

"Maybe I want that," she murmurs, jacking my length from tip to base—I can't help thrusting, now, and she settles into a rhythm, plunging her hand down as I thrust up. "Maybe I want to watch you come all over yourself, right here in this open compartment for anyone to see."

"Bryn," I growl, back teeth gritted as I fight for my fucking life, trying like hell to hold back when my orgasm is an imminent detonation throbbing in my balls and pulsing throughout the length of my cock. "Fucking *please*, sweetheart. I need that pretty mouth on my cock. You want to watch me come? I'll get us a room as soon's we get there and you can make me blow anywhere you want it to go. On my belly, on the bed, on the sink…on your face, all over those perfect tits of yours."

"You want to come on my tits?"

"No," I snap. I wrap my hand around her throat, holding without applying pressure. "Right now, I don't *want* anything. Right now, I *need* to come down this lovely throat of yours."

Her gaze softens at my touch, a hot grin curving her mouth at my words. "Show me how you want it, then, Rush."

"Say my name again, Gorgeous."

"Rush." It's a whisper.

"Once more," I breathe. "I like how you say my name. I like knowing my name is the last thing on your lips before they wrap around my cock."

"Oh fuck, you say such filthy things…*Rush*."

And then her mouth is opening and her tongue flits against my tip, tickling my opening as she licks away the bead of precum, humming her approval at the taste of me. She strokes my shaft, and another bead drips out of me, and she licks that one away too.

God, I can't last much longer.

"Fuck, woman. I'm gonna come in a second. I've begged you every way I know how."

"Rush," she whispers, lips moving, brushing against my sensitive tip.

And then I'm sliding into her mouth, and I swear on everything holy, nothing has ever felt so good as that moment when I fill her mouth, when her lips wrap around me, and her wet, hot, tight mouth takes over.

"Fuck," I snarl, the word barely a breath. "Bryn. Jesus."

She lifts her eyes to mine, a smirk on her lips. God, that's so fucking sexy it hurts—that smile of hers, bright and bold and beautiful. She smiles as she takes me in her mouth. Eager. Hungry. Wild.

Her eyes flick to the window—a middle-aged couple passes our compartment just then, and they see us. The woman's eyes go wide as saucers, and she pushes her husband onward. He resists, and she snaps something in German that I don't hear through the glass—and the roaring thunder of my runaway-train pulse. Bryn grins, looking right at them as she slathers her suctioning lips down my shaft.

Now they're both stopped, watching. The woman's mouth is hanging open, almost in awe, as Bryn takes all of me, backs away so my cock sways in the cool air, her saliva glistening on my length. The man says something to the woman—she gasps in shocked outrage, shoves him angrily onward.

She does take one last backward glance, though.

"What do you think he said?" she asks.

"Why doesn't she suck him off like that, probably," I answer.

"Think she will?"

"If he's as lucky as I am, yes."

She caresses my length, watching her hand slide down, up, down, twisting around my base. I thrust into her hand, shaking all over as my orgasm wells up within me, pressing hard against my self-control.

"It's not lucky," Bryn whispers. "Make me come as hard as you did, and I'm pretty open to suggestions."

"In that case, come here so I can eat your pussy. I've a suggestion to make."

"What's that?" she whispers. "I'm still shaky from the last one."

"Let me have you up against the window."

She strokes my length faster and faster, until my hips are pumping and my breath is shaky and ragged and I'm grunting and gritting my teeth in an effort to hold back my orgasm.

"You won't last that long, Rush."

"Try me," I bite out. "You'd be surprised what I can manage when I put my mind to it."

Lies.

I'm riding the edge as it is. And my god, she knows it. She's watching my every movement, every facial expression, every twitch and gasp. She knows *exactly* how close I am.

"You'll come when I let you come," she whispers. "And not a moment before."

"Gonna make me beg again, is that it?" I snap.

She pumps my length faster and faster, and as much as I hate to admit it, I can't hold out any longer. I'm gonna come all over myself like a boy and there's not a damn thing I can do to stop it.

"Fuck, fuck," I snarl. "Bryn…I'm—oh god. Fuck. Fuck!"

"Yeah?" She breathes, slowing her strokes. "Gonna give it to me?"

"No stopping it now, love," I grumble, arching up off the bench as my climax shudders through me.

"Say my name," she demands.

"Bryn!"

"Who's making you come, Rush?"

"Bryn!" I snap. "Fuck, I'm—oh god."

"Ask me nicely again," she whispers, pulsing soft, shallow, twisting strokes around my cock-head.

"Please, Bryn. Please. I need your mouth!" I feel it happening and I'm helpless to stop it. "Now, Bryn. Please. I'm coming—Oh, fuck. I'm—-I can't…Ahh fuck…*Bryn!*"

At the last second, she covers me with her mouth. I tangle my hands in her hair, fisting handfuls of her dense black curls as I unleash everything inside me with a shout—I shove my fist against my mouth and bite down—Bryn bats my hand away, covering my mouth with her hand, jacking my cock at the root while slopping her mouth around my head.

She hums around me as I explode in her mouth, and then I hear her gulp, and then my blood is rushing in my ears as I come harder than I ever have in my life. Her fingers circle around my base and squeeze hard while her lips suction around my shaft and slide down and down and down. I'm not a small man, mind you, but she takes it all without a sound, and I feel her throat rippling around me, and it's so tight and so hot that I sag, boneless and limp and helpless to do anything but hold onto her hair and keep coming.

One hand covering my mouth, she releases my cock with the other, and now a renewed flood of intense orgasm crashes through me, and I go haywire, jerking helplessly, thrusting, shoving her head down. She moans as if enjoying every second of this, and her palm cradles my balls, caressing and cupping as she continues to work my cock with her throat, her lips tight around my root. She bobs on me, swallowing and gulping and humming her encouragement.

Just when I think my orgasm is subsiding, she backs her mouth up around my head, now taking my length in one hand and pressing the middle finger of the other along my taint. She works my cock-head with quick short bobs of her lips, pumping my shaft to milk every drop of out of me, massaging my balls and pressing a finger to my taint, and a fresh wave of release smashes through me.

Even when I can come no more, she sucks around my tip and caresses my softening length, until finally she lets me go with a soft plop as I smack against my belly.

She tosses her jacket over us and snuggles her cheek on my chest and pretends to sleep just as the conductor waltzes past us. I watch through slitted eyes as he pauses, suspicious, before continuing on.

When he's gone, Bryn lifts her head from my chest with a quiet giggle. "Almost got caught."

I'm still more than half-delirious, and all I can do is stare at her, shaken to the core by what just happened.

A blow job, yes.

But it was more than that.

To me, at least.

It was the start of a very, very major problem.

"You ought not to have done that, Gorgeous," I murmur when I can summon language once more.

She frowns. "What? Why not?"

"Because now I need to fuck you." I swipe my thumb over the corner of her mouth, catching a stray bead of my cum; she opens her mouth for me and I fit my thumb into her mouth. "Good girl."

Her eyes flare, aroused at my words. "You gonna prove it, right here?"

"No, I'm not." I pull up and fasten my trousers. "I'm going to wait until we're alone, and I'm going to press your perfect, naked body against the hotel window for the whole city to see, and I'm going to fuck you until you don't know your own name."

The grin that spreads over her face is predatory. "You'd better be a man who keeps his promises, Rush."

"You'll find out soon, won't you?"

A few minutes later, the train pulls into the station in Lyon. As we make our way forward past compartment after compartment, we pass one that's still closed. In it, a familiar-looking couple is still seated. The man's head is thrown back, his eyes closed, mouth open. A blanket covers his lap…and that blanket is moving up and down, a woman's lower half bent over him.

Bryn stifles a giggle, watching as the man arches, crying out loud enough to be heard through the closed door. A moment later, the woman sits up, hair all askew, lipstick smeared, looking dazed. The four of us trade looks, and then the crowd behind us pushes us onward.

"Looks like we inspired them, ey?" I say.

"Looks like it," Bryn agrees.

I'm playing casual, but inside…I'm shaken.

It's not the blowjob. It's not the public setting. It's just…*her*. The way she looks at me, the way she gives back every shred of my own attitude. The way she sounded when she came. The hum of eager enjoyment as she went down on me.

Everything about her is unlike anyone I've ever met.

I need more.

I need all of her.

And fuck me, but I'm not sure I'll be able to give her up. Not to *him*. Not to anyone.

Not ever.

7

THE PRICE OF ENTRY

UNEASE PRICKLES THROUGH ME—A TICKLING DOWN my spine, a raising of the fine hairs on the back of my neck. We're strolling down a street whose name I can't even begin to pronounce, just outside the train station in Lyon. Once again, Rush seems in no hurry at all, holding my hand as we walk; we must seem an ordinary couple on vacation—sorry, *holiday*.

I'm not at ease, for a lot of reasons.

I was okay on the train, mostly because it didn't seem likely that we'd encounter any bad guys—our ticket purchase was cash, and last minute, so unlikely that anyone could know where we were going and get on the train with us. Plus, that little nap, and then…

The hotness.

Good lord, the hotness.

The man's cock is divine. Truly. I know I'm somewhat prone to exaggeration and hyperbole, but in this case, divinity isn't much of a stretch. Godlike, but little g—not God as in the Big Kahuna, the Almighty, with whom I have a distant and pretty disinterested relationship. Recent events do, I must admit, have me rethinking that position, but waiting until I experience attempted rape and murder seems like a shitty time to find Jesus.

Is it a sin to think about Jesus one second and Rush's big, beautiful dick the next?

If it is, I'll say a Hail Mary or whatever—I don't know, I'm not catholic. I just know that first, the man gave me an orgasm I won't soon forget with no more than a finger or two, and then….hoo-boy. That dick.

I'm a horny bitch, okay? I get it from my mama, I'm pretty sure, although to be honest, I don't really want to think about that. I just know that Killian and I learned very early on to give their wing of the house plenty of distance whenever they disappeared together. Which is *frequently*. I'm sure I may get some of it from Dad, but for some reason, it's less icky to think about Mom's sexuality than my dad's. Not looking at that too closely.

I digress. Where was I?

Rush.

The things he says? Dirty, aggressive. Commanding. I'm not a girl who typically likes being told what to do—in fact, I'm pretty sure Mom would say I'm allergic to obedience. But when Rush tells me to swallow his cock and tells me I'm a good girl for swallowing all of his cum? Ooh, *girl*—I am *not* okay.

There might be a certain amount of distraction value to the situation, though. I mean, this is life or death—or worse. I'm far from home, alone, and being pursued by sex traffickers. I've killed people. So yeah, it's a nice, welcome distraction to put all that out of my mind and just focus on the much more pleasant subject of sex. Meaning, my favorite subject.

I'm under no illusions as to the score with Rush, though. He's going out of his way to help me, to protect me. Which is nice. And I doubt he'd say so in so many words, but I feel like there may be a certain expectation of us playing together in exchange for his protection. It's not…explicit. He hasn't even hinted at that. The moment on the train seemed very organic to me—it just happened.

Maybe I'm overthinking things. Another fun gift I have courtesy of my genetics—although I think that's from Dad.

Maybe I should feel Rush out on this.

"So, you, umm…do this a lot?" I ask.

He looks at me. "Do what?"

"Rescue girls from sex traffickers and have them blow you on the train."

"Preceded by me fingering you, I'd like to point out. Don't forget that." He eyes me suspiciously. "I gotta say, sweetheart, I *really* hope you're not implying there's any expectations on my end. Because if you think I'm only helping you so you go down on me or what'ave-you, I'll be a bit miffed. I ain't that sort of bloke."

"It did cross my mind afterward," I admit.

He stops walking. "What'd I do to give you that impression?"

"Nothing, overtly."

"Look, Bryn. I'm a lot of things, not all of 'em very

good. But one thing I'm *very* fucking much *not* is a man who has to coerce women into doin' things with me."

He's *pissed*. His gaze is gray and sparking with arrogant fury. "You wanna know the truth? I can walk into any bar or pub or club and crook my fuckin' finger, an' I'll have my pick of slags gaggin' themselves for 'alf an hour with me. I don't say that to be crude or to brag, but so's you under-fucking-stand. I don't need to help you. I don't even know if I *want* to help you. I certainly don't need to help you to convince you to have my cock down your throat. And don't forget, love, *you* came *first*."

I grin at him. "Good answer. And just F-Y-I, you're not the only one who can walk into any bar, pub, or club, crook your finger, and have anyone you want. Doesn't make you special…*love*."

He smirks back. "Good to know you don't hold that against me."

I shrug. "Why would I? You don't owe me any explanations. Also, I know a fuckboy when I meet one."

"Fuckboy, ey? What gave me away?"

I flick a finger at his face. "The smirk."

This gets me a puzzled frown. "Smirk? I'm not followin', mate."

I roll my eyes. "Fuckboys tend to employ a particular kind of smirk. Some may call it a smolder. You look at us with a cocky little smirk that says you know you're hot shit and that it's only a matter of time before we give in to the inevitable and beg you to dick us down."

"Bleh." It's a non-word sound of disgust. "I fuckin' *hate* that phrase. Dunno why, I just fuckin' hate it."

I laugh. "To be honest, I don't like it either. But I only use it when I'm being funny or sarcastic."

"Or insulting."

"You're insulted by me calling you a fuckboy?"

"Nah, love. I'm insulted that you think what happened on the train was somethin' I expected because I'm helping you. If I thought you thought that, I wouldn't have so much as looked at you." A tip of his head to one side. "But that said, calling me a fuckboy *is* an insult. Just because it's true don't make it not an insult."

"You're not denying it."

"Nah. I like sex, I'm good at it, and I've never fucked around with the whole 'feelings' and 'relationship' shite. I believe in havin' a good time and makin' sure expectations are set out clearly from the jump." He looks at me. "What about you?"

"What about me, what?"

"Are you workin' up to tellin' me that givin' me a gobbie on the train wasn't really like you? That you're not really that type of girl?"

"A *gobbie*? Really right now?"

He adopts a nose-in-the-air, hoity-toity expression. "Well, *excuse me* for using such crude terminology, your highness." He even does a remarkable high-brow accent. "I meant performing the act of fellatio."

I can't help a laugh. "I don't mind slang, but I draw the line at 'gobbie'. It feels juvenile to me."

He snorts. "A fair point, that is."

"So." I look around pointedly. "Again, where are we going? Because it seems like we're just sort of strolling around aimlessly."

"That's cause we're bein' followed." His tone is as breezy as ever. When I go to look around, he briefly squeezes my hand hard. "Nah, nah, don't look. Jesus. I clocked the clumsy fuckwits ages ago. They picked us up in the station." He stops walking abruptly and yanks out his cell phone, putting it to his ear and carrying on a fake conversation—it's all a ruse to give him an excuse to pivot in the street. "Yeah, yeah, got it. Right—right." To me, in a low voice, then. "Two fat blokes in trackies."

I spot them immediately when I turn sideways on the sidewalk to face him, as if waiting for him to finish his call. Like the assholes back in Berlin, these guys are on the wrong side of middle age sporting beer bellies, heavy stubble, and matching tracksuits, the halfway-zipped tops of which bulge obviously with guns.

"Jesus, whoever is doing the hiring has a typecasting issue."

Rush glances at me. "Say what?"

"The guys in Zermatt, Berlin, and now here? They're all basically the same dude."

He snickers. "Oh, yeah. Hired guns is all. The sort of chaps who'll sell out their own grandma for a handful of euros. They're in plentiful supply, unfortunately." He grins. "Means I won't be bothered merkin' 'em." In his accent, "bothered" comes across with a 'V' sound instead of a 'th'.

I frown at him. "Merk?"

"Do in. Off." He does a finger gun, complete with a soft "pew" noise. "Murder 'em."

"Oh."

Rush pretends to end his call, pockets his phone, takes my hand, and sets off again the way we were going.

"So, what's the plan?" I ask.

He shrugs. "Dunno yet. Lead 'em on a merry chase till they're knackered, and then find a likely spot to do a nice little renovation on their skulls."

"So if I'm interpreting you correctly, you mean to tire them out by walking around a lot, lure them into an alley, and shoot them?"

"Right-oh, love."

"Can't we just skip right to the murdering?" I suggest. "As much as I'd love to explore the city of Lyon on foot, that nap on the train was the only sleep I've had in forty-eight hours, unless you count a good twelve hours of being drugged unconscious."

He glances at me. "Good point. Drugged sleep ain't exactly restful."

"You know this from experience?"

His expression shutters. "I know a lot of unpleasant shite from experience, love. Among those experiences is being drugged against my will, yes."

"You know my story."

He sighs. "Mine's not got the happy ending yours has. I mean, I survived, so I suppose that's happy enough." A gruff, annoyed growl. "Fine. But only because that gobbie you gave me was some serious fuckin' top work."

"You're a dick."

He just grins. "I know, love. Don't forget it." He waves a hand. "So, Afghanistan. Chasin' an' H-V-T— high value target. Taliban bigwig, a right nasty cunt. My unit lit'rally stumbled on a fuckin' hornet's nest of tangos. Hell broke loose, we offed a bunch of 'em, lost a couple blokes of our own—not a nice situation. Details don't really matter, but due to no error on my part, I got separated from my mates. Got captured, stuck with a big fuckin' needle, and ended up with a smelly sack over my head in the back of a cave in the mountains."

"Oh. That doesn't sound fun."

He looks at his fingernails. "Nah, it wasn't. Learned a few valuable lessons, though. Like, it takes a good four months for fingernails to grow all the way back. Didn't much like that. Rather get my head done in."

"What did they want?"

A shrug. "Usual. Information, on the face of it, but really, just to fuck with me. Sleep deprivation, sound assault, the odd beatin' here and there, hot needles under my toenails, um…what else? Electrocution via jump leads an' a car battery."

"Jesus, Rush."

"Jesus wasn't much part of it, I don't think." He laughs. "Nah, I'm just jokin'. I'm alright. You get the odd nightmare now and again, but that's why God invented drinkin' problems, innit?"

"You're very casual about torture."

"Well, I ain't gonna stand around havin' a cry about it, am I?"

"How'd you get away?"

"Mates came for me. Tell you what, though, love, you'll never in your life be as happy as when your mates kick the door in and take you home. Don't mind admittin' I cried when I saw Freddie, Reg, and Beaners bash in the door to my cell."

"Beaners?" I ask. "How does someone end up with a nickname like Beaners?"

"No point tryin' to understand military nicknames. Even if I told you the whole story, you'd still not understand it, mainly cause it's fuckin stupid." He glances at me, then at the two men who are now only some thirty feet away and closing. "Fine, fine. I'll just be done with it, then. Take all the fun out of things, why don't ya?"

His hand vanishes behind his back under his leather jacket, which is when I realize he intends to just whip out his pistol and shoot them right here and now, on the sidewalk, surrounded by people.

"Holy shit, Rush, you can't just shoot them right here! Jesus!"

He frowns at me, hand still on his gun butt. "What? Why not? Not like I'm gonna miss. I can shoot the wings off a mosquito from the far side of a pitch."

"Um?" I gesture at the crowded sidewalk. "Witnesses? Bystanders? What if someone does something unexpected? What if the bullets go through and ricochet?"

He rolls his eyes again but drops his hand. "Fuck me. Why you gotta bother me with silly shit like logic? Fine. C'mon, then. I'll find a more private spot to do in the clumsy fuckwits."

He hauls me into motion without another glance at the two men. We reach an intersection and cut right, away from the larger thoroughfare to a smaller side street. Here, the buildings are 8- or 10-storey apartment blocks built in a square to comprise a full city block. There's graffiti on the walls in places, compact sedans and hatchbacks parked on the left side of the one-way street. We round the corner, and Rush pulls me into a run—we sprint flat-out until we reach a closed garage door leading down into an underground parking garage. Rush pushes me into the corner, wedged between the garage door and the wall. He presses his back to me, his gun held in both hands, arms extended, barrel angled at the ground at his feet. He waits, motionless, listening.

I hear heavy footsteps, voices grumbling in either Russian or a related language; I've always felt a little self-conscious about my lack of linguistic skills, seeing as pretty much everyone in my life except Rinna, Killy, and Cal are fluent in at least three languages. Even Mom, who claims to hate learning new languages, is passable in Spanish and Russian, with a smattering of Greek.

A foot, wearing a sparkling-white ADIDAS trainer, appears first, followed by a meaty, tracksuit-clad leg. Rush waits until the men, walking side by side in near-perfect unison, are parallel with him. The one closest to Rush must sense movement out of the corner of his eye, because he reacts faster than I'd have expected, lurching into his partner and stumbling backward as he fumbles for his gun. Rush is faster, though, by several orders of magnitude. The other two may as well be moving in slow motion, compared to the brutal efficiency with which Rush moves.

He slams into the nearest attacker, pinning his gun-hand between them, and jams the barrel of his pistol into the underside of the attacker's chin. *BAM!* The report is deafening, and a chunky pink mist sprays upward. A split second later—*BAM!* The other tango didn't even have time to reach for his piece before Rush's bullet enters one temple and exits the other at an oblique, downward angle, ricocheting off the road and smacking into the rear bumper of a nearby car.

Rush makes an "oops" face at me. "Good call, I guess."

I roll my eyes. "Men are so impatient."

He grins, shrugs. "C'mon. Best keep moving."

The whole process, from the appearance of the sneaker to both men dead, took less than thirty seconds, total. But there are people looking—faces in windows, a couple on a corner at the end of the block.

Vanishing his pistol, Rush takes my hand and we step over the bodies, avoid the pools of spreading blood, and carry on down the sidewalk.

The couple on the corner sees us coming and scurry away, furiously texting on their phones.

"How did they know where we were?" I ask.

He shrugs. "Dunno for sure. Most likely, they've got some pencil-neck nerd at a computer in a basement tracking ya with cameras or the like. Not that hard, if you've a bit of trainin'. Probably saw us buying tickets." *Saw us* sounds like *saw'r'us*.

It sounds true—and I know from spending time with Uncle Lear that it really is that easy if you have the right software and skills. But yet, it's too easy of an answer. I don't know. Something about it sticks in the back of my mind. I can't figure out what about Rush's answer doesn't sit right, though, so I let the question simmer in my subconscious.

We take a circuitous, winding path away from the scene of the killings, taking a left here, a right there, but always heading in the same general direction.

Rush glances at me after a few minutes of walking. "You're not bothered by that?"

"By what?" I ask.

"Me killing those blokes. You don't seem bothered a bit."

"I guess I'm not. I dunno. I threw up when I killed those guys on the train, if that makes you feel any better."

What I'm not sharing is that part of the training Killian and I both received when we expressed interest in being part of the family business was watching body-cam footage of various A1S operations—both real, live missions and training exercises. Which included seeing bad guys get offed. The idea behind making us watch the videos was two-fold: to see the tactics and practices we'd learn in action, spot mistakes, and see how it all works in real time when real lives are on the line, and to desensitize us to the sight of death—if the first time you see someone's head explode is on your first mission and you have a bad reaction, you could compromise the whole team. And it worked. I only threw up because no amount of video-watching or training can truly prepare you for the feeling of stabbing some asshole in the eyeball with a Ticonderoga #2 pencil.

I'm not gonna say any of this to Rush, though. He doesn't need to know who I really am. Once I'm sure this shit isn't going to spill over to the rest of my family, I'll get ahold of them and come home, but for now, he's right. I brought this on myself with my stupid decision to sneak out. It's on me to clean up my own mess.

I know if I called Mom and Dad, they'd be here

faster than I can blink, cleaning up my mess for me. But I'm an adult. I can take care of my own mistakes.

Mostly. I didn't ask Rush to help me, but he is, and I'm not one to look a gift horse in the mouth.

"So, your friend." I look around us—we're in a more affluent area, now. "Who is he? How can he help me with these sex traffickers who keep showing up wherever I go?"

"He's an executive officer for Interpol," Rush answers. "He's got resources most blokes can't even dream of. A few phone calls and you're in the clear."

"You met him when you were in the military?" I ask.

"Somethin' like that, yeah."

He's on edge, for some reason. His attention is elsewhere—not on me, and barely on our surroundings. I'd expected him to haul me to the nearest hotel to make good on his promise, which I admit I was looking forward to. I enjoy giving head—maybe I'm weird, I dunno. It's fun. Men get so gooey and stupid when you've got their cock in your mouth. You can convince a man to do just about anything while you're sucking him off. I like the power. But also…it's just hot. His reactions, his powerful body helpless under my hands. I just like the way it feels. That said, it doesn't satisfy my deeper need for sex. and if Rush is that hot while I'm blowing him, fucking him would be on a whole other level.

But I can tell his mind is a thousand miles away from banging me.

"Where'd you go, Rush?" I ask.

He frowns at me, blinking as if coming back from being lost in his thoughts. "Oh. What? Sorry."

I laugh. "You're somewhere else, all of a sudden."

He shrugs. "Nah. Just…thinkin'."

"About?"

We reach yet another intersection. A taxi sidles by, and Rush flags it down. Nudges me to get in first and slides in after me, rattling off something in French that's as rapid and excellent as his German.

"German and French, huh?" I ask.

He nods, twisting to look behind us, and then settling against the seat. "My French is better than my German. I can speak Italian passably well, but I wouldn't call it very good."

I huff. "I have a lot of honorary aunts and uncles, and they're all fluent in like half a dozen languages, and here's me who can only speak English. I feel stupid, sometimes."

"What's an honorary uncle?" he asks.

"Someone your parents are so close to you grew up calling them Uncle or whatever, even though they're not actually related to you."

"Oh. And you've a lot of them, 'ave you?"

I nod. "Yeah, I do."

He glances behind us again, briefly. "Not knowing a language doesn't mean you're stupid. It just means you didn't have a reason to need it. My best mates from the streets growin' up were lads who spoke French and German and not much English, so I learned them that way. Then, when I joined up, I had reason to keep current on it, professionally. Trainin' exercises, joint operations, shit like that. Now I'm out, I do work in France in Germany and use both a lot."

"This may be an insensitive question, but—"

He laughs, cutting me off. "Nah, love, I can't read or write in either language. Shit, I'm barely literate in English. I speak and understand, but put a newspaper in front of me or whatever? Nah. Not a word. May's well be Swahili."

"Did that affect your career in the military at all?"

He shrugs, nods. "A bit, yeah. My best mate in my unit, Reg, found out I was dyslexic and he'd cover for me. Help me with paperwork, sit near me in briefin's and tell me what was on the board, shit like that. I'd do anything for him, I would."

"Good to have friends like that. Rin is that for me."

"Rin?"

"Yup. Short for Corinna. She's basically my sister."

Rush leans forward and says something to the driver—we make a sudden turn, accelerate, make another turn, and then pull off to the side. Rush watches our backtrail for a few moments, and then tells the driver we can go.

"Someone's following us?" I ask.

He nods. "Think so. Not a hundred percent sure, but best not to take any risks." He growls wordlessly—a sound of irritation. "Best not approach my friend, yet. Not till I'm sure we've lost our tail."

A funny thing I've noticed: he refers to friends from his youth as mates, and his teammates from his unit in the SAS as mates, but this contact here in Lyon is always his "friend." I wonder what that's about.

He gives the driver more instructions, and we pull onto the road. A few minutes later, we're braking to halt under the portico of an upscale hotel in what Rush informs me is the 6th arrondissement, one of the wealthiest areas of Lyon.

In the lobby, he approaches the clerk and strikes up a friendly conversation, keeping me tucked against his side with an arm slung low around my waist, one hand casually resting on my hip. I figure I'd better play along, so I lean into him and gaze at him like he hung the moon. I don't follow the conversation, obviously, but it ends up with Rush forking over a stack of euros and receiving a single keycard.

Which, it turns out, is for a suite near the top of the building. It's not a penthouse, but it's close. There's a big seating area furnished with white leather couches on three sides around a glass coffee table decorated with a bowl of wicker balls and giant candles on antique wooden candleholders. A print of a famous Degas painting occupies the space over the electric fireplace, and floor-to-ceiling curtains frame acres of massive windows.

The bedroom is huge, with a king bed draped in high-thread-count linens and a luxuriously appointed bathroom.

"You sprang for a nice place," I remark, taking it all in.

He grins. "No point slumming it. Plus, we're close to where we need to go tomorrow." His eyes morph to green as he glances at the windows. "I've not forgotten what I said, Bryn. You can't get windows like that in a pay-by-the-hour motel in the red-light district."

"No, I don't suppose you can." I glance at the window as well, trying to imagine being pressed up against it, Rush behind me…

His eyes blaze, his grin widening. "Yeah, you're thinkin' about it, aren't you?"

"About what?" I ask, eyes wide and innocent.

His grin shifts, becomes that cocky, heated smirk—full of teasing promise and arrogance. "Oh, I dunno." He moves into my space, and even though he's only got four or so inches on me, he seems to tower over me, all broad shoulders and hard chest. "Didja forget what I said I'd do to you once I had you alone?"

"I've got a terrible memory," I lie, my voice unintentionally breathy.

God, this man affects me. My pulse pounds, hammering in my veins, roaring in my ears. My thighs press together as he occludes the world around us until there's nothing but him. His eyes are fiercely green, now, sparking fire.

He takes a step, forcing me backward. "You're a shit liar, Bryn."

"No I'm not."

He unzips my jacket, slides it off. Tosses it carelessly aside. Forces me another step backward.

"You remember. I see it in your eyes, love. And you want it. Don't you?"

"Want what?"

"By all means, carry on playin' dumb. It's cute, but I know better. You're razor sharp, and make no mistake about that. Much smarter than me, I'd wager." He presses me backward another step, two, three.

He bends down, nipping my earlobe in his teeth, breath hot, body hard against mine. His hands grasp my ass, squeezing hard enough that I squeak in protest.

"This fuckin' arse, Bryn. Jesus. Taut as a fuckin' drum." He yanks my pullover fleece up and off, hurls it one way. Shirt next, gone like the other. "You need a reminder of what I said I'd do?"

Another step backward, and then I catch up against cold glass with a hollow, echoing thump. "I…I might need a brief refresher, yes." I'm proud of how casual I sound, when inside, I'm anything but.

Nervous, excited, maybe a little afraid. Desperately shielding myself from thinking about anything or anyone that might pull me out of this moment, I run my hands up his chest, palming the firm swell of his powerful pecs. Brush his leather off, let it flop to the floor.

He toes the jacket aside. Kneels in front of me, lifts my foot, and tugs my boot off. My sock. The other foot. Rises to his feet and runs a fingertip down my centerline from throat to navel.

"Fuck, you're beautiful, you know that?" He hooks a finger behind the button of my jeans.

"It's nice to be told," I answer. "Remind me what you said, though. I really don't remember."

He opens my jeans. Steps back. "Take 'em off for me, Bryn."

In just a maroon Henley, his arms cross over his chest, thick and rippling in the tight sleeves. His chiseled jaw is hard, eyes burning with erotic promise.

I wiggle my hips to shimmy out of the jeans, which I toss to him. "Shirt off, Rush."

He lets the jeans hit his chest and drop to the floor, that damned cocky smirk on his lips. "I don't think so."

He steps into me, framing me with his huge, powerful

arms, hands on the glass beside my ears. His lips touch the side of my neck, and I tip my head to offer him better access. "Take off your bra, Bryn. I need to see those perfect tits."

"Shirt first."

He rumbles a laugh. "Funny, you thinkin' you're in charge." He nips my earlobe, sending heat shimmering through me from chest to core, making butterflies flutter in my belly. "You want to do what I say."

"Do I, though?"

I do. I really fucking do. But I'm not about to let him know that.

He touches his lips to my breastbone. The swell of my breast. "Yeah, love, you do. Wanna know why?"

"Yes," I breathe.

"What I promised you back on the train was I'd get you naked, press you up against this very window, and fuck you until you don't remember your own name." His voice is dark and rough and heavy with arousal, a hoarse, raspy, rumbling growl that makes me shiver and shake. God, I could almost get off just from the shit he says in that low, throbbing voice of his.

"Fuck," I whisper—the epithet ripped out of me at his dirty promise.

"You want that, don't you?" He cups my sex over my panties.

"Maybe."

"I like this game." He trails a fingertip up my seam over my underwear.

"What game?" I breathe.

He tips my head up with a finger to my chin, kisses

my throat. With his other hand, he teases my pussy over the fabric, finger sliding up and down, up and down, always lingering over my clit, reminding me what he can do to me with just one finger.

"You wanna play?" he asks, his voice rife with amusement. "Fine, then, we'll play. But you don't get what *you* want until I get what I want."

He sinks to his knees in front of me and presses his mouth to my seam, huffing a hot breath over my flesh. I wiggle, biting down on a whine. He reaches up to cup my ass, nips the tender skin of my thigh with his teeth. Breathes on my pussy again.

"Rush," I whisper. "Fuck."

"That's the idea, yeah. I could be inside you right now, but you're playin' games."

I feather my hands in his hair, but he grabs my wrists and presses my hands against the glass.

"No touching. Not till I get what I want."

"What do you want, Rush?"

"Take your bra off."

"You do it."

He shoots to his feet, a sly grin on his face. His hand flashes, blurring with blinding speed. There's a snap, and the dull back of a knife is cold against my sternum, the tip of a wicked, black, serrated, folding knife nicking the bottom strap of my bra.

"Your way, or mine?"

I'm tempted to call his bluff, but I know damned well he's not bluffing. I hold his eyes as I peel the sports bra off; my nipples pebble into hard little nubs as his eyes take in my bare chest.

"Jesus, woman. Fucking perfect." He folds the knife and shoves it into a hip pocket, then cups my tits in his hands.

"Keep calling me perfect, and you're gonna give a girl a complex."

He doesn't respond to that, a soft grumble of male appreciation rattling his chest. "Pants off now, Gorgeous."

I frown at him. "My pants are already off."

He snorts a laugh, toeing my jeans. "These are jeans, or trousers." He hooks a finger in the elastic of my underwear. "These are pants."

"Oh," I breathe.

"Now. Pants…off. Show me that pretty pussy."

He stands back and stares at me, thumbs hooked in his belt loops, his gaze heated.

I slide the underwear down, and his eyes follow my hips as I wriggle to shimmy my panties off, and now I'm nude, and he's fully clothed.

I gesture at him. "Shirt off."

He swaggers toward me. "I'll take it off when I'm ready."

"I gave you what you wanted. Now it's my turn." I reach for the hem of his shirt.

He grabs my wrists and shoves them up over my head—and just like that, I'm reminded of the strength difference between us. I'm a fit, strong girl. I lift weights, I spar, run, do yoga, surf, and paddleboard. I'm not some dainty little Pilates princess. But Rush's strength is on a whole other level. He pins my wrists to the glass and nips my earlobe again.

"It's your turn when I decide it's your turn, Beautiful.

And I've decided I'm feeling a bit…peckish." He moves his lips to my jaw, my chin, my throat. "Leave your hands up there or I'll stop."

"Wouldn't that be tragic?" I quip, going for insouciant.

It backfires immediately.

Rush releases me and steps back, hands in his pockets. "Wouldn't it just?" He leans into my space, close enough to whisper without touching me. "That orgasm I gave you on the train? That was nothing. I've been told I have a magic tongue."

"I don't believe in magic."

"You ever come so hard you forget your name, Bryn?"

"No." It's a breath, barely audible.

"Put your hands over your head and spread your legs." His command is quiet, insistent, dripping with promise. "Be a good girl for me. Let me show you what *real* ecstasy feels like."

"I'm not a good girl, Rush."

"No, you're not. I like that about you. But you'll be a good girl for me, won't you?"

Fuck.

I'm shaking with need. My thighs squeeze together, heat pulsing through me. My nipples are so hard they ache, and my clit is throbbing.

I refuse to give in so easily, however. I just stare him down.

"Stubborn one, aintcha?" He grabs my hands and moves them behind my back, pinioning them in one hand. "Maybe you need a little reminder of what you're missing out on, then."

"Perhaps I do," I whisper.

His fingers walk down my belly, and then I gasp as he presses the pad of his index finger to my clit; he lets out a rough, dark chuckle at my sharp inhale. "Like that, do you?"

"A little."

"A little, she says. As if I can't smell the need dripping out of this sweet, hot, tight, wet, little cunt."

I hate that word. I *hate* it. It's gross. Yet from him? Maybe it's the accent, I don't know. I just know when he says it—with a crisp enunciation, the 'T' popping—my core spasms.

He traces a finger up my seam. "See?" he shows me his glistening fingertip. "Drippin' for me."

Fuck, fuck, fuck. I want his mouth. I need to come. It's an inferno inside me, pressure building in my core like a malfunctioning steam engine

Touch me—touch me. Goddammit, touch me.

The words won't come out; sometimes I hate how stubborn I am.

"Still not convinced, are you?" he grins. "Very well, then. This is fun for me. Maybe I'll take my time. Tease you for fuckin' hours. You ever been edged till you're ready to kill someone for an orgasm?"

I just stare at him, refusing to answer.

"It's a simple question, Bryn. Have you?

"No," I whisper.

"Is that what you want? Want me to finger your hard little clit till you're right about to come, and then stop? Do that again and again and fuckin' again until you're ready to fuckin' snap?"

"Maybe I do," I snarl, lying through my gritted teeth.

"Or maybe I just want you to stop goofing around and fuck me already."

He laughs. "Oh, no, no, no. That won't do at all." He touches his lips to my ear. "I like to play with my food."

I shudder at the tickling of his hot breath, my core clamping, thighs squeezing. "Rush…"

"Wossat, love?"

I can't bring myself to ask him to touch me. Capitulation isn't in my blood.

He swipes a finger against my clit and I twitch, gasping. He keeps my wrists pinned behind my back, his forehead against mine as he watches his finger slide upward over my seam, pause, and then he scrapes a fingernail over my clit. A ragged moan escapes me, then, and that's when he plunges his two middle fingers inside me without warning, scooping my essence and smearing it over my clit—my knees almost give out. He hooks those fingers inside me again, and I'm held up by his touch inside me.

"Fuckin' hell, Bryn. So fuckin' tight, so fuckin' wet. Drippin' for me, you are." He withdraws his fingers and drags his wet middle finger over my lips. "Taste yourself, Gorgeous. Tell me. Do you taste as sweet as you smell?"

I feel my traitorous tongue ghost over my lips, and the flavor of my own juices bursts on my tongue. "Yes."

I've forgotten what it was he wanted me to do that I wouldn't do or say. I don't know. He scrambles my brain.

He slips one finger inside me and swirls it around, pulls it out. Pops it into his mouth. "Mmmm. Sweet as sugar."

Again, that finger dips into me, and again he tastes

me as if sampling the finest dessert. I whimper every time he takes his touch away, the sound ripped out of me against my will. He does it again, but this time instead of tasting me, he smears my essence over my clit and circles. Circles. Swipes. Brings me to the edge, until I'm shaking and panting, knees dipping every time he makes contact with my clit.

And then, an instant before I topple over the edge into release, his touch vanishes and he's licking his fingers clean.

I growl in desperation. "Rush!"

"What, love? You need somethin'?"

"Dammit!" I press my thighs together in a vain attempt to get more friction, more pressure. "What do you want, Rush?"

"Hands over your head against the window. Spread your legs apart. Don't make a sound."

Holding his hot gaze, which is now a greenish-gray shot through with streaks of brown, I slowly drag my arms over my head, clasp them together, and press them against the glass.

"Good girl," he murmurs, and dammit all to hell, the praise makes my thighs quake. "Spread your legs for me, now. Let me see all of you."

Gritting my teeth in embarrassment, I wiggle my feet apart inch by inch until they're about shoulder width.

"Wider."

I comply, taking another half step until I'm in a sumo squat stance; Rush stands in my space, gazing down at me, smirking. "Now what?" I ask.

"Now…" he taps his foot against mine, nudging it

further, and the other side; my balance is compromised, now—one wrong move and I'll fall over. "You stay just like that until I say otherwise. Don't move. Don't make a sound." He drags his finger against my clit—I gasp involuntarily, and his touch is instantly gone. "Hush, now, Lovely. The quieter you are, the more you get what you want."

"I want *you*," I hiss, hating how needy and pathetic I sound.

"Then you'd better not make a peep, ey?"

One finger slips inside me, squelching deep. His other hand steals to my chest, carving up my diaphragm, cupping my breast. He pinches my nipple, hard—I grit my teeth and hiss.

"Good girl," he whispers. "Just like that."

Fuck, this is hot. It shouldn't be. I should hate it. But I want his touch. I want to come—I need to come. I need him. I need more. So, I play his game.

And I find myself liking it.

He dips at the knees, lifting my breast to his mouth and suckling my nipple between his teeth, flattening it between his tongue the roof off his mouth; all the while, he's slowly drilling his middle finger in and out of my pussy, slowly and teasingly fucking me with it.

A whimper crashes against the gate of my clenched teeth as he tongues my nipple and teases my clit—it takes all of my self-control not to use my hands to push him down, to guide his mouth where I want it. Fuck, at this point, I'm close to begging. His finger isn't nearly enough.

I'm breathing hard, my knees dipping every time

his finger drives into me, every time his mouth assaults my nipples.

Within a few minutes, I'm on the cusp of orgasm again, shaking all over, panting hard through gritted teeth, hips rocking, pushing, driving into his pumping finger while I arch my back to press my tits against his seeking, licking, nibbling mouth.

"God, you're a greedy one, aren't you?" he whispers. "Need more, do you?"

I don't answer out loud, but I do meet his arrogant, aroused gaze and nod.

"Want to come, Bryn?"

I nod again.

He laughs. "Nah. Not yet. You're not ready yet."

Not ready yet? Bastard. I'm losing my mind over here. I clench hands into fists and press them against the glass—it only occurs to me now that it's broad daylight and my bare ass is up against the glass for everyone on the sidewalk below to see.

Why does that turn me on even more?

Maybe I am, as he puts it, a slag.

He brings me to the edge again with his fingers plunging inside me and his mouth on my nipples, taking me to the shaking, shuddering edge of climax before abruptly taking away his touch.

This time, I can't keep a scream of infuriated frustration from escaping.

Rush just laughs. "Gettin' closer." He pops his finger into his mouth again, eyes closed as he hums his enjoyment of my taste. "Dunno if I can hold out anymore. Need to taste you for real."

I pant desperately, hips rocking against nothing, a keening whimper seeping out of me.

"You're gonna come all over my face, aren't you?" he asks. "You can answer, Gorgeous."

"Yes!" I cry. "God, yes."

He drops to his knees in front of me, staring up at me. "When you come for me, I want to hear you scream my name, all right?"

I nod.

"Tell me what I'm gonna hear when I make you come."

"I'm gonna scream your name."

"Yeah, you are." He flicks his tongue against my clit. "What's my name?"

"RUSH!"

He growls, one hand raking up my body to clutch at my tits, the other fitting under his chin, driving one finger and then two inside me. His mouth fuses to my clit and for a few moments, it's all syrupy slow touches, his fingers slicking into and out of me in slow motion, his tongue lazily flitting against my clit.

When I buck and gyrate, he growls ravenously, and now there's no more teasing, no more games.

Just his mouth ravaging my clit, his fingers fucking my pussy and pinching my nipple. Helpless to stop myself, I knot my fingers in his hair and buck against his mouth.

"RUSH!" I cry, shaking as the orgasm builds to a wild crescendo. "Oh fuck…fuck. *Fuck!*"

Closer…closer—I'm rocking, bucking, grinding,

wallowing in ecstasy as the orgasm starts to shatter through me.

And then he stops.

"FUCK!" I scream. "Rush, goddammit! I did everything you asked."

He's on his feet in front of me, ripping his shirt off. "Hands over your head, Gorgeous."

I move so fast the window shudders when my hands smack against it.

Lazily, he bends and unties his boots. Tosses them aside. Socks, next. His eyes hungry on my body, he flips open his fly, lowers the zipper. Steps out of his jeans. Shoves his underwear down and kicks them up, catches them, and tosses them aside.

He's naked, at long last.

And holy god, the view was worth the price of entry.

He's a god.

Truly.

Carved from marble, he's a sculpture of male perfection. Thick, heavy muscles, hard, broad shoulders, massive arms, corded forearms. A rippling, shredded eight-pack. Those fucking grooves at his obliques—I want to run my tongue along them, taste that huge hard cock that bobs at his belly, swaying with his breathing.

He steps close, cock nudging my belly. Whispers in my ear. "You want to come, Bryn?"

"Yes."

"Yes, what?"

"Yes, please?"

"Then get on your knees and show me how that mouth looks wrapped around my cock."

I'm so pathetic. Quivering with need, I'm at a place of desperation where I'll do just about anything he asks. I sink to my knees and eagerly, greedily capture his huge, hard cock in my hands. And my god, what a magnificent instrument the man has. Thick enough that my thumb and forefinger don't quite meet around his girth, it's just… beautiful. Slightly lighter in shade than the rest of him, so long I can fit both hands around him one atop the other, and studded with delicious veins. His balls are heavy and tight against his body, wreathed in closely-trimmed black body hair.

I give him a few introductory strokes with my hands, watching his face for reactions. His eyelids flutter at my touch, and his abs harden, pull in.

"Fuck," he growls. "As good as that feels, I asked for your mouth, love."

I wrap my lips around him, stretching my jaw to accommodate his massive size. He groans in relief as I bob on him, taking more of him inch by inch. His hands go to my hair, holding onto my head, guiding me, gently but insistently pressuring me lower. He knows I can take him—and I do. I open my throat and take all of him—I start from the top, licking his tip, and then I wrap my lips around his glans and suckle there, and then I slowly take his length inch by inch, until his balls tap my chin. I grab the hard bubble of his ass and gulp, breathe raggedly through my nose as I work his swollen, pulsing shaft with my throat.

With a rough snarl, he drags himself away from me, cock leaving my lips with a loud *pop*.

"*Now* you can come," he growls in my ear.

He twists me to face the window, the movement rough and unapologetically aggressive. Cold glass crushes against my tits. Below, a clutch of people pass by, heedless of the view a few dozen feet up.

His fingers find my clit and swirl, swipe, and circle—plunge in, fuck deep. Pull out, smear against my clit. Drag teasingly up and down my seam, and then drive into my pussy, ripping a cry from me. All at once, I break apart, screaming his name.

"RUSH! Ohmygod ohmygod ohmygod! RUSH!"

"That's it, Beautiful Bryn. Come for me. Come all over my fingers."

Three fingers inside me, he fucks me hard with them, thumb pressing against my clit, and then those fingers withdraw and drag my wetness against my throbbing clit, and I come all the harder.

"You on birth control?" he growls in my ear.

"Yes."

"You believe I'm clean?"

"Shut up and fuck me, Rush."

"God, you're amazing." He dips at the knees and I feel his cock nuzzle my entrance. "Put me inside you, Bryn."

I reach between my thighs and grasp his immense shaft and guide him to my pussy. Notching him just barely inside me, I twist my head to look at him over my shoulder. "It's been a while since I've been with anyone, and you're *really* fucking big, so be careful at first, okay?"

He doesn't answer me with words. Instead, he snags my hands and stretches them at arm's length overhead, using his body to press me flush against the cold glass of the window. His lips press to my ear, and for a moment, I'm lost in sensation—there's nothing in the whole universe except Rush. His massive body, hot skin, and hard muscles pressed up against me, my back to his front. Chest to my spine, hips to my ass, thighs to my hamstrings. That fat, plump head of his cock splitting my pussy apart. His breath on my ear, his rough, powerful hands grasping mine. He's imprisoning me between the window and his huge frame, and it makes me delirious with arousal and excitement.

"Is this how you want it, Bryn?" He rocks his hips a fraction, driving ever so slightly further inside me. "Slowly? Gently?"

I can only whimper, mainly because I'm desperate for more of him, for all of him. I tip my hips toward him, rocking in an attempt to get him deeper inside me.

Instead of giving me his whole length inside me, he teases another infinitesimal, fractional thrust. "Wouldn't want to hurt you, Beautiful Bryn. I want you to feel better than you've ever felt."

He writhes against me, abs tightening against my spine. His breath is rough in my ear, telling me he's more affected by his game than his casual, teasing tone implies.

"You want more, Gorgeous?"

"*Yes,*" I breathe. "More."

I'm aching for the rest of him, my pussy spasming to swallow his thick, hot, rigid length.

"Like this?" A thrust, but another small one. Not enough.

"More," I whisper.

"Is it gentle enough?"

"Don't be—" I start, and then he thrusts deeper, cutting me off. I start again. "Don't be an asshole, Rush. You know what I meant."

He rumbles a laugh, his chest vibrating against my back. "Well, never let it be said I don't listen. You said to be careful, so I'm being careful. If you want something different, all's you gotta do is ask, love."

"I need all of you inside me, Rush. Give me your cock. Please. All of it."

"Ahhh, god, fuck me, I thought you'd never ask." His mouth rests on my shoulder, and then his teeth sink into the ridge of muscle as he slides into me, inch by endless, massive inch. God, it takes an eternity for him to fill me, and the more he does the more I ache, the more my pussy has to stretch to accommodate him. It's almost too much—almost.

He growls as he seats himself inside me, teeth digging into my skin and muscle. His hands crush-grip mine. After what feels like a thousand years, Rush is finally fully impaled inside my pussy.

"Rush!" I whimper. "You feel—oh god."

"Tell me, Beautiful Bryn. Tell me how I feel inside your hot, tight, wet, perfect little pussy." He thrusts against me, hips pushing against my ass cheeks to slide his cock just a little deeper. "Fuck, Bryn. Tell me how I feel. Tell me it's as good for you as it is for me."

"Rush, I—" I swallow, gasp, gagging on my ragged breath. "Fuck. Too good."

I'm dizzy, delirious, my knees weak—the only thing keeping me upright is Rush, his cock inside me, and his body all around me. I lift on my tiptoes, driving my hips forward, and I feel him slip out of me a few inches.

"That's it, Bryn, take me. Show me how you like it." His voice is raspy and rough, hoarse with strained need.

I let myself fall onto my heels, and he's driven into me to the hilt—we both groan in unison.

"Oh *fuck*, Bryn," he breathes. "It's like that, is it? That's how you want it, ey?" He nips my earlobe—the man likes to bite, apparently. "Seems like you *do* like it a bit rough."

"Maybe," I groan. "Or maybe it's just you."

"You want it rough like that, then this won't be a long fuck. You feel so fucking good, Bryn. You want it rough, then I'm gonna come really fucking hard and really fucking fast."

"God, yes," I hiss, rocking my pussy around him. "Give it to me, Rush. Hard and fast."

He presses my hands flat against the glass. "Leave 'em there," he orders. I nod, but he doesn't let go. "Yes, Rush. Let me hear you, Beautiful."

"Yes, Rush."

Fuck, I shouldn't like this so much. I shouldn't secretly love being ordered around. I shouldn't be so close to orgasm, I'm shaking when he hasn't even thrust twice. But I am. I do love it. I'm getting off on submitting to him. Obeying him. It's fucking hot, and I don't know why.

Worry about that later.

For now, just enjoy being fucked.

His hands skate down my arms, tickle my armpits, and then cup my tits. "Love these tits, Bryn. Fucking perfect. Know why?"

"Why, Rush?"

He grips them and holds on tight, using them to pull me backward as he draws out and slams back into me. "Because they're perfect handholds for fucking you. Just the right size. A nice, plump handful each."

"Ohhhh, fuck. Fuck. Yes. So good, Rush."

He plunders my pussy like that for several minutes, then, and I lose track of time, thoughtless but for the gasp and groans of pleasure as he fucks me, his fat hard cock throbbing through me, pulsing inside me, stretching me to a glorious burn. Each thrust is unhurried and measured, sliding into me until his hips clap against my ass, and then ending with him driving in that last inch or two with a hard push.

I feel myself rising to orgasm slowly—slowly. Each slow, hard thrust takes me higher, until I'm shaking and shuddering, whimpering and whining, wanting to push into him to get him deeper, to take him harder, to make him fuck me faster. But I can't. I'm helpless. Pinned against the glass, arms overhead, fucked up onto my toes, I have no leverage, no leeway for movement. All I can do is take what he gives me.

And what he's giving me is glorious—and not enough.

"Rush, goddammit, please. I'm so close."

"So'm I, sweet thing. But I'm not ready to be done yet."

"I need to move."

"You move, you'll make me come."

"I want it. I want you to come, Rush."

"Contrary to my name, though, I don't like to rush

a good fuck. And you, Beautiful Bryn, are giving me the best fuck of my life."

I laugh. "You don't have to—oh god, oh fuck—you don't have to flatter me, Rush. I'm a sure thing at this point."

He laughs, a rough bark of amusement. "You're funny, you are. But I'm bein' serious. You feel—" he cuts off with a grunt as he delivers another hard thrust, his hips slapping my ass. "So—fucking—*good*. Taking all the control I have to not cut loose and fuck you so hard your teeth rattle."

"Don't tease me with what you won't deliver, Rush."

His laugh is predatory, dark, dangerous. "Ohhhh, love. Now you've done it."

8

CAN'T STOP THIS

This girl is a fucking menace. Literally and metaphorically. I'm resorting to every trick I know to hold back my release—nothing's working. She's too fucking sexy. She feels too goddamed incredible.

Tight? As a vise.

Hot? As the face of the sun.

Wet? As a Slip 'n Slide.

She's a goddess. Her body is divine, taut and lithe and svelte and curvy in all the right places. The way she wants me, though. She takes every thrust with a greedy zeal that says she wants more and more and more.

And now she calls my bluff?

I am in so much trouble. I've always had a knack for getting myself into pickles, but this one is particularly tricky.

I'm meant to do something horrible to her. Betray her in the worst possible way. I should've already done it, but I couldn't. And now I'm literally balls deep in her hot wet cunt and she's gagging for more. Fuck her 'til her teeth rattle, she says.

Jesus.

How'm I meant to send a woman like her to hell? She's bold, tough, smart. Doesn't scream or carry on like a fainting priss when I blast a hole in a man's stupid skull. Resourceful. Clever. Sexy—did I mention that bit yet? By which I mean hot as fucking sin. Miles of lush brown skin, wild, untamable curls. Deep, dark eyes that see my very soul. Those fucking curves. A pussy that squeezes my cock so hard I can barely move.

All that, and she's willing to play along with my silly games? Does what I say and begs for more?

Jesus.

I'm fucked. Fucked, I tell you.

Wanting to delay my orgasm as long as possible, I pull out of her and step back. My cock aches, my balls throb, but I grit my teeth and tolerate it. I'll be back in her wet heat in a moment.

"Bend over the bed for me, Bryn," I command.

She pulls herself away from the window, turning to face me. Stalks toward me, each step lithe and graceful, tits jiggling hypnotizingly. She grips my cock, pumping my length. Teasing me. Torturing me. Each stroke is agonizingly slow, her fingers gliding down my length, which is slick and slippery. I grit my teeth, feigning indifference when I'm frantically clenching every muscle in my body in an attempt to keep from squirting my cum all over her hands.

She wins.

I yank myself out of her grip, snarling as I pace away, furiously tightening myself against the hot release pounding in my balls. "Fuck, woman. You're killing me."

"I thought you could fuck for hours, Rush."

I whirl, giving her a taste of my aggression. I stomp toward her, scoop her airborne, both hands digging into the plump, taut perfection of her tight little ass. Her legs wrap around my waist instinctively, and I rock into her. Split open, her pussy swallows my length with a slick penetration that has us both groaning. I walk across the room and crush her back against the window.

"When I'm fucking someone else, I can. But you, Beautiful Bryn—you're a fucking menace. You do me in. You ruin me." I drive into her, hard, and she cries out, pussy spasming around me. "I'd love nothing more than to be able to fuck you for hours, but you make it impossible. I won't last another minute, and it's your fault. You feel too fucking incredible."

"Again, Rush!" she screams.

"See? You take everything I've got and demand more." I give her another slamming thrust, and I drive so deep my balls ache, so deep my cock throbs and there's no more of her to fill, and yet she claws at my shoulders and uses her weight to sink down on me, forcing me deeper inside her than I thought possible. "Fuck, Byn. Jesus. What are you *doing* to me?"

She knots her fingers in my hair and yanks hard as she meets my thrust, wailing. "Shut up and make me come, Rush."

"D'you need to touch your clit?" I ask.

"Yes."

"Then do it. Touch that clit, baby. Make yourself come on my cock." I nip her earlobe, growling. "But fair warning—I'll come when you do. And I won't be nice about it."

"You don't have a nice bone in your body."

I thrust. "This ain't nice?"

"Nice?" She laughs. "No, it's not nice. It's wicked."

Her fingers slide between our bodies and she touches herself—the result is immediate. She cries out, arching backward as she pulses around me. "Oh fuck—fuck—fuck! Rush, holy god, fuck!" She thrusts against me, one hand gripping my shoulder while the other works between her thighs, rocking up and down on me, demonstrating absolute trust in my ability to hold her as she rides me.

"Bed!" she snarls at me. "Bed, now. Bed, goddammit, bed."

I stagger across the room on shaky, gelatinous legs, grunting in shock at the intense potency with which her pussy squeezes around my cock with the waves of orgasmic release smashing through her beautiful, perfect body.

When we reach the bed, she lets go of me and topples to the mattress, scrambling away from me and moving to her hands and knees. She spreads her legs wide, pushing her shoulders and chest into the bed to present her ass to me like the precious gift it is. "Fuck me, Rush. God, please. I need more."

"Fucking insatiable, aren't you?" I murmur, crawling onto the bed after her. "Just when I think you can't get any better, you fuckin' do."

She reaches between her thighs for me as I line up behind her, groaning as her eager fingers clutch my slick, aching cock and fit me into her slit. The moment I'm notched inside her, she pushes backward to take all of me, and her growl of need is ragged and breathless.

And if I'd thought she felt good before, she feels even better like this. I get a good grip on her ass cheeks and pull them apart to drive deeper, and she growls like a feral animal, hands curling into the mattress in shaking, white-knuckled fists.

"Ohhh *fuck*—RUSH!"

"Bryn!" I growl, hunching over her for a moment. "Beg, Beautiful Bryn. Beg me for what you need."

She obeys instantly. "Rush, please—fucking goddammit, Rush, please fuck me. Please fuck me. Come inside me, Rush. Fill my pussy."

Jesus actual fucking Christ, this woman. Gonna be the death of me, one way or another.

I've been holding back for so long now, I'm nearly mad with the need to come. My balls pulse and ache and burn, and my cock throbs and pounds, and she's so fucking wet and hot and tight, so lush and perfect around me.

I pull back slowly, pause, and then pound into her with a wordless shout. She pushes into my thrust eagerly, rising up on all fours and crashing back into my thrust as hard as she can. Her scream is ragged and wild, head hanging, and I feel her pussy spasming, preparing to come again.

She's a sex goddess, I tell you. I can die a happy

man after this fuck, because I know I'll never have a better one.

"Again!" she snaps. "Give it to me, Rush. Fill me. Come inside me. Fuck me until my teeth rattle."

Begging on her own—how can I deny her?

I give in. Let go.

Gripping her hips, I jerk her backward as I fuck into her, and this time I don't stop. I cut loose with everything I am, and the wet sounds of my cock plunging inside her and the rhythmic slap of my hips into her full, round, perfect ass is the most beautiful music I could imagine. Except maybe the way she screams through her orgasm, guttural wails and shrill, breathless cries again and again as I fuck her relentlessly, pounding her pussy with hard thrust after hard thrust.

"Ah lord god oh fucking Jesus," I say, feeling my orgasm work its way through me, preparing to rip me apart in a way I know I'll never be the same. "Bryn! I'm—oh fucking god in heaven, Bryn. I'm gonna come, oh god I'm gonna come so fucking hard!"

"Yes! God, yes. Give it to me, give it all to me!"

She's coming yet again, screaming and crying, literally sobbing and wailing, losing the ability to function as I fuck her into oblivion. She collapses forward onto the bed, but I'm not done—I hold her in place and keep fucking.

And then the sun explodes inside me.

My soul shatters.

My body is obliterated.

This isn't an orgasm, this is…rapture.

I don't know what sounds I make, what I say, what

I do—all I know is the sweet wet heat of her spasming pussy, the lush wonder of her body taking everything I'm giving her and demanding more and more. The rush of cum is an endless flood spurting out of me and filling her in wave after wave, and I pound her through each surge, cracking my hand on her ass cheek and then gripping the meat of it, driving deeper as my orgasm destroys me and keeps on going.

I come back to myself slowly, dizzy and breathless. "Holy fuck." She sags forward, and I slip free. "You're dripping my cum, Bryn."

She rolls to her back, panting. "I really, *really* hope you're clean, because that was seriously reckless of me."

"And I really, *really* hope you're on birth control, because same."

She looks at me, her expression carefully neutral. "I am. Never missed a dose. I know I'm clean, because I haven't been with anyone in almost a year, and only one person for several years before that."

"Neither are true for me, I admit, but I *am* clean. I was tested just a month ago, and I'm not normally so reckless as to go without a rubber. I can show you the report, if you like. It's on my mobile."

She shakes her head, a small smile on her lips. "No, it's okay. I believe you."

You really shouldn't trust me—is what I think, but don't dare say. The fucking irony of it is that I *want* her to trust me—I've never craved anyone's trust more. Yet here I am, deserving that gift, the very least of anyone alive.

Fucking monster, me.

"Gonna clean up," I say. "Right back."

"Bring a washcloth?" she yells after me.

God, I'm a fool. Fucking her bare? What the *fuck* was I thinking? I don't do that. It's my one unbreakable rule. I may be a randy horndog with a wandering dick and too few scruples, but I keep my shit bagged up. The world only needs one of me, and even that may be one me too many.

I wet a washcloth and clean myself up, then wet another and return to Bryn. She's laying on the bed watching me, smiling, hands laced behind her head, legs crossed ankle over ankle. So fucking beautiful.

I don't believe in love, but I think if I did, I might be tempted to think I'm half in love with this girl already.

God, that would be stupid, wouldn't it? Falling in love with the woman you're supposed to sell into sexual slavery?

Good thing I don't just not believe in love but am allergic to it. I repel it. Based on history, at least.

She reaches for the cloth, but I keep it out of reach. "Nah, love. Let me. Please."

She drops her hands, but hesitates, searching me. Now that we're done and the wild heat of the moment is spent, she's shy?

She keeps her legs crossed and pressed together, swallowing hard.

"Cmon, love. Open for me." I sit on the bed's edge next to her, waiting.

She covers her face. "It's a *lot*."

I lean over her. "Hey. Nothing to be embarrassed about, sweetheart. Sex is messy."

I press a palm against her thigh, and she slowly relinquishes the pressure, opening her legs for me. I swipe the cloth down through her folds, gathering my seed. Fold it, drag it down again, and a third time.

But then…

I can't help myself. I'm sat there staring at the prettiest pussy I've ever seen. I mean, it's perfect. A delicate pink flower, lips like silken petals, clit an elegant pistil. Her folds glisten, beckoning.

I drop the washcloth to the floor beside the bed and settle myself in the cradle of her thighs and feast upon her. Gently, however. Tender licks and soft kisses, slowly, purely for the enjoyment of tasting her sweetness.

"Rush, what are you—oh. Oh…*god*. Wow, I…oh god, that feels good." Her fingers bury in my hair, but not to pull or knot or yank. There's no desperation, no ferocity in this. It's almost…affectionate. "Rush. Your mouth…oh god. Fucking magical."

I take my time kissing and licking. I'm not trying to make her come, I'm just…giving myself a little treat.

"God, you taste like fuckin' sugar, Bryn." My words are muffled in the silk of her thighs. "Love the way you taste."

She pulls her heels up against her ass and holds my head, hips tipping and rocking subtly as she gasps quietly, each breath a soft whimper that shoots straight to my cock.

Her sounds, though. Bloody hell, the sounds she makes are fucking erotic. Sensual. The soundtrack of pure female ecstasy.

Her hips lift off the bed as she nears her climax,

and I push her over the edge without preamble, tonguing her to orgasm as unhurriedly as I began. There's no screaming, no thrashing, just her quiet gasps and breathless sighs and rapturous whimpers.

I keep her coming until she's trembling all over and arched off the bed, mouth open in a silent, shuddering cry. I devour her hungrily, growling my enjoyment of the way she arches, gasps, and whimpers.

Finally, she pushes me away. "Stop, stop. I can't—I can't handle any more. I need a minute."

I crawl up and flop to my back beside her, wiping my lips with the back of my hand.

She covers her face with both hands, panting raggedly, shuddering occasionally, "God, Rush. I just came, like four times, and you go down on me *again*?"

I grin. "Sorry, not sorry. Couldn't help myself."

She shakes her head. "I mean, I'm not complaining. I've just never had anyone go down on me minutes after we finish fucking."

"I'm not most blokes, am I?"

"No, you're not."

She yawns. "Sorry. It's been a lot, and it's catching up to me."

I have a freakishly strong urge to pull her into my arms. To hold her. Nuzzle her hair. And I've gotta ask myself: the *fuck*, mate? I don't *do* that. I don't *snuggle*. I fuck and get gone.

But this is Bryn.

And this isn't a normal situation.

The choice is taken from me when she rolls into me, the soft press of her breasts against my chest making my heart skip a beat. I swallow hard, finding it difficult to catch my breath.

Bryn chuckles, patting my pec. "Relax, Rush. We're just enjoying a nice little post-coital cuddle. I'm not expecting a proposal. Breathe, Jesus, you're as tense as a rock."

I will myself to relax, but that's sort of a contradiction in terms and doesn't exactly work. I focus on breathing, but that's ineffective as well. Eventually, I zero in on her—categorizing and memorizing the sensations of her: her scent; the warmth of her skin, the silk of it against my body; her breath on my chest; her hair tickling my chin and nose; her fingers curled on my pec.

That relaxes me.

Slowly, slowly, I drowse.

Bryn twitches, sighs. I feel her drop off into sleep, growing heavy against me.

My throat is tight and hot—what am I doing? Making everything harder on myself, that's what. I should get up and leave. Sneak out like I usually do. Call him and give him her location. Wash my hands of this whole thing. Take my money and run.

I have to.

Saving Bryn isn't an option—I've only room in my life for one girl, and it's not Bryn, unfortunately.

I'm almost asleep myself when I hear my mobile buzz. It's across the room in the pocket of my discarded jeans. Moving slowly, I worm out from underneath Bryn, holding my breath when she stirs. Asleep, there's youth and innocence in her features that makes my heart clench. So damned beautiful.

She's no idea what's going to happen to her. What I'm powerless to stop.

Fuck.

I tiptoe across the room, snag my phone, and take it into the bathroom.

It's him.

I shoot back an SMS rather than answering: *can't talk. What do you want?*

> Him: *Where is she? You should have delivered my merchandise by now.*
>
> Me: *Close.*
>
> Him: *Not having second thoughts, are you, Rush? Need I remind you why you're doing this?*
>
> Me: *No.*
>
> Him: *You have until noon tomorrow. Or instead of receiving the money you need, you'll get her head in a box.*

Fucking goddammit it all to motherfucking bloody shit-eating cunt ass hell.

> Me: *If you so much as breath the same air as her I swear to god I'll rip out your eyeballs and skullfuck you.*
>
> Him: *How eloquent. You should know better than to threaten me, Rush.*

Perfect grammar and punctuation, even in a text message, uppity fucking prick bastard.

> Me: *I don't make idle threats*

Him: *Nor do I.*

A moment later…

Him: *I'll sweeten the pot for you, because it has come to my attention that the particular…item…in your possession is of higher value than I'd originally realized. Bring her to me as soon as possible, and not only will I increase your payment to an even 500k, I'll cut you loose. Done. No more jobs for me. Ever.*

Damn. She must be really valuable if he's offering that. I wonder why?

Me: *Tomorrow noon cash legally binding contract you miserable sadistic evil fucking cunt.*

Him: *Deal.*

I'm about to click the button to put my mobile to sleep when it dings again.

He always has to have the last word.

Him: *Enjoy your stay at the hotel. I've heard the Salade Niçoise is particularly excellent there.*

He knows where we are? How? What I told Bryn was the truth—I assumed they lucked out on finding us here. But if he knows which hotel we're in? Not good.

A tracker, I can only assume. Implanted while she was drugged and unconscious.

I have neither the skill nor the tools to remove or neutralize an embedded tracking device.

Why would I? I'm giving her over to him. I have to. My threat wasn't idle—I'd put a slug in his brain without a second thought, and then I'd follow it with two or three more just for good fucking measure. But he's immensely well-protected. If I had a team of six highly skilled operators, eyes in the sky, and a solid plan, I'd go after him in a heartbeat. But alone? Nah. I'd be dead, and the one human on the planet I refuse to fail will be alone and helpless.

I let my phone clatter to the bathroom counter before I either crush it in my hand or huck it at the mirror. My head hangs, and I struggle to pull in a breath. My heart hammers. The image of the sink below my face wavers and distorts. There's a fat fucking elephant on my chest. Guilt rages through my veins in place of blood, along with an acidic dose of venomous rage.

I hear the door creak, but it doesn't register. I can't breathe. Can't breathe. Fuck.

What do I do?

Bryn is clueless. She trusts me. She's so fucking beautiful. Inside, I mean. Strong, smart, resilient.

I can't give her to a monster like that. He'll use her for himself until he's had his sick fill and then sell her to the highest bidder like an old used Ford Fiesta at auction.

But if I don't? Well, that doesn't bear thinking about. I nearly vomit even considering the idea of not following through.

At what would happen.

"Rush?" A soft hand rests on my shoulder.

I flinch violently. "Fuck off." It comes out in a ragged croak.

"Hey, it's okay." She doesn't fuck off. She leans against my back, arms wrapping around my shoulders. "You don't have to tell me what's wrong. But you're not alone in it."

Fucking hell—that just makes it all the worse. She's *comforting* me.

"You don't know the first fuckin' thing about me," I murmur, my voice rougher than 24-grit sandpaper.

"No, I don't."

"You dunno wha'I've done." I can't totally make my London accent go away, but if I focus, I can smooth it out a bit, which I've done for her since she mentioned not being able to understand me. But right now, this upset, it's back with a vengeance and thicker than treacle.

"What have you done?"

"Wrong question, swee'art. What've I not done, more like." I growl. "Answer is, not fuckin' much. I might 'ave a pretty face but I'm a fuckin' *monster*."

"I've seen no evidence of that so far, Rush. You've been rather sweet with me, actually."

This gets a laugh out of me. "Sweet? Lay off the drugs, love. One thing I ain't is *sweet*."

"It's all an act, baby." She rests her cheek on my back, breath plosive on my skin. "I see who you are under the cocky bad boy exterior."

"You ain't seen shit," I snap. "An' if you do see that, you're fuckin' 'allucinatin.'"

She worms her arms under mine, hugging my torso from behind, hands on my chest. "Hey, don't be grumpy with me, Rush. I know what you're doing."

"What am I doin', then?" I snap. "Coz it seems like I'm tryin' to make you understand that I'm not who you think I am."

"Pushing me away."

"Yeah, so get pushed, bitch."

She snorts. "Oooh, the B-word. If you think that's all it takes, then you don't know me very well, either."

"Nah, I don't. Don't want to, neither."

"Sorry, not buying it."

I hate her touch—because I crave it. I hate the soft bite of her words—because they sear my soul.

Her soft, small hands drift down.

"Don't," I whisper.

"Why not?"

I can't tell her. I try—I fucking swear I do. I open my mouth to tell her the truth, but nothing comes out.

I'm weak. So fucking weak.

Her hands glide down, down. Rest on my hip bones. I look in the mirror and see her molten brown eyes find mine in the reflection. Hers are filled with compassion, interest, and mischief—a complicated assortment of emotions.

Mine? Tortured.

My cock doesn't care about any of that. All it knows is that her hands are ghosting closer to it, and it likes what that portends.

"Bryn," I whisper, struggling to push the hot ball of truth past the lump in my throat. "I'm—"

She grasps my semi-erect cock in her hand, lazily rolling the pad of her thumb over my tip. I groan, hang my head, because I can't meet her eyes.

"Ssshh," she breathes. "Just hush. And watch."

I should never have touched her. Not once. I know better. But she's under my skin. I crave her. I can't bring myself to look away from our reflection, from her small hand sliding and clutching and playing with my growing erection—I can't look away, much less stop her.

I groan as she toys me to full erection. Like when I went down on her earlier, she takes her time. This is more for her than it is me. Just playing with me, enjoying the feel of my body, my response to her touch.

She leans against me, giving me her full weight against my back, breasts firm against me, skin soft and warm, breath hot on my shoulder.

Gradually, I feel myself rising toward orgasm, pressure welling in my balls, need building. I grip the edge of the sink and brace, breathing hard as she works my length with one hand, the other delicately cupping and massaging my balls.

"Fuck," I breathe.

"You like that?"

I nod.

"Need to hear you say it, Rush."

"Yes, Bryn, it feels good." My voice is rough, a hoarse croak.

I push into her hand, grunting as my orgasm wells within me. I don't have it in me to hold out. Shit, I'm barely hanging on to my sanity as it is.

I couldn't stop this if I tried.

The closer to climax I get, the slower her hands move. I feel her lips curve in a smile against my shoulder, watching me grind into her hand, grunting and growling as I reach the cusp of climax.

Right as I'm about to blow all over the sink and mirror, she drops to her knees on the tile and twists me in place. There's no warning or lead up, just her hot mouth around my cock, tongue sliding past my frenulum as she takes me. She doesn't deep-throat me this time. There's nothing to prove. She squeezes my balls and presses that wicked, teasing finger against my taint and pumps my cock at the base and moves her tight, wet, sucking mouth around my head—slowly, unhurriedly, lazily.

I groan raggedly, burying my hands in the soft curly mass of her hair. I arch, head thrown back, legs shaking and threatening to give out entirely as she utterly destroys me with her mouth. Time ceases to exist, and my lungs sear as I struggle to breathe past the spasming ecstasy of wave after wave of climax. The hot, wet suction of her mouth is an endless wonder, and even when I can't come anymore, she keeps going, fondling my balls and suckling and bobbing sloppily around my cock.

I have to grip the sink with both hands to keep myself upright as she takes me to a level of orgasmic delirium I've never dreamed was possible. Finally, she releases my cock from her mouth and sits back on her heels, grinning up at me like the proverbial cat who ate the canary.

With a raspy gasp, I sag to the floor, staring at Bryn in pathetic, stunned awe. "Bloody…fuckin'…hell."

She drags her wrist across her lips, looking almighty pleased with herself. Rightly so, I'd say. "Feeling better now, I bet."

My brain is scrambled senseless, and all I can do is give her a dazed nod. "Uh-huh."

This gets me a breathy giggle. "Good. I don't know what just happened to make you look so…I don't know…sad and angry, but hopefully that helps a little bit."

I stare at her, guilt shattering through me like a riptide as my cognitive function slowly returns. The guilt is fucking lava in my gut. I could vomit from it.

"You're a fuckin' wonder, Bryn," I whisper. "I don't deserve any part of who you are."

"Rush," she whispers back to me. "Don't say that."

"Just the truth, love." I shake my head, scrubbing my face with one hand. "If you knew. If you could see my rotten, black soul…" I swallow hard, each breath searing my throat with the infernal heat of guilt ravaging my insides. "You'd run as far and fast as you could. And you should, Bryn. If you had an ounce of sense in that…that perfect fucking head of yours, you'd put a hole in my fucking skull and run. And you should, Bryn. Run and don't fucking look back."

My eyes burn. Everything burns.

I can't…

It has to be now or I'll cock it all up.

"My mobile," I say, my voice shredded as if I'd

swallowed razored blades. "It was my friend. We can go see him now. He'll…he'll sort you out. But it has to be now."

Hope blossoms in her eyes. "He can help me get home? This won't touch my family?"

"Yeah. Home." I can't look at her or she'll see the lie on my face. "Won't touch your family."

She scrambles to her feet, grabs my hand, and hauls me to my feet. "Well, come on then! Let's go!" She's so eager, the poor doomed creature, pulling on her clothes as fast as she can.

I just watch from the doorway for a moment. "I'm so sorry," I whisper.

She doesn't hear.

Not that it matters. There's no forgiveness for the likes of me.

Not after this.

9

THE EVILEST HUMAN BEING I'VE EVER MET

Rush is…off. He's been off since we got to Lyon. I don't know what to make of it. The cocky, smirking, teasing, "love" this and "mate" that brash bad boy is gone. He's withdrawn, silent, and brooding. Dark and angry. Whatever happened in that bathroom was not good.

A venomous little serpent of suspicion wriggles in my belly—what if he's not who he says he is? What if there's something he's not telling me? What if…what if…what if?

I wonder a thousand things, ask a thousand what-ifs, worry about a thousand hypothetical scenarios as we walk the streets of Lyon. I'd thought we would take a taxi, but Rush insisted on walking. I only slept for an hour and a half at most, so I'm still physically exhausted. Plus, I'm now deliciously sore down between my legs—the man is hung like a horse. There is such a thing as too big of a dick, and his is *just* barely this side of that line. Any thicker and it'd probably hurt in a not good way. As it is, he pounded me into next week, so yeah, I'm walking a little funny.

No regrets, but I'm gonna need a day or so to recover before I ride that train to Poundtown again.

For some reason, I hear Corinna's voice in my head: *Brynnie-baby, are you in a dick-haze? Because in your situation, you can't afford to let yourself get lost in the cock, no matter how good the fucking is. You gotta be thinking clearly.*

You don't know how good the fucking is, I tell Corinna's voice in my head. *It's world-class. Top work, as Rush would put it. And his cunnilingus game? Stellar. A-plus. Ten stars out of five. The sex is so fucking amazing I had to bring my A-game. And not to toot my own horn, but I like to think my A-game is pretty damn good. That BJ I gave him in the bathroom? Might be my best effort to date. So yeah, I might just be a little cock-lost. You would be, too. I mean, for fuck's sake, look at you, Rin. You and Apollo got it on like Donkey Kong all over the world, and the man fucking KIDNAPPED you and held you hostage in his own personal fucking castle like some demented, horny version of Beauty and the Beast. So bitch, you can miss me with the dick-haze warning. My eyes are open. This is just good sex—okay, GREAT sex, the best, the most amazing sex I've ever had—with a sinfully, wickedly hot man who just happens to be helping me escape sex traffickers. It's a situation of opportunity. You would, and did, do the same. Of course, you fell in love with your captor, you Stockholm Syndrome-having slag. I'm not falling in love with Rush. I mean sure, I'd kill to have a week alone with him in a hotel with nothing but room service and a lot of good, hard fucking. That's not love, though. That's lust. I'm a lusty gal, and I'll take all the world-class sex I can get.*

I end my mental diatribe with an internal sigh as I take in my changing surroundings.

This area of Lyon is upscale. The buildings are all those fancy French ones that you see all over Paris. Fancy hotels. Fancy coffee shops, fancy restaurants.

I point at one of the buildings in question. "Is there a word for that style of building?" I ask Rush.

"Haussmann, I think." His response is absent-minded, his thoughts clearly elsewhere.

Well that was a dead-end conversational gambit. He's not holding my hand like he did the whole time we've been together. Not looking at me. Responding in as few words as possible. His hands are fisted in his leather jacket pockets, jaw clenched and hard.

We're stopped at a crosswalk, waiting for traffic to clear. I grab his arm, turn him to face me. "Rush."

He jerks his arm free. "What?"

"What did I do?" I ask.

He frowns. "Do?"

"I clearly pissed you off, somehow. You've barely said two words to me since we left the hotel." I hate how needy I sound, how desperate for his approval.

He sighs, scrubbing his face. "It's not you, Bryn. I promise. You've done nothing wrong. I just…" He trails off, shaking his head. "It's not you."

"Feels like it's me."

"It's not." He starts across the intersection without a glance either way, boldly ignoring the blaring horns and screeching tires.

I follow after him at a trot until I catch up. I want to cut through his taciturn armor, find something pithy, witty, or helpful to say. But I can't think of anything, and one look at the storm cloud that is Rush's expression deters me from trying.

So we walk in silence.

We turn this way, walk a few blocks, turn that way, walk a few blocks. He doesn't watch for tails. If I didn't know better, I'd think he was walking to his own gallows.

After thirty minutes of trudging through Lyon's wealthiest arrondissement, Rush stops in front of a gate. It's huge, a ten-foot arch of wrought iron. An eight-foot-high wall of aged white-gray stone blocks stretches in both directions for a full city block. On the other side of the gate, the driveway is red cobblestones older than the US government. Shrubs line the driveway, carved into perfect rectangles. The driveway curves, obscuring any view of the house.

For a long moment, Rush just stands at the gate, hands in his jacket pockets, staring at the intercom and keypad box as if he's waiting for it to strike him like a cobra.

"Rush?" I ask. "Are we…going in? Or…?"

He swallows hard. Nods once. "Yeah. We're going in." His voice is a hoarse whisper.

"You're worrying me a little," I murmur.

He turns his head to stare at me, his eyes a darker

gray-brown than I've seen them yet. His mouth opens, but no sound comes out, and he clicks his jaw closed, shaking his head.

That serpent of suspicion is writhing in my guts, now. Something is wrong—very, *very* wrong.

For a moment, I'm tempted to just run. But… where would I go? Who would I turn to? How would I get home? How would I escape the traffickers who seem able to find me no matter where I go or how I get there?

No. For better or worse, I've tied my fate to Rush. Maybe I'm a fool, but I see good in him, no matter what he may say. I feel a little like Luke Skywalker, thinking that: I see good in you, the innocent farm boy said to the powerful villain.

Rush jabs the buttons of the keypad with a thumb, each stab staccato, angry. There's a buzz, and the gate ghosts open on silent hinges. I hesitate, and then follow his lithe, furious predator's gait down the winding cobblestone path. I turn back to see the gates swing closed, clanging ominously.

Rush notices my absence, follows my gaze to the closed gates. "No turning back now, Beautiful Bryn."

I don't like how he said that. "Rush? What are you not saying? Something is wrong. I know there is. Just tell me what it is. Please."

He just shakes his head. "It's too late." He holds out his hand to me. "Come on, now, love. Let's get this over with."

"Too late? Rush, I really don't like the sound of that."

His gaze is dark, baleful, tragic. "Now you notice,

do you? I told you, sweetheart. I've a black, rotten soul. I hope you understand that I've no liking for what I'm doing. It's just that I've no choice. Now come on. No point in delaying the inevitable."

When I don't move, he crosses the space between us in a few short, furious strides, grabs my wrist in a biting, painful grip, and drags me into a fast walk.

"Rush—stop!"

"No stopping it now, I'm afraid."

He hauls me at a trot around a curve, and the hedgerow opens up into an expansive, verdant, manicured lawn. The ochre cobblestones give way to raked white gravel in a circle around a marble fountain. The house facing me is a stunning display of French palatial architecture, with gables and peaks and turrets, stained glass and gargoyles, tiny balconettes and soaring rooflines.

Roaring stone gargoyles flank flagstone steps leading up to a wide front porch covered by a two-story portico. Men wearing black suits, mirrored sunglasses, and earpieces stand guard on either side of the staggeringly enormous main doors, which had to have come from a medieval castle, being black with age, wrapped with black iron straps and fist-sized studded bolts. The men wield Steyr-Aug assault rifles.

Um. Shit.

Shit, shit, shit.

This is bad.

I halt at the bottom of the steps, yanking against Rush's implacable hold. "I…I don't like this."

"You're gonna like what's next even less, I'm afraid." He jerks hard, tripping me up the stairs.

"Rush…" I whisper, fighting tears of fear and confusion. "What's going on?"

He ignores my question, hauling me to the doors. The guards ignore him as he shoves open the fifteen-foot-tall doors, which may well be a thousand years old. Beyond, the floor is a black-and-white checkerboard. A heavy round table is centered beneath a candle chandelier that looks every bit as authentically ancient as the doors…and the suits of armor that flank the curved staircase…and the vases on pedestals covered by thick glass cloches.

There's not a sound…until the heavy doors slam closed with a shuddering echo that shivers down my spine with an awful finality.

"Rush? Where are we?"

"The belly of the beast," he murmurs, his voice barely audible, scratchy and ragged and freighted with darkness. "The mouth of hell. Abandon all hope, ye who enter here."

That sounds really fucking bad.

Footsteps echo, growing closer. A trim, thin man with white hair slicked back approaches us—he's wearing a tuxedo, an earpiece wire trailing down behind his left ear. "Welcome, Rush and…*guest*." His voice is crisp, arch, and faintly French-accented. "Monsieur Pugli will be with you in a moment."

"Pugli?" I repeat. "I've heard that name."

Rush doesn't move. Doesn't speak. I don't think he's

even breathing. There's more life in the suits of armor on the wall.

The butler or whoever he is leaves us, returning the way he came, touching his ear and murmuring in French into his left sleeve.

Minutes pass.

Abruptly, Rush speaks. "I can't do this."

I swallow hard, look at him. "What?"

He whirls to face me, shaking and trembling. "I can't do this. I can't fucking do this."

"Do what?" I ask. "Rush, *talk* to me."

The haze of horror clouding his face clears. Resolve turns his eyes the color of cold steel. "I'll ask you this only once, Bryn, and I know I've no right to ask, considering where we are and what I've done. But…" he takes my hands in his, crush-gripping me until the pain brings smarting tears to my eyes. "Do you *trust* me?"

I have roughly a quintillion questions. But it's not the time—I sense that as clearly as I sense the awful miasma of evil in this place.

I hold his eyes, search him. I see guilt, fury, self-loathing, horror, rage, confusion.

And above all?

Guilt, guilt, guilt.

"Obviously I've made a terrible mistake in trusting you this far," I whisper. "But as they say, in for a penny, in for a pound. Yes, Rush. I will choose to trust you."

He barks a laugh. "God, you're mad, aren't you?" He shakes his head, amused—or perhaps bemused is the better word; his expression sobers, then. "Stay with me. Do as I say when I say without fucking hesitating. And just…be ready. Shit's about to pop off."

Footsteps again. Distant, measured. Unhurried. I didn't know mere footsteps could drip with malignant arrogance, but somehow, these do.

I notice Rush's right hand moving. Stealing behind his back and secreting his gun into his jacket pocket.

"When I say run," he breathes, leaning close so his lips brush my ear, "you fucking run like the devil himself is on your heels, because he fucking is."

"Which way?"

"Outside. I'll be behind you." He grabs my hand and presses his knife into my hand. "If by some chance you get captured, take as many out as you can and then cut your wrists."

I stare at him. "What the *fuck*, Rush?"

His gaze is humorless—deadly serious. "This cunt you're about to meet is the evilest human being I've ever met, and trust me when I say I've met some *really* fuckin' evil people. He gets his hands on you, you'll beg for death. But it won't come."

"And you brought me to him?"

"I had no choice."

"There's always a choice, Rush."

"Folks like to say that, don't they?" His eyes are cold and hard. "But it's not always true, is it? Sometimes, there's only one real choice to make, and you fuckin' make it, because you've got to." The footsteps are closer, now. "Don't say nothin'. Not one fuckin' word, you 'ear me?" His Cockney is back and thicker than ever. Funny how it comes and goes, sometimes.

"I hear you." I take his hand, squeeze it. "I believe in you, Rush."

His eyes fly wide, shocked at my words. It's too late to respond, though. He yanks his hand free of mine and grabs my arm in a vicious grip that'll leave bruises on my bicep. His other hand in his jacket—on his gun.

I don't have to dig deep to summon the fear boiling my veins—I let it out. All the fear, all the confusion. The horror of killing. The exhaustion. Everything. I let it all out, and suddenly I'm hyperventilating, crying, struggling in his grip. It's not fake. He's not letting go, even when I thrash as hard as I can, keening in my throat like a trapped wildcat.

"Rush, Rush, Rush." The voice is deep, stentorian, smooth, articulate, arrogant, condescending, authoritative. "You came through. I have to say, I'm somewhat surprised. I thought our lovely Miss Bryn Harris here would get her hooks in you." His accent is complicated—there's hints of Italian, French, and English in there.

He's imposingly tall—between my even six feet and Rush's six-four. His body is lean and fit inside a hideously expensive bespoke suit. His hair is jet black and swept back, glossy and gleaming. Clean-shaven, his jawline is sharp and aristocratic. His eyes, though—fuck me. They're black as coal and radiating pure evil.

The evilest human being I've ever met.

Yeah, accurate.

I swear the temperature in the foyer dropped by several degrees when he entered.

I've gone still, hanging from Rush's implacable grip, staring at the man.

I've seen his face.

I've heard the name.

Pugli…Pugli.

It comes to me in a flash—I attended a meeting Dad had with the heads of his various units. This was last year, I think. Before Zero's death. I shove that aside and focus on the memory. Dad was giving a presentation, going over the dossiers of people he considered a threat—warlords, kingpins, arms dealers, traffickers in humans, traffickers in stolen or illicitly acquired information. The worst of the worst. This man was in that presentation.

My excellent memory comes through: Roberto Pugli. Interpol official, middleman between terrorists, arms dealers, and drug lords. But not just a middleman, oh no. A terror in his own right. The boogeyman. Some of the crimes against humanity Dad said Pugli is known to be responsible for were truly nauseating. Words like "flayed alive" and "burned alive" and "melted in vats of acid" were used. Those were just the crimes Dad could list without puking, and Dad has seen the worst the world has to offer.

I resume thrashing, flailing, kicking, spitting, screaming.

"For fuck's sake, Rush, *handle her*," Pugli snaps. "She's annoying me."

I prepare myself, knowing Rush isn't going to play this safe or nice.

He doesn't.

The backhanded smack is hard enough to make me see stars, rocking my head around. I sag in his grip, weeping, cupping my throbbing jaw.

"I thought you would have fucked some sense into her by now, honestly," Pugli says, gleeful at my visible pain; his hand goes to his crotch, fondling himself as if my pain is making him hard. "Although, I must say I'm glad you haven't. I like to take my merchandise through their paces before I sell them. It's more fun if they're… still spirited."

Oh god. Oh god. Now the knife and the warning make sense.

Rush still hasn't spoken.

Pugli sighs. "The silent treatment, is it? You're not *really* bitter, are you? You knew what you were getting yourself into the first time you took my money. You can't *really* have thought I wouldn't find out everything there is to know about you, can you?"

Rush doesn't answer.

Pugli is annoyed now—this is a man who likes to see his effect on people. "Hand her over, now. I'll get you your money and your contract."

"The price has tripled." Rush's voice is hard and low.

Pugli rolls his eyes. "Too late for that, I'm afraid."

"You're desperate for her," he says. "Means she's someone important. Triple. Or she dies, right here, right now."

Oh fuck, oh fuck.

Pugli just chuckles. "You've no idea who she is, do you?"

Rush stares, baleful and vibrating with wrath.

"Bryn Eloise Harris. Twenty-four years old. Daughter of the one and only Nicholas Harris and his equally impressive wife, Layla Harris. Who, together, own and operate the world's most successful security contracting service, Alpha One Security. They're bona fide heroes, Rush. And do you know who she calls aunt and uncle? None other than Kyrie and Valentine Roth." He tuts, mocking. "The poor thing has suffered a loss recently. Her fiancé, a rather talented musician named Zero, died in a tragic car accident only a few months ago. Now, what I can't figure out is how she ended up in that nightclub, and how those incompetent apes I hired managed to get their hands on a very real princess like this. Even more interesting is her escape from the train. Killed two men—one with a pencil. Imagine that! A pencil! Unfortunately, my original merchandise was allowed to escape in all the hubbub, which is…well, rather inconsiderate of you, Miss Harris." His black gaze meets mine, jovially depraved. "I had a buyer for her lined up. A deposit was laid out. And he doesn't want any…*darkies*, as he put it. I know, I know—how offensive. He's a true reprobate, I don't mind admitting, but we can't judge who we do business with. I don't ask questions, I merely provide. I offered you to him at a significant discount, too, but no. I'll have to acquire someone else who fits his desired profile."

I'm so terrified and horrified that the disgustingly racist remark barely registers. It's the least of my concerns, at the moment.

He shrugs, then claps his hands. "Well, now. That's enough pleasantries. Rush, let her go."

"Triple the cash, and the contract first."

"I'll wire it to you. Hand her over."

Rush jerks me closer. "Cash. Contract. *Now*. Unless you want to see her brains splattered across your fucking floor."

With a heavy sigh, Pugli snaps his fingers. Moments later, the butler apparates from nowhere—Pugli murmurs to him, and the man nods, vanishes again.

"Triple!" Pugli says, conversationally. "Going to start a new life for yourself, are you? Somewhere warm, maybe? Tired of the drab London weather, I suppose." He looks at me speculatively. "Did you tell her why you're doing this? No? Well, I won't spoil it, then. I know how to keep a secret, and you can trust me when I say yours is safe with me, Rush."

Secret?

Rush flinches at Pugli's words, his grip on my arm clamping down so hard I squeak in very real pain.

I hear a faint, muffled *click*—a hammer being pulled back. His grip is still viciously tight—it's a warning: *be ready.*

The butler returns with a black duffle bag in each hand. He sets the bags on the floor in front of Rush and then reaches into his tuxedo jacket pocket and produces a folded sheet of paper and a pen.

"Sign, and you're a free man," Pugli says. "And a million euros richer. Yes, I kicked in an extra hundred thousand to make it an even million. Call it a tip for bringing her to me early."

A million euros—the price of my life.

Rush inhales deeply, holds it, lets it out slowly, his eyes flickering down to mine.

There's no warning. Not so much as a twitch of his eyes.

His hand blurs—*BAM!* The butler's head snaps backward, blood and brain matter spraying.

BAMBAMBAM!

Pugli jerks and twists as the slugs hit his chest, three of them dead center.

"RUN!" Rush's shout is deafening.

The heavy doors creak open and the guards fill the space, assault rifles tucked into their shoulders. I don't know which way to run—Rush said outside, but the only way out is past the armed guards. Pugli is on the ground, writhing, gasping—there's no blood, though.

BAMBAM—BAMBAM!

The guards drop in near unison, twin holes in each of their chests over their hearts.

That's the only opening I need—I burst into a flat-out sprint, hurtling over the bleeding bodies, tripping down the stairs, and skidding on the gravel.

Rush's hard hand impacts the back of my left shoulder, spinning me to face right. "That way," he barks. "Go."

Shouts ring out somewhere in the house or behind us; I don't know from where—there are a lot of voices shouting. I don't look back, I don't check to see if Rush is with me. I'm under no misapprehensions that I could ever outrun him. I just run parallel to the wall, feet digging into the grass, sprinting for all I'm worth. Which, apparently, is a million euros. Or, actually, three times less than that, since he tripled the cost at the last second. Quick math, which is not my strong suit…three hundred thousand?

That's a little depressing. It's not exactly chump change, I'm aware of that. But my perspective is a little skewed. I grew up on a private island with private jets taking me wherever I wanted to go. My father has freaking fighter jets, for shit's sake. Three hundred grand is peanuts, where I come from.

Rush accelerates past me as the far edge of the property comes into view—the wall. Sunshine streams through the canopy of trees lining the road, glittering off the glass shards embedded in the rim of the wall. With one of the Steyr-Augs slung across his back, leather jacket off and in one hand, he skids to a stop at the wall, leaps and tosses his jacket over the rim, and then lands in a crouch, back braced against the wall, fingers interlaced to create a basket. I need no instructions for this—it's a standard part of training. I don't slow my pace—I sprint harder. My lungs burn, my legs ache. But there's no time for weakness.

I take a leaping step, plant my foot in Rush's interlocked hands; I feel him lift as I leap, boosting me upward. I go airborne, Rush's immense power launching me so hard I clear the wall entirely. I windmill my arms, desperately flailing in an attempt to keep my body oriented. The ground hurtles up to meet me, and I fight panic in the stretched-out instant before I land. My feet hit the sidewalk and training kicks in—the hundreds and hundreds of reps of pratfalls, shoulder rolls, and drops from walls that Mom and Dad forced me and

Killy to take part in show their value. It's instinct to throw my weight and tuck my shoulder to absorb the momentum in a roll. Shocked voices squawk at me in surprised, indignant French as I bowl through a forest of legs. I make my feet just in time to see Rush plant his hands on his jacket and vault over the wall in a neat body roll, dropping the eight feet to land in a crouch like it's nothing.

"What are you, fucking Spiderman?" I mumble, annoyed at his physical prowess.

He just stares at me, expression blank and unreadable. He has the Steyr-Aug in his hands, which causes the formerly indignant passersby to scatter in fright. Well, that and the fact that a jacked, six-foot-four man carrying an assault rifle just vaulted over an eight-foot wall.

"Let's go," he growls. "They're tracking you."

"Tracking me?" I ask. "How?"

"GPS chip. Probably planted it in you when you were unconscious."

"So take it out?"

"Oh yeah, just like that? You know where it is? No? Me neither. And how, even if I did? Just cut it out with my fucking knife?"

Anger explodes in me, and I yank the knife out of my pocket, flip the blade out, and slam it against his chest. "*Yes*, asshole. That's *exactly* what I fucking want. Better yet, just fucking cut my throat and be done with it." I take the knife back and put the edge to my throat. "C'mon, Rush. *Do it*. You sold me to Roberto *fucking*

Pugli. You lied to me. Tricked me. You fucking *sold me* for three hundred grand!"

He moves so freakishly fast my eyes can't track his hand's movement—the knife is just gone and my wrist is stinging. "Don't fuckin' tempt me, *slag*." His eyes blaze.

"Oh, there we go. Here's the real you." I shove him as hard as I can. "Slag. Cunt. Bitch. Got any more names? Hit me with 'em, Rush. I've heard them all from better men than *you*."

Agony blazes across his face. "And well I fuckin' know it!"

"I can't help who I was born to!" I shout.

"Neither can I!" he shouts back, and then abruptly goes silent, head cocked. "C'mon, princess. This ain't the place for a row." He pronounces *row* to rhyme with *cow*. "Unless you'd rather go it alone?"

I wave a hand vaguely. "Just…fucking go. We'll have our *row* later."

He stalks forward a few steps and then stops, jogs back to the wall, hopping up to retrieve his jacket. "My best mate gave me this," he says by way of explanation, as if I'd asked.

"Wonderful." I follow after him.

A taxi is stopped a few feet down the road from us, and a well-dressed young couple is preparing to get in. Rush levels the rifle at them. "Fuck off, the both'a ya."

He shoves me toward the car and then plants his hand on the back of my head like a cop does to a perp on TV; I shake my head. "Get off me, asshole, I'm going. I know how to get into a fucking car on my own."

I slide over to the passenger side as Rush piles in

after me. The driver, a young African man, glances nervously at Rush, who settles the rifle across his lap while barking out a clipped phrase in French.

The driver nods jerkily, planting the accelerator. The taxi jolts forward with a squeal of tires. I turn to look behind us—half a dozen suited men wielding assault rifles jog to a halt, watching us depart. One of them lifts his wrist to his mouth, giving a report that we escaped.

Rush exhales shakily, scrubbing his face. "I don't suppose you know anyone who can get that fuckin' tracker outta ya, do ya?"

"Yes, as a matter of fact, I do. I'll have to contact my parents, though. I was hoping not to involve them in this." I glare at him. "Weren't you SAS? You don't have any contacts?"

"I wasn't exactly thrown a parade when I left, love."

"Do *not* fucking call me that shit, Rush. I'm not your fucking *love*. I'm not your fucking *anything*."

That agony passes over him again. "I know." He closes his eyes. "Fuck. I fucked up. I *really* fucked up, Bryn."

"Selling me out to Pugli? Not sure 'fucked up' is a strong enough phrase. When did he get ahold of you, anyway? The bathroom? That was him?"

"No, Bryn." His voice is a razor-sharp whisper. "Well, yeah, it was him. But it was always me, luh—it was always me. From the start. Runnin' into you in Berlin wasn't an accident. I was sent to get you."

"Jesus," I whisper. "I'm a fucking moron. A blind fool. Blinded by a pretty face and a hot body. God, I'm such an *idiot*. It was never real, was it? None of it. Just getting your rocks off before you sell me to a sex slaver."

"It *was* real." I barely hear him. "Sellin' you out wasn't the fuck-up."

"Bullshit." I frown at him. "So what *was* the fuck-up, then?"

"Savin' you."

"Oh. Wow. Okay. You wanna go back for the money?" I laugh. "How much do you want, Rush? Did you miss who my parents are? Who my aunt and uncle are? A million dollars, is that it? Give me your phone and I'll have a fucking *billion* dollars in your account by noon."

He snaps, then. Lunges across the car at me, knife at my throat, face a rictus of rage and agony. "IT'S NOT ABOUT THE FUCKING MONEY!" he screams, his voice ragged and raw as if he'd swallowed a handful of gravel.

I go stone-still, not blinking, not breathing. Slowly, he backs away, dropping the knife to his lap from shaky fingers. "I'm sorry. Fuck me, fucking fuck me. I'm sorry, Bryn. I'm sorry."

I can't move.

"It ain't about any goddamn money."

"That was incidental, then, huh? I snap, my voice venomous, acidic. "Just a perk? The real payment was *me*, I bet. Getting to sample the *merchandise*?"

"No. That was real."

"Right," I say with a bark of sarcastic laughter. "You said triple it, and he gave you a million. Threw in an extra hundred grand. That means nine hundred thousand. Which means your original fee for coercing, tricking, and seducing me into Pugli's mansion was three hundred thousand dollars. Sorry, euros." I snort, shaking my head. "But yeah, it's not about the money."

"Fine, yeah, it is. It *is* about the money, sort of. It's about two hundred and seventy-six thousand, four hundred and eighty euros and sixty-six cents. To be precise."

I blink at the specific number. "I…I don't understand."

"No, you don't. Coz you fuckin' *can't*."

"So tell me."

"You…" he shakes his head. "Nah. You wouldn't fuckin get it, princess."

"Because I was born rich?"

"Because you've never had to fucking struggle!" he snaps. "You've never known. You'll *never* know."

"Oh for fuck's sake," I snap. "Fine. Keep your secret. What-the-fuck-ever. It's not like you sold me for it or anything. But no. I won't fucking get it because I was born into wealth. Fuck you, asshole."

Silence, then.

Rush says something to the driver, who pulls over, looking relieved. We're in a poorer section of the city now. No more elegant Hausmann buildings, no more quiet, tree-lined streets. Here, it's tumbledown apartment buildings covered in graffiti and suspicious-looking men slouching in doorways smoking cigarettes as they watch us as we exit the taxi.

Rush leads us to an alley, which dumps us onto a narrow side street lined with parked cars, most of which are aging compacts. He stops at once, tries the handle.

Locked. On the third attempt, the door opens...probably because the car is such a piece of shit the owner likely didn't care if got stolen.

Flicking his knife open, Rush pries open the steering column and has the car hot-wired in seconds. It's been less than thirty seconds from sitting down to pulling away from the curb. He settles the rifle between his leg and the car door.

Instead of driving like a maniac, however, he keeps a sedate pace, following the posted speed limits. He must sense my confusion. "I told you already—play it cool and you'll likely get away. Driving like you stole it is what gets you nicked by the bobbies."

I just stare at him, uncomprehending.

"Oh for..." he rolls his eyes. "Caught by the police."

"Right, but don't we need to get away from Pugli?"

"They're *trackin'* you, love. We *can't* get away till we get that thing outta ya's. So no point driving crazy. We're just putting miles between us and his goons till we can figure out a plan."

"So, if you were always assigned to bring me to Pugli, then why were those guys after me?"

"Pugli likes to double his coverage. Any job he needs done, he hires more than one crew or person to do it, but he don't tell them there's others. If they brought you in, they'd get the payday. If they killed me on the way, so what? No skin off anyone's back." He glances at me. "You sound like you know who he is."

"My father is Nicholas Harris." I figure it's all I really need to say.

"Operator royalty, he is. Him and his men. They're

all famous. Duke, Thresh, Puck, Lear, Anselm. Fuckin' the best of the best. And you grew up with 'em?"

I nod. "Those are the uncles I mentioned."

He scrubs his forehead. "Jesus. And they trained you some, didn't they?"

I nod. "They won't let me on the teams, though. Pisses me off." I make a snooty, disgusted face. "I'm not ready, they say."

Rush sighs. "You're their daughter, Bryn. The teams, military or otherwise, are deadly work. Even if you're the best in the world, bad shit happens. Did to me."

"I froze. That was my fucking moment, and I froze. I guess they're right, huh?"

"Not for that, nah. Promise you, every one of them uncles will tell you how they froze at some point. And when it really counted, when your skin was on the line, you did what you had to do. Like a fuckin' pro, love. They'd be proud."

"Proud? I don't think so, Rush." I shake my head, eyes blurring. "I ran away like a spoiled brat. I didn't tell anyone where I was going. After all my parents have been through, I pull that fucking childish stunt?" I bury my face in my hands, unable to stop myself from crying. "God, I'm the worst."

His cell phone appears in my eyeline. "Call 'em."

"What?" I lift my head, blinking away tears.

"Past time for playing about, Bryn. They're way past angry and into into full-on panicking by now, I'll bet. They're involved. Call and ask for help."

Goddammit.

I hold the phone, but don't dial. I stare at him. "Why did you change your mind? What changed?"

He sighs, leaning against the window, driving with his right wrist draped over the steering wheel. "Call 'em. Set something up to get that chip out your fuckin' neck or wherever the dozy pillocks put it. Then I'll tell you everything."

"Everything?"

He nods. "Every last sordid, cocked-up, bastard detail, Bryn."

10

A STUDY IN PAIN, STUPIDITY, AND DEATH

S HE DIALS AN EXTRAORDINARILY LONG SERIES OF numbers. Puts the phone on speaker, holds it near her face, parallel to the floor. It rings three times.

"Acme Concierge Service, how may I help you?" The voice that answers is a smooth, accent-less female voice, a professional phone operator.

I stifle an involuntary snicker at the name Acme, though. What is this, Bugs fucking Bunny?

"Hi, my name is Jane Smith," Bryn says. "I need to get in touch with a travel agent." Bryn's voice is even, expressionless.

"I see. Do you have a particular agent in mind?"

"Yes, actually. I was hoping you could connect me to Doc Smith."

There's a pause. "I see. And this is Jane Smith, you said?"

"Yes."

"Do you have an ACS identification number?"

"I do. It's one-six-five-bravo-echo-hotel."

Another of those pauses. "Very good, Miss Smith. Category?"

"Um. Just…code red."

"I'm sorry, Miss Smith, but that's not a recognized category."

"Goddammit," she whispers, her voice losing the even, measured quality for a moment, going shaky. "I need a return ticket."

"Thank you, miss. Shall I have your agent return your call to this number?"

"Yes, please."

"Very good, miss." A pause. "I have contacted your agent. Doc Smith will be contacting you *very* shortly. Will that be all?" The emphasis on 'very' seems intentional and important in this coded conversation.

"Yes, ma'am. Thank you."

"It's my pleasure, Miss Smith. Take care and thank you for contacting Acme Concierge Service. Goodbye."

Bryn ends the call and sets the phone on her thigh, staring at it expectantly.

"Sorry, but Acme—?" I start.

She holds up a finger, indicating I should shut up and wait, so I do. At literally the very moment she lifts that finger, the phone rings. She answers on the first ring, putting it on speaker.

"Hi, Daddy," she whispers, her voice shaky. "You're on speaker and I'm not alone, but I…well, it's complicated, but I'm mostly safe and able to speak freely."

There's a significant pause, and then a low,

silky-smooth, hard-as-nails voice slides across the line. "When you, your mother, your brother, and I spent a week at Disney World when you were nine, I purchased a souvenir for you. What was it, and what did you call it?"

She licks her lips, exhaling slowly. "A stuffed llama. I called her Yammie, because I'd just started taking Spanish lessons and figured they should be called yammas rather than llamas."

"If you are able to speak freely, tell me five significant details of the person you are with."

"His name is Rush. He's former SAS. He works, or worked, for Roberto Pugli, who is responsible for this whole…situation I'm in. He needs, for a reason I have not yet discovered, a quarter million dollars. Two hundred and seventy-six thousand and change—it's a very specific number. Um. He…Oh, he's fluent in French and German."

There's another heavy pause. The voice returns—Nicholas Harris, I assume. The legend is real. "Bryn. Sweetheart. I love the shit out of you, girl, but what the actual *fuck*?" The last word is furious, snarled.

"I'm sorry, Daddy."

"You give your bodyguards the slip by picking a fight—" I hear Mom's voice in the background, muffled and unclear. "Do *not* encourage her, Layla. And then you fucking *vanish* off the face of the earth. In the wake of your little Houdini act, at least six men have turned up dead. Two of whom were brutally murdered in what I can only describe as clever ways that tell me you've taken a few situational survival lessons from your mother."

"That's…accurate."

"Elaborate, Bryn. *Now*."

Oooh boy, Daddy is *peeved*.

Bryn launches into a facts-only retelling of the events, and it doesn't seem like she leaves anything out except for our little sexual side quest.

And my betrayal.

Once she's done—having made it seem like Pugli captured us rather than the truth, her father is silent again. "You're lying about something." His voice is cold. "Don't."

"Daddy, I—"

"I have four fucking fireteams scouring Europe for you. I pulled your Uncle Lear away from a very important case to track your movements. Your mother is frantic. Your brother and Cal are beside themselves. Law enforcement from three different countries have *your* fucking face on their wanted lists." His voice rises in volume—just a hair above the quiet, conversational tone he's used so far. It seems significant, though I don't know the man from Adam. "So, I will say this only once, Bryn Eloise Harris. Do—*not*—fucking—*LIE*—to—me." He bites out each word, snapping the world "lie" with vicious intensity.

"Tell him the truth, Bryn," I murmur. "I'll accept the consequences."

"Consequences?" Nicholas says, the question ominous.

"I told you he works for Pugli." She swallows hard. "I didn't know that at first. He…he was, um…"

"Pugli has leverage over me, sir," I say. "Significant leverage. Enough to force me to do things that go against everything I am. I was tasked with bringing Bryn to Pugli. And I did. But I couldn't go through with it. I don't say that to justify anything, though. I did what I did, and I ain't gonna deny it."

Harris is silent. "I assume your relationship has crossed into…personal territory."

Bryn snorts. "That's none of your business."

"He betrayed you. Tricked you. Lied to you. Sold you to one of the most notoriously vile human beings on the planet. Yet you're still with him."

"I told you, it's complicated."

"I suppose that's your choice, and I'll have to let you make it. God knows we've all made weird choices in this fucked up family." He sighs. "What do you need? Why call now? I assume because you thought you could handle it on your own and have come up against something you can't handle by yourself."

"Rush thinks they're tracking me, somehow. Like a chip or something. They keep showing up everywhere I go, when there's no way they should be able to."

"You're using the evasion strategies we've taught you?"

"And then some. Rush knows what he's doing, Dad."

"Ah, here we go." A lengthy pause. "I just received Rush's dossier from Lear."

"Shit," I mutter.

Bryn glances at me. "Something to hide? Something else, I mean?"

I snort bitterly. "You might say that, yeah."

"You're a complicated man, Rush Bellamy."

"Bellamy ain't my real last name," I answer. "I just picked it for the military forms coz it sounded good."

"Then what is your last name?"

"Ain't got one, sir," I answer. "I was left on the steps of a vicarage in central London when I was not even a week old. No clue who either parent was. Raised in an orphanage till I was eight and then put in various foster homes till I ran away and lived on the streets. I was given the name Rush by a nun at the orphanage because I had too much energy and was always rushing around causin' a ruckus. Before that, I was just 'you, boy.'"

"I see." A long pause. "Recruited into the military at seventeen, SAS by nineteen. Top marks across the board in all disciplines. Multiple honors, decorations, and medals, including the Victoria Cross." Another pause; the man uses pauses like weapons. "But…you've also been demoted several times for a variety of offenses, mostly to do with insubordination, assault, and…oh." He actually laughs. "You were discharged rather abruptly two and a half years ago, but the details are heavily redacted."

"Yes, sir."

"I'm curious about that."

"Um." I really, really don't want to get into that.

"Dad," Bryn says, admonishing. "I'm not sure this is the right time for an interrogation."

Harris sighs. "I guess not. But son, we're gonna have that conversation."

"Ain't your son, sir. Respectfully."

"Understood." Another of those damned dreadful pauses—I see where Bryn gets her penchant for using silences as interrogatory weapons. What's he going to say next? "What's he have on you?"

I clear my throat, reaching deep for a calm I do not feel. "So you can have it on me, too?"

Bryn takes the phone off speaker and puts it to her ear. "Dad. I'll handle Rush and his secrets—yes, I'm aware. No, I don't want you to intervene, I can handle it. I just need this tracker deactivated. I didn't want to drag you all into this—yes, Dad, I know, *god*. I've already apologized for—right, I forgot I have to use Dad's Official Apology Script or the apology doesn't count." She speaks in a mocking, annoyed, monotone. "I accept responsibility for my decision. Regardless of extenuating circumstances which may or may not apply, I made choices and they are mine alone. I'm sorry, Dad. I should not have ditched my guards, snuck out to a club for some unmonitored alone time, and gotten kidnapped by sex traffickers while trying to stop a kidnapping." A pause. "There—happy? Yeah, well, me neither. This hasn't exactly been fun, Dad. Jesus! Can you just fucking stop *parenting* me for six *goddamn* seconds and help me with my actual problem? Or is this phone call just a waste of time? Maybe I should have asked for Uncle Lear instead. I mean, silly me, I thought you'd want to *help*."

She listens for a while after that outburst,

interjecting the occasional "right" and "yeah" and "got it."

After a few minutes of this, she says goodbye and ends the call, tossing the phone at me. "Good lord. He can be such an uptight jackass, sometimes."

"He cares." I give her a long, hard look. "Be grateful you have that, Bryn. No one on the planet has ever given a single solitary flying fuck what I do or what happens to me except as it affects them."

She scrubs her face. "You're right, I know you are. He just can't help himself."

"So. Is there a plan?"

She nods. "There is. We have to get to Lisbon—there's a contact there who can get this thing out of me."

"And then?"

She shrugs. "Kill Pugli. Go home."

I growl. "Still pissed that the fucker had a vest. Shoulda put 'em in his fucking forehead, but he was a good distance away and I didn't want to miss. Won't get that chance again." I shake my head. "He didn't plan beyond deactivating the tracker?"

She eyes me, shrugging again. "That's step one."

I feel my heart sink. "Meaning you don't trust me with the rest."

She stares at me. "And why should I, Rush? You fucking *sold* me for a goddamned pittance. If I knew why, I might understand. I don't think you did it maliciously, and I believe it wasn't about the money. But if you won't tell me the fucking truth, what am I supposed to believe?"

My tongue is adhered to the roof of my mouth—I

couldn't speak if I wanted to, and I don't want to. I don't dare trust anyone else with that secret. Not even Bryn.

She shakes his head, hissing in disgust. "Fine. Just put me on a bus to Lisbon and go fuck yourself."

"I'll drive you," I rasp.

"I don't fucking want you to."

"Too bad."

We're rounding a curve, going fairly slow, but still fast enough that I panic when she shoves open her door and unbuckles.

"Pull over," she snaps.

"No, Jesus. Shut the fucking door, you daft bitch!"

"I know how to tuck and roll, Rush. I swear to fucking god I'll jump out of this car and *you* can explain to my dad what happened to me."

I jam the brakes and haul the wheel over. We skid to a halt on the shoulder. Bryn is out of the car before it's even stopped, marching furiously away from the highway toward the rooftops in the distance to the east.

I get out and jog after her. "Bryn, wait!"

"Fuck off, Rush."

"Just wait! God, just fuckin' wait a goddamn second!" I jog past her, turn and grab her shoulders.

She does a hold-break move followed by a viciously hard shove that sends me stumbling backward several steps. "Do *not* fucking touch me." She flips me off with both hands, thumbs out, putting her hands directly into my face, spitting snarled words. "You can fuck all the way off, *love*."

"Bryn, just—"

"You're a *liar*, Rush. You *used* me." She shakes her

head, holds both hands up. "This isn't about the sex, by the way. I knew going in that it was casual. I was and am fine with that. We were in a whole…situationship. I'm not mad because we fucked. I'm a big girl and I knew what I was getting into before I jumped into bed with you."

"Bryn, I—" I can't find words to explain anything I'm thinking or feeling. "I ain't good at this shit."

"What, telling the truth? Being forthcoming about literally *any*thing?"

"Yes. Well, no. Talking about myself."

"Try." She takes a step toward me. "I hope you see that I'm trying *really* fucking hard to give you a chance, here. I like you. I may or may not have felt something for you at some point. I don't *want* this to be the situation we're in, but it is. And you did it. *You* put us here."

The panic I've been refusing to let myself feel starts to take over, like it or not. I know the signs; I've been here before.

My hands start to tremble. My lungs get tight and hot, and I can't take a full breath. Racing thoughts. Narrowed and blurred vision.

No, no, no. Not now. Not here. Not in front of her. Fuck!

I turn away from her and go back to the car. Sit behind the wheel, let my forehead thump against the wheel. Grip it in shaking, tingling hands. Try to breathe slowly like Dr. Parvati told me: in for four, hold it for seven, out for eight. Repeat. Repeat.

Focus on the world around me, sensations: the peeling leather of the steering wheel in my hands. The emergency flashers tick-tick-tick-ticking. The blue sky through the windshield.

"Rush?" Her voice comes from a million miles away.

I shake my head. In for four, hold for seven, out for eight.

"Panic attack?" she asks. I nod my head against the steering wheel.

I hear the other door open. Her hand is soft on my forearm—she slides her hand down my arm and laces her fingers in mine. In a soft, low, beautiful voice, she sings a lullaby—I can't focus on the words or recognize the melody, but it's soothing. Slowly, my breathing calms and the panic gradually recedes.

When I feel more normal, I look at her. "Thanks," I croak.

She leans closer. Touches her forehead to mine. "Rush, just talk to me."

I swallow hard. "Six years ago, I was in London on leave. I'd just gotten back from a really bad stint in Afghanistan. Lost my best mate." I tug at my leather jacket. "The one who gave me this. Arjun. Went through training with him, made the SAS teams with him. Got assigned to the same unit. Fought with him. Bled with him. Did everything with him. He was the brother I've never had, and he—he…he fuckin' died in front of me. Stray round to the fucking face. No sense in it. Alive one second and dead the next. Wasn't even a firefight. Just some fuckin' asshole taking potshots at us."

"I'm sorry, Rush."

"Thanks. But that's just context. I was in bad shape,

mentally. Went out with some of the lads, hit a few too many pubs, got mad pissed." I lean back in the seat and scrub my face with both hands, exhaling raggedly. "Met this girl at the last pub. Rachel. Lovely girl. Went back to her place and we…well, you know. Didn't think much of it, just a good tumble in the sack, so I thought. Only, I was pissed so I fell asleep in her bed. Never done that before. And it sorta turned into a thing. Didn't mean for it to happen. I was shipping out again and I knew it. Had no business gettin' involved with anyone. I was just…I was fucked up, and I went and fucked up both of our lives."

Bryn winces. "Oh dear."

"Yeah, bet you can guess where it's going?"

"Knocked her up, huh?"

I nod. "Yep. Got her up the duff." I swallow hard. "I tried to do right by her. I sent her money while I was deployed. Talked to her. Stayed in contact. I…I'd *never* fucking abandon a child. Not like I was. I didn't abandon her—them. I made it back to London for the birth. She, um…we decided we weren't gonna be a thing. It was mutual, I swear. Not just me deciding it."

"I believe you."

I fucking loathe the way my eyes burn at her words. Ignore it. Keep going—too late to stop now. "For the first few years, I spent as much time as I could with my daughter, Eliza. Darling girl. Sweet, beautiful. Silly. I…" I squeeze my eyes shut. "I fucking love her so much it's mad. Do fucking anything for her. Whenever I wasn't downrange, I was with her. Sent her mum gobs of money. Toys. Clothes. Diapers, everything."

"Rush. What *happened*? How did Pugli get involved?"

"The world is a terrible place, that's what. Rachel died. I was home with Eliza, and Rachel was out running errands. She got hit by a car. Dead on the spot."

"My god. No!"

"I had a job to do. I couldn't just…quit. So Eliza went to live with Rachel's parents. Good folks, overall, but they've no love for me nor me for them. We're just different sorts of people, I guess, from totally different worlds, and we don't get along. There's no, like, hate… we're just totally different. I…we have an arrangement. When I'm home, Eliza is with me full time. When I'm gone, she's with them. We don't see each other except for pickup and dropoff, and it works for us. No drama, no mess. Easy."

"But?" she prompts.

"But then, a year and a half ago, Eliza got sick. She has an extremely rare form of leukemia."

"Rush," she breathes. "My god."

"Yeah. Chances of survival are pretty much nil. We've tried everything. Literally. Every kind of chemo and radiation there is. Alternative therapies, eastern medicine, extreme diets. They've even put her under the knife trying to…what's the fuckin' word they use? Excise, that's the one. They excised a shitload of the cancer not once or twice, but *three* times. I've spent every last fucking penny I've ever made trying to save her life and I've thrown myself to the wolves tryin' to earn more." I throw my head back and growl as a helpless, agonized sob catches in my throat. "None of it—fuck. FUCK! None of it's working, Bryn. She's fuckin' *dying*."

"Rush." Her voice is soft and quiet and horrified. "I had no idea. I'm so fucking sorry."

"Course you didn't, love. No one fucking knows. Even my best mates from the service don't know about Eliza, let alone that she's sick. Only her parents and me know. I keep her separate from the rest of my life." I scrub my face again. "I ain't a good man, Bryn. I know it. I don't fuckin' lie to myself about it. I done a lot of fucking bad shit and I'll probably do more because I'm…back in the old days they'd have called me a blaggard."

"Rush," she murmurs. "You're not—"

"Oh save it, Bryn. Don't let your pity for my poor innocent dyin' little girl distract you from what I done to ya."

"But Rush, I have to believe a monster like Pugli has something on you. You said you needed a very specific amount of money that Pugli was paying you for bringing me to him."

I nod. "Yeah, I…there's an experimental drug program startin' in the States and it's gotten the most promising results anyone could hope for, specifically for Eliza's type of leukemia. But it's very fuckin' far from free. It's not a public drug trial, see. And like I said, I've spent all I've got. Sold my house, rentin' a shitty little flat in a shitty part of London. Sold most of my gear. I take every job I can find, good or bad, long's I'm not murderin' innocent folks or the like. I…" I blink hard. "I done a lotta bad shit, mostly to other bad sorts like me, but still. Blowin' an 'ole in some bastard's head because he's shootin' at you is one thing. Doin' it because some other greedy bastard doesn't like him is a whole other bit of fuckery."

"And then Pugli got ahold of you."

"Yep. Right you are. He heard, somehow, that a highly decorated SAS operator had been summarily booted from the service under some rather suspicious circumstances and was taking the odd violent job for cash. He got in touch with me and gave me jobs. Big'uns. It was these jobs that've kept a roof over my head and paid for Eliza's care for the last year. I send pretty much all I make to Rachel's parents for Eliza's care, which is costly even without the experimental shite."

"And Pugli found out about Eliza, I'm guessing," Bryn says, anger tingeing her voice.

"Right again. How, I don't know. He's got spies everywhere. At the base of it, that's what he does—he deals in information. Trafficking in people and drugs and guns is just sort of gravy for him. A bit of fun and some extra cash. Really, he's a middleman. A connector. He puts terrorists in touch with gunrunners and bomb-makers and the like. Puts drug dealers in touch with arms dealers. Gathers nasty intel on politicians and sells it to the highest bidder—and I don't mean just in Europe. In the US, Canada, Australia, Africa, everywhere people want leverage over their opponents, he's got people lookin' into people, listenin', diggin', sniffin' around. And he found out about Eliza. Her cancer. The experimental treatment that's her last hope, which is as out of reach for me without him as the fuckin' moon.

I can make an easy ten or twenty or even fifty grand doin' in some gang's big boss for another gang. I can pull in five grand for puttin' the hurt on some fucker who owes some other fucker. I can make twenty-five grand for escortin' assorted illegal cargo across international borders—guns, drugs, people. I don't mind the guns and drugs, but I've always drawn the line at people…till now, at least. Anyways, he found out. He knew I couldn't bring in that kinda cash on short notice—I need to pay that quarter-million deposit by next month or she's lost her chance. And if she loses the trial, she's dead in three months, six on the outside. And this… this trial, it's…they say it may buy her a few years. It won't cure her, most likely, but it'll give us more time. And she's my little girl, Bryn."

I can't stop the tears from burning my eyes. I look away, out the window, hating myself, hating life, hating everything. I'm just…so fucking *angry* at the unfairness of it all, really.

"Fucking hell, Rush. I…I get it. He gave you a chance to save your daughter's life. Even just giving her more time, of course you'd do it. Even if it meant… well, what you did. It explains how conflicted you've been. Back and forth. Hot and cold."

I nod. "I hated every second of knowing what I was tricking you into. Because I know what he's like. I know the ugly, awful details of what's left of girls he gets his rotten fuckin' hands on. And after you embarrassed him, lost him that deal, cost him a hit to his reputation as a bloke who *always* delivers, and killed his hired goons in the process? Oh love, you'd *suffer*.

The devil himself ain't as inventive about suffering as Roberto fuckin' Pugli." I force myself to look directly and unblinking into those deep, dark, knowing brown eyes. "What we shared, though, Bryn? In the train, in the hotel? It wasn't a trick. It wasn't supposed to happen at all. I shoulda just clocked you upside the head, tied you up, stuffed you in the back of a stolen car, and dropped you at Pugli's doorstep. But I talked to you. Got to know you. And the more I did, the less I felt able to do that. To treat you like…like nothing but goods. A product. I couldn't. I *can't*. You're fucking *real*, Bryn. You're the most amazing woman I've ever met. And in the end, I couldn't do it. And now…"

"Rush," she whispers again, speaking my name in a tender, understanding voice that cuts me deeper than any razor blade could.

"Now my girl's gonna die." I collapse against the steering wheel. "Fuck. What've I done? Bryn? I traded her life for yours. What kind of a choice is that? What've I done?"

There's a long silence.

"Rush, I'm gonna ask you the same question you asked me."

I force myself to look at her again. "What?" I ask, even though I know the question that's coming.

"Will you trust me?"

I shake my head. "How can you ask me that, Bryn?"

She lets out a sigh. "Listen. This is when you need to dig deep into that reserve of professionalism, Rush. Turn off your personal feelings. Look at this situation objectively. Where are we? Not geographically, but situationally."

"Fucked, that's where." Something in her silence has me sitting up and looking at her. And the daft bitch is…grinning? "What's that look for, then?"

"You've evidently forgotten who I am, Rush."

I frown her way. "Meanin'?"

"I'm Bryn motherfucking Harris, bitch. I have the full weight and might of Alpha One Security behind me. I have Valentine Roth behind me. And to be honest, Rush, I don't think you have the first goddamn clue what that really means."

A tiny seed of hope germinates in my gut. "Whassit mean, then, love? Hope is a hard thing to feel when my whole life has been a study in pain, stupidity, and death."

She takes my hand. "You're about to find out."

11

AN INTERLUDE IN LISBON

My heart aches for him. For what he's endured. All the loss he's experienced. It doesn't seem like he's ever known a kind word or a tender touch, someone who cares for him just because. Generosity without strings. Compassion without expectation.

He's a hard man, no doubt. He's had to be. He's had to claw, scrape, and fight for every last thing he's ever had. And yet, despite that, I can see as plain as the nose on my face the love he has for his daughter. I don't doubt for a second that if a doctor told him he could trade his life to heal her, he wouldn't even blink.

His gaze is skeptical, wary. "So what are you proposing?"

"I'm not proposing anything, Rush." I squeeze his hand. "I'm asking you to have faith in me. In my family. You rescued me. You've saved my life time and again. And when it came down to the choice, you saved me.

And what I'm telling you is that that choice will not have been in vain. I won't allow it, my parents won't allow it, and Aunt Key and Uncle Val won't allow it." I cup his hard jaw. "Look, the honest truth is that I can't make any promises as to what will happen, but the promise I *can* make is that whatever we *can* do, we will."

He shakes his head. "Why? After what I done to you, why would you help me?"

I turn his face to mine. "Because I *see* you, Rush."

He tugs his face away, refusing to look at me. "Dunno what that means."

I pull him back to eye contact. "Hey." I stare at him, hard, until I'm sure he's not just hearing me but listening. "It means I understand. It means I know how to forgive you, and I do."

His eyes squeeze shut, and he shakes my head. "Nah. That's bullshit. Don't bullshit me, Bryn."

"If you'd left me there, obviously we'd be having a much different conversation," I say, and then bark a bitter laugh. "Or actually, no, we wouldn't be. But you know what I mean. The point is I'm not bullshitting you. I forgive you. Keep me alive and out of Pugli's hands, and I'll do everything in my power to help Eliza. You want to look at it as a deal, then that's the deal."

"And you..." he glances at me sidelong. "You don't hate me for what I done to you?"

"No, Rush. I don't hate you. I was angry and shocked at first because it ...well, it was a shock. To find out the whole time you were playing me for your own ends? Yeah, I was pissed. But you had a pretty good fucking reason, not just avarice or greed or whatever.

And in the end, you were faced with an impossible choice. Obviously, I'm really fucking grateful you made the choice you did, because I really don't want to end up Pugli's sex slave. Or anyone else's. And what kind of a person would I be if I didn't do everything I could for your daughter, after the choice you made?"

"Wasn't a choice, Bryn," he whispers. "I couldn't do it. Fuck me, but I tried. I did. I just couldn't do it."

"And that says a lot about your character, Rush. I think deep down, you actually are a good man. It's just…maybe no one has seen that in you, maybe no one has given you a chance to be that man. And maybe I can."

He swallows hard. "I'd like that."

"Well then, get me to Lisbon." I grab his cell phone from where it rests on his thigh. "First things first…" I look at him. "You have your important numbers memorized?"

He shrugs. "Of course, but—"

I toss the phone out the window. "We're not taking any chances."

"That phone was encrypted," Rush grumbles.

"Do you know for one hundred percent certain that Pugli has not and cannot track it?" I ask.

"No, nothing is ever a hundred percent anything, but—"

"Then we aren't taking the chance. The number one thing my Uncle Lear taught me was that any cell phone—*any* cell phone—can be hacked and tracked by someone with the right tools, training, and enough time. The second most important thing is that cards are even easier to track."

Rush snorts. "Well, that second one I know well enough, but I paid a lot of fuckin' money for a mobile no one can track or crack into."

"And what I'm saying is that in a situation like this, we can't afford to gamble. Pugli has immense resources—beyond those that mere wealth can provide, given his position within law enforcement."

He sighs. "You're right. We'll pick up a burner when we get to Lisbon."

I wave at the road ahead of us. "Well, then? Let's go! I want this tracker out of me post-fucking haste."

Lisbon is ancient and beautiful. In other circumstances, I'd be all over the opportunity to explore a place like this. Alas, this is not such an opportunity. Seeing as I'd tossed Rush's phone out the window, and with it our sat-nav, as Rush calls it, we had to stop once we arrived in Lisbon to pick up a burner and ask for directions—we're to meet our contact at a cafe on Almirante Reis near Alameda Park. Rush has never been here either, so it takes us a few wrong turns before the shopkeeper's instructions made sense—neither of us speaks either Spanish or Portuguese, which made the process even trickier.

Eventually, we found Almirante Reis, and then after traveling in the wrong direction we found the park—a long, somewhat narrow rectangle of green space running perpendicular to the street, which cuts the park in half. The cafe is only a block or so away from the park, and Rush finds an alley near the cafe where we stash our stolen ride. He deftly un-hotwires the car, replacing the cover to a degree that it doesn't look obviously stolen, and we set out for the cafe on foot.

"You're pretty handy with the hotwiring," I say, smirking at him.

He shrugs. "Me and the lads watched a movie once, when we was waitin' on orders. Some stupid shit from a long fuckin' time ago, and this character said a line I've not forgotten, even though I couldn't tell you a single thing from the rest of the film. He was pickin' a lock I think, and he said it was the skills of a misspent youth. That's me. I've got a lot of skills from a misspent youth."

I snicker. "Seems like a lot of words for 'I was a trouble-making hooligan.'"

"I was bein' interesting and tellin' you something about myself." He arches an eyebrow. "Most women I've known are always after me to use more words, share more about me."

I lean into him hard, making him stumble to the side. "I'm just fucking with you, Rush. I do want you to share."

"Hard to tell when you're jokin', sometimes."

I snort. "The laugh didn't give it away?"

"I mean, people laugh when they're saying something true but mean."

"That wasn't mean, Rush. At least, I didn't think so. You were a homeless orphan, which is, in my understanding at least, not a socio-economic status that engenders a law-abiding lifestyle."

Rush shrugs and nods. "I suppose that's true, innit? But it's true mainly because the world ain't a fit, proper, or safe place for homeless orphans. Folks don't know what to do with the likes of us."

"No, I suppose most people don't," I agree.

Rush scans the signs and points at one. "Here we are, this is us."

We enter the cafe and Rush orders us meals. We find an open booth and sit on the same side, facing the doorway.

Rush, on the outside, glances at me. "Never sat in a booth with someone like this, both of us on the same side. Not sure if I like it or if it's weird."

I laugh. "Same, to be honest. I kinda like it, though. I can do this." I curl my hand around his bicep and rest my head on his shoulder.

"Well, that's a good point, that is." He turns his head to mine, inhaling my scent, and presses a soft kiss on the top of my head. "Coz then I can do that."

I feel my heart flip at the casually tender affection he's showing me, something I wouldn't have expected from a man like him in a million years. "Rush," I whisper.

He sniffs a soft laugh. "You say my name like that a lot. I never quite know what to make of it." I feel his attention, his thoughts going deep. "Why've you forgiven me so easily, Bryn?"

I sit up, sighing. "I take after my mother in a lot of

ways, Rush. Sadly, I didn't get her tits and ass, but I did get her mercurial temperament."

"Okay, two things here," Rush says. "One, I've not met your mum, but I personally think the tits and arse you've got are pretty fuckin' spectacular. An' two, what's mercurial temperament mean?"

"My mom's a lot curvier than I am, is all I'm saying. I'm tall and lean like my dad. But I'm glad you like my body, Rush."

He snorts. "'Like' it ain't quite the phrase I'd use."

"No? What would you say, then?"

"Fishin' for compliments, are you?"

I nod, laughing, as I mime casting with a fishing pole. "I'm not good at fishing for fish, but I'm *great* at fishing for compliments."

"Fair enough. I actually *hate* fishing. Boring and pointless. I want a fish, I'll pop down to the grocery and buy one. Waste of fuckin' time sittin' around in a stupid tin boat throwin' hooks about hopin' some manky fish is idiot enough to try an' eat one."

I cackle. "Same! Now, deep sea fishing is a different story. That can be fun."

"Wossat like then?"

I grab his hand and squeeze. "Stick around and maybe we'll take you."

He looks at me. "Bryn, I…"

Our food arrives then, and we both begin eating.

I see the doubt on his face, hear the hesitancy in his voice. "Rush, listen to me." I set my fork down and take his other hand in mine, pivoting on the bench to face him more directly. "I forgive you. Okay? Maybe no one else on the planet will ever understand why, but I do. What you did was not done maliciously. You're not a bad man. You're a good man in a bad situation faced with no good choices. You did a bad thing for a good reason. When I say I have a mercurial temperament, I mean I get angry fast, but I let it go just as fast. My anger burns hot and intense, but it cools off in equal proportion. When I'm happy, I'm over the fucking moon. When I'm sad, it's like the world is ending. When I'm horny, I could fuck all day and all night and never get enough. So yeah, I was shocked and hurt and angry when you told me the truth. But Rush, the important thing is that you didn't follow through—you saved me. You fought for me, as you have since the moment I met you, regardless of your original intentions. And you did tell me the truth."

His eyes drop, full of intense emotion he's visibly uncomfortable with. "Bryn, I…fuck me, mate. I've no clue what to say. I'm not good with emotions."

"I know, and that's okay." I see a figure enter the cafe and scan the patrons as if looking for someone. "I think that's our guy, so we'll pick this up later. But Rush, just keep being honest with me. Good, bad, ugly, or weird, just be truthful with me. I'm an open-minded and generally understanding sort of girl."

The figure is a tall, whipcord Black man, built lean and of middle age, wearing fitted khakis and a red polo with impeccably clean vintage Jordan 1s, mid-height in red and black—Killy is a sneakerhead, and I've developed the bug myself. His wary, restless gaze stops on me, and I see recognition flare in his eyes. He beelines for us and settles in the booth opposite Rush and me.

"Bryn Harris?" He's American, his accent vaguely and broadly Midwestern.

I extend my hand to his and we shake. "Yes. This is Rush." I indicate him with a jerk of my head.

"Nice to meet you. I'm Alexander Ludwig. I'm a friend of Lear Winter." He withdraws his hand from mine, shakes Rush's, and then immediately squirts sanitizer on his hands from a spray bottle produced from his pocket. "So. I hear you have an unwelcome bug hitching a ride."

"I don't know for sure, as in I don't have any evidence other than the fact that the bad guys keep showing up wherever I go," I say, "and trust me when I say the two of us know how to lose pursuit."

Alexander nods. "I believe you. Finish your meal and come with me."

Rush and I hurriedly scarf down the rest of our food, Rush tosses a handful of euros on the table, and we accompany Alexander out of the cafe. He leads us on foot away from Almirante Reis—our route is squirrelly and indirect, doubling back and circling the same block more than once, before he seems content that we're not being followed at this exact moment. They're probably confident knowing my location and don't see a point in wasting resources following me in person.

Alexander finally leads us in a direct line to a narrow side street, where a small white van is parked in a line with other vehicles. He unlocks the rear doors with a key, opens them, and ushers us in. Within is a mobile computer lab Uncle Lear would be jealous of. Taking a seat on a rolling stool, he indicates a small bench at the back near the doors. "Sit, sit. Give me a few minutes to get things going."

He boots up a myriad of computers, spends minutes typing on one and then another, and then rummages in a cabinet along the roofline and produces a handheld device that wouldn't be out of place on a Star Trek set. He spends minutes more fiddling with that device, connecting it to a computer and doing more… things. I don't know what—I'm great with a cell phone, okay with computers, and hopeless with anything more complex than an app. This is far beyond my meager skills.

Eventually things seem ready, and he unplugs the device and rolls over to me. "Arms out and hold still."

I hold my arms out at my sides while he waves the device around my head, over my shoulders, along my arms, and down one side and the other, over my lap, my legs, my feet—he even has me stand hunched so he can scan my butt and the backs of my thighs and my back and my crotch.

The first circuit produces nothing I can identify as a hit of any kind; he fiddles with the wand's settings and scans my body again. This time, it emits a quiet beep when it passes over my left side, up near my armpit and side-boob area.

"Ah, there we are." Alexander adjusts the settings again and scans the area repeatedly, scans the rest of my body again, and then goes back to where it produced the beeping. "Gotcha, fuckers."

"So now you take it out?" I ask.

Alexander tips his head to one side. "I mean, I could. But that's a medical procedure and I'm a computer engineer. I could try to dig it out with a pocketknife and some isopropyl."

I blink at him. "Or?"

He grins. "Or, we leave it in place and fuck with them."

"That sounds less painful," I say. "Fuck with them how?"

"Like this," he says, and proceeds to spend the next thirty minutes typing at machine gun speed on one computer and another. After hitting the "Enter" key with a dramatic flourish, he grins at me. "There. Take that shit, motherfuckers."

I blink at him again. "Wow. Fascinating. You typed a lot."

He chuckles. "I did indeed type a lot. What it amounts to is I wrote code and uploaded it to the chip inside you. So now, instead of sending your location, it cycles through locations at random." He indicates a screen that shows a flat Mercator projection of the Earth, with a blinking dot somewhere in Africa. "Right now, it's showing you in Djibouti. In about thirty seconds…" He stares at his vintage wristwatch, pointer finger extended; he points at the screen. "Now you're in Moscow." The dot blinks in Russia. "Every thirty seconds, it'll show you somewhere else. But not static, oh no. It'll show you moving as if you're walking around or driving a car."

"So it's not, like, bad for me to have that thing inside me?" I ask.

He shrugs. "Nah. It'd do more harm than good to take it out, in this setting at least. And now they're gonna be confused."

Rush pats my thigh. "I've got a couple rounds stuck in me, still. Never notice them except going through a metal detector."

I frown at him. "A *couple* rounds?"

He shrugs. "Sure." He reaches around and pats his back near his left lat muscle. "Took one at an angle off a ricochet, went in and stuck near my spine. Doesn't hurt me or cause any issues, and it's too risky to take out, being as close to my spine as it is. A quarter of a millimeter and I'd be paraplegic." He taps his belly, next. "Got another one in me innards, close enough to major organs that it's not worth the risk to remove since it's not doing much but floatin' about inside me."

Alexander eyes Rush. "Sounds like you've had some luck, friend."

Rush nods. "Guess so, yeah. Never been one to play the lottery, but maybe I should, ey?"

Alexander shakes his head. "I wouldn't. You might use up all your luck, and the next one won't miss."

Rush snorts. "Not sure if you're jokin' or not, mate."

Alexander shrugs. "Why take the chance?" He shuts down the various machines. "Sit tight. We're moving."

"Moving?" I ask.

"Yeah, well, this is your last known location, right? Letting you get out and walk away from here is rank idiocy, and none of us are rookies. So yeah, sit tight and I'll drop you guys off somewhere else."

He squeezes through a narrow gap to the driver's seat and then we're moving. There are no windows back here, but we make roughly a hundred and twenty different turns, so I'm guessing we take another long, circuitous route across the city.

"Fancy bit of work, that," Rush says, indicating me with a jut of his chin.

"If he's a friend of Uncle Lear's, then that's probably child's play for him," I say.

Eventually, Alexander pulls over, parks the van, but leaves it idling. He wiggles back to us. "Either of you have a cell on you?"

Rush digs the burner we just bought out of his hip pocket. "Cheapo burner we just bought here in Lisbon."

Alexander takes it, shakes his head, and produces a Faraday bag from a drawer. "Trackable." He rummages in a cabinet and comes back with a different Faraday bag, which has a newer model smartphone inside it. "This is not. I wiped the software completely and programmed a totally bespoke operating system. End-to-end messaging encryption for SMS and email. And it doesn't use towers for cellular connection—I, um, sort of hijacked a telecom satellite and slaved it for my own purposes, namely, this. Absolutely no one on the planet can intercept your calls with this, or learn your location from it. I've programmed in Lear's direct number as he has a similar device. You'll only contact him from here on out, okay? Any communications to your parents or anyone else *must* go through him or you risk detection."

"I understand," I say. "Thank you, Alexander. I, um, I hope my family has arranged payment for you."

Alexander snorts. "I'll pretend you didn't just ask me that. I owe Lear my life several times over. I'd do anything for him."

"Well, thank you, regardless."

He nods. "My pleasure." He gestures at the doors. "I've brought you to the train station. Get away from Lisbon before making any plans with your family, or even contacting them. I'm familiar with Pugli, and the worst thing you could do is underestimate both his vindictiveness and his resourcefulness."

"That ain't a word of a lie," Rush says. "You stay off his radar, too, mate. I know the evil bastard all too well myself, and I know he ain't kind to those who help his enemies."

Alexander grins. "Oh, I'll be halfway across Europe before he knows what happened to the two of you, but thanks for the word of warning. Be safe, you two. And tell Lear I said I still owe him."

A few hours later, we're on a train rocking back across Europe, cutting across Spain, again because it was the first train going anywhere.

I feel like I've crossed Europe several times over the last…well, you know, I don't even know how long it's been? Three days? Four? Feels like a lifetime ago that I was innocently skiing the Matterhorn with Killy and Cal.

Slowly, the rocking of the train lulls me to sleep, my head on Rush's solid shoulder, his hand on my thigh.

12

DADDY'S ON THE JOB

I SPEND THE LONG TRAIN RIDE DOZING AND THINKING. Reflecting, really—something I generally make a concerted effort to avoid doing.

I've never had anyone stick by me like Bryn has. I mean, my mates in the service, obviously, but that's different. We trained to be a team. We had no choice but to learn to trust each other. We killed and bled side by side, suffered the hell of war together. This whole experience with Bryn…it's all new. I don't run from fights, typically. If this was just me on the lam from that festering pustule Roberto Pugli, I'd go after him. Invade his fucking house and burn it down around him. Kill as many of his goons as I could before they put a round in the old brainpan. I've never much cared whether I lived or died. In a way, it's probably what made me such an effective operator. I was willing to take risks that other blokes might not, simply because there's never been a single soul on this godforsaken planet who would mourn me if I ate a bullet. Even my mates in the service would look at it as just another soldier dead in the line of duty—they'd be sad a bit, maybe tip a pint in my memory once a year. I'm not reckless, mind you. I like being alive. I like life. I like sex and good booze and a good eight hours' sleep. I like a scalding shower in the morning. I like a basket of fish and chips from my favorite chippie. I like a long morning run along the Thames.

But when I'm out there, on mission downrange, all of that vanishes. My focus becomes singular. Accomplishing the objective is the only thing that matters.

This ain't that. Bryn ain't another lad from the service. She *is* the objective. But she's also someone who sees me. Hears me. Understands me. Even though it's been a matter of days, she sees my fucking soul in a way no one else ever has. And it's freaky. Disconcerting.

She forgives me. It might be an overstatement to call what I did the ultimate betrayal, but not by much. And she just…let it go. Got mad and let me know it. But she still heard me out. Demanded the truth from me, and when I gave it to her, she listened. She understood.

She forgave me. She doesn't seem to hold it against me, either. I mean, in my experience, it's still likely she'll trot it out when she's cross with me. But she don't seem the type for that. Hopefully not, at least.

I don't deserve her.

Not after all the shit I've done, not with all the blood on my hands and the skeletons I've got jam-packed in every closet, cabinet, and nook, and cranny of my rotten soul.

She stirs, and slowly slumps lower and lower until she finally gives a wordless, grumbling snurk and topples down to lay her head on my lap.

And here we are, on a damned train again.

Barcelona. Sunny, hot, and beautiful.

It's hard to enjoy it, though—for the last few hours, I've had a gnawing sense of unease in my gut. At first I thought we were being followed, but I've used every trick I know to spot a tail and haven't seen the same person twice in our hours of playing tourist. So it's not that.

I ask Bryn if she feels anything weird, and she just shrugs and says no, for once she's feeling hopeful.

I can't fucking shake it.

Finally, I decide to check in with Eliza's grandparents—I have a voicemail I've set up so they can leave a message if they need to get ahold of me. I had it set up to send an alert to my mobile, but Bryn yeeted that out the window somewhere between Lyon and Lisbon.

I lead Bryn to a bench beneath a massive palm tree near the beach. "I need to check in with Eliza," I tell Bryn. "I've a bad feeling I can't shake."

I pull out the fancy mobile Alexander gave us and dial into my voicemail box, input the password. I've one new message.

It's Richard, Rachel's father. He's frantic, nearly incoherent—left not an hour ago. "Rush! They took her.

They took her. She's gone, man, she's gone.. She's bloody gone. Eliza…oh god, oh god, she's bloody gone, Rush. Oh god, oh god."

My heart freezes solid in my chest even as incandescent rage boils in my veins. "Fuck me bloody," I snarl under my breath. "I'll bloody murder the cunt."

Bryn rears back at the savagery in my voice. "Rush? What's wrong?"

I don't answer—I can't. I dial Richard's number with a shaky finger. It rings once.

"Rush?" It's Evelyn. "Is that you, boy?"

You, boy. Fuck, I hate that phrase. I ignore that and focus. "Yeah, Ev, it's me. Tell me you've found her."

"Oh, Rush, it was awful. We were sat to lunch and these horrible men just…" she whimpers. "They crashed the door in, smashed everything to bits, and-and-and…" she pauses, sobbing. "They put guns on Richard and me, didn't they, and told us to sit down and shut up or they'd kill us slowly. They just *took* her, Rush. They took Eliza. Put a bloody black bag over her poor darling head and *just…left* with her. She was crying for you, Rush. Crying for her daddy as the men carted her away like a sack of potatoes. We couldn't do a damned thing, Rush. Oh god, I'm sorry. I'm so sorry, Rush. She's gone. I don't know—oh god. I don't know who or why. If it's money they want, we'll—we'll sell everything we have, I promise you we will, Rush."

"Ev, Ev—stop!" I have to shout to get her to shut up and take a breath. "It's not your fault, Evelyn, it's mine. This is about me. You've done nothing wrong."

"What's it about, Rush? What've you done? Don't those bloody monsters know she's a dying child?"

Hot bile rises in my throat, presses against my teeth. I can't answer, can't breathe—I shove the mobile at Bryn and stagger to the nearby trash bin and vomit into it.

When I return to the bench, Bryn is speaking. "…promise you we will do everything that can be done to bring her back safely. I know you don't know me, ma'am, but I come from a very wealthy and powerful family. We will move heaven and earth for that girl."

The rage, guilt, horror, and worry are a tangled knot in my throat, making me dizzy. Fuck, not another goddamned panic attack—I'm outside myself, almost, observing me having the mother of all panic attacks. All the ones that have come before seem like the miniquakes that come before the big one that brings down skyscrapers. It feels like a heart attack.

"—eathe…Rush. Breathe. In through your nose." I hear her voice, see her face wobbling and blurry.

The ground is hard under my hands and knees, grit sticking to my palms. An ant crawls at the edge of my vision.

Why did I think he wouldn't do this? What kind of a fool am I that I didn't take precautions to keep my girl safe?

He'll do horrible things to her just to fuck with me, to hurt me. He probably doesn't even want anything from me, he just wants me to suffer.

"No, no, no," Bryn says, and I realize I've been

talking aloud, ranting. "She'll be okay. You'll see. We'll get her back."

"You don't know him, not like I do."

Instead of arguing, she rings the sole contact in the sat phone. "Uncle Lear, hi. Not good, unfortunately. No, I'm fine. But my—Rush, his daughter. Pugli took her, Lear. From London, right, Rush?"

I shake my head. "No, erm…South—Southampton."

"You hear? Yeah, okay. We're in Barcelona. What do we do, Lear? She's sick. She's dying of cancer. YES! Exactly—that's exactly the kind of monster this motherfucker is. He kidnapped a dying six-year-old girl to get at Rush and me. I know I caused this whole situation, but—" she sniffles. "I need everyone, Lear. Fucking *everyone*. I don't care what it takes. I'll answer for it. Yes, it's *my* fucking fault! *I* ran away. *I* stuck my nose in shit that had nothing to do with me. *I* caused all of this. Call in fucking *EVERYONE*. And let me put this as plainly as I can—Roberto Pugli dies. We don't stop until I personally see his fucking corpse with my own two eyes." A pause. "Yes, perfect. Have Dad call me. Thanks, Uncle Lear. Yeah, love you too. Bye."

Less than thirty seconds later, the mobile is burbling, and she answers it. "Hi, Daddy. Yes, I'm fine. No, I'm not—Dad, listen. No, you don't understand—SHUT THE FUCK UP AND LISTEN TO ME, GODDAMMIT!" She lets out a harsh breath. "Pugli kidnapped Rush's daughter…she's six. No, her mother died. Dad, Jesus, stop with the irrelevant questions. She's got leukemia and that fucking evil monster had her kidnapped out of her home. YES! Exactly. Sick or not, he stole a child. Yeah, that's what I fucking thought. And if you won't mobilize literally every asset we can field, I'll hunt him down and murder him myself or I'll die trying. Yes, I mean fucking *EVERYONE*, Dad. The uncles. Cuddy. Raze's crew. Call in every favor you're owed. I'll do whatever it takes to cover the cost—no, I just…it's my fault, Dad. Yes, it is!"

I snatch the phone from her. "Harris, it's Rush."

"Rush. What does he want, do you think?"

"For me to suffer. I double-crossed him to save Bryn. I…fuck, I should have known he'd do this. I guess I…I thought if he had even a smidge of humanity, he'd leave a dying child out of it. It's one thing to use her as leverage to get me to do what he wants. That's indirect and I hate him enough for it as it is. But this? This is a step too far, mate. I know I don't have any right to ask your lot to help me, but I am. Please, *please* help me. Not even me, help my daughter. She's an innocent girl, sir."

"Rush, you don't have to even ask. This is what we do, and we're the best in the world at it. We'll get your daughter back and we'll make Pugli pay for his sins. And you can trust me when I say I'm not going to be leaving justice up to the courts." Harris's voice is cold and vicious. "I have assets in the UK mobilizing as we speak. Give me an address and they'll start the investigation. I've got Lear doing his thing—he'll be able to track their movements and give us a place to start."

"I can't wait for an investigation, Harris," I snap. "I need to find my daughter. I need to find Pugli."

"You can't do both, son." His voice is stern but not unkind. "You're gonna have to trust us to handle one of them. You call it. Are you going after Pugli or your daughter?"

I look at Bryn—the guilt ravaging her beautiful face is utterly heartbreaking. "I trust Bryn and she trusts you. If you can promise me you'll track her down and get her to safety, then I'll take the promise and go after Pugli."

"Rush, you have my vow—as a man, as an operator, and as a father, I will personally rescue your daughter. I'll find her, I'll kill those who took her, and I won't let her out of my sight until she's back in your arms."

My throat is hot and tight. "That's good enough for me. Get me a lead on Pugli."

"Done. You'll have something shortly."

"Harris, sir—"

"Save it, son. I know who you are and what you do—I've had a better look at your file, and even with what's been redacted, it's obvious you're one hell of an operator. So now it's time to do what we do. Set your personal feelings aside. Trust me and my men to do our jobs, and you do yours. And right now, you have *one* fucking job: hunt down and kill Roberto Pugli."

When you've spent the kind of time I have in the military, you automatically respond to the tone of authority. This man's voice snaps with that authority. I find myself straightening. "Sir, yes sir."

"Good man. Now. Hang up and keep this phone ready. And tell my daughter…" There's a significant, heavy pause. "Tell her Daddy's on the job. And for god's sake, son, *take care* of her."

"With my life, sir."

"Harris, out." Click.

Even in the circumstances, I can't help but find it funny that the man ended the call with "Harris, out."

Bryn notices my half-hearted sniff of laughter. "He said it, didn't he?" She shakes her head, bemused. "He can't help it. Mom and I have both told him repeatedly how cringey it is when he ends a call with 'Harris, out', but he just can't help himself."

I take her hand. Hold her gaze. "It's not your fault, Bryn. I don't blame you."

The humor in her eyes and voice evaporates. "Yeah, well…I do."

"I know. But you shouldn't. There's no one to blame but the people who did it." I scrub my face. "I should've known better. I should've hidden her or gotten one of my old mates to watch the house or something. I didn't do nothin'. I underestimated how evil that man is."

"Will he…" she stops, shuddering. "I can't even think it."

'Will he actually hurt her?" I nod, shrugging. "Got to assume he will. The stories I've heard? I heard one about this gypsy lad who crossed Pugli, tried to investigate him, take him down. Pugli hogtied him, pried his eyes open, and made him watch as his wife and infant children were burned alive in front of him."

Bryn covers her mouth, shakes her head. "My god, no. What? How can—how could anyone *do* that?"

"Mankind is capable of incredible acts, Bryn," I say. "The worst evil and the greatest good. And Pugli takes a twisted sort of joy in being the evilest cunt who ever lived."

"I know you're British and it's different over there, but I *really* hate that word," Bryn says. "In this case, however, I'll make an exception."

"Your dad told me to tell you he's on the job, by the way."

"Alpha One Security is the best in the world at recovering kidnap victims," she says. "It's how Dad got his start. Well, that and working for Uncle Val."

I can't help a snort. "I'm not sure I'll ever not find it amusing that you refer to the richest man on the planet as Uncle Val."

"So what do we do?" she asks, ignoring my non-sequitur about Valentine Roth.

"Your dad is getting us a lead on Pugli's location. We go after him."

She nods. "Good. Dad will take care of Eliza. You can count on that. He's never once failed."

That does make it a bit easier to breathe, but I won't be able to take a full breath until I've got Eliza back in my arms.

It ends up being two hours later before Lear pings over a last known location, along with a contact number for Alexander, who has been brought in to help so Lear can focus on finding Eliza.

Within forty minutes of receiving that message, I've stolen us another car and we're heading out of Barcelona—Pugli is heading for Italy and Lear thinks he knows where he's going. We just have to get there first.

Alexander helps us evade border security, taking us into Italy via a long, slow, circuitous route, which I take at ill-advisedly fast speeds. Bryn says nothing, just stares out the window, stewing.

Blaming herself.

I know the feeling—I blame myself, as well.

Pugli's destination, as best Lear can figure, is a country estate in Tuscany. It's another beautiful place that we've no time or emotional space to appreciate—I blast up and down the hills at breakneck speeds, pushing the battered old Lancia I stole to its limits. We're only half a dozen or so miles from the estate when the sat phone rings.

Bryn answers it, puts it on speaker. "What's up, Uncle Lear? You're on speaker."

"Perfect. I have some updates. The original six are en route via hypersonic jet to Europe. I've tracked the van the kidnappers took Eliza in across the Channel. They're heading east. We have Sasha on the ground with two more fire teams loaded for bear. We have a plan, and will intercept them." He pauses, typing. "Second, I've confirmed that Pugli is arriving at his estate in Tuscany as we speak. You two are *not* to engage on your own. He traveled with at least thirty men; I have eyes in the sky on his estate now, and I'm seeing at least that many more. No matter how badass you may be, Rush, that's beyond any one man's ability to deal with. And Bryn, I know you've done some training, but—"

"If you think for one bloody fucking second that I'm gonna sit on my bloody fuckin' hands while those cunts have my bloody fucking daughter, you ain't been payin' attention to the sort of bloke I am, mate."

Lear hesitates. "*Sixty* men, my guy. I've got RMI crews en route to your location as we speak—they're coming from Rome via Osprey. Just…be smart. You do your daughter no favors by dying. She'll need her dad when this is over, Rush."

"RMI?" I echo. "As in Johnny Raze and that lot?"

"Yes."

"Fuck me, you bastards are well fucking connected, ain'tcha?"

"Yes. We are." Lear pauses, typing again. "Raze's crew is led by Chico. I know him personally, and he's a hard-ass motherfucker who also happens to have four daughters. When I tell you he's pissed off on your behalf, you should be very, very glad he's on our side. He says they're thirty minutes out from target."

"I've heard stories about that lad," I mutter. "Be glad to work with him." I scrub my face with one hand as I pull over onto the shoulder. "Fuck me. I'll wait thirty minutes, but if I've not heard from you by then, I'm dealing with these fuckos myself."

"Not by yourself," Bryn snaps. "If you think you're going in without me, *you* haven't been paying attention."

Lear chuckles. "Yeah, good luck with that one, kid. Bryn doesn't do 'no.'" He hums, thinking sound. "Oh, by the way, when you see Chico, tell him Cuddy says fuck you."

"Will that get my block knocked off?" I ask.

"Preface it with 'Cuddy says' and you should be fine."

"*The* Cuddy is your *wife*? Jesus," I mutter. "Wound up in the Premier League, haven't I?"

"Alright, kids," Lear says. "That's it for now. I'll give you a heads up when Chico and company are close. Sit tight, don't forget to breathe, and remember that Pugli himself doesn't have your daughter. We'll have her in hand…" he goes quiet as he consults something or other on his end. "By eighteen hundred at the latest, according to current data."

"The second you know anything about Eliza," I say.

"The very instant, Rush. Trust us. This is what we do."

"Well, what I do is violence," I say. "And I'm about to fuckin' pop. So your boy Chico had better be here on time or I'll take out these sick fucks with my bare fuckin' hands."

"I hear you. Thirty minutes."

The call ends, then, and I'm left antsy, agitated, and fidgety—my pulse hammers with anticipation and fury, making each second last hours.

When thirty minutes nears, I'm pacing circles around the old Lancia as the late afternoon Italian sun beats down mercilessly, sat-phone in hand.

Eighteen hundred hours, the man said. I check my watch yet again—sixteen-thirty. Almost two hours to go, still. Fuck.

Knowing Pugli, he wants to do the honors himself,

so my guess is that Eliza is unharmed for now. And as long as she stays out of Pugli's hands, she should stay that way.

But Pugli won't live long enough to know anything's gone wrong.

Exactly thirty minutes on the dot from Lear's update, I hear the distinctive sound of an Osprey—it's flying low and fast, skimming the hilltops like a dragonfly. It roars overhead, flares to a halt, the rotors rotating upright to let it hover and then descend. Its door opens and ten figures clad in full battle rattle emerge, jogging toward us. The lead figure is short and stout, carrying a black duffel bag that looks heavy from the way he's carrying it.

Once the men are on the ground, the Osprey takes off again and is gone in a cloud of swirling dust.

The lead figure approaches me; he's brown-skinned, with a shaved head and a thick black beard. His dark eyes are hard and restless, scanning our surroundings, taking in the things operators take note of—possible cover, where an ambush might come from, where you'd dig in for a prolonged firefight.

He drops the bag at his feet and extends his hand to Bryn first. "Miss Harris. I am Chico. I know your father and mother." His accent is Latin American. "I am hearing that there is a sick fuck who has stolen an innocent child."

I step toward him, give him my hand. "Chico, I'm Rush. And you heard right—Pugli kidnapped my daughter."

"Pugli?" His expression darkens with fury. "I hear

of him. He is a bad, bad, bad man. I am glad to be part of killing someone so evil as him." He indicates the bag. "I bring goodies. Tony, what is the latest intel?"

A tall bloke with a nasty scar curling his upper lip into a permanent sneer steps forward, tablet in hand. "Same as before, sir." His voice makes him from the American South. "No movement, no additional arrivals, no departures. An estimated sixty targets."

I'm rummaging in the bag—there's vests, assault rifles, mags, sidearms, shotguns, grenades, flashbangs, NV headsets…he brought the goodies alright. I speak while sorting out my kit. "What's the target like? I assume he's got defensive measures of some sort."

Bryn is alongside me, pulling on a vest and choosing weapons.

Tony answers. "Bet your ass he's got defensive measures. Walls around the house, for one. Fuckers posted at the corners, the gates, all over the place. No easy in, that's for damn sure."

"We will get closer and do some recon," Chico says. "But I think we will have to come up with some kind of clever plan. We are too few to directly assault this place."

"Well then," I say. "Let's get clever, shall we?" I pause, a hand on Chico's shoulder. "By the way, Lear told me to tell you Cuddy says 'fuck you.'"

Chico gives me a flat stare, and then bursts into laughter. "Oh, Cuddy. I miss that *loca putana*." He hesitates. "Please do not tell her I called her that."

Yeah, nah. Not on your life, mate. I've heard the stories.

Pugli is no one's fool. He expected us. This place ain't an estate, it's a small fuckin' fortress is what it is. He's got men posted on the walls with sniper rifles covering all lines of approach, and there ain't no cover to be had for miles in any direction. More men patrol the grounds beyond the walls in ranged patrols. I'd also wager he's got a bloke on the inside with a shoulder-launched SAM or some shit like that in case we decide to try and fast-rope in.

Once we've established the situation, we retreat half a click further back to come up with a plan.

"So, as you said, a direct approach is suicide," I say to Chico. "Using the Osprey to get closer is risky too—I wouldn't put it past the bastard to have some sort of defenses in place against aerial attacks." I give Chico a long, hard look. "So, mate, what's our clever plan, then?"

Chico stares into space over my left shoulder, gaze vacant as he considers the problem. I can almost see the wheels turning in his shrewd brain. Definitely not a bloke I want to be on opposite sides of, I can tell you that without having watched the man work. Sometimes, you can just get the measure of a person at first meeting. And, as advertised, this is a hard, confident man who knows what he's about.

"Guerilla warfare, I think," Chico says. "Pick off their snipers, for a start. Pick off the roving patrols. Keep them wondering where we are. Draw his men out. Perhaps even draw him out, force him to try to flee this place, and then when he does?" He mimes firing a shoulder-mounted rocket. "He dies. Bada-boom."

"Right, so we split up into groups," I say. "Surround the place and make him wonder how many we have."

"What if he doesn't come out?" Bryn asks. "What if he's set up to be able to outlast exactly this kind of thing?"

"We pick off his men until we have cut away his numbers and we can attack," Chico answers. "It is not the fastest solution, but it is the one that prevents us from wasting our lives. We can get supply drops from our Falcon One—food, water, ammunition, things like this. He can maybe last, but so can we."

"Well then," I say. "Let's pick teams and start doing violence."

13

ATTACKING TUSCANY

I'M WITH RUSH, UNSURPRISINGLY, ALONG WITH another man from RMI; we've split into four groups of three. Each team has a man with a scoped rifle—RMI didn't come to play around. We go over the plan once more and then break, splitting away and slinking around to our various positions. The one thing working in our favor to a degree is geography—the rolling hills of knee-high grass may not provide enough cover for us to approach the walls undetected, but they do allow us to slither close enough to put the crosshairs on the men on patrol and the men on the walls.

Rush and I are both armed with M-4 carbines and sidearms, and our RMI companion is armed with a sniper rifle—I'm not familiar with the exact make as my training never covered that kind of work.

We creep up the side of a hill on our bellies, the grass waving restlessly in the ceaseless wind. Ulrich, our sniper, is in the middle with Rush on his left and me on the right. We've all got fancy bone-conduction comms keeping the four teams in contact. I know I shouldn't, but I feel…excited. I'm part of something. I'm finally using the training I worked so hard at my whole life—literally, all I've ever wanted since I was old enough to understand what it was Dad did is this. To do what he does. To be an operator. I've never really wanted anything else. Never thought about anything else. I don't have a mind for business like Corinna. Killian is always out with Dad, these days, learning the ropes of what it takes to administrate a company like A1S—and honestly, truly, that's great. I don't want to be in charge. I don't want the desk and the responsibility and the numbers—Killy is good at that shit. *This* is what I want. And my experiences so far, as scary as they've been, have shown me that I'm good at it.

Ulrich—a German national in his late thirties or early forties with salt liberally sprinkling his dark blond hair—creeps closer to the crest of the hill, and carefully creates a little nest in the grass, going so far as reaching out to break off individual stems of grass with his fingers in order to open his sight lines. Once his nest is arranged to his liking, he settles on his belly with his rifle, spending several minutes fine-tuning his position and weight distribution and grip until he's fully satisfied. Only then does he whisper, "U-Boat in position."

I glance at him. "U-boat?"

He shrugs. "I am German and my name begins with U. And also, before I became a sniper for the KSK, I was a submariner."

Rush eyes him. "KSK is army, I thought."

"Ja, it is. My path to KSK was not…direct."

"I'd say," Rush says, chuckling. "Submarines to spec ops—I don't think there is a direct route, ey?"

Ulrich sniffs a soft laugh. "Nein, there is not." He looks at me. "You are the Harris girl, ja?"

I nod. "Yes. I'm Bryn."

"I am told you prevented a kidnapping, and in the process killed a man with a pencil to the eyeballs."

I snort. "Close, but not quite. I *tried* to prevent a kidnapping and got myself taken with the girl I was trying to save, because when it came time to shoot a man for the first time, I froze. And *then* I killed a man with a pencil."

Ulrich laughs at this. "That is funny. You freeze with a gun and come through with a pencil." He must see something on my face, because he amends his reaction. "I froze, once. My second mission with the KSK. There was a hostage situation, and I was ordered to take a shot. But the person I was meant to shoot was a woman. She had a gun to a little girl's head, so she was a threat, but I still froze when the order came to shoot her. I could not do it. My spotter took the gun and made the shot, but it was messy. He did not kill her as he intended, and her gun went off. Innocent hostages were killed for my split second of indecision."

"Jesus, Ulrich," I say. "That's horrible. I'm sorry that happened."

"I only say it so you know everyone has a moment of hesitation when they must take a life. If you did not, I would worry for your mental health." He claps me on the shoulder. "You stepped up to stop a situation when most would not."

A moment later, another team gives the ready signal across the comms, and within a few minutes all the teams are in place.

"Shooters, on my signal," Chico says. There's a pause of five or so seconds, and then: "Three…two…one…fire."

Ulrich's rifle cracks, and from four cardinal directions come three more simultaneous reports. Rush, on his belly with a spotter's scope, gives a quiet scoff. "Well fuck me, that worked a treat. Tango down times four. Good shootin', everyone."

"Move to position two," Chico orders.

We crawl forward through the grass at an oblique angle, stopping every few feet to watch and listen. We can hear shouts in the distance coming from the estate. Creep and crawl, pause. Creep and crawl, pause. Rinse and repeat until we're a hundred and some yards closer—all four teams moved clockwise east to west so no one is in the same vector as their previous shot.

"Spotters, report," Chico orders.

"We poked the nest, boss," a deep, gravelly male voice says. "Lots of activity on the walls. They're looking for us."

"Pick a target and fire at will," Chico says. "And then move to position three."

Ulrich settles into position much faster this time, and now Rush and I are within reach with our carbines, so Rush puts away the spotter's scope and levels his carbine. I pick a target on the wall—a dark smudge at this distance, but I'm not really meant to hit anyone from this position, only to keep their heads down and cause chaos while our snipers do the real work.

"One away," Ulrich mutters, and squeezes the trigger.

His rifle bucks with the deafening crack; I put my crosshairs a good inch above my target and pop off a round, re-aim and fire again. I've no idea if I hit my target or not, but the smudge is gone.

"U-boat reporting," Ulrich says. "Three tangos confirmed down. Moving to position three." He glances at me. "Excellent shot, Miss Harris."

Rush snorts. "Oi, mate—what am I, chopped liver?"

"No, friend, you are a professional operator with years of experience whom I know could make the shot. She is a rookie. We must encourage her."

"Yeah, yeah," Rush drawls, sarcastic and snarky. "Be all right and whatever."

Ulrich snickers at this. "I'm sorry, friend. Good shot. I am proud of you."

"Yeah, nah, it's too late to butter my biscuit now, mate."

Ulrich blinks at Rush. "I do not understand this, to butter your biscuit."

I pat Ulrich's shoulder. "Don't worry about it, U-Boat. He only makes sense half of the time at best."

"What, is it pick on Rush time?" Rush mutters. "C'mon, you two. Position three. Unless you'd rather stay here and take the piss outta me."

We belly crawl through the grass at a snail's pace, trying like hell to rustle the grass as little as possible, moving back west this time rather than eastward again. Shots ring out from the walls, but none come close to our position.

"They know we're in the grass somewhere," Chico says. "Expect to take fire, now. Fire at will from position three and move to position four at your discretion."

We're now close enough at position three that I can make out the humanoid shape of my target as he crouches on the wall, peering through the reticle of his assault rifle, sweeping the grass. We wait for Ulrich to settle in, and at his rifle's report, Rush and I open fire. This time, we rake the walls after dropping our initial targets, and Ulrich's rifle cracks a second time, and a third. The chatter of fire from the other teams overlaps ours, coming in staccato bursts. Even to me, it seems like there's more of us than there is. Activity on the wall is frenzied, figures rushing this way and that, dragging the injured out of the way, rolling corpses off the wall to tumble to the ground on the outside.

"No respect for their dead," Ulrich remarks. "Savages."

A bee buzzes angrily past my ear, a hot buzzing that's felt as much as heard. It's followed by a second and a third, and that's when I realize it's not an errant bumblebee.

"We're taking fire," I say, dropping lower in the grass.

"Noted," Ulrich says, his voice dryly sarcastic. "Let's move before near misses become hits."

We crawl straight forward this time, with bullets whipping and buzzing overhead—they know roughly where we are and can now see the grass waving and wriggling with our movements.

"The gate is opening!" Chico snaps across the comms. "Concentrate suppressive fire on the walls. Abraham, ready the Stinger."

As he's speaking, the gate in the ancient compound's wall swings open and a line of glossy black Range Rovers bolts through at breakneck speed. A figure pops up in the grass in the distance, hesitates, and then a corkscrewing streamer of whitish-gray smoke streaks into the lead SUV. The explosion shudders the earth as flames leap skyward, debris raining down for yards in every direction. The second of four SUVs has no time to react and plows into the wreckage, but the third vehicle skews sideways under hard braking, rocks off the road and bounces around the wreckage, followed by the fourth.

Another missile makes a flat arc toward the fleeing SUV, impacting its hood. The explosion sends the car flipping up and forward end over end. The last remaining vehicle tries to swerve out of the way, but the embankment is steep and it topples sideways to roll down into the grass. The nearest fireteam opens up from their position, pouring fire into the side of the upturned Range Rover. After a pause, the fireteam approaches warily to peer inside—a few minutes later, the report comes across the comms.

"It was a fakeout," I hear. "One body in each car. It's doubtful Pugli was in any of these."

That's when I hear it—the distinctive thump of a helicopter's rotors. And even to my civilian's ears, I know that's not the Osprey. Seconds later, a helo rises into the air and peels away, nose angled down as it accelerates.

"FUCK!" Rush snaps, kicking at the grass. "Bastard had a bolt hole. The fucking Range Rovers were a distraction."

The satellite phone burbles in the pocket of my vest, then. I hurriedly dig it out and move to stand by Rush, putting it on speaker. "Dad?"

"We have Eliza," Dad says. "She's safe, she's unhurt. Scared out of her mind, but she's okay."

Rush drops to his knees with a relieved sob. "Thank fuck. Oh god, thank you." He takes the phone. "Can—can I talk to her?"

"Of course. Here. Eliza, sweetheart, your daddy wants to talk to you."

A small, high-pitched, sweet little girl's voice, adorably British-accented, fills the line, then. "Daddy? Is it really you?"

"Yeah, lovey, it's me." His voice is rough and ragged. "You alright, Lizzy-Bean?"

"Well, I'm not hurt. But they were rather mean. They just smashed *every*thing, Daddy. Even grandmama's favorite china, just because. Why did they break things, Daddy?" She says it *grandmah-MAH*.

"Because they're right awful bastards, that's why," Rush snarls. "They didn't hurt you?"

"I was very afraid, Daddy. They said if I didn't do as I was told they'd kill me. But I knew you wouldn't let that happen, Daddy. Where are you?"

"I'm…I'm somewhere else, lovey. I had to…the

men who took you were following the orders of another man. I'm looking for him to tell him what he did was bad."

A pause. "Daddy, I'm not a baby no more. You're not going to only talk to him, are you? I'm a big girl, now. You can tell me the truth."

Rush laughs, nodding. "Yeah, sweetheart, right you are. I'm gonna…well, I know you're a big girl, but you ought not know the things your daddy does. They're not very nice."

"Daddy, don't be silly. You're nice to me, and you're sometimes nice to grandmama and grandpa, but to other sorts you're quite mean. And I heard grandmama say you're a killer. I wasn't meant to hear her, though. *Are* you a killer, Daddy?"

Rush doesn't answer, struggling to contain a tumult of emotions. I have to do something.

I take the phone from him. "Hi, Eliza, my name is Bryn. I'm a friend of your father's."

"Hello, Bryn. You sound American."

"I am. And you sound British."

She laughs, a merry, tinkling bell-like sound. "Well, of course I do, silly. Because I am!"

"Well, then, I sound American because I am." I let my voice go serious. "Eliza, you must know that your daddy only does what he has to do to keep you safe and take care of you."

"I know that. But…he *does* hurt people sometimes, doesn't he? That's what grandmama said."

"Only if he has to, and only bad people. Your daddy is a good guy."

"Well of course he is!" she answers immediately, as if it's the most obvious thing in the world. "He's my daddy. Sometimes he has to go away, and I get quite sad. But he has to. For work. And I'm not meant to know what he does because it's adult things. But I know he's a good guy. He's the bestest good guy there is. D'you know why I know that?"

"Why?" I prompt.

"Because he gives me kisses and tickles me and reads me stories at night, even though it's hard for him because his brain is a little different about letters and such, and he loves me. A bad person wouldn't do those things. So that's why I know he's good."

Rush is on his knees in the grass, tears flowing down his face. His rifle is forgotten, off to the side. "I'm not. I'm not," he whispers, rocking. "I'm not good. I'm not good."

"Can you say that again?" I say to her. "A little louder."

"Daddy? Are you there?"

"Yeah—" he clears his throat, trying to sound unaffected as he rises to his feet on shaky knees. "Yeah, lovey, I'm here."

"I love you the most in the whole wide world, Daddy," Eliza says. "And if you have to do bad things sometimes for work, that's okay. I do bad things sometimes, but it doesn't make me bad, right?"

"Right," he whispers.

"Are you coming home soon, Daddy?"

"Soon as I can, Lizzy-lovey. Soon's I can."

"Are you sad? You sound like you've been blubbing."

Rush bursts into helpless laughter. "I wasn't blubbing, you cheeky little shit. I was worried for you."

"Daddy, you ought not say swears at me. I'm only six."

"I know, darling, I'm sorry. You're such a big, bright girl that sometimes I just forget."

"Well, don't. Grandmama says I should be a proper girl, even though you're not a gentleman."

Rush snorts. "I'll have to have a word with Grandma about speaking out of turn around you."

"Oh, well, no, Daddy, it's not her fault. I sneak out of bed and listen to them talk at night when I can't sleep because you're gone."

Rush sighs. "I'm sorry you were so scared, Lizzy-Lovey. This ought not to have happened to you. It's my fault, darling. Do you forgive me?"

"Silly Daddy. Of course I do." A pause. "Daddy?"

"Yes, my love?"

"The medicine I had last time didn't work."

"I know, Eliza. That's…that's where I'm…that's what I'm doing. I'm trying to find a way to get you better medicine."

"I…I don't think there is any, Daddy. I think sometimes, people just get sick and you can't fix them."

Rush's face contorts in agony. He turns away, head hanging, shoulders shaking. "I'll find a way, Lizzy-Lovey. I won't ever give up. Not ever."

"I know, Daddy. Oh, Mr. Nick wants to talk to you now. Bye, Daddy! I love you!"

I hear Dad's voice speaking to Eliza. "Can you go with Miss Cuddy? If you ask nicely, she might have candy for you. just don't tell anyone—she doesn't like to share." On the line, now. "Rush, you there?"

Rush clears his throat. "Yeah," he rasps, his voice wet and hoarse.

"You've got one hell of a brave girl on your hands, son. We caught up to them in a hotel outside Paris. The second she saw us break down the door, she crawled onto the floor between the beds and didn't make a sound. How, I don't fucking know, but she knew we were there for her."

"Did she see—" Rush can't finish.

"No," Dad interrupts. "She got down and stayed down with her hands over her ears and her eyes shut until I picked her up. Not a tear, man, not one. Steady as a rock."

"She shouldn't have had to be," Rush says. "But after what she's been through medically, not much fazes her. She handles a blood draw better than I do."

"Rush, about that." Dad clears his throat. "I may have stepped out of line on this, but I, um, I made some calls."

"For what?" Rush asks, suspicious.

"Well, I only made one call. I'm sure Bryn's told you that Valentine Roth is like a brother to me."

"Yeah?" Still suspicious. "So what?"

"So Valentine got your girl into that program. He, uh, well, it's Valentine Roth, and he doesn't do anything by half measures. So he arranged it so she can receive the treatment from home. You don't have to go to the States. They're bringing everything to you. They're getting everything together right now."

"Fuck me, mate, that must've cost a fortune. I ain't got that kinda cash, Harris, and I never will."

"Exactly. Listen to me, okay? It's what he does. You can't stop Val when he decides to do something. Honestly, you're lucky he didn't just buy a whole hospital and put it in your name."

Rush looks at me. "Is he takin' the piss?"

"Like, is he joking?" I ask, and Rush nods. "No. That's how Uncle Val is. He takes the notion of philanthropy and…" I explode my fingers apart. "Goes nuts. You can't stop it, even if it's ridiculous."

"My wife, about three or four years ago, had an idea." Dad pauses, grunting, and I hear Eliza's laugh in the background. "Here we go, darlin'. Buckled? Alright. Hold on tight. You ever been on a helo before? No? Look out the window. And if you wanna go faster, just tell Captain Beth faster, faster."

I hear her tiny voice shouting "Faster! Faster!" And then whooping in childlike glee.

Dad's back on the line, then. "So anyway. My wife thought it would be a cool idea to host free swimming clinics in some select, um, urban areas of Miami. She heard about a spate of kids drowning because they never learned how to swim due to a lack of access to swimming safety education."

"Not to be rude, mate, but so fuckin' what? We're still on the ground, here."

"So, Val heard about this and created a billion-dollar foundation that installs public pools in inner city areas all over the US, with free swimming clinics every weekend, and they also hand out free life jackets and floaties. Layla was just thinking a single weekend event at a public pool, and Val went and spent a billion fucking dollars on it. That's my point. That was because his wife had a random idea. Your girl is sick—this is personal. He can bring the experimental drugs to you, so he did. It wouldn't happen for anyone else, but he probably made a massive grant to them or something, and now your girl is gonna get the treatment she needs in the comfort of her own home. And knowing him, he's probably not done."

"Jesus. I…" he covers his face. "I dunno know what to say."

"Well, when you meet him, start with thank you."

"Mr. Harris, sir." Rush swallows hard. "You and your crew. I…I owe you. All of you. You saved my girl. I'll never be able to thank you enough. Not ever."

"Son, when people involve kids in adult shit, we get pissed. And trust me when I say that these fuckers who took her weren't the end of it. We won't stop until every last sad sack of shit who was part of this thing is six feet under being eaten by worms." He clears his throat. "Sorry, sweetheart. Don't repeat any of that, yeah?" He laughs. "Sorry, man, forgot she was here for a second. Point is, I'll bring her home to her grandparents and post a crew to keep watch until we're sure shih—things are settled. The medical people will be meeting us there. I also took the liberty of arranging for repairs to your in-laws' home. These fuh—um, morons made a heck of a mess."

Rush tips his head back, sniffing hard. "God, what's happening to me? I'm all…ah, fuck." he scrubs his face, shakes his head like a bear stung by a bee, stomps a foot. "Thank you, Mr. Harris. Thank you."

"Just Harris is fine, son. Kill the mister and the sir. You're not in the service anymore."

I notice Rush isn't correcting the "son" comments anymore. Interesting.

"Now," Dad says, his voice all business once more. "Sitrep."

"Sitrep is Pugli fucking got away. Had a bolthole and a helo."

"Shit. Well, Lear's on it. And when Lear wants to track someone, there's no getting away. The man could track a mouse fart in a tornado."

Rush snorts a laugh. "Descriptive."

"Just facts, kid. Lose anyone?"

"Nah. We took 'em by surprise, but he bugged out rather than fight. Pussy."

"Well, get airborne and wait for Lear to update you. This ain't over until Pugli is dead."

"That's a fact."

"And for what it's worth, I don't know if I would've done anything different, Rush. With Pugli, your daughter, and the situation with Bryn. It was fucking impossible. If Bryn is still by your side, then that's good enough for me."

My eyes burn a little at Daddy's casual statement.

"You shoulda seen your girl work, sir. I mean, Harris—that might take me a minute. She dropped a tango from two hundred yards, clean as a whistle. She knows her business, and I say that from a professional standpoint."

"Well, she's our kid. Just…stick with her, Rush. That's my daughter."

"You take care of mine, sir, and I'll take care of yours."

"You know it, son." A pause. "I've got a call coming. Gotta go. Talk soon. Harris—"

"Daddy, do *not* say that," I say, leaning closer to the phone. "It's embarrassing for everyone involved."

A pause.

"Harris, out." Click.

I groan. "He's such a troll, sometimes."

"It is the way of fathers," Ulrich says—I'd forgotten he was there, honestly. "My daughters are always embarrassed by me no matter what I do, so I must have fun with it, since I am such an embarrassment simply for existing."

Rush looks at him. "Lucky me, I'm still my girl's hero." A disgusted sigh. "Try convincing Evelyn of that, though. I'll never be good enough for her."

Ulrich nods. "This I understand and empathize with, very much. My wife comes from a very important family. Her father worked for the Chancellor, and her mother ran a fashion magazine. I came from a very poor family from a very rough part of Berlin. Plus, when I met my Gisela, I was only a lowly submarine sailor. Gisela loves me, but her parents have never learned to do the same. They tolerate me at best."

Rush nods. "Richard and Evelyn ain't rich or nothin'," he jerks a head at me. "But they're good, solid, Christian folk who go to church on Sundays and have tea every afternoon and talk about the bloody Royals like they fart rainbows and shit glitter." A shrug. "They don't understand me, or my life, or anything. Thanks for your service an' all that, yeah, but they don't get it and they don't get me."

Ulrich claps him on the shoulder. "Who can, my friend? Only we who have done the job can understand."

"Pugli's men are watching us," Chico says on the comms. "They don't seem interested in pushing their luck, but let's not take any chances."

"The rat bastard really just left his men here?" Rush asks. "Guess he either didn't care or figured we ain't the slaughterin' types."

"A bit of both, I think," Chico answers. "Falcon One is en route. Gather at the E-Z."

Not long after, I'm strapped into a jump seat in the back of the Osprey.

Yay, more traveling.

14

AMBUSHED

We follow Pugli's path across Italy and into Switzerland. He puts down at an airfield outside Geneva, but he's in a car and gone before we're even close. Lear tracks his progress across Geneva while we land and divide into a quartet of old but serviceable four-by-fours.

What follows is a comically long-distance chase across Geneva—we close in on his position, and he bugs out again. And I have to admit, I like Pugli being on the run, the mouse to my cat. I hope the fucking twat is out of his mind knowing we've got his ass on the run.

It's the effort of a lifetime, though, to keep my focus on the task at hand rather than Eliza. In my mind, I know she's safe. But I've not seen her or held her. I can't comfort her or read her a story. I can't do anything but trust people I've never met to protect my little girl.

I've always been good at compartmentalizing my

personal shit while I'm working. But lately, I'm starting to realize that was mostly because I never had any real personal shit to deal with. Then things happened with Rachel, and then we had Eliza, and then Rachel and I broke up, and then Rachel died, and then Eliza got diagnosed, and then Eliza got sicker…

Turned out I'm not so great at compartmentalizing. Not when serious shit is happening in my life. When you've got a dying child, however, everything is serious.

"Rush?" Bryn's voice brings me out of my thoughts.

"Wossat, love?"

"Why were you kicked out of the SAS?"

We're side by side in the back of a jeep, trying to make up time as we chase Pugli across the mountains.

I sigh. "That ain't a nice story, Bryn."

"Are any of your stories nice?" she asks.

I snort. "Nah, guess not. But it ain't something I'm proud of."

"Well now I'm even more curious," Bryn says. "Out with it, bub."

I groan. "Fuck. It's…well, not classified or nothin', exactly, but what really happened ain't on record."

She snorts. "Oh my. That sounds ominous."

"Definitely not what you're thinkin' it is, I can all but guarantee you that." I look at her, shaking my head. "Can't believe I'm telling you this. I'm really not supposed to—I signed an NDA an' all."

She gives me a wide-eyed stare. "Holy shit, you had to sign an NDA? What did you *do*, Rush?"

I grimace. "I, um, well, I sort of shagged the wife of the commanding officer of the entire SAS."

Silence.

"No shit."

"Not my brightest idea."

She huffs a laugh. "Yeah, I guess not. But…how? I mean, I can't imagine the average soldier really comes into contact with top brass all that often, let alone their wives."

"Nah, not really, no. And to be fair, it wasn't all me. I hate sounding childish or whatever, but she started it." I blow out a breath. "It was an accidental meeting, an' that's the honest truth. I was having a pint with the lads near base, as you do, right? Some of the lads left, and then more, and then more, and then suddenly it was just me halfway to rat-arsed with a fresh pint of bitters. Well, in walks a lady. By herself, which in that area ain't a commonly done thing, mind you. Bit of a rough place, it was. Still dunno what Vivian was doing in a place like that other than hunting the exact sort of trouble she found. Meanin' me. Now, mind you, I was straight carparked by then, but I'm the sort who don't show how pissed I am till I'm arse up in a ditch outside Tisbury with a sausage in one hand and a biscuit in the other."

Bryn stares at me. "What the fuck did you just say? I know you used English words, but…*what*?"

I snicker. "I was hammered, babe. Proper shitfaced. But you can't really tell how drunk I am."

"Okay, but what the fuck is Tisbury, and what do a sausage and a biscuit have to do with anything? And furthermore, carparked? How many different words and phrases do you Brits have for drunk?"

"Tisbury is a place," I answer. "West of London and north of Southampton where Eliza's grandparents live. Me and the lads stole a caravan and went on a drive out into the countryside. Ended up in a pub in a place called Tisbury, got colossally pissed, and wandered off by myself. The lads found me face down in a ditch with a half-eaten sausage in one hand and a biscuit in the other. Because I was carparked. And to answer your question, we've got as many different ways to say drunk as the beach has grains of sand, love. Think of any word and we can find a way to make it mean drunk."

"Got it. But…when you say you and a lad stole a caravan?"

I sigh. "Gettin' pretty far off track here, but this was before I joined the service. Some lads I ran about London with, causing trouble, if I'm being honest. Mostly boosting cars and being vagrants, with the occasional bout of drunkenly picking fights with rich wankers."

"And you stole a caravan? Which is…?"

"I think your lot call it a camper."

"I'm confused."

"Oi, keep up. A big thing with wheels what you can live in. Got a kitchen and a shitter an' all, yeah? But you've got to have a jeep to tow it with. We stole a jeep and a caravan and did a runner right out of London. Made it as far as Taunton before the law caught up to us."

She blinks. "Well, I have no idea where Taunton is, but I guess it doesn't matter. So what then?"

"I get sent down. Went to jail, meanin'. That's where Leftenant Rodrick Ulysses found me."

"That's his name? For real?"

I nod. "Absolutely. He was an absolute unit, too. Sort of bloke who could crush bricks with his bare hands. Saw him do it, matter of fact. And the short version of that story is that jolly old Leftenant Ulysses told me I could rot in prison for a laundry list of crimes—which, by the way, was only what they could pin on me and not even the half of what I actually done—or I could join the military and he'd fast-track me into the SAS. Turns out I'd taken some test or other during a short stint of attending a proper secondary school, and that test showed an aptitude or something? I dunno. They heard about me somehow and decided an orphan with no family and no education would make a great fuckin' operator. Guess they was right, ey? Coz I was. I am. I'm a legit fuckin' top-tier operator. But what I'm not is a good *soldier*. Which brings me back to the original story."

Bryn grins at me. "See what I did there?"

I frown. "No, I don't."

"I got a whole bunch more information about you out of you and you didn't even notice."

This gets a laugh out of me. "You're a sneaky one, you are. Make a hell of an interrogator."

"So, you're carparked at a pub, and in walks a woman." Bryn rolls her hand. "Carry on."

"She was a proper fit, Vivian was. Had no idea who she was, or I'd not have touched her with a ten-foot pole. But then, all's I saw was a gorgeous woman. Some bit older than me, maybe, but so what? I've had some great sex with older women."

Bryn arches her brow at me. "Nice."

"What? It's true, and it's context. You wanted to

know. I didn't know how old she was or who she was. She didn't look her age, and she didn't introduce herself as 'Vivian Goddard, wife of Major-General Albert Goddard, Director of Special Forces.' Nah. She sat down next to me, ordered a G-and-T, and chatted me up. Said her name was Viv. I had no reason to think she was anyone special. So, you know, we shagged. She paid for a room at a hotel. I assumed she was in town on business or something—I didn't ask. Wasn't that kind of thing, I thought. Figured we'd just shag a time or two and she'd pop along her merry way."

"I'm guessing that's not what happened."

"Not exactly, no. She showed at the pub again the next weekend. Same hotel, same room. This time, she gave me a key and told me to be there at the same time the next week. And it *was* just sex. She was Viv, I was Rush, we didn't talk about our lives, or who we were, or our jobs. Nothing personal, ever. Figured she came into town on business every week, and I was her little plaything while she was in town. I was fine with the arrangement when that's all I thought it was."

"But then?" Bryn prompts.

"Bu then..." I sigh. "There was an event. We all had to dress out in our parade uniforms and attend some ball or other. Stuffy, boring, formal bullshit. We all hated it, but when brass says dance, you dance. And guess who I saw waltzing with her husband, the commander of all special forces in the UK? Viv. Gussied up in an expensive gown, dripping in diamonds and looking quite different from the lady who was laughing in bed with me just a few days prior."

Bryn laughs. "Oh god. I bet that was a shock."

"To say the least, yeah. Nearly fainted, honestly."

"So how did the commander find out?"

"He started to suspect something and had her followed. Had photographs of us together."

Bryn winces. "Oof. Not good."

"Yeah nah," I drawl. "I got a summons to Goddard's office. Which I don't have to tell you don't bode well. A nobody soldier like me don't get summoned to the office of the D-S-F. It just ain't done. But that's what happened. Found myself sitting in his office getting the dressing down of a lifetime. Didn't matter I didn't know, obviously. But it was delicate, it turns out. He didn't want to risk social or political embarrassment as he had political aspirations or some such, so he needed me to keep quiet about it. But he also couldn't let it go that I'd shagged his wife. So I signed an NDA, got summarily booted, and got a referral to work for a bloke who could use my skills."

"Pugli?" Bryn asks.

I laugh. "Nah, nothin' like that. He was former SAS like me doing security work. Pugli came later, when the more above-board work dried up and it was take the offer or start working the grease baskets at the local chippie."

Zurich, 0700 hours. Bryn is asleep against the window, mouth slightly agape as she snores softly. We've chased this fuckstain from Geneva to Zurich and now we've lost him in Zurich—he played a trick on us, using several identical decoy cars in a game of shuffle. I'm exhausted, irritable, hungry, and antsy for the boring fucking slow chase through the lush Swiss landscape to be over.

We make a turn onto a narrow side street, guided by Lear's instructions piped into our comms via some sort of techno-wizardry.

"Shit, shit, shit," Lear mutters. "Stop. Go back. I don't like this."

I sit up, roll down my window and lean my torso out to see ahead of us around the lead car—we're second in the line. Black SUVs are parked across the road a hundred meters ahead. I crane around to see behind; our parade slows at Lear's instructions, but it's too late. Two more SUVs squeal to a stop, blocking us in.

"FUCK! Ambush!" Lear shouts.

Everyone reacts instantly. Our cars brake to a skidding halt, angled across the narrow street to provide cover. Bryn blinks awake, stretching and yawning. "Where are we? We catch up yet?"

I roughly cup her cheek, tugging her lower lip with my thumb. "We're bein' ambushed, love. It's bang-bang time."

She's fully awake almost instantly, shaking her head to clear it of the sleepy cobwebs as she tightens her vest and checks her rifle—eject mag, check load and replace, hit the charge handle. "Ready." She's an old hand already, going from asleep to gung-ho in seconds.

That's when all hell breaks loose.

Automatic weapons fire rattles and chatters from every direction, glass shatters, and rounds thunk into metal. On either side of us, apartment or condo buildings rise three and four stories, full of innocent bystanders. This is where they choose to ambush us? Where the chance of collateral damage is highest?

Fuck these bastards.

"TIGHT CLUSTERS, LADS!" I shout. "WE'RE SURROUNDED BY CIVILIANS!"

I wrench open my door and hit my knee behind it, pop up and squeeze off a quick trio of rounds at the enemy SUVs—my shots put silver holes in the driver's door and shatter the glass. I see a muzzle flash and drop to my knee again as rounds zip overhead with a vicious buzz, one shattering my window and showering me with glass. I tip my head forward and shake like a dog. Bryn is huddled at my back, crouched and facing the opposite direction. I hear her carbine bark thrice in quick succession—more like three individual shots in close succession rather than a true three-round burst, but this is a firefight, not a training exercise.

I hear a grunt from the other side of the SUV—an RMI operative drops, a round through the throat. Fuck, this is bad.

Rounds zing, zip, whip, and buzz back and forth, shrieking as they ricochet off the ground and smack into the stone facades to one side or another. I glance up at a window and spot a woman peering down at us, face pressed to the glass; I press my flattened hand downward as I hold her gaze, and she vanishes from view. Just in time, too: a stray ricochet shatters the glass where she was standing moments before.

Bryn's rifle goes *crack-crack-crack* behind me,

pause, *crack-crack-crack*. "Eat that shit, fucknut," I hear her mutter.

"Drop one, didja Gorgeous?" I ask.

"Well, his ugly-fuck face exploded, so hopefully, yeah."

It shouldn't be arousing, watching Bryn work, but it is. She's fucking magnificent. No wasted movements. Just pure grace and lethal efficiency as she pops up, rips off her burst, and hits the deck again, never in the same rhythm. I take a moment to watch her shots, as well, and her clusters are goddamned brilliantly tight.

It's awfully bizarre having a chubby in the middle of a firefight, but here we are, ey?

The next time she drops back down, I wrap a hand around the back of her neck and kiss the hell out of her.

She laughs in surprise. "What was that for?"

I laugh as well, leaning around the edge of the door this time, firing with the rifle tilted at a 45-degree angle—a tango appears in the V of a doorway, his rounds slicing air where I would have been if I'd gone up instead of to the side. Thus, he misses and I do not. His head jerks back with a burst of red-pink spray.

I pull back and grin at her. "Cuz you're bloody fucking amazing, that's why, and I had to kiss ya."

She grins back, opens her mouth to respond; a bloodcurdling scream cuts through the chattering chaos of the firefight—a woman in absolute terror.

Bryn stands full upright to look, and I follow suit. A little girl, no more than four or five, has somehow managed to appear in the street, right smack in the middle of the kill zone. Bullets whip this way and that, snapping and buzzing, zinging off the blacktop and smacking into the tube frames of bicycles.

The girl is standing stone still, frozen in terror, screaming, hands fisted out to the sides and shaking. Her hair is a messy mass of blonde curls. Her mother is huddled in a doorway, reaching for her helplessly, sobbing.

All I see is my Eliza, and there's no choice but to do something stupid.

"Fuck me," I snarl. "Bryn, down."

She glares at me. "Fuck that. The girl!"

"On it, love." I suck in a quick breath. "Cover me!"

Bryn pops up and rakes a long burst across both SUVs while an RMI operative does the same the other way, keeping the enemy's heads down.

I lurch into a sprint, skidding around the hood of the SUV and diving for the girl. At that moment, a tango rises over the hood and pulls a bead on me. I see it happen in slow motion, and there's not a damn thing I can do. I've got the girl in my arms, my rifle hanging by its strap behind me. I drop to a crouch and turn my back to the shooter, curling my whole body around the child. She's gone silent but I feel her shuddering uncontrollably. *CRACKCRACKCRACK*! Something hot sears past my left ear. Another round creases the outside of my left arm. The third digs into the blacktop near my left knee.

CRACKCRACK—

Overlapping reports conflict, one burst cut short. An elephant kicks me in the back, shattering the air out of my lungs and sending me toppling forward. I curl my arms in a vise around the girl and twist my torso as I fall, taking the brunt of the impact on my shoulder, log-rolling several times toward the doorway where the mother huddles, still screaming hoarsely in an extremely Swiss mixture of German and French.

I can't breathe, can't draw in a breath. Spots dance across my vision. My limbs won't cooperate. I can feel my toes, at least, so I'm not fucking paralyzed, but this shit is not fucking fun.

I hear Bryn yelling my name, but it's all I've got to force my body to obey, shoving a knee under me as I gag for oxygen, mouth flapping emptily, vision blurring and narrowing. The girl has my vest clutched in her little fingers, face buried in my throat. For a moment, it's Eliza.

"I've got you, sweetheart," I whisper—or at least, that's the intent. All that comes out is a hissing croak.

A horde of bees swarms past my skull. I've got to move. Through sheer stubborn determination, I force my body to move despite the lack of oxygen. I lurch to my feet and stagger forward, half-tripping on the low kerb. I slam into the door beside the girl's mother, mouth working as I struggle to suck in a breath. The mother is speaking, but I can't hear anything over the roaring in my ears.

My knees give out, and I sink to my ass, panic bubbling in my gut as I feel darkness welling up inside me—how long have I been unable to draw a breath? Thirty seconds? Longer?

I still have the little girl in my arms. I look down at her. Big, frightened blue eyes meet mine. A tiny soft hand touches my cheek. Her little mouth moves, asking me a question, but the roaring in my ears drowns it out.

I fight the panic, draw my knees up to my chest and push my stomach out slowly, focusing on trying to force my diaphragm to move. Pull my belly in, force it out. When you've had the wind knocked out of you like that, especially as hard of a hit as I took, you have to learn how to do something that goes against everything your body is trying to tell you—you have to forcibly relax yourself. Don't panic, get your diaphragm moving, and try to get little sips of air as you can.

Very, very slowly, my breath comes back. At first, it's like wetting your lips when you're near dead of thirst, and then drawing in enough to coat your tongue, and then finally allowing a full swallow. Bit by bit, my lungs start to work again, and the roaring in my ears fades, and the crackle and chatter of the firefight return.

"*Hallo? Herr? Bist du verletzt?*"

"Nein, nein." I look down at the little girl, addressing her in German. "You're okay. You're not hurt."

She shakes her head, patting my cheek with her warm little hand.

I can't help but hug the girl tightly, until she squirms.

"I have a daughter," I say to the mother.

She gathers her child to herself, her tear-wet eyes wide. She doesn't say thank you, too busy weeping and kissing her daughter, but she doesn't have to. I see it in her eyes, the gratitude, the relief. I look out at the scene, assessing what's happened while I was fighting for my breath.

Enemy bodies lay slumped by tires and beneath doors—I count six. We've lost three RMI guys, but I see two of them still moving so hopefully they're just wounded.

Bryn is edging around the back of the SUV as if about to make a break for it, but I hold out a hand to stop her. I don't need her here—the doorway isn't big enough for three adults and a scared child.

An RMI operative rises to send a burst over a hood—and takes a slug to the eyeball, rocking backward, dead instantly; an instant later, another operative retreats to the next SUV down the line, leaving Bryn isolated. Pugli's men sense an opportunity and pop up in unison, laying down heavy fire. I assume a firing position, one knee up, elbow braced on that knee, sending rounds at the enemy, but that only draws their fire my way—and toward the mother and child.

RMI guys are retreating—the tangos at the rear of our line are all gone, dead or wounded, leaving only the six now working in coordination. Bryn is alone. They're making a play for her.

"BRYN! Retreat!" I shout.

"Not without you!" she shouts back.

"I'm fine! Go!" I gesture furiously at the RMI guys scuttling backward as they fire at the enemy—most of their rounds going high.

Stubbornly, Bryn refuses to retreat.

I've nowhere to go.

If I fire, I risk drawing their rounds this way, endangering the innocent mother and child. If I dart out,

I'll make it maybe ten steps before I catch a round—the bullets whip back and forth in a thick, whining hail.

And caught in the middle is Bryn.

With Pugli's men advancing.

I peek out—there's another doorway a dozen or so meters further down. I hold the mother's eyes. "When I say go, you take her and you run like hell for that door down there. Understand?"

She nods, scooping the girl up in her arms and cradling her against her chest, crouching at the ready.

A round ricochets off the stone wall near my face, spraying my cheek with tiny stinging shards.

I roll out, raking the enemy line with a long burst. "GO!"

The mother darts out and sprints faster than I'd have thought possible for the indicated doorway, vanishing behind the meager cover just as more bullets whizz past, digging into the road and the wall.

The bastards are shooting at anything that moves.

Fury ignites in me. It's one thing to shoot at another armed combatant, it's another to fire on innocent civilians—women and children in particular.

Bryn rolls out from behind the SUV, firing in a low crouch. I see it happen—the bullet striking the grip of her rifle, severing the tip of her middle finger. The rifle goes flying, and she drops to a knee, clutching at her bleeding hand. Another round smacks the road near her feet. I fire at the enemy, but they're firing back, and I have to duck. RMI is doing their best to lay down suppressive fire, but they've got no good angles and they're dragging their wounded with them.

One of Pugli's men makes a break for Bryn, sidearm raised and bucking. No, no, no. I fire at him, miss, fire again, catch the side of his knee. He topples, but not before a round from his pistol hits Bryn square in the vest, knocking her backward. I finish him off, but then I'm taking heavy fire and have to shove myself into the opposite corner, and Bryn is writhing in agony from the close-range strike—she'll be alive but stunned, possibly a bruised or broken rib, depending on where it hit. They know I'll make a play for her and they lay down a heavy tirade of fire, the rounds divoting and whining and shrieking off the walls and ground near me, keeping me huddled in the corner, helplessly watching as another Pugli's men sprints to Bryn, grabs her by the vest and hauls her across the blacktop. She fights him weakly, helplessly, the air still knocked out of her. RMI guys push forward, trying to assist, but it's too late. Pugli has Bryn.

Careless in my fury, I break out of cover, ready to throw my life away to keep Bryn out of their hands, but with bullets whipping past my face and snatching at my sleeve and trousers leg and snapping past my ear, I can do nothing but fire after them as I slam into the body of one of our bullet-riddled SUVs.

They drag Bryn behind their line. I hear her screaming, fighting. A gun goes off, and she goes silent.

A hard, heavy body crashes into me from the side, knocking me sprawling before I can make a break for the enemy line—Chico.

"You cannot, amigo," he murmurs in my ear, pining

me to the ground. "They have her, for now. We must regroup."

"*You* regroup, motherfucker!" I snarl, thrashing in his grip. "Let me go! BRYN! *BRYN*!"

"RUSH!" Her voice is faint—I hear the pain, the rage, the fear.

"I'LL FIND YOU!"

An engine howls, tires squeal, and then I know Bryn is gone.

They've left three men to hold us—RMI makes quick work of them, now that we outnumber them.

Chico lets me up—I scramble to my feet and slug him on the jaw. He takes it without complaint. "You know I am right," he says. "But I know also your pain."

"Oh yeah?" My voice is nakedly skeptical.

He nods. "My wife was taken by the cartel. To make me work for them. I rescue her and kill them all… eventually."

"Shit." I scrub my face, scanning the bloody, writhing bodies. Fucking Pugli.

Full of incandescent rage, I plug Pugli's wounded men from where I stand, finishing them off.

Harris's voice snarls in my ear, fed into my comms somehow by Lear. "What the *fuck* happened?"

"Ambush," I grit out. "They took Bryn. They have her." I choke, gagging on a hot ball of acidic rage. "I fuckin'…I let it happen."

"He could not have stopped it," I hear Chico say. "It was cleverly done. It was planned, I can promise you this."

"We've got no ride," I say, seething. "Everything's all shot to shit."

"I'm tracking them," Lear says. "We'll get her back."

Chico has me by the vest. "You did the right thing," he says, holding my gaze. "The child. You save her. Bryn would say it as well."

I hear Harris growl a sigh. "The reports I'm hearing say you saved a little girl who got caught in the crossfire and took one to the vest in the process."

"Yeah, well, I couldn't very fuckin' well leave the innocent little thing stood there to die, could I? The fucking shiteaters were targeting her."

"Are you okay?" Harris asks.

"Fucking fine," I snap. "Must have been a ricochet or something, coz we all know these vests can't stop a NATO round at that range."

"Bryn was alive when they took her?" Harris asks.

"Yeah. Lost the tip of her middle finger and took a nine mil to the vest, but she was yelling for me. She was alive." I feel the adrenaline flood out of me all at once, the reality that Bryn is gone hitting me like a mule kick to the belly. I hit my knees. "I let them take her—I…I let them. I let them."

"Quit hogging all the fucking blame, Rush," I hear Harris snarl. "We've had you chasing that fucker thinking we had him on the run. This isn't on you. You could only have gotten yourself killed, son. All you can do now is sack the fuck up and find a way to get her back."

Chico hauls me to my feet. "Come. We have a plan."

Dazed, I let Chico haul me into a jog.

Pugli has Bryn—it's the only thought rattling in my stunned, exhausted, rage-addled brain.

Pugli has Bryn.

Pugli has Bryn.

Part of me, though, wishes I could be a fly on the wall to see what happens. I doubt he has any clue the kind of tiger he's caught by the tail.

15

ACROSS THE POND; A MOTHER MURDERED

WELL THIS SUCKS.

These asshole have me trussed up like a Thanksgiving turkey, wrists bound behind my back with law enforcement-grade zip-ties, elbows tied together to force my shoulders back. My finger hurts like a bitch, throbbing and pulsing, smearing blood everywhere. Not that they care. I'm also gagged and have a smelly burlap sack over my head. Feet bound, knees bound. No chance of escape; clearly, they're not taking chances of a repeat of what happened on the train. Word must get around in the small world of villainous henchmen.

Stab a guy in the eyeball one time, and suddenly you're a problem.

The driver is driving like a bat out of hell, squealing around corners, braking hard at the last second and wrenching the wheel, then gunning the accelerator. The net result is that I, not seat belted and unable to see where we're going or brace against momentum, am tossed this way and that violently, slamming against the window again and again, until my head is pounding.

To say I'm getting pissy would be an understatement.

The next turn throws me across the car, so I land against the guy in the back seat with me. He pushes me away, but I react out of purely vengeful, childish, rash anger. I lash out with my head, the only part of me that I have any control over. I feel something soft crunch under my skull and it's a very satisfying feeling, so I do it again.

And again.

And again.

As hard as I fucking can, feeling that soft wet something get softer and wetter and mushier.

The car brakes, tires squeal, and the car slews around to a tire-stuttering halt. Click.

Something hard touches my forehead. "You be still. No more."

"FUCK YOU!" I scream. Of course, I'm gagged so it comes out *HUH OO*, but still. I think he got the message.

The gun barrel presses harder against my forehead. "I am already paid." His voice is low and nasty, with an accent I can't place. "Be still." The gun moves to my knee. "Maybe I don't kill you. Hey? Which are you choosing?"

I don't move.

"Is what I am thinking." A sigh. "Fuck. He is dead?"

A long, vicious flood of curses, or what I assume are curses in his language, based on the tone.

A door opens, and then the door back here. I hear rustling, and then the thud of a body falling to the ground. My door opens and I smell too much shitty cologne as my captor buckles me in. The door closes. The other door. The engine howls, tires squeal, and then we're bolting forward.

Holy shit, I killed the guy? With my fucking head? Nice one, Bryn. I feel pretty badass. Wait till Rush hears about that one.

Although now my head is sticky with hot, drying blood.\

Now that I'm not being thrown around the back of the car, I can properly consider my situation.

Clearly, that was a planned ambush. They knew exactly what they were doing. That little girl was just a poorly timed distraction—Rush couldn't have done anything else, and I wouldn't have wanted him to. But it did give Pugli's fucktards the chance to isolate me, which I think was the goal all along.

Being hogtied like this definitely makes things harder, but there'll still be an opportunity. I just have to stay calm and be ready to seize it and make the best of it. I have to steel myself against what I might endure, also. No matter what, I have to stay alive. Rush will come for me. Mom, Dad, my uncles…Pugli really doesn't have a clue what he's done.

Long minutes of this jackass driving like he's a stunt driver in a Tom Cruise movie. Which after several minutes of it, gets pretty tiring and boring.

But what can I do? Not a damn thing but tolerate it.

Eventually, he must feel like he put enough distance between us and my people, because he slows down and drives normally.

This lasts a long, long time. No clue how long, but my joints are sore and my shoulders hurt from the unnatural position, and my finger is on fucking fire. I can't believe my middle finger is missing a piece. No chance of reattachment, either.

I bark a laugh—I'm twinning with Uncle Puck, now. He'll get a kick outta that.

"Shut the fuck up, bitch. Nothing is funny."

"Huh Ooo, ish."

"I said shut up, bitch." The gun at my head again.

"Huh ooo, ish. Eye ee."

A disgusted sigh. "I don't know if you are worth the trouble. Maybe I leave you here, hey?"

I shrug. Fine by me.

The gun touches my knee. "Maybe I kneecap you first and *then* leave you."

Less fine.

I don't react, though.

We've stopped—I missed that, somehow. I hear and feel the earth-shaking roar of a jet taking off. Airport? They sound like civilian jetliners, so it's a public airport.

The door beside me opens, and hard hands haul me out of the car and set me on my feet. The gun presses into the back of my head. "I cut your feet loose, now. I *will* shoot out your brain, so do not be trying anything."

No promises, my guy.

I hear a knife blade snick open, and then the

pressure binding my ankles and knees snaps away. I'm shoved forward.

"Walk." The hands guide me forward. "Stairs."

My feet clomp on steps; I hear jet engines whining nearby, which means I'm getting on a jet. Super.

I fight down the boiling ball of panic that rises in my throat. This changes nothing. They'll find me. They'll rescue me.

Stay calm. Stay alive.

Shaky, wobbly kneed and panting, I stumble forward—the noise from outside is hushed, and then goes muffled as the door closes.

"Anatoly, my god. No need to treat our guest like a savage." The voice is familiar, dark and smooth and dripping with arrogance and superiority.

"She kills Oskar with only her head, sir. While tied up as you see."

"Be that as it may, I feel confident I will be able to handle her. Let me see her face."

I'm shoved down into a luxurious leather seat—a private jet, obviously. The bag is whipped off my head, the sudden light blinding me.

Pugli. Patrician, handsome. Dark hair swept back and glossy. Clean-shaven. Dark eyes vicious and cruel and cold and amused, wearing a stone-colored suit with a white-button down and no tie. "Well, there you are." A sigh. "My god, you really are remarkably beautiful."

If I wasn't gagged, I'd spit in his face. As it is, I stare at him with all the hate inside me. Too bad looks really can't kill.

"Mmm," he hums. "Such fire. Such spirit. I really wish I could break you myself."

I can't help my face betraying my confusion.

He sees it. "Ah, you're wondering where we're going. And, most likely, who *will* be the one to break you, if not me."

The door to the cockpit opens, and the pilot pokes his head out. "We're ready to take off, sir."

"Very good."

With deft, nimble fingers, Pugli removes my gag, buckles me into the seat, and then buckles himself. A few minutes later, we're roaring into the sky.

I really hope Uncle Lear is watching.

Once we've reached a cruising altitude, Pugli unbuckles himself, but leaves me. \

"I would relish in your suffering, my dear. Your screams, I think, would be delicious. But alas, I've found a buyer for you. And what a bargain we've struck, Miss Bryn Eloise Harris. What a bargain, indeed." His voice is low and smooth and articulate, educated. Arch and crisp. Subtly accented with his Italian heritage. When I don't betray my curiosity, he seems annoyed. "You see, I have a problem. And there is a man across the Atlantic who can help me with my problem. But he, like me, has all the money he could ever want and much, much more. I'm a pauper next to this man. So what bargain do you strike with a man who has everything?" He flicks manicured fingers at me. "You cater to his…tastes. And it turns out this Mercado fellow and I share certain… predilections. Which is where you come in."

Mercado? Never heard of him.

DELTA

I stare at Pugli, waiting for him to keep monologuing at me like a James Bond villain. The pretentious fuck.

"He's quite a big deal, apparently. He controls much of the global drug trade, I'm told, but has recently fallen afoul of a certain organization of…hmmm…unpleasantly altruistic former soldiers. Not unlike your own family. So, we have decided to help each other, this Mercado and I. I'm bringing some of my best men, and I'll help him eliminate his…problem. He then will help me with mine, which is where our problems intersect. And this is where you come in. You're a peace offering, of sorts—we're both suspicious men, you understand. Nature of the business and all. You also serve another purpose—bait. Your lot will surely come to save you, and that's when Mercado, relieved of the burden of those pesky…Broken Arrows. And they *are* pesky—I should know, after all, as I've recently tangled with them myself. But Anatoly and his crew will make quick work of them, I'm sure. Right, Anatoly?"

"Yes, boss."

"I've lost my train of thought. Oh, right. Once Anatoly and friends have rid us of Mercado's and my Broken Arrow problem, we turn our attention to you, your boyfriend, and your family, who, I'm sure, will show up en masse to rescue you. Which is all part of the plan, of course." Pugli looks at me, licks his lips. "Once all the killing is over with, Mercado and I will trade. I give him you, and he gives me a delicious little thing from his part of the world." He leans toward me, whispering conspiratorially, as if I were in on his joke.

"When I say I've been craving Mexican, I'm not talking about burritos."

Oh god, gross.

Bile rises in my throat at how he's so casually discussing human beings like…like a commodity. Something worth less than a bag of French fries.

He doesn't miss a thing, Pugli. He sees my expression and laughs. "No stomach for that, eh? Well, you'll certainly not enjoy what Mercado has planned for you. He shared it with me in some detail after I sent him your file."

He has a file on me?

"We sort of bonded, he and I. It's truly wonderful to connect with someone who operates on one's own level, to freely discuss one's…pecadillos."

This guy is fucked in the head. But the good thing is I know his plans, so I'm that much closer to knowing how to foil them. I also know I'm not going to be immediately tortured, raped, and killed. Just eventually. Although going off of what he's saying, I'm starting to think torture, rape, and murder would be the easy way out of what's actually coming my way, if this freaky fucker's frank admiration of Mercado is anything to go on.

He leans back in his seat, scrutinizing me. "You're a calm one, Miss Harris. I find that admirable, truly, but foolish. There is no escape. There will be no daring last-minute rescue by your delightful band of do-gooder paladins." A shrug, a flip of his hand. "That said, hysterics will do you no good either, I'm just not accustomed to a lack of theatrics when my merchandise discovers the fate awaiting them."

I feel a vicious surge of disgusted hatred at the use of the word "merchandise" to describe human beings.

I've kept silent thus far, but since I've got very little to lose at this point, I may as well indulge in my curiosity. "Tell me, Bob, what happened to you? I mean, who hurt you? For real."

His dark eyes narrow at me. "Bob? I think not." The hardness in his gaze belies his jovial, charming speech patterns. I hit a nerve, I think. "And I've no idea what you mean."

"Well, Bobby-boy, what I mean is that I just can't figure out how the fuck you become such a vile, disgusting, evil, demented, filthy, depraved, rapey piece of shit. It's truly mind-boggling." I roll a shoulder, or at least, as much as I can while my hands are still bound behind my back and my elbows cinched inward. "The only option, as far as I can tell, is that you were badly abused as a kid. That's how monsters like you are made, right? Daddy beat you? Mommy called you mean names? Uncle Al diddled you in the basement?"

I'm making light of such awful things on purpose—to get a reaction.

And it works.

His hands curl into claws and dig into the armrests, savage, insane fury lighting his features. "What would *you* know about such things, you pretty, privileged princess?" he spits each plosive P-sound with venomous rage.

"Nothing whatsoever, Bobby-boy. *My* mommy and

daddy love me. My uncles gave me perfectly appropriate hugs. I've never been beaten or diddled in the basement—at least, not as a child and not against my will." I shrug, faking an insouciance I do not feel. "There was that time Zero and I got it on in his mom's basement. The man had a talented mouth, I'll tell you that much."

"Stop calling me that."

I lean into the restraints, letting him see my hate. "Or *what*, bitch? You think I don't know what's coming? Fuck you. You can't do shit to me. Your sick little buyer across the pond wants me untarnished, am I right? That means *you* can't do shit to me. I have to be unspoiled so your kinky little bitch of a buddy can have all the fun with me."

His eye twitches. "I warn you, Miss Harris, I am not a man to provoke."

"Oh, I bet. Big bad man like you? You're the type who likes to pretend like he does his own dirty work, huh? Get in on the action? Cut off a few fingers, throw a few punches, maybe even finish them off with your special gun?"

Another eye twitch—bullseye.

"C'mon, Bobby-boy. What do you have to lose? If you're right and my fate is sealed, you've got nothing to lose by telling me a bit about yourself. Who am I gonna tell? This Mercado prick? According to you, I'll be too busy being tortured or whatever it is you sick fucks like to do to innocent girls."

"Innocent? You, Miss Harris, are very far from innocent."

"I mean, until your pet apes tried to kidnap that

poor girl in Zermatt, I was. I'd never killed anyone. You brought this on yourself, Bobby-boy." I shake my head, sighing. "Regardless, my question stands. What the fuck happened to you? For real. How do you become what you are? I mean, you have to know that you're a sick, twisted, horrible creature from the deepest, darkest pits of hell, don't you? People don't just suddenly turn evil. Things happen. Evil in human beings is created by other humans. We all have the capacity for good, and we all have the capacity for evil. It's the things that happen to us in our formative years that determine which way we go. And you, obviously, had truly awful things done to you as a child to make you the kind of person who gets off on the suffering of innocent girls."

Jaw grinding and ticking, narrowed eyes fixed on me with blatant fury, Pugli is silent for a long, long time. Several times he opens his mouth to speak, but thinks better of it, clicking his jaws together with an audible snap.

Eventually, he glances over his shoulder at Anatoly. "Sedate her before I give in to the temptation to teach her a lesson. It would not do to raise the ire of Mercado at this juncture, after all."

Is he...*scared*? Of Mercado?

That gives me major pause. If *Pugli* is afraid of Mercado, then the guy has to be a big fucking deal.

Anatoly reaches under his seat and comes up with a black hard-sided case. He opens it, revealing, in true Bond-villain style, black foam encasing four identical, pre-filled syringes. Selecting one, Anatoly approaches me with it. Eyeing me warily, he pauses, draws his pistol from the shoulder holster, shoving the barrel against my crotch, angled so the bullet, if he were to fire, would go through my pelvic bone. "I do not give a fuck about his friend. If you so much as breathe wrong, bitch girl, I shoot you. Right…*here*." He digs the hard barrel into my groin, eliciting a shocking burst of agony—I can't stop the gasp of pain from escaping. He grins. "Now think of how much hurt it will be if I shoot you here. Hmmm? You like it? No? Do not even fucking blink."

I hold absolutely still as he injects me with the sedative. Feeling it take hold almost instantly, I grin at him. "Scaredy-cat. Afraid of little ol' me, are you?" Darkness is pulling me under. "You're gonna die, Anatoly. My face will be the last thing you ever see."

"Bitch, I will—" Anatoly starts.

I don't catch the rest, because I'm unconscious.

I come back to consciousness slowly. At first, it's just a sense of heaviness, a slow, dense kind of quasi-awareness. That sensation gradually gives way to an awareness of light on my eyelids and the bounce and jolt and rock of an SUV on a rutted road. I can't make my eyes open for a long time, can't make my limbs function—I'm mostly conscious but unable to surface the last of the way to fully awake.

I hear the suspension protesting, the rattle of objects in cupholders. There's a sniff and snort, a window humming open, and the gross sound of a loogie being hawked.

I'm on my back, stretched out. I'm still bound, but my hands are in front and my elbows are loose. It's a relief, honestly.

I crack my eyes open cautiously. I'm in the trunk/cargo area of an expensive SUV, most likely another Range Rover, which this pretentious jackass seems to prefer; the bouncing and jolting of a backroad abruptly gives way with one last violent bounce to the smooth hum of blacktop.

"Finally," I hear Pugli mutter. "My teeth were rattling."

"Sorry, boss," Anatoly says. "I cannot fix the bumpy road." "I'm aware. We are behind schedule, however. We're due to meet Mercado's lieutenant in Austin in less than two hours, and we're at least two and a half hours away."

"I go faster, boss."

"Very good." A pause. "But within ten miles per hour of the posted limits, please. An encounter with American law enforcement at this juncture would be regretful."

"Yes, boss."

Austin? *Texas?* The fuck? When he said across the Atlantic, I assumed we'd be somewhere in South or Central America.

I'm considering the possible implications of being on American soil when a cell phone burbles.

"Silence, please, Anatoly. I must answer this."

"Yes, boss."

"Yes, hello? This is Pugli."

"Señor Pugli, I am Luis. I am *el numero dos* for

Señor Mercado." The voice is nasally and heavily Spanish-accented.

"Hello, Luis. We are about thirty minutes behind schedule, I'm afraid. We encountered heavy winds crossing the Atlantic."

"Is no problem, *jefe*. We, um…there was a problem."

"Oh. I see. Meaning what?"

"We are attacked. A very dangerous woman attacks our safe house in Austin. She is bad-bad, *jefe*. Our people took the woman and the boy, but *La Víbora* got away, and so did Lorenzo."

A pause. "You refer to people whom I do not know, Luis. Is there one woman? What child? And who is Lorenzo?"

"*Lo lamento, jefe*. I talk about two women, one boy, and one man. The dangerous woman is *La Víbora,* The Viper. She is bad-bad, very dangerous. Escape Mercado and cause big trouble, kill many men. The other woman is…" a pause, a frustrated sigh. "I do not know all these words *en Ingles*. She is not mother, but she raises boy like a mother. The boy is Mercados's *hijo*. Mercado, he wants his *hijo*. La Víbora does not want this."

"I follow so far. And I'm guessing this Lorenzo is another troublemaker. One of the Broken Arrows, perhaps?"

"*Las flechas rotas*." A pause. "The Broken Arrows. Very hard men. Bad-bad. No can be stopped. Lorenzo, he is no Arrow-man, but he fight with them. He and La Víbora, they are *amantes*. They are also amigos with the Lash, who I think you know."

"Lash, is it? I see," Pugli says, his voice dangerously quiet. "And?"

"Lorenzo escape with the woman and the boy. Mercado sends us to find them. La Víbora finds them first. There is much shooting, and only Raul gets away with the woman and the boy. Raul is injure, very bad. We must find Raul and the boy. This is Señor Mercado's only…ah, *enfocar*? Is all he want, now. You help find *el nino* for Mercado. Nothing else matter. Your woman, these Arrow-men, everyone. They all die. Only the boy is *importante*."

"I see. Where should we begin looking?"

"I send you where he is last time I speak with him."

"And where are you?"

"Going there also. But you are closer."

"I see." A ding of an incoming message. "I have the location. We are…forty-five minutes away."

"I am one hour."

"What about the woman?"

"*Ella no es andie*. Sell her, kill her, is no matter to Señor Mercado. But the boy…no hurt him. Keep safe for Mercado."

"And if I encounter…what did you call her? La Vibra or something?"

"La Víbora. The Viper." The laugh is cruel, almost malicious. "Pray you do not, jefe. El Diablo wakes at night, frighten of La Víbora. She has no blood inside, only *hielo*. She is *la Reina de Hielo*."

"*La Reina de Hielo*? I do not speak Spanish."

"You are Italian. Is close, no?"

An irritated sigh. "Hielo…ice? The Ice Queen?

She's The Ice Queen? Or The Viper? Which is it? She seems to have a multitude of melodramatic nicknames." He ends with a biting, sarcastic laugh.

"You laugh. But you do not know, jefe. La Víbora…I tell you, *El Diablo* dreams of her coming for him and he is frighten. And now she is *angry*."

I don't know who this Viper woman is, but I like her already. The Devil himself is scared of her? Fuck yes. Let's go, bitch. You and me. Let's fuck these sickos all the way up.

I'm excited just imagining what kind of badass human being she must be if these Narco shitstains are so scared of her they give her wicked nicknames like The Ice Queen and The Viper. I'm picturing knives for fingers like a murdery version of Edward Scissorhands, or laser-beam eyes like Cyclops; hopefully both. Narcos aren't scared of fucking *anyone*, but this bitch has them pissing in their big boy pants.

Can I be her when I grow up?

Gives me something to focus on, a reason to keep my wits about me, stay calm, and when the opportunity arises, raise hell and hope La Víbora is as vicious a killer as I'm picturing.

Forty-five minutes is a long time when you're awake, bound, and staring at the ceiling with nothing to do but think and wait.

We must arrive at whatever location Luis gave to Pugli, because we stop, engine running, and both Pugli and Anatoly get out. They're gone about five minutes and then return, Pugli on the phone.

"...Just fucking find them, Connor! I don't care what you have to do. Fucking find them. I'll give you an incentive, alright? If you locate my quarry for me, I'll give you a bonus that will make your holiday bonus look like a pittance. Call it…a quarter million? And if you fail to locate them, I will take your girlfriend and your new infant son and I will rape your girlfriend myself while you watch and then throw your child out a fucking window. Alright? I don't want to, Connor. Really, I don't. Harming children gives me no pleasure. But I require results. Understand? Very good."

Jesus. This is how he treats his *employees*? Good lord. Succeed and I'll pay you a quarter million dollars. Fail, and I'll rape your girlfriend in front of you and defenestrate your infant son. Charming.

A few minutes later, there's the burble of his cell phone.

"Connor. See? I knew you could do it. Excellent work. Yes, yes, Olivia and James are safe." Pause. "Your bonus should hit your account within twenty-four hours. Keep your phone on and within reach, though. I doubt I'm through with your services."

We're in motion again, racing this time. The powerful engine bellows as Anatoly floors the accelerator, and I'm thrown backward. I'm hoping they don't know I'm awake yet, so I have no choice but to go limp and let the momentum roll me like a rag doll.

We're only in motion for maybe ten or fifteen minutes when our brakes bite and tires squeal, and I'm rolled back the other way, slamming into the back of the second row bench.

"There!" Pugli shouts. "They're running. Anatoly, get them. And remember, the boy is important so you can't hurt him. He's a little boy so you should have no problem restraining him without causing harm." A door opens, stays open. Pugli sighs. "The poor man is still alive? Good heavens. Well, best end his suffering."

Another door opens and stays open. I risk detection to lever myself so I can see out the window. An old, battered silver pickup truck is angled across the shoulder, halfway into the ditch beyond—I can just make out the silhouette of a man slumped over the steering wheel. I can see hints of movement, but he looks weak.

Pugli, in that impeccable stone-colored suit, strides toward him, withdrawing a pistol from a shoulder-holster and I shit you not, the thing is platinum-plated. What'd I say? Fancy gun for a man compensating for something…

Such as a lack of a soul, and probably a very small dick.

Pugli levels his pistol at the man behind the wheel and blasts a hole in the side of his head, replaces the gun, and then swaggers back this way. He doesn't get in the car, though, but rather leans his backside against the hood of the Range Rover, watching as Anatoly jogs across a wide, empty field. I see two figures running in the distance, one larger and one smaller.

Anatoly isn't even running very hard, but he catches up easily. He cracks the woman across the head with his gun, scoops the boy up over his shoulder, and marches back this way.

The woman scrambles to her feet and follows, begging, pleading, battering her fists on his back, grabbing at the boy...Anatoly ignores it for a while, and then when he gets fed up, he pistol-whips her again. She goes down once more, writhing and scrabbling at the tall grass.

Oh, god.

Stay down, lady. It's all you can do. They'll kill you.

She gets up.

No, no, no.

I watch, unblinking, eyes tearing up, as Anatoly strides toward us with the boy over his shoulder; the boy struggles and fights with admirable ferocity, for all the good it does him.

The woman staggers toward her son. Her face is a mask of blood, but she's visibly distraught, scared, and hurt. Sinks to her knees, arms outstretched, pleading, sobbing.

Casual as you please, Pugli draws his pistol, stalks with singular purpose toward the woman, halts a couple feet away, levels his pistol at her, and blows her brains out. The boy sees the whole thing from Anatoly's back, watching as she slumps bonelessly to the ground.

The boy's screams reach me, awful and shrill.

I flop to the floor when Anatoly strides this way with the boy's thrashing form.

"Anatoly, wait." Pugli puts his gun away and slimes

his way over to the hatch of the Range Rover, opens it. "You can end the charade, Miss Harris. I know you're awake."

I open my eyes and glare at him.

He indicates the boy. "Keep him calm. The calculus is different, now. I have leverage over Mercado that isn't you. Which means I can keep you for myself. So what I'll say is this, my dear: you keep the boy calm and I'll keep your suffering short. If you do not keep him calm, I'll chain you to my bed and show you the true meaning of suffering." He leans in, dark eyes insectile in their cold, lifeless savagery. "I might even give you a taste of what was done to me to make me this way, since as you so astutely pointed out, evil things were indeed done to me. I learned to enjoy them, in time, but I doubt you will." The real threat is in the void of his gaze more than the horror of his words. "Do you understand me?"

I nod once.

"Very good." To Anatoly. "Toss him in. The Harris bitch will take care of him for now."

Anatoly tosses the boy in like so much garbage. Scrambling for the hatch, the boy would have had his fingers smashed if I hadn't lunged for him at the last second, looping my bound arms around him.

He thrashes in my arms, screaming.

"Hey, hey, hey," I murmur, trying to stay calm. "I'm a friend. Amiga. I'm an amiga. Calm. Calm."

He slows a little. "*Madre. Mamá, mamá. Le dispararon.*"

"I know," I whisper, guessing at what he's saying. "I know. I know."

He twists. "*Cómo te llamas?*" His eyes are big and dark and wet, intelligent and scared.

I know enough Spanish to answer that. "Bryn."

"Soy Renihno." *Ren-IHN-yo.*

"Hi, Renihno."

"*Hola.*" he blinks hard. "*Mi Madre…*"

"I know," I whisper again. "I'm sorry. But you have to stay calm. Okay? Calm."

He blinks hard, nodding, visibly gathering his courage. "*Sí. Tranquilo.*"

"*Sí*," I echo. "*Tranquilo.* Stay calm and they won't hurt you."

He nods—I get the feeling he understands a bit of English, even if he can't speak it.

He twists in my arms again, putting his back to my front. For a few moments, he's still, but then I feel his shoulders shake.

He weeps quietly for a long, long time.

What do you say or do when a kid just watched his mother get shot?

Not a damn thing. I just keep my arms around him and let him cry.

The longer this shitshow goes on, the more it feels like mere death is too good of an ending for these soulless monsters.

Objectively, torture is wrong. I know this, okay?

But these people? Maybe it'd be a little *less* wrong.

16

MEETING OF THE TITANS

Thanks to Alexander, we know exactly where Bryn is—the techno-wizard extraordinaire was able to remotely undo what he did, somehow. He tried to explain it, but only Lear followed any of it. The upshot of it we—the surviving RMI blokes and me—are doing my least favorite thing in the whole bloody damned world: waiting.

We're sitting around in a hangar at the arse end of a shitty, rundown old airfield just across the border in Germany. It was likely a Nazi staging ground or supply depot back in the second World War. The hangar, if you can call it that, is little more than an overgrown Quonset hut without a front, open to the elements and stuffed full of derelict aircraft parts. I'm sitting on an old jet engine manifold, cleaning my rifle with a kit borrowed from Chico.

We're waiting for Bryn's dad to arrive in some

sort of fancy super jet that's able to make the trip from France to Germany in a fraction of the usual time. On board are the legendary original six Alpha One Security members; every operator on the earth knows their names: Harris, Thresh, Duke, Puck, Lear, and Anselm. The baddest of the bad. Their exploits are damn near mythological, at this point.

Fuck me, I'm nervous.

I get jittery before a firefight, especially if I know I'm going into one. I feel fear when Death brushes up against me.

What I don't get is fucking nervous. Ever. I wasn't nervous when I stood before Vivian's husband, the DSF; I was scared shitless I was going to be thrown in the brig, or worse— vanished into a blacksite, for example. Officially, our lot don't use them. Unofficially? There's always a place where undesirables can be disappeared and questioned using "advanced interrogation techniques." I was convinced I'd find myself on the wrong end of such a one.

So yeah, scared shitless. But not nervous.

This is *nervous*. I'm not afraid—they're not here to kill me, after all. Harris has assured me he knows Bryn's abduction wasn't my fault, and there wasn't shit I could've done to stop it. RMI vouched for that.

I'm just flat fucking nervous. Not just because these blokes are the most legendary operators on the planet, but because they're Bryn's family.

Bryn means something to me.

The longer she's gone, the more obvious that becomes. I'll tear apart heaven and earth to get her back, and I'll gut anyone who tries to fucking stop me. You don't feel that way for someone who's just a fun, easy fuck.

Of course, Bryn was never that. It was always complicated. Now, it's not complicated. She's mine. I'm hers. However you want to put it, that's what it is. I don't use the L-word except with Eliza. But consider it used.

And she's being held by fucking Pugli. To say I'm unhappy is a bit of an understatement.

A low rumble shakes the earth—an approaching aircraft. But this ain't your typical jet, I can already tell by the engine signature. The power of it even at this distance is just fucking bonkers.

The others are standing up, gathering their gear, stretching, doing the things career soldiers do once the hurry-up-and-wait period is finally over.

The rumble becomes an earth-shaking roar that shocks even me, and I've been around the most powerful aircraft any military can field. The jet that approaches, however, puts all of that to shame. It actually somewhat resembles an SR-71 Blackbird, the only aircraft I know of that can threaten this thing for speed—at least, that's what Harris told me.

I watch in awe as it shunts toward the ground almost recklessly fast, flaring at the last second to kill airspeed and then touching down as delicately as a butterfly landing on a daisy. Whoever the hell is at those controls is a right fucking master of their craft, I'll say that—a real artist.

Moments later, the long, low, sleek black aircraft—all angles to deflect radar—scuds to a halt outside the hangar, and a ramp at the rear lowers. Chico doesn't wait for a written invitation, jogging toward the ramp with the rest of RMI on his heels. I follow suit, mixing in with the pack.

The ramp leads up to a fairly small cargo space—enough to pack in luggage, gear bags, and shit like that. Huge black duffel bags are secured to the walls…six of them. Chico and his guys—and two gals, if you wanna be all politically correct about it, even though I use "guys" interchangeably—find places for their gear and move toward the door in the back wall of the cargo area. So, I do the same, strapping my carbine with my bag, although I do keep my sidearm in its holster on my right thigh.

Through the door and into a different world.

Everything is white. White carpet, white ceilings with embedded, hidden lighting along the ceilings above the rows of individual captain's chairs. Which are white leather.

"Fuck my eyeballs," I mutter. "Bloody blinding in here, innit?"

I hear a laugh. "I've repeatedly asked Val to redo the interior so it's less…this." The voice is familiar—I've been speaking on the mobile with him regularly: it's Harris himself. "But so far, he thinks I'm being funny. You get used to it."

He's about six feet tall, built lean and rangy, with a buzzed head and piercing green eyes, a short blond beard dusting his jaw. He's dressed in all black, with a sidearm on his thigh, a tactical knife on the opposite side, and another, smaller pistol in a shoulder holster.

He's in his late fifties, maybe early sixties—it's hard to tell, although I know it has to be closer to sixty based purely on Bryn's age, unless he was quite young when they had her.

His gaze rakes over me, scrutinizing me, assessing me. "Rush Bellamy. Nice to meet you in person."

I shake his hand, going for firm but not trying to prove anything. "You too, sir."

He rolls his eyes. "Harris. I've told you."

I wince. "I know. Habit. You know how it is when you've been in the service for a long time. Old habits are hard to break."

He chuckles. "This I know, son. Val was 'sir' to me for years, too. I started out as his driver and bodyguard. Eventually, I became his best friend, and now we're more like brothers. So yeah, I do know how hard it is to kill old habits, especially ones ingrained into you by the military." He gestures for me to sit in one of the seats. "Sit, sit. Mercedes is a stickler for that kind of thing."

"Who's a stickler for what?" I ask, clicking my belt into place.

"Mercedes. My—well, Val's pilot. The pilot of this aircraft. She won't even taxi until everyone is seated and buckled, and she's got a monitoring system up there, so she knows."

I look around. "Everyone seems sat to me."

He raises his voice to address the aircraft at large. "If you are not buckled, please buckle *now*. We can't taxi until every seat that bears an ass is buckled."

There's a chorus of clicks; the instant the last click sounds, the engines whine with an increase of power.

Harris grins at me. "Ever fly hypersonic?"

"No, sir."

"Hold onto your tits, kid. This shit is *wild*. We don't often fly at the threshold of this thing's capabilities, but this is my daughter we're talking about. Mercedes is under orders to push as hard as she can."

"What *is* the threshold?" I ask.

"Mach...six? Seven? Somewhere in there. I know Val's got his engineers constantly tinkering with this thing, trying to squeeze every last ounce of speed out of it."

"Mach *six*?" I mutter, stunned. "Jesus shits."

He fiddles with something in the armrest of his seat—I look at mine. It's a small touchscreen with haptic buttons. Seat controls—tilt, recline, bolster, massage, heating, cooling, bed. Wait, *bed*?

"What's the difference between recline and bed?" I ask."Oh. Well, recline means lean back, but not flat. Bed mode turns the seat into a cot, basically. Pretty damn comfy, actually. Not that we'll be sleeping this trip." He winks at me, clicking his tongue. "Assuming Bryn keeps you, you might get a chance to try it out another time, though."

Oh. Oh man. That was...weird. Awkward? Nicholas Harris is...awkward? I notice him watching me, though, and I get the impression he's playing a character or something.

Testing me? Checking me out? Seeing how I'll react

to Bryn's dad being a bit of an awkward doofus? I mean, who winks at another man? Fucking weird.

When I don't react, Harris bursts into laughter. "Okay, you passed."

I frown. "Huh?"

"Oh, c'mon, kid. Bryn thinks I'm an awkward weirdo. The thing is, I just do it because she's so easily riled up."

"Oh." I sigh. "Sorry, mate. I'm a bit preoccupied."

The humor fades. "I know. You can't dwell on it. You'll go nuts. You gotta save your energy for the hunt, the fight." We've finished taxiing and have turned and halted at the end of the runway. A smooth female voice fills the cabin from hidden speakers. "Prepare for takeoff."

That's all the warning we get, and then the Fist of God smashes me back into my chair. I flex every muscle in my body to keep the blood flowing as the pressure increases with our building speed. My vision wavers and blurs, and it feels like my limbs are made of lead. And that's just the initial burst to hit takeoff speed. I feel my stomach drop away as we ascend.

Across from me, I see Harris straining to move a finger—he taps the screen in his seat's armrest, taps again, and then a third time.

A chorus of terrified shouts echoes throughout the cabin as the floor, walls, and ceiling go transparent. As in, suddenly we're sitting suspended over nothing, like we're in that one superhero's invisible jet, only we're visible and it's not. Harris is grinning again, getting a kick out of it. Once the initial shock wears off, it's actually fascinating. The sense of speed is incredible—the ground falls away and blurs beneath us. And even as we reach cruising altitude, it's still visibly apparent how incredibly fast we're going.

We level off at cruising altitude, and the pressure slackens. I let out a breath and move to unbuckle.

"Seven minutes until hypersonic acceleration," the same female voice says.

"That wasn't hypersonic acceleration?" I ask.

Harris chuckles. "Nah, son, that was just takeoff. We can't break the sound barrier over cities."

I look down and see that the landscape has changed in the seconds since I last looked. We're passing over a fairly large city. As I watch, the city falls away rapidly. And this isn't even hypersonic? Oi. That's gonna *hurt*.

Minutes pass, and the landscape changes, becoming the patchwork quilt of farmland. We're also steadily rising, I realize, the sky going darker and darker blue.

"Prepare for hypersonic."

"We can't have reached the Atlantic yet?" I ask.

Harris shakes his head. "No, we went south to the Mediterranean first. It's faster, apparently, to fly subsonic toward the nearest ocean, cross the barrier, and then find your vector. Hypersonic flight is a whole other ballgame."

"Hypersonic in five…four…three…two…one…" A dramatic pause. "Now."

I've been donkey-kicked by The Almighty. The breath wheezes out of me, the immense pressure on my body so intense it feels like I've been teleported to the bottom of the Marianas Trench. My vision narrows, darkens, tunnels.

It goes on and on.

For several seconds, at least.

How long?

I flick my eyes down and see the rippling blue water of the sea winking far, far below. As I watch, I make out the distinctive formation of the Strait of Gibraltar—we're going so fast that no sooner have I spotted it than we've passed it.

Jesus, *what*?

"Fuck, this is one hell of a long burn," Harris mutters, the strain evident in his voice.

Spain and Africa fall away behind us rapidly, replaced by endless blue ocean. We're banking, now, angling north toward the States.

And then, finally, the pressure slackens as we reach cruising speed, and I can breathe again.

"Hypersonic cruising speed attained."

"No shit, Mercy," Harris mutters. To me, then: "She takes her job very, very seriously. She's the best damn pilot I've ever seen, and generally speaking, I'm the best pilot I've ever seen. But even if it's just Val in the cabin, she announces everything."

"I suppose when operating something like this, you want someone who don't cut corners, ey?" I say, unbuckling when I see him do so.

"Damn right."

"Can I ask you a question, mate?" I say.

"Shoot."

"No judgment on this, trust me, but…how can you

laugh and joke when Roberto fucking Pugli has your girl?"

He sighs. "It's a coping mechanism I've developed over the years. In the past, I'd be all broody and pissed off and serious, like you are. But that doesn't help anyone. I'm in charge. Everyone is looking to me, watching me. If I panic, they panic. If I'm angry, they're angry. But if I'm calm and at ease…"

"We will be," I finish.

"Right." He shows me his hand, which is trembling slightly. "See? I'm so angry I'm shaking, Rush. The shakes will pass when it's go time, but for right now, I gotta act cool as a cucumber. We're up against a seriously bad dude, Rush. You know it as well as I do."

"Yeah, I do."

"But what you may not know is that it's not just Pugli we're facing. He's teamed up with someone just as bad as him, if not worse."

I stare, my mind momentarily blank. "Scuse me, sorry, but…it sounded like you said *worse* than Pugli?"

"I did." "Fuck me. He's nigh on the devil incarnate. Who's this other fella and how the fuck can he be worse?"

Harris growls, his fury showing through his easygoing facade. "His name is Rafael Sousa, better known as Mercado. But when I say better known, I mean to the very small handful of people who even know he exists. He's one of the most powerful and secretive drug lords on the planet. He makes Escobar and El Chapo look like Sesame Street characters."

"Fuck that. You're takin the piss, aren't you?"

Harris shakes his head, expression solemn. "No, son, I'm not. He's that bad. And apparently, his interests and Pugli's intersect. According to Lear's latest report, Pugli has taken Bryn to Texas, where we happen to know Mercado has been operating. We have a handshake agreement with another security operation known as the Broken Arrows, who have been working to take down Mercado. One of their members also has a vested interest in taking down Pugli."

"How do those two kingpins intersect, then?" I ask.

A shrug. "Don't know for sure. I think Mercado is having trouble fielding enough of his agents on the US side of the border, whereas Pugli, with his connections through Interpol, can more easily get armed men into the US. I'm just guessing, though."

"So what *do* we know for sure?" I ask.

"There was a hit not long ago on a safehouse in Austin—someone connected to the Broken Arrows was staying there, hiding from Mercado. I don't know the particulars, but that much is established fact. Someone got away, and someone else didn't—again, I don't have a full brief on the details, but we'll know more when we reach the States and rendezvous with the Arrows. Hopefully by the time we're feet dry over US soil, I'll have more details. The other known fact is that one of the people who escaped the hit is a woman named Inez, the estranged wife of Mercado and now his mortal enemy."

I rub my jaw. "Turnin' into a bit of a soapie, innit?"

When Harris frowns, I roll my eyes. "Soap opera? All drama and shite. His ex-wife is now his mortal enemy, and she leads the daring Broken Arrows in a crusade for justice against her villainous former husband?"

Harris laughs. "Oh. Yeah, I guess, when you put it like that. But my own story is no less dramatic, so I can't talk."

It's my turn to laugh. "Well, yeah, but everyone knows your story. Seen it on the telly, ain't we?" I wave a hand. "Nevermind. Go on."

He shrugs. "That's about it. We're not just rescuing Bryn, is the point. This is an all-out war. Pugli and Mercado against the Broken Arrows and A1S." A rueful laugh. "It is pretty dramatic, I guess."

We're quiet for a few minutes, and then he looks at me speculatively. "So, you and my daughter."

I sigh, wincing. "Figured this was comin' at some point. Look, the truth is, I don't know what it is. I know I've got real feelings for her, but I also know how things started between us ain't exactly conducive to…well, anything." I rub the back of my neck. "It's all been a bit of a whirlwind, and then she's gone, and I couldn't stop it." I shake my head. "I just don't know, sir. Wish I did, but I don't. A lot depends on her. On what happens. What she wants. Plus, I've got my girl to think about, and…"

"She's a remarkable child, your Eliza," Harris says. "She never cried. She didn't ask questions, or ask for snacks, nothing. Cool, calm, polite, and sweet."

I sigh. "She's a miracle, alright. But I wish…I dunno how to put it. She had to grow up too fast, Harris. She's like that because she's been sick. Faced death. Surgery. Chemo. Radiation. Watched other sick kids in the beds around her die. Grows you up, I guess. She knows there ain't no cure for what she's got. Meanin' she knows she's gonna die. What's that do to a young mind? Gettin' kidnapped an' all? Probably not much to be scared of, if you think about what she's already faced. Look your own death square in the eye, and some ugly blokes cartin' you around ain't much to be afraid of, I guess."

Harris doesn't reply beyond a nod. His gaze flicks down to the view of the endless azure ocean scudding beneath us, vacant and thoughtful. "She's immensely proud of her dad," he says, eventually, green gaze finding mine. "You're all she could talk about."

My stupid eyes burn at this. "I don't spend near enough time with her. Fuckin' kills me, having to leave her to go do…" I flip a hand vaguely. "The shit I've had to do since she got sick. My little girl is…an' I should be with her every moment, but I…" Harris leans forward, one strong hand gripping my knee and shaking it. "Things will be different, now, Rush. You have my word on that." I shake my head. "I don't know how to make sense of anything. What I did to Bryn, tricking her and leading her to Pugli, and then choosing her over my daughter? I don't know to…fuck me, mate, I ain't even got the words for it all. And then feeling things for her, when I'm…and my daughter? It's all gone fucked in my head, Harris."

To my surprise, Harris laughs. "Son, what you're going through is called falling in love. You've never had any real exposure to love, have you? Never seen it. Never received it."

All I can do is shake my head.

"No, didn't think so." He pauses, thinking. "You did what you had to do for your daughter. I get it, and while I haven't had an in-depth conversation about it with my daughter yet, I'm gonna guess she does too. But in the end, you knew what you were doing was wrong. Your conscience won. You made an impossible choice." He leans forward again, elbows on knees, fingers steepled in front of his face. "Your subconscious helped you make that choice."

I frown at him. "Not following that bit. My subconscious helped me? How?"

"You knew, somehow, deep down, that by making the right choice for Bryn in that moment, it would work out. You knew your daughter would have told you to make the choice you did."

More burny, salty eyeballs, the traitorous fucks. "She would've done, yeah."

"You acted out of faith that saving Bryn wouldn't doom your daughter. And it didn't."

"Hell of a fucking gamble," I mutter.

"It wasn't a gamble, son."

"Why d'you call me son?" I ask. "Never had no father. Never been a son to no one."

He just shrugs. "Dunno. Maybe I feel a kinship to you. Maybe I see something of myself in you."

I spend the rest of the shockingly short flight working through the chaotic muddle of thoughts and emotions inside me.

Falling in love?

A kinship to Harris.

Everything will be different, now.

Never been a son to no one.

Acted out of faith…

"How d'you know?" I ask Harris, as we slow out of hypersonic in preparation for landing.

He doesn't have to ask what I mean. "Think about your life tomorrow, next month, next year…is she in it? Does the thought of her not being in your life in a day, a week, a year, or a decade make your stomach hurt? Does it make you feel all panicky? If it does, then you love her."

"Then what?"

He grins. "Then what? Son, that's the good stuff. *Then what* is putting your lives together. Leaving behind who you were and figuring out how to be you and her. How to be the man she sees when she looks at you. Because, Rush, when the women who love us look at us fucked up, fight-or-flight, never-show-weakness warriors, they see the real us. The us we don't see. They're not seeing potential, they're not seeing who we *could* be and trying to make us into someone we're not, they're seeing who we really are, who we *should* be. Our job is to take all that effort we spent defending our hearts and being the being goddamn soldier we could be, and put it into being that man. *Her* man. The man she sees. Because son, I guaran-fucking-tee you, that man is infinitely better than who we would be otherwise, without her."

The man's a font of wisdom, too?

"Is there anything you're not good at?" I ask, shaking my head.

"Cooking. Sewing on buttons. Knowing when to stop. Basketball."

"That's funny, though, coz I'm a proper killer on the court."

He grins. "Well, then, I'd like to see you and Killy go one-on-one. That kid's a sniper from the outside."

"I'm an inside bloke. Can't hit shit but bricks from beyond the free throw line, but put me in the paint and let me cook, bruv."

"Look forward to it," Harris says, and somehow, I realize he's not kidding or blowing sunshine up my ass.

I've been pulled in, it looks like. And again, I'm not sure how to categorize the feeling that knowledge puts inside me, other than warm, weird, shaky, and… addictive.

We put down for a landing at the Austin airport, taxiing to the business aviation area. There's yet another parade of black SUVs, but these are definitely not your run-of-the-mill government issue Suburbans. Even as I descend the ramp and approach one, I can tell it's been heavily modified.

I'm stood there trying to sort out what's been done to them when the sun is blotted out by a mobile cliff on my right.

I turn, wondering if the jet rolled backward or something, and instead encounter the most enormous human being I've ever seen. Seven feet tall if he's an inch and built like Arnie in his prime…and this man's pushing sixty if not beyond it. Blond hair gone half silver, cropped close on the sides and messy on top, a trim beard squaring off a hard jaw.

"So you're Rush." His voice is as deep as you'd expect, rough and hard and curious.

"You must be Thresh," I say.

He just nods. "You here for a good time or a long time?"

"Um. Sorry, mate, but what?"

"Brynnie."

"Oh. Hopefully a good long time."

He grins. A massive, heavy, cinderblock hand crashed down on my shoulder with casual power that makes me realize this fella's as much stronger than me as I am your average doughy, pencil-pusher type. "Good answer, kid." He glances down at me. "We're gonna get her. Nobody fucks with us."

"Think I'm workin' that one out on my own, mate," I say. "Not sure these wanna-be warlords know what they've bitten into."

"No. They don't."

"But that said, it don't do to underestimate Pugli. I've done work for him for a couple years now. He's a canny, cunning, unpredictable fuck. We've got to assume we're walking into a trap."

Thresh nods. "Rule number one of hostage extraction is always assume everything is an ambush."

The telltale scent of cigar smoke wafts across my

nostrils, and I glance to my right—the man who is suddenly there is quite short but as broad as he is tall, with shoulders so broad you could land a Harrier on each one. Arms near as big as Thresh's. His head's shaved to skin, and a long, thick black beard brushes his diaphragm—incongruously, there's a trio of clumsy braids woven into the beard down the center, the ends knotted with pink, purple, and baby-blue bows.

He's got a fat cigar clamped between his jaws on one side, acrid smoke curling upward, small, deep, dark, wickedly intelligent eyes scrutinizing me. "I'm Puck."

"Rush," I answer. I extend my hand to him.

He takes it in his and crushes mine, a smirk on his mouth. I notice he's missing the tip of a finger—same finger of the same hand as Bryn is now missing. I indicate the finger in question. "You and Bryn have matching missing fingertips."

Puck plucks the cigar from his jaws and taps it with his missing fingertip-hand. "That a fact?"

I nod. "Lost it in the firefight right before she got taken."

"How'd she handle it?" he asks.

I shrug. "Pissily."

This gets me another smirk. "Thatta girl." He eyes me, popping the cigar stump back into the corner of his mouth, on the opposite side, now. "Dyin' to ask, ain'tcha, bub?" He strokes his beard, fingering the incongruous bows.

I nod, biting down on my tongue to keep from letting out a comment about him being a Walmart Wolverine. "Bit out of place, is all."

"Granddaughter wants to braid Papa's beard, granddaughter braids Papa's beard," Puck answers, shrugging. He shows me his other hand, which features fingernails messily painted—respectively from thumb to pinky—red, orange, yellow, green, blue, and indigo. "She was mighty annoyed I didn't have a sixth finger to make it a full rainbow."

"You have a granddaughter?" I ask.

He nods. "Colbie and I's daughter had a little oops when she was sixteen. We take care of the li'l stinker while her mama finishes her degree."

I think back to conversations Bryn and I had, and what I know from media coverage of the A1S guys. "Didn't know you and Colbie had a granddaughter."

Puck nods. "Chloe's seven." A blinking, thoughtful expression. He eyes me. "Internet stalking us, are you?"

I snort, shake my head. "Nah. Talked to Bryn a good bit. Done a fair whack of traveling since I ran into her, and not much to do but talk."

Puck snorts. "Ran into her? Is that what you're callin' it, bub?" A rough bark of sarcastic laughter. "Whatever helps you sleep at night."

"Puck," Harris snaps from the SUV trunk he's loading gear bags into, not looking up. "Belay that shit."

"Sir." This is accompanied by a sarcastic little salute.

"It's fine," I say. "Can't exactly say I don't deserve it."

Puck smacks my shoulder. "That's the spirit, kid. If you own your shit, folks aren't as likely to try an' hold it against you. And I dunno about you, but I don't like shit being held against me. It stinks."

I snicker a laugh at that. "Right you are there, mate."

A man I can only describe as nondescript approaches from…somewhere. "Unassuming" also comes to mind. Medium height, medium build, brown hair, brown eyes. Nothing about him screams operator or badass extraordinaire, but I know this man is Anselm, one of the deadliest men on the planet—past, present, or future.

He extends a hand to me. "I am Anselm."

"Rush."

Anselm grins at me. "We like to call him Grampy, now." He points at Puck. Puck's eyes narrow at me. "Don't even think about it, kid."

I chuckle. "Warning heeded. I like my insides on the inside, after all, don't I?"

Puck nods, expression serious. "Good plan, kid."

A thick, heavy, hard hand rests on my shoulder like an anvil. "Don't listen to Grampy, kid. He was just born salty."

I look at the owner of the hand—Duke Silver. Two inches taller than me and carrying something like twenty-five pounds of muscle more than me. And I'm not small. Red hair with streaks of silver at the temples and along the hairline, buzzed close on the sides and longish messy on top.

He grins at me. "Welcome to the club."

"Which club is it I'm in?" I ask.

He gestures at the men around us. "This one. We've all been where you are right now—rescuing a beautiful woman from a complicated and dangerous situation, and tryin' to figure out how we feel."

"Oh." I let out a breath. "Quite a club. I'm alright

with the rescue part—done more than a few hostage rescues with the service, but the feelings bit is a whole other thing."

Duke nods, clapping me on the shoulder; again, it's like having an anvil give me friendly crushing; as I've said, I'm not a small man nor a weak one, but these blokes are just built different. "Feelings are tricky little fuckers, bud. The more you try an' ignore 'em, the more insistent they are."

"Tricky little fuckers, indeed," I echo, getting weirded out by the immediate familiarity with which these men are treating me.

Puck puffs on his cigar and then plucks it from his jaw, rests a hand on Thresh's mammoth arm to balance himself while he stubs it out on the heel of his well-worn combat boot, and then pops it back in his mouth, unlit. "He's still in the denial phase, Dukey-Doo. You can tell he's scared shitless of the weird, squishy feelings." He strides toward the SUV nearest us. "Let's go, young blood. Assholes don't kill themselves."

Duke stares after his friend with a pissed off expression darkening his features. "Little fucker. Told him a billion times to stop calling me that."

"It's Puck, bro," Thresh rumbles. "Listening is not one of his top attributes."

"I ain't afraid of the weird, squishy feelings," I mutter. "It's just new. And weird. And squishy."

Duke laughs at this. "Can't fight it, kid." He gives me a playful shove toward the SUV. "She forgive you?"

"Yeah."

"Then you're fucked." He grins at me. "May as well just accept your fate as a kept man, now, kid."

I climb into the third row to make room for the two massive bodies that are Thresh and Duke; Thresh, in particular, has to hunker down with hunched shoulders and a ducked head, even with his knees drawn up like a grown man sitting in one of those little kid seats at the library. Puck is driving, Harris is in the front seat next to Puck, and Anselm is in back with me; the RMI guys take up the rest of the SUVs, behind ours.

"How'm I fucked?" I ask.

Duke just laughs. "Bro, c'mon. You tricked, lied, and manipulated her into the hands of a notorious trafficker in all things nefarious. A woman isn't going to just forgive that unless she's in love with you. Not even Bryn."

"Whassat mean, not even Bryn?"

"Oh, well, she's just…she burns hot, temperamentally. Gets pissed off easily, but forgives and forgets just as easily. Like her mama. You just don't want to get on her bad side, because if you do manage that, she won't ever forget." Duke rolls a shoulder. "Bryn is super understanding, kid. Open-minded. Caring. But not especially given to handing out her heart. She's never brought a guy around, except Zero."

The Suburban goes quiet, then.

"R-I-P, Zero," Puck says. "You were a one-of-a-kind weirdo."

"She hasn't said much about him," I say. "Just that he died in a car accident not long before the wedding."

Harris sighs. "It's hard for her to talk about. He's

hard for her to talk about. We all got worried about her when that happened. She'd lived a pretty damn charmed life till then. Zero was…" he sighs again, shakes his head. "He was cool. I don't say that lightly. He just had this way of…I dunno."

"You wanted to hang out with him," Duke says. "He was one of those people that just has music inside them. It was as much a part of him as his name or his hands or whatever. He could play just about anything. Just pick it up and play, whatever it was."]

"Took some of us a bit to accept him for her," Puck says. "He was fuckin' weird. Goofy. Unpredictable. Fuckin'…*zany*. But yeah, he was the epitome of effortlessly cool. She loved the shit outta that boy. She was damn near ruined when he died. Didn't smile for months."

"Layla had to physically drag her out of bed and force her to shower and eat," Harris answers, his voice heavy with memory. "We forced her to talk to a therapist. She hated us for that, but when she realized it was helping, she threw herself into it."

"That and training," Duke says. "She must've spent hundreds of hours at the range, practicing room clearing, sparring, stripping weapons, and all that shit."

"She's like both of us in that sense," Harris answers. "Needs to stay busy to cope. She was happy as a clam touring with Zero, acting as his manager and assistant, making his life easier so he could focus on music. When that ended, she didn't know who she was or what she wanted anymore."

"I think she's found it," I say.

Harris turns to look at me. "Meaning?"

I gesture at the occupants of the Suburban. "This. The family business. I say this as an operator, not someone who's got feelings for her—she's a goddamned bloody natural at this shit. Cool under fire. Doesn't hesitate—except that once, and we all know how that goes. She does what needs doing, learns fast, and listens. Her aim is fuckin' spec*ta*cular."

Harris thuds his head against the headrest. "Wonderful."

I laugh. "Not happy with that news, ey?"

He rolls his head against the headrest. "Would you want your daughter to follow in your footsteps?"

I consider that. "Fuck no."

"Exactly."

"You have men watching them, yeah?" I ask. "My girl and her grandparents."

"Six of them. The house is being renovated after what happened, so Val sent them to Disney World. Private jet, armed escort, line passes, the works."

I lean forward. "Wait, what?"

He snorts. "Oh, I must've forgotten that part. My bad."

I rest my face in my hands. "I had plans of taking her to Disney World after her treatment." I savagely suppress my disappointment. "Glad she's getting to go, though, even if it's not with me. God, I've got a lot to thank Mr. Roth for, don't I?"

"Son." Harris's voice is surprisingly gentle. "After her treatment, you're gonna wanna take her home and baby her like a princess. Not traipse around that place."

"That place, is it?" I ask. "Not a fan?"

He tips his head to the side. "Eh, not really, personally, but the kids love it. She'll have a blast. Go right to the front of every ride, eat all the terrible shit there is to eat, meet all the characters. Good for her grandparents, too. That shit was scary for them, too, y'know. When it's your time with your girl, please trust me when I tell you that you want it to be simple, easy, and stress-free. And as the adult, Disney World ain't that."

"Oh."

The question that repeats in my head the rest of the drive, though, has nothing to do with Disney World, though.

It's much simpler: Where is home?

I've dozed off, apparently. I blink awake as the Suburban pulls into the parking lot of a deserted strip mall—there's a smoke shop, a Thai food place, a chemist—which apparently the Yanks call a drug store—and a resale shop. There are only a handful of other cars in the lot, making me wonder if these businesses are even still open. Puck pulls around the back of the lot, passing trash bins and employee cars on the right, a brick retaining wall on the left anchoring a steep hill sparsely dotted with short pines and low shrubs. It looks hot outside.

There are a pair of top-end G-Wagens parked nose-to-tail near the middle of the back lot. As our parade of SUVs approaches, the two vehicles disgorge seven men, who, speaking in strictly professional capacity, are each more improbably more impressive than the last, regardless of which order you look at them in. They're massive blokes, hard, capable, and confident. Operators, like myself, and the men with me.

A minute later, we're standing in a lopsided oval—the Original Six Alpha One men, myself, the seven surviving RMI operatives, and the seven new guys. Fourteen hard men, all pissed off and ready to eat lead and shit gravestones.

"Right, intros," Harris says, taking the lead. "I'm Harris." He points at each of us in turn. "Duke, Puck, Thresh, Anselm, and Rush. Chico? Your guys?"

Chico jerks his thumb at himself. "I am Chico." Like Harris, he points at each man as he names him. "Tony, Ulrich, U-Boat, Larson, Epson, and Stinky."

The one named Stinky is a tall man, closer in age to the A1S blokes, with silvering brown hair and a short beard. "Ask me why they call me Stinky, and I'll fuckin' shoot your ass."

No one says a word in response—we all know how military nicknames get attached to you. And pro tip, it ain't because you did something badass. I just got lucky because my name *is* a cool handle. No stupid nickname to make me remember my worst moment.

Harris juts his chin at the new guys. "Solomon?"

A tall, trim, Robert Redford-looking bloke answers. "Right. I'm Solomon. We're the Broken Arrows. This is Rev, Chance, Kane, Lash, my brother Saxon, and my other brother Silas."

Rev is brown-skinned with a wide, black mohawk

of tightly-curled hair. Chance is nearly as big as Thresh, Hawaiian or Polynesian or something, based on the tattoos I can see, though I could be wrong. Kane is six feet even with a bodybuilder's physique, a blond beard, and a black ballcap. Lash is shorter, like Puck, and similarly built—wide, broad, and dense, with short black hair and a neat beard; ethnically, I can't place him, as his brown skin and black hair could mean anything. The brothers are all very similar—over six feet, lean and hard and muscular, the sort of blokes you'd see playing the dashing hero in a Hollywood shoot-em-up flick with big explosions and lots of slow-mo running from said explosions. Solomon has copper hair, the other two are golden boys.

Harris consults a tablet device. "Right. Now we know our names. Sol, last intel we had put Bryn not far outside Austin, in motion. We know Pugli is here, and we know Mercado is…somewhere, but his men are Stateside."

Solomon nods. "We have several objectives. One, rescue Bryn Harris. Second, find Lorenzo. Third, find Inez. It's likely they're together, and if they are, they'll be going after Mercado. Fourth, find Beatriz and Little Ren." He has a tablet as well, which he spends a moment tapping and swiping on—a second later, Harris's tablet dings, as does Chico's. "That's what we know. Lorenzo was with Beatriz and Little Ren in a safehouse in Houston. That got hit, and Inez tracked them to *another* safehouse in Austin, which was hit as well by Mercado's men."

"Shit." Harris hisses a sigh. "Lear just updated

me—Bryn's location stopped for a few moments on a highway not twenty minutes from here, and then kept going southwest, roughly in the direction of the border."

"Well, then, let's fuckin' go," Puck says. "We can share intel over the comms."

"Hold up, though," Harris says. "Who are Beatriz, Ren, and Lorenzo?"

"Oh," Sol says. "Right, forgot you don't know. So, Inez is Mercado's ex. Well, technically they're still married, but she's out for his blood. Little Ren is their child, who Inez stole from Mercado after his birth. She hid him with a woman in Colombia named Beatriz, who raised him as her son. Little Ren doesn't know who his father is, or that Beatriz isn't his mother. Mercado needs an heir to take over the throne of his narco empire, and he wants Little Ren. Lorenzo is Inez's…umm…" he glances at his mates. "Former lover, I guess? An old flame. He's an operator, too, and a damn good one. He was taking care of Beatriz and Little Ren while Inez tried to take out Mercado on her own, but it seems like Mercado got them first. We haven't heard from him since the hit on the safehouse in Austin, and we're worried about him. His body wasn't there, and if they'd killed him, it would be, so we're reasonably sure he's alive. We also don't know where Inez is, but she's…well, she's our boss. Our leader. And our friend. She wanted to handle Mercado on her own, but we decided to ignore that order. She didn't leave us to handle our shit alone, and we're not about to leave her to handle hers alone, either. Even if she *is* who the boogeyman has nightmares about."

Chico is frowning. "The wife of Mercado? You mean Sophia de Silva?"

Sol's gaze snaps to Chico's. "Yes. You know her?"

"Do I *know* her? No. Do I know *of* her? Sí. Before Raze hires me, I work for the Tri-National Anti-Gang Task Force to fight human trafficking. I make enemies of Mercado's men. They kidnap my wife. I make them talk before I kill them very slow." He spits on the ground. "This was many years ago, when I was a very young man. They speak of Sophia de Silva with…" he trails off, hunting for words. "Reverence, I think you say. And much fear."

Solomon nods. "That's her."

"She is no longer cartel?"

"Nope."

Chico's grin is wicked. "May god have mercy on Mercado, in that case, for what I have heard of Sophia de Silva tells me that she will not."

"No," Solomon answers, his voice hard. "She will not. And neither will we."

Harris clears his throat. "Excellent. We've cleared that up. I want my daughter back. Let's fucking go, already."

17

HERE WE FUCKING GO. AGAIN.

Ren moans now and then, muttering to himself in Spanish. A lot of the murmurings contain "mamá" however, so I can imagine the kinds of things he's saying. God, the poor, poor boy. Kidnapped, carted who knows where by these monsters, and then his mom is murdered in front of him. I can't help but cry for him—and stew in my rage.

After an endless hell of heat, thirst, sweat, and the hum of the road beneath us, the car stops. I hear muffled voices—I can't make out what they're saying.

The hatch opens, and blinding light sears my eyes—I squint, shielding my face with my hands.

"Out," Anatoly says. "No stupid stuff. Let's go." He grabs my arm and yanks.

I stumble, and something inside me snaps. I yank my arm free and kick him in the nuts as hard as I can. "Do *not* fucking touch me, you piece of shit fucking *cock*roach," I snarl. "I was just in the trunk of a car for who knows how fucking long, so how about you give me a goddamn second, asshole?"

He whimpers, dropping to his knees. I see Pugli a few feet away, pistol in hand, waiting for me to make a further move. I glare at him. "You need to hire better help, dude." I indicate Anatoly. "This cocksucker isn't worth whatever it is you're paying him."

Pugli sighs. "Don't I know it. But it really is impossible to find good, trustworthy help, these days."

"You know, it's really not?" I answer, making my voice sweet. "I think it's just you."

"Charming." He gestures with his pistol, and I realize we've come to a motel—an off-brand, just-off-the-freeway shithole. "Inside."

It's evening, the sun red and huge and hot as it rests on the flat, endless horizon. The room is standard motel fare—two small beds with cheap, scratchy linens, filthy carpet, popcorn ceilings, a thirty-year-old TV, and a tiny bathroom.

Pugli stands in the middle of the room, looking around in palpable disgust. "What a shockingly vile place."

I snicker. "Not up to my standards, either, Bobby-boy. Couldn't afford anything better, huh?"

He whirls on me, face a rictus of rage. "You *will* stop calling me that infernal name. Mercado doesn't much care about what happens to you anymore—your utility to me now rests upon your ability to keep that brat quiet and compliant." He stalks over to me, gun in hand. "I am a patient man. I have no issue waiting as long as necessary to see you properly punished for your impudence."

I grin at him, a grin I do not feel. "Too bad you won't live that long."

"So you think. But we have surprises in store for your friends, my dear girl. While you were enjoying your stay in the trunk of my car, Mercado and I were planning."

"You mean your new daddy was telling you how it'd go," I say.

He hisses. "My god, the mouth on you, girl." He slaps me, hard—an open-hand slap. It stings like a bitch of course, but I've done full-contact, no-gear sparring sessions with my various uncles, so I can take a man's punch and stay on my feet. His little bitch-slap barely fazes me.

"You'd better learn to curb your tongue, girl. You really do not want to provoke me." He slips a hand into his pocket and flicks open a long folding knife, pressing the flat of it against my mouth, the razor-sharp blade biting into my lips. "The next time you speak out of turn, I'll cut your tongue out."

A small hand tugs on mine. "Bryn? *Cállate. Por favor.*" I hold still until Pugli removes his knife. "Listen to the boy, Bryn. Shut up. I've tolerated your nasty invective for far longer than I'm accustomed to, and I am swiftly running out of patience."

He paces away to the window, gazing out with distaste. The door creaks open on protesting hinges and Anatoly limps in, hate burning in his eyes. He drags himself to me, hauling out his pistol and pressing it to my temple.

"Anatoly," Pugli snaps. "Put that away, you fool."

The hate in Anatoly's eyes doesn't dissipate when he regards Pugli with a baleful glare. "I have had enough of this bitch. Control her or I will."

I snicker at this. "Okay, then, shit-fucker. You don't control anyone. Fuck off."

The gun presses harder into my temple, and I lean into him, nose to nose, his foul breath huffing against me. "Pugli doesn't pay me enough to deal with you, bitch."

"Pull the trigger or fuck off, you slimy cock-stain," I snarl at him. "Your breath will kill me if you don't."

Pugli physically drags Anatoly away from me, shoving him across the room to the door. "Go find us food. Preferably something more palatable than the dog food served at American fast food establishments."

Grumbling under his breath in his native language, Anatoly limps out.

Pugli watches him leave and then sits on the edge of the bed, his posture stiff and perfect as he stares at me, slightly shaking his head. "Your sense of self-preservation is massively atrophied, Miss Harris," Pugli says to me. "Push that man any further and his reaction will be beyond my ability to curtail."

"Thanks for the warning, Señor Thesaurus."

Another shake of his head. "You weren't beaten enough as a child and it shows."

"You weren't hugged enough as a child and it shows," I retort.

Renihno tugs on my hand again. I look down at him and he gestures at the bathroom. I walk him that way, but I'm stopped by Pugli's voice.

"I am aware of the window in that bathroom, Miss Harris. You won't get far with a child in tow, and if you attempt to escape, I'll let Anatoly have his way with you while the child watches."

"Yes, I'm aware of your obsession with making people watch horrible things." I flip him off. "Fuck you."

His growl is nearing irate. "Miss Harris, this is your last warning. Your utility is limited."

"And you have no utility, so I'm ahead of you." I flip him off.

God, I really am an idiot. Pissing off these awful, evil, violent, horrible men is a terribly moronic idea. Yet I just can't seem to stop my mouth from running away from my brain.

I take Renihno to the bathroom and turn away to give the boy privacy. He pees for longer than I'd have thought possible for a body as small as his.

He washes his hands, dries them, and then looks up at me with large, tearful brown eyes. "*Mamá esta muerta?*"

I'm familiar enough with classroom Spanish to know what he's asking. I crouch in front of him and take his hands. Hold his eyes. "Yes, your mama is dead."

"*Por qué la mató?*" he asks.

"Why…?" I shake my head. "You're at the limit of my Spanish, kid."

He stares at me. Looks at the door, points. "*El hombre malo…*"

"The bad man?"=

"Sí. The bad man." He makes a finger gun and points at the ground, and makes a soft explosion sound with his mouth. "*Por qué? Mi Mama es buena.*"

My eyes burn. "Oh. Why did he kill her?" =

"*Sí. No se por qué. Mi Mama es buena. Fui malo?*" His voice cracks at the end.

I gather him against my chest in a hug. "No, Ren. It's not your fault. Esta no…tu…um…problema?"

He manages a tiny quirk of his lips at my godawful Spanish. "*No es tu culpa. No es mi culpa.*"

"*Sí,*" I whisper. "*No es tu culpa,* Ren. *El es malo.* That's the only reason. *El es muy, muy malo.*"

A fist pounds on the door. "That's enough. Come out."

"Come on, then." I stand up and take his hand.

We enter the room, and Ren goes immediately to the empty bed nearest the bathroom, curls up on the edge of it, and closes his eyes.

I lounge on the bed next to him, considering my options for getting out of this mess. Number one, I need to learn how to bite my tongue. Between Pugli and Anatoly, I'm going to piss one of them off and get myself shot. The problem here is that controlling my sass has proven, thus far in my life, to be impossible.

Second, I need a plan for what to do once Ren and I are away from these fuckers—killing Anatoly and Pugli will be the easy part. It's the "what then" that's the sticking point—this Mercado guy has Pugli nervous, at very least. Wary, perhaps, is a better word. I'm not sure Pugli is necessarily *scared* of him, exactly, but he's definitely got a healthy respect for him.

Which means I should be terrified. Pugli is the Devil incarnate. In which case, there's a level of evil beyond the devil, and that's where Mercado lives.

Which means, assuming I can kill Anatoly *and* Pugli, I still have to keep us out of Mercado's clutches. With a terrified, traumatized child in tow, with whom there's a bit of a language barrier going on.

Working in my favor, however, is the fact that A1S is on the case. Rush is on the case. They're looking for me, at least. I don't know who this kid is or why he's suddenly so important to Mercado, but I have to imagine if he's involved, people are looking for him. Hopefully, good people who are dangerous to these very bad people.

My fury is a simmer, bubbling away just beneath the surface, hot and full of seething violence and ready to boil over at any moment. I have to wait. I have to bide my time. I have to keep my fury banked until the moment is right.

Which means I have to stop baiting Pugli.

And then…an idea occurs to me.

A very bad idea.]

But I'm far, far too impatient and reckless to sit around and wait to be rescued.

Anatoly returns a while later with two large brown paper bags filled with white Styrofoam clamshells which contain a variety of Tex-Mex dishes. Pugli selects what he wants first, and then Anatoly, leaving Ren and me what's left. Which is fine—there's a chicken quesadilla with beans and rice and a giant burrito, also with a side of beans and rice. Ren takes the quesadilla and nibbles at it, making the occasional face, muttering to himself in Spanish. I hear the words "Mamá and "Comida." Mama's food was better, or something like that.

No shit, kid. Tex-Mex from a crappy restaurant in the middle of nowhere can't touch a Hispanic Mama's home cooking.

So far, Pugli has claimed one bed, leaving the other for Ren and me, while Anatoly eats at the small desk in the corner by the window. Once he's done eating, Anatoly stands at the foot of the bed Ren and I are on, the TV remote in his hands.

Here we go.

"Move, bitch."

I can't help it. "Get out the way, get out the way… move, bitch," I chant, finishing the line from the song.

He blinks at me, confused. "Shut the fuck up, bitch, and get off the bed. Is mine. The little shit, too."

Pugli ignores this exchange, although I note his gaze flicking to us briefly before returning to his phone.

"You know," I say, "You keep calling me a bitch like it's the worst thing you can think of. What's funny about that is I really *am* a bitch and I know it. So, do you think you can come up with a different insult? Or is that too taxing for your pathetic little squirrel brain?"

Out comes the gun, as expected. He braces his hand on the edge of the bed and levels the gun at my knee. "I will call you bitch or anything I like and you will shut the fuck up about it, *whore*."

I do a mocking little series of claps. "Good *boy*! You learned a new word! Can you spell it with me? W...H...O...R...E. Whore!"

Anatoly's eye legit twitches. "That is it. You learn a lesson now, stupid American whore." I shove Ren unceremoniously off the bed as Anatoly lunges for me, grabbing my ankle and hauling me toward himself with the gun pointed in my general direction.

Cue the pain, dumbfuck.

My hands are still bound, but I'm a woman: my real physical strength is in my legs, and a lot of my self-defense lessons have been focused on situations exactly like this, where my hands are bound and I have to perpetrate violence on assholes.

I curl my body in on itself, yanking Anatoly toward me by his grip on my ankle. He topples forward, off-balance, gun-hand smacking into the mattress to catch himself; I kick him as hard as I can, square in the nose with my other foot as his momentum carries him forward. His nose crunches with a beautifully brutal crack of cartilage, loosing a curtain of blood and ripping a howl of shocked pain from Anatoly.

He braces himself with his gun-hand and puts his other to his nose—perhaps five seconds have elapsed. Pugli's attention is just starting to cut to us, his mouth opening to settle our squabble as if we're recalcitrant children on a road trip: *Now, now, kids, don't fight or I'll turn this car around.*

I hook my legs around Anatoly's neck, bracing one

thigh against his torso for leverage. I roll hard against the leverage point, and I'm rewarded by the loud, sickening crack of his neck snapping. I already have his gun in my hand, Anatoly's now-dead body locked between my thighs. We're only a handful of feet apart, but Pugli is moving, rolling off the bed as he recognizes what's happening—there's no chance of a headshot, so I pop off a quick pair of shots at his torso.

I fucking hit the bastard, dammit, square over the heart—I know my aim is dead-on at this range. But there's no blood—just the flutter of his suit jacket and shirt as the bullets strike…revealing the black of a bullet-resistant vest underneath.

Dammit—Rush did the same thing. I should've remembered, should've gone for the headshot.

Pugli hits the ground groaning. I wish to god my hands weren't bound. Anatoly left the key fob for the Range Rover on the desk by the door—I shove the gun in my hip pocket, scoop Ren off the floor with my bound hands, and drag him to the exit. He finds his feet and scrambles into a run, leaving my hands free to grab the keys.

Pugli is on the floor, gasping for breath, eyes wide with pain, panic, and rage. Ren has the door open for me, and we rush outside into the hot black night. An amber lamp flickers at one edge of the motel's parking lot, casting short, stuttering shadows. Despite the gunshots, no one has come to investigate. Lovely.

I bolt for the driver's door, transferring the keyring to my teeth so I have my bound hands free for the door handle. Yank it open, physically hurling Ren in;

the boy wastes no time scrabbling over the console to the passenger seat as I throw myself in after him. The gun topples out of my pocket and wedges between my hip and the console—stupid girl jeans with these stupid, useless tiny pockets. If I were a dude wearing dude jeans, I could fit a whole-ass AK-47 in my hip pocket, and maybe an extra mag or two. Girl jeans? You can barely fit a fucking key fob.

I stab the ignition button and the engine catches with a powerful snarl; I yank the shifter toward myself into Drive, thanking stupid dead Anatoly for being one of those pretentious jackasses who back into every parking spot just to show off. It means I can floor the accelerator and haul ass out of the parking lot just as Pugli staggers out of the hotel room, blasting shots after us. One shatters the rear window, the round thunking into the ceiling. Another thuds into the back of the passenger seat headrest, and a third slugs into the dashboard in front of the passenger seat—good thing Ren is a smart boy, having curled his tiny body down inside the footwell the moment the rear window shattered.

Driving with your hands bound is tricky, it turns out, something that probably should be covered by training. I'm all over the place as I wrench the wheel around to get the big, heavy, powerful SUV onto the road—we go flying as I launch over a curb, tires barking as they catch pavement, the body rolling precariously. Ren chatters in scared, panicked Spanish. I have to ignore him for now, though. Just drive. I get the heavy, powerful Range Rover under control, gunning it for the freeway. I have no doubt Pugli can track this thing—if this Connor dude is even half as skilled as Uncle Lear, following my getaway will be child's play. I just have to stay free and find a way to contact my family.

By sheer accidental luck, I took the ramp going north, so at least I'm going away from Pugli and, I assume, Mercado. And hopefully toward Dad and Rush.

God, I miss Rush.

I shouldn't. I should still be mad. Shit, more than mad. But I'm not. I understand why he did what he did. I can't say I blame him—I can't say I wouldn't make the same decision in his shoes. Hell, the kid down in that footwell isn't even mine—I just met him a few hours ago—but I'd do what I have to do to protect him. I dunno if I'd sell someone into sexual slavery, but if he was my son? I can't say I wouldn't.

Looking back, I can see the moments he fought himself, the times he had second thoughts, the times he hated himself for what he was doing.

Ren pokes his head up after several minutes have elapsed with no further gunfire; I smile at him and pat the seat. He climbs up and sits, dutifully clicking the seatbelt across his lap; it's too high, the strap going across his neck. I can't do anything about that while driving ninety on the freeway with my hands bound, though. That said, I do slow to posted limits, because I'm not sure how I'd explain…well, anything to do with this whole situation if I were to get pulled over—I remember Rush's lessons on the subject, also.

The buffeting of the wind through the shattered hatch precludes conversation, even if Ren and I were able to communicate beyond simple phrases.

He looks at me with a curious expression. "*El hombre malo esta muerto?*"

I nod. "*Sí. Muerto.*"

He looks forward again for a moment or two, and then back at me. "*Te sientes mal por ello?*"

"Um?" I shrug at him. "No comprende, buddy."

He frowns, thinking hard. "*El hombre malo.* Tu…" he wrenches his neck to the side with a click of his tongue, eyes rolled back in his head, tongue sticking out in a freakily accurate miming of Anatoly's neck snapping.

"Sí," I answer. "I killed him."

"You…not…" he trails his finger down his cheeks.

"Oh!" I say, putting it together. "No, I don't feel bad for killing Anatoly."

"*El gran hombre malo no esta muerto.*"

"El gran…" I echo. "Oh. The big bad man. Pugli."

"Sí. Pugli." He mimes shooting, the way Pugli shot his mother.

"No, he isn't dead."

"*Pero…pero le disparaste.*"

"Pero…but…" I shake my head. "I don't know *le disparaste.*"

He mimes shooting again, twice.

"Oh, yeah. Yes, I shot Pugli." I thump my chest. "He had on a vest."

Ren looks confused. I thump my chest again, driving with my knee briefly, touching my fingers to my chest, and then exploding them away with a "ping!" sound. He only looks more confused. Shit. How do you explain what a bullet-resistant vest is to a kid who doesn't speak your language?

I mime the same thing again. "I shot him, but he's no muerto."

Ren seems frustrated by the exchange and just shrugs. "*El hombre grande y malo le disparó a mi mamá. Debería morir.*"

"Yeah, I didn't follow any of that. Sorry, kid. You got stuck with the one person in this whole fuckin' shitshow who doesn't speak forty-two languages fluently. Sorry about that luck, kiddo."

He says something back, his Spanish so fast it becomes obvious he's been slowing way down for my benefit. He sounds…angry. His brown eyes blaze, and he stabs the air, slams his fist on the dash, tears gathering. I give him a sympathetic look. "Let it all out, kiddo. You've got every right to be mad as hell."

More machine gun-fast Spanish, the tears falling now, stumbling over his words, stuttering, punching the dashboard.

"I know, buddy. It's not fucking fair. I don't know who you are that this Mercado monster wants you so bad—you're just a kid. His kid, maybe?" I look at him. "*Tu padre?*"

He just shrugs. "No se."

"Well, then either you're *not* his kid and there's something else fucky going on, or you *are* his kid and you don't know. I wonder if your mama knew." I sigh. "No matter. Not like she can tell us, now, huh?" Ren draws his knees up to his chest and stares out the window. I wish I could comfort him, but…how? Even if I spoke perfect Spanish and we weren't fleeing for our lives from not one but two deadly foes, what do you say? The kid watched someone blow his mother's brains out in front of him. What do you say to that? How do you comfort that?

I drive until my eyes cross. Ren fell asleep at some point. I need to pee, I'm thirsty, I'm hungry, and we're running out of gas—the tank was less than half when we got in, and these big Range Rovers are thirsty.

I have no money. No cell phone. My hands are bound by law enforcement-grade zip ties that make me look like an escaped convict or something, and I'm driving a stolen car with a shot-out window. Well, wait—do I have the cash I stuffed in my bra back in… Europe somewhere? I drive with my knee and pat my boobs—no. Must have fallen out one of the times Rush and I got busy. Ugh. I mean, it was euros, so it's not like a random gas station in Buttfuck, Texas would've accepted it anyway.

Fuck. So what do I do? Ask for help? Go to a police station? I don't trust that someone as connected to law enforcement as Pugli can't easily buy the services of the local sheriff's department. Or Mercado, for that matter, especially this close to the boarder—guys like that tend to have their fingers up the assholes of cops and politicians everywhere around here. Likely as not, I'd go to a cop for help and get locked up until Mercado or Pugli show up and plug me right there in the cell.

So no, I can't risk that.

The car dings at me, alerting me that our fuel level is low. It'd be stupid to let this thing die on the side of the freeway, though. Might as well put a big flashing neon arrow over my head as do that. So, off the freeway we go and into the pitch-black void of the Texas night. The wind noise fades as I slow around the off-ramp and then stop at the two-way intersection. To the left, I see the orange glow of a Shell Station sign, a Taco Bell, and a few other places now closed for the night. I have no confidence that I'm doing the right thing, but what else can I do? I have no idea where to go or what to do, I just know I can't risk the Range Rover dying on the side of the freeway—the pursuit I know for a fact is after us will see us and it'll be over that much faster.

I head for the Shell station and pull up to a pump. Ren wakes up, looks around, sleepy and confused, but follows me inside without a word.

The person behind the counter is a young dude, a few years younger than me, bored-looking, wearing a battered camo hat with a plug of chewing tobacco bulging his bottom lip. He has his phone propped up on the counter next to his cowboy-booted feet. When we enter, he glances at us but doesn't otherwise move or greet us.

When I stop at the counter, he deigns to look at me. "Help ya'll?" His thick Texas drawl makes it sound like *he'p yawwwwl*.

I hold up my bound hands. "My boyfriend and I got carried away, and then we got into a fight and…" I wince in what I hope looks like embarrassment. "Nowhere's open. I just need scissors or clippers or something. Can you help me out?"

His eyes narrow. "Lady, ain't no scissors in the world gonna cut them off ya'll. Them is *po*-lice ties.".

"There's an auto garage right there," I snap, my patience at an all-time low. "There's got to be wire cutters or something."

"Closed. Ain't got the key."

"Fuck, man." I lean forward. "Look. I'm in trouble. It's not the law, though, so it won't blow back on you. I just need help. Please."

His frown deepens. "Trouble is trouble, law or not. I don't want none of that. Buy something or get out."

"Goddammit," I hiss. "Fine. Have it your way."

Like an idiot, I left the gun in the car. So I march back out, grab it, and march back in. Point it at him. "Now you've got trouble with *me*. Find the fucking cutters, my dude. *Now*. Do *not* fucking test me."

His eyes fly wide. "Alright, alright, Jesus, lady. You on the rag or somethin'?"

Disbelief leaves me stunned for a solid ten seconds. "Are you stupid? You've got to be legitimately stupid to ask me that." I fire, putting a round into the counter near his foot—he jerks away, toppling backward out of his chair and hitting the ground in a tangled sprawl of limbs.

He comes up choking on his chew, gagging, staggering to his feet, bent over. He pukes brown tobacco juice everywhere. My stomach roils at the sight and scent of it.

"Fuck, lady," he rasps. "I was just fuckin' with you."

"Pro-tip, dumbass—don't *ever* ask *any* woman that question again. Especially not one who has a *fucking gun*." I flick the gun in the direction of the darkened auto garage. "Clippers. *Now*. I won't kill you unless you give me a reason, but I swear to fucking god, if you fuck with me, you'll regret it for the rest of your short, pathetic, stupid little life."

"I got it, I got it," he mutters.

He goes right in and flicks on a light—it wasn't even locked? My god. What an idiot. I'm sure Texas is filled with a lot of very smart people, but this kid ain't one of them.

He's gone for a few minutes, the sound of clanking tools echoing from the garage. He trots in, triumphantly wielding a massive pair of wire cutters, as in the type used for clipping through very large locks. But, they'll do the job.

I level the gun at him. "Cut 'em off. Try not to be stupid."

He wedges the mouth of the cutters sideways against my wrists, managing to snag one end of the tie with the jaws. Click—one hand is free. He repeats the action on the other side, and my hands are free.

He backs away, holding the cutters. "You know we got cameras, right? Cops are gonna find you."

"Cops are the least of my worries, kid." I sigh, annoyed. "Look, I don't want to do this, but I'm going to have to ask you to get us a few bottles of water and some protein bars or something."

"Just…don't shoot me, alright?" He holds up his hands, the cutters in one hand still. He sets them on the counter and then goes to the fridge case and gets two big bottles of water and a handful of protein bars.

"You need gas, too?" he asks. "Already shot up the place, held me at gunpoint, and robbed me. Might as well fill up the gas while you're at it." I gesture at him. "Good idea. Go to it."

He goes behind the counter, glances to see which pump I'm at, and does whatever he has to do to get the pump going. He's rounding the counter when headlights rake the windows, tires squealing.

He stops, frowning. "Um. Think you got company, lady. And it ain't the cops."

The words are barely out of his mouth when gunfire erupts, shattering the glass.

Here we fucking go.

Again.

18

A GOOD HURT

"Vehicle spotted on the shoulder," Chico says across the comms. "All stop."

Moments later, a couple RMI guys are checking out the truck stopped at an angle on the side of the highway. Chico glances at us through the windshield. "One occupant. He was shot in the torso. There is much blood—he drove away while bleeding. Passenger door is open, and there are footsteps in the dirt—it looks like a child and a woman, I think. The driver was shot in the head from close range."

Solomon's voice comes from the comms, next. "Let's check it out—this might be Beatriz and Little Ren. RMI, form a perimeter and watch our backs. Arrows, fan out and search the field. Harris, you wanna have your guys come with us?"

Harris's jaw ticks—I don't think he likes taking

orders from this Solomon fella. "Roger, copy you." To us, then. "You heard the man."

We pile out and adjust our gear, although I'm missing an important piece of kit for a night search. "Anyone got a spare torch?"

Puck eyes me. "Ain't the fuckin' Middle Ages, bub. No torches 'round here."

Thresh leans into the open hatch of the SUV, grabs something, and then tosses me a long, heavy, military grade torch. He glances at Puck in amusement, his gravelly voice shaking with laughter. "Dumbass. Like you ain't done your share of work with the Brits before." His tone goes mocking, imitating Puck's Southern American drawl. "'Ain't the Middle Ages, bub, no torches 'round these here parts.'"

Puck flips him off with his stubby middle finger. "Hey, Thresh, buddy, how about you dig a hole and go fuck yourself in it?"

"Cut the chatter, gentlemen," Harris says, his voice low and even and measured; despite that, both Puck and Thresh go tense.

"Sorry, Hare," Puck says. "You know we're focused."
"Yes. I know."

Harris strides out into the field beyond the road. "I'm just not in the mood for the bickering. Every second my daughter is in Pugli's hands is a second she's closer to…" he cuts off with a click of his jaws. "Just scan the fucking field, goddammit."

Puck and Thresh trade looks but say nothing. Everyone except four RMI guys, who stay back to keep watch, forms a search line. We scan the ground in front of us with our torches—flashlights, to the Yanks—looking for anything out of place.

We're maybe a hundred and fifty meters away from the shoulder when I hear a voice call out. "BODY HERE!"

Everyone converges on the other giant guy—Chase? Chance? Chance, I think. He looks godawful pissed. "Why?" His voice is low, shaky with fury. "The woman was innocent in all this. Why kill her?"

"Didn't need her," Duke murmurs. "If all they want is that boy, she's dead weight."

Chance exhales heavily. "Ain't leavin' the poor woman here to rot. She deserves better, even in death."

"Roger that," Chico says. "I have a contact near this place. He will come. Do you know her people?"

"I don't," Solomon answers, "But Inez does. Can you arrange for her to be prepped for burial?"

Chico tips his head to one side. "My friend is not one who buries the dead. He cleans up when those like us have made our messes. He can hold the body until your Inez can make arrangements, though."

Sol nods. "That works. He'll be paid."

Chico nods as well, already on his mobile and murmuring in rapid Spanish. A moment later, he hangs up, does something on his mobile, finishes, and pockets it. "He is coming. I pin him this location."

Harris's mobile rings, then. He answers it on the first ring. "Lear." A moment of listening, and then a hiss. "Fuck. Thanks. Send me the coordinates." We all look to him. "Bryn's stopped again, less than twenty minutes from here. We gotta haul ass. I have a bad feeling."

Sol nods. "Mount up! Let's Roll!"

This Solomon cat is a confident leader; even the A1S men snap to at the command, jogging toward the vehicles. Harris is already halfway there; he's behind the wheel by the time we reach the blacktop. Seconds later, we're squealing away, and Harris is driving with the needle buried in the ass-end of the speedo.

No one speaks.

We're on the highway for less than ten minutes before Harris pulls onto an exit ramp, tires squealing and smoking as he drifts around the long curve, the big Suburban leaning heavily to one side. Down a long, narrow, two-lane rural highway, empty fields on both sides.

Puck tips his head toward the window, leans forward. Rolls his window down—now I hear it too: automatic weapons fire.

"Fuck, that's them," Harris growls. "Get ready, boys."

We check loads, tighten vests, and exhale a few times. Fiddle with the fire selector switches.

We approach a gas station in the distance, an island of light in the endless dark. Flashes of muzzle-burst bloom from one edge of the island—too many of them. You can't reliably count tangos based on muzzle-flash because people tend to move around during a firefight, but you can get a rough estimate. And my estimate is there's at least a dozen tangos out there, and Bryn is fending them off alone.

"One thing we should have mentioned," Solomon's voice comes across the radio. "Except for Lash, we Broken Arrows don't shoot to kill. We took an oath."

"The fuck?" Puck grumbles to himself, then, across the comms: "Operators who won't kill? Time for a new career, boys."

"Watch us, buddy," a different voice snarls. "Takes a fuckuva lot of skill to stay alive in a firefight while intentionally taking down but not outright killing people."

"What my brother is saying is that you don't need to worry," Solomon answers. "We'll hold our own. Just understand that we aren't missing our shots."

"Don't worry," I say into my comm. "We'll bag the lot of them for you."

"Arrows," Harris snaps, cutting through the cross-chatter.. "Form the center. Suppressive fire. Keep their heads down. RMI, flanks. Use the darkness to pick them off from the wings. Alpha team, get Bryn and the boy back to our side."

There's a chorus of affirmations across the comms. Taillights fade away and blink out behind us as Chico and the RMI blokes dissolve into the night. Our headlights wink off, bathing us in darkness; We creep forward foot by foot as the firefight continues. Although firefight is a loose term—it's massively lopsided. Closer now, I count at least a dozen tangos, hear overlapping chatter in Spanish.

"This is Mercado's men," someone says across the comms—a smooth, deep, accented voice—the Lash lad. The accent is European. Romani, maybe, though I'm far from an accent expert.

"So then what happened to Pugli?" Someone else asks—with so many new faces, I've no way of knowing who's speaking.

"An excellent question indeed," says the accented voice—definitely Romani, definitely Lash; I did some… erm, extra-legal work with a Romani fella, a year or so back. Excellent chap. Sticky fingers, smooth talker. "Until you see that lice-ridden, cockroach-infested pustule bleeding out before your very eyes, you cannot ever count him out. He will make himself known in some manner, assuming Bryn evaded him but did not kill him."

"Oi, mate," I say into the comm, "don't insult lice and cockroaches that way. They're just innocently following their natures. Pugli is lower than the stains left on the toilet bowl after you've taken an epic shit."

Laughs and snickers greet my comment, but not from Lash. "I appreciate the sentiment, but Pugl's evil is no laughing matter. I merely lack the English to fully and accurately capture the depth, breadth, and intensity of my hatred for Roberto Pugli." A pause. "He killed my wife and children."

"Funny, mate," I answer, "Seems like you speak English better than I do. But point taken. Let's just agree he's an evil fuck who needs killin' post-fucking-haste." My turn to pause. "Sorry for your loss, mate."

"Thank you."

I hesitate. "Wait…I heard a story about a guy who had info on Pugli…"

"That was me."

I exhale. "Jesus fuck. No wonder you hate him."

"No wonder indeed, sir."

"Sir, he calls me," I mutter to the men around me as we creep forward closer to the firefight—we're intending to surprise them from behind. "Ain't been called sir since I got busted down for insubordination."

"Rush?" Harris's voice float to me from the front of the Suburban.

"Yeah, mate?"

"Shut the fuck up."

"Sir." I've a tendency to ramble before a firefight like this.

Arjun was always giving me shit for it. Fuck, I miss that lad. He could take the piss outta me and have me laughin' at myself. Brave, funny, clever lad.

"Here's good," Harris says, and the Suburban brakes to a halt. The Arrows stop behind us, and we kill the engines, slip out of the vehicles, and take up positions behind wheels, boots, and bonnets.

"RMI, status?" Harris says.

"In position," Chico says. "On your order."

"Arrows ready," Solomon adds. "On your order."

"Light 'em up on three," Harris growls. "One—two—*three*."

The crack, rattle, and crash of M4s, HKs, and Steyr-Augs is sudden and deafening, my ears immediately ringing and going muffled. It's hard to see shit with the muzzle flashes. I spot a shadow illuminated by a burst and put a trio of rounds into it.

Again.

Again.

These fuckers are no untrained thugs, though. They spot the threat immediately and adjust accordingly, sending suppressive fire at us while they shift behind cover, deeming us more of a danger than Bryn.

Perfect.

I pay close attention to the way the Arrows work, and I'm impressed. They pick their targets carefully, and their shots are calculated to inflict damage and pull the focus of the others to care for them. Nontraditional, but effective. Anselm has vanished into the night, and I hear the boom of a rifle—a big one.

The enemy's return fire picks up intensity, becomes withering, forcing us to duck as their rounds smack into the body of the Suburban—it's armored, thank fuck, with heavy duty, bullet-resistant glass.

Rifle chatter from the flanks changes the calculus of the firefight as RMI makes their presence known.

I pop up, spray a burst their way, scanning the battleground: shadows move, shouts in Spanish echo, groans flutter. A shadow moves near the tail of a pickup; an arm slicing through the air. A dot-shadow arcs through the illumination of the gas station lights.

"Grenade!" I shout, scrambling around the bonnet of the Suburban.

The grenade clatters across the cement and skitters toward me, so I do the only logical thing—wind up and boot the thing as if this is the Emirates Stadium and I'm taking a corner kick for Arsenal.

I dart away as something hot snaps past my ear, whickers over my head, and buzzes angrily around me. Fuck, fuck. I'm out of cover, now, in the open. "RUSH!" Harris shouts. "Get the fuck back here!"

I dart the other way, but a burst of fire rakes the cement inches from my feet, forcing me to scramble the other way. More fire blatters at me, rounds hissing all around me like a swarm of hornets.

KA-BOOM!

The grenade detonates—good thing I don't play for Arsenal, though, as my kick was total shit. The thing went nowhere near the enemy, blowing up an air pump off to the side rather than the petrol pump I'd been aiming for.

Shrapnel dings and tinkles all around us, but no one pays any attention. No. They just shoot at me. Bullets snap perilously close to me on all sides, chewing up the concrete behind me, preventing me from returning to the protective cover of the armored SUV.

"RUSH!" I hear a blessedly beautiful voice call from the gas station shop.

Fuck this. Sometimes the only way out is through, yeah? So fuck it. Time to make a break for it.

I bolt forward into the teeth of the enemy fusillade, bullets whipping all around me, plucking at my shirt sleeves and trouser legs as I zig, jog, zag, and jig toward the shop. A figure looms in front of me, an M16 leveled at me, the barrel a huge round hole. I fire from the hip, catching the shooter in the thigh. He buckles, goes to a knee, but still gets off a burst at me. A sun-hot hammer slams into my left arm, jerking me around off-balance. There's no pain at the moment, just the tremendous impact with crushing heat spreading to my shoulder, chest, and forearm. I let my carbine go, and it swings from the clip attached to my vest. Draw my sidearm without losing a step, sprinting through the scrum of tangos—now no one dares shoot, not with me in the mix. The tangoes don't want to hit each other, and our lot don't want to hit me. Which means for a split second or two, the firefight is paused. I use the lull to run even harder, until my lungs scream and my thighs burn and the pounding hot ache in my arm slowly becomes a pulsing mass of agony that I have no choice but to swallow. I'm even with the tango who shot me, his eyes wide, teeth bared as he swivels on his arse in an attempt to bring his rifle to bear on me.

Too late.

I fire across my body—my pistol is in my right hand, and the target is on my left. I catch a glimpse of red blooming at his throat, and feel a little zing of pride. That was a good shot, if I do say so myself.

The shop is mere meters away now, and I feel a dozen pairs of eyes on me, feel iron sights settling on my back. Instinct screams in my gut, that sense of danger. You wouldn't think it would be helpful in the middle of a firefight, because obviously there's danger: motherfuckers are shooting at me. But it's more subtle than that, if you care to pay attention. This instinct is telling me to drop, *now*.

You don't survive in this job for long without those instincts, without the ability to react instantly to nothing more than a warning tingle in your bollocks. You gotta learn to listen. I learned a long time ago—it's how I survived on the mean streets of London as a homeless little gutter rat and it's how I made it through all those missions when so many didn't. That and blind, stupid luck, of course.

This time, it's not luck. I feel the tingle in my nuts

telling me to hit dirt, so I tuck my shoulder and cradle my rifle against my gut. Throw myself forward into a roll. The concrete is unforgiving as I hit it, and the magazine jabs my diaphragm like a mule kick, and grit scrapes my cheek, bitter on my lips and dusty in my nostrils, stinking of old petrol. My shot arm screams agony as I roll over it. A long chainsaw rattle of automatic fire cuts the air where I'd been a mere heartbeat before, and now I'm rolling to my back and kicking myself along the ground toward the shattered doors of the station shop as hell breaks loose now that I'm out of the way.

I crack off a shot with my pistol down the length of my body, and I'm rewarded by the muzzle-flash raking skyward as the shooter goes down. A hand grabs my vest and pulls—I crack off shots in rapid succession, kicking my boots into the concrete to help Bryn pull me along, as there's no time to make my feet. Rounds buzz and snap and hum all around us, and I glance up to see a tendril of Bryn's curly black hair jerk, wisps fluttering in slow motion down to me, severed by the round whickering millimeters from her ear.

I'm firing indiscriminately in the direction of the enemy, just trying to keep their heads down. Our lot are pouring fire on them as well, and I see one tango twist awkwardly as a shot from the flanks jerks him in a wild, ungainly pirouette.

Something sharp slices at my backside and the gap between vest and trousers—glass shards digging in as I half-crawl and am half-dragged across them.

A tango appears over the bonnet of a truck stopped

between the pumps, black hair and brown skin, a blue kerchief tied around his mouth and nose. Bryn, dragging me with one hand, puts a slug right through the fucker's teeth.

And then I'm across the threshold and she's hauling me behind the cover of the clerk's counter, and the relative silence is deafening.

For a moment, it's all I can do to catch my breath, my oxygen-starved lungs searing with each breath, a stitch in my ribs stabbing me like a needle.

Bryn's face appears above me, her mouth moving. Blood roars in my ears, adrenaline pounding my veins, tinnitus ringing like feedback squealing from an amplifier.

"…Ush? Rush!"

I see the lock of hair that got shot away, and I reach up and pinch the severed end between finger and thumb. "Nearly had your number on it, this one." I'm speaking too loudly, I think.

"You're hit," she says—I read this on her lips as much as hear it.

"Yeah, I noticed," I say, grunting as I lever myself more upright against the counter. "It don't fuckin' tickle."

"Stay here," she orders.

"No worries, love, I ain't in no hurry to go back out there."

"Rush, sitrep." Harris's voice crackles across the comms.

I key the comms. "Yeah, yeah. I'm all right. Took

one to the wing, but I've had worse. Bryn's alive. Saved my arse, too."

"The boy?"

I cast a look around, but all I see is scattered crisps from bags burst by stray rounds, cereal boxes trickling their contents, fizzy drink spraying and leaking, cans rolling this way and that.

"Bryn?" I call out.

She appears from one of the aisles, ripping into a first aid package as she hits her knees at my injured side. "Hold still, Rush. You're bleeding everywhere."

I pull my comm out of my ear and stretch it to her, and shove it into her ear. "Say hi to your dad, love."

She lifts my arm, checking for the exit hole, grunting when she sees it. "Went through the meat. Good thing you've got a big-ass arm." A pause. "Hi, Daddy. I'm good. Yeah, I've got him. He's under a desk in the office."

She digs through the first aid kit and finds a package of gauze pads, rips it open, and presses one to the exit wound. "Hold that," She orders me. I do, and she presses another to the entrance, and then winds a bandage roll around it, cinching it as tight as she can.

"No, he's fine," she says. "I mean, physically. He watched Pugli kill his mother, so mentally he's a lot less fucking fine, but he's a tough kid…Pugli? No, he's alive, unfortunately. He has a vest on under his suit. I shot him point-blank three times. Oh, he'll hurt alright, but he's alive. I know. I know. Well, the situation here isn't good. I'm down to…" She checks the load of her pistol. "Two or three rounds. We have Rush's rifle and his sidearm. Rush, honey, how many spare mags do you have?"

I grin at her. "Honey, is it? Can't say I don't love the way that sounds, Gorgeous."

"Answer the question, you hopeless flirt," she snaps.

I check my vest pockets, locating two spares for my carbine and two for my pistol—a damned Beretta, since RMI didn't think to bring the right size ammunition for my Browning and neither did Harris's lot, so I've had to trade my trusty old Hi-Power for this shitty fucking Beretta. Operators are particular about their sidearms, you see, and that Browning has been to every corner of Hell and back with me.

Bryn reports our ammo situation to her father, listens, occasionally interjecting an affirmative sound. Finally, she hands me the earpiece back. "They're gonna regroup and make a push. We need to get Ren out here so we can be ready to make a break for it."

"Go get him, then," I tell her. "I'll see what's doing out there."

"Rush," she says, hesitating. "I'm glad you're here."

I grin at her. "I'd rather be on a beach on Tortala, sipping a G-and-T and wondering when we can go back to the hotel so I can do bad things to you again." I lean in and kiss her, softly and quickly. "But I suppose this'll do."

She rolls her eyes, but can't suppress a grin. "Rush. You know what I mean."

"Missed you too, love." I eye her. "Pugli…he didn't do nothin' to you, did he?"

"No," she answers. "He wanted to, but he's scared of Mercado. Or maybe not *scared* exactly, but…Mercado wants me. Or wanted me. He wants the boy more. Why, I don't know."

"Cuz he's his father, that's why. The woman who got killed wasn't the boy's actual mother, like biologically. There's another woman named Inez who those blokes out there are scared shitless of—she's his mother, I guess. It's fuckin' complicated, is what it is."

"Ah, that makes sense. But no, Pugli didn't hurt me. He really fucking wanted to, but he didn't. I'm okay. Just…very, very pissed off."

"These narco wankers are pissing off a lot of the wrong people," I tell her. "Your lot is out there, Inez's lot, and RMI."

"Inez's lot?"

"Weird bunch, but damn good shots. Call themselves the Broken Arrows."

"Ah. The Arrow-men. The broken Arrows. Inez must be La Víbora."

"Who? The Viper? Who's that?"

"Mercado's ex-wife. Those guys out there are scared shitless of her. And the Arrows."

"Rush," Harris says in my ear. "Ready?"

"No. Give us two minutes."

"Get the boy and my daughter to us, Rush. We'll hold them. You just get them here."

"Copy you," I answer. To Bryn: "Get the boy. It's go-time."

She crouch-runs back across the destroyed shop—there's a door at the back, which she shoves open. I catch a slice of an office—a desk scattered with papers, a dark computer screen, a filing cabinet, boxes of cigarettes, and cases of liquor. Fuck, I'd kill for a shot of something to dull the pain, but I need my wits about me.

I see two figures huddled on the floor under the desk, a young Hispanic boy of six or so, and a young man of twenty wearing a ballcap and a flannel shirt with the sleeves cut off. Bryn pulls the boy by the hand, and he follows her to me, doing a good job of staying low.

I address him in Spanish. "My name is Rush. You're Ren, aren't you?"

He nods. "Do you know Big Ren?" he asks.

I assume he must mean Lorenzo. "No, but I'm friends with his friends. They're out there." I gesture at the doors. "We're going to make a run for it, okay? There's gonna be a lot of shooting and scary noises, but I'll keep you safe."

He looks at my arm, where the bandage is stained red as I bleed through it. "You are shot."

I grin at him, lift my shirt to show him the various places I've been shot. "Not my first time. I'll be fine. Just my arm."

He frowns at me. "Are you ever afraid?"

I nod. "Sure, all the time. If you're not afraid when someone is shooting at you, you're either crazy or a liar."

"You have been shot, and you are afraid, but you are still here."

"That's the job, mate." The word "mate" comes out in English, the rest in Spanish. It's as weird as it sounds. I indicate Bryn. "But mainly, I'm here for her."

He smiles at this. "She is crazy! She says crazy things to the bad men, until they are very angry."

Bryn watches this exchange suspiciously. "He's talking about me, isn't he? What's he saying?"

"The little bad man, Anatoly," he stumbles over the unfamiliar name. "She killed him with her legs."

I laugh at this. "She what?"

"She broke his neck with her legs. It made a sound like this." He jerks his head up and to the side with cracking noise. "And then he died."

Bryn shakes her head at his reenactment. "I wish he hadn't seen that."

I grin at her. "Proper mankiller, you are."

"Unfortunately, yes."

"Turns me on, watching you kill people," I tell her. "I'm a sick fucko like that."

She's about to respond when Harris's voice fills my ear. "Ready?"

I exhale sharply, work to my feet, ignoring the scream of pain from my arm. Times like this, all you can do is gut through the suck.

I undo my vest, awkwardly shrug it off and drape it one-handed over Bryn. She starts to protest, but I ignore it and tighten it to create as proper a fit as possible. I replace the mag in my pistol, rack the slide, and shove it behind my waistband at my back. Curl an arm around the boy, crouched, feet braced to sprint.

"Bryn, you're going first. Spray the fuckers down, yeah? If there was ever a time to spray-and-pray, this is it, love. We'll be right behind you." I don't give her a chance to argue. "Harris, we're ready. On your order."

"On three," he says. I hold up three fingers for Bryn

and the boy, waiting, pulling down a finger each time Harris counts. "One...two...three!"

On three, I scoop the boy into my good arm and sprint. Bryn is already through the door, carbine spraying rounds across the battlefield, thunking into the truck bodies, keeping their heads down. Gunfire crackles from the wings, muzzle-bursts flashing in blinding yellow stars from the darkness like sunfire blossoms as Chico's RMI operators lay down an enfilade across the enemy position. I hear several grunts and cries of pain as RMI bullets find targets.

Bryn spots a tango rising from behind a brick column and puts rounds into his chest, knocking him backward; his vest stops them, but he's in pain, groaning, gasping, gagging. I know the feeling. Bryn finishes him off as we pass him, cratering his skull with a single shot on the run. I have the boy, Ren, clamped against my chest one-armed; his legs are locked around my waist, his arms around my neck. Something hot sizzles across the back of my neck, leaving a scorching line of pain.

Bryn's rifle cracks in staccato bursts. From our line, muzzles flash, putting down suppressive fire even as RMI keeps up the withering enfilade from the wings.

We're almost there—just a few more meters to go. With the enemy behind us, Bryn breaks into a flat-out sprint to reach the cover of the Suburban, immediately spinning and dropping into a crouch to fire over the bonnet, her rounds whickering shudderingly close past my ear.

Each step takes an eternity, now, for some reason.

Wait, I know what's happening—something bad. I'm about to enter a world of shit. I've been here, before. I dunno, why, but every so often, when shit really hits the fan, things slow down. I feel the iron sights on my back as a prickle of awareness.

Six feet—two meters. I'm fucking *there*. Not now, goddammit.

That old bitch, instinct or gut feeling or seventh sense…she's nasty. Insistent. Telling me to toss the boy.

Just do it, Rush. Throw him.

Fuck if I know why, but I don't argue with her.

I see that seven foot tall monster, Thresh, rising to his full, massive stature, his M4 looking like a kid's toy in his giant paws. "THRESH!" It's a desperate shout.

I hurl the kid like a rugby ball with every last ounce of strength in my arms, the injured one screaming in protest as I force it to do my bidding.

Thresh's eyes go wide. He drops the rifle and moves with lightning speed, a man of his gargantuan size shouldn't be capable of, snagging the boy out of midair.

BAMBAMBAMBAM!

Bullets walk up the concrete, hit the bonnet of the SUV.

BAMABAMABAMBAM!

Return fire from our side is a deadly barrage, but it's too late.

God kicks me again, the bastard. Right in the back. The hot hammer slams into me once, twice, three times, hurling me forward. I hit concrete on my bad arm, but that's nothing against the breathless scorching agony radiating through me. For a moment, I think it'll be okay—I'm wearing a vest. And then I remember—no, I'm not.

Well, fuck.

I see Thresh moving—whirling in place, curling his mammoth torso around Ren. I see the rounds hit his back, dimpling the vest, rocking him forward. The big fucker barely moves, doesn't make a sound. I took one ricochet to the chest and couldn't breathe for five fucking minutes. That goddamned ogre took three to the back and seems unaffected.

Some blokes are just built differently, I guess.

The dirt tastes like oil and petrol. It's gritty under my cheek. Something wet is spreading under my belly. I don't like that.

I like even less the elephant sitting on my chest. I can't open my lungs, can't catch a breath.

I'm trying not to panic, but I'm not succeeding. This could be bad. There are sounds, but it's hard to make sense of anything—the adrenaline can't mask the crushing mass of excruciating agony searing through me from where stupid God kicked me in the back.

Wait…

Right.

I've been shot.

Again.

Go me.

Woo.

Hands drag me, which doesn't feel entirely wonderful.

Voices overlap.

Hands do things.

"Ca—can't…b-br—" I rasp. "C-can't…breathe."

"We gotcha, kid," a gruff voice says.

A knife blade rakes up my back, the dull side cold on my skin as it slices open my shirt. Something is pressed to my skin. I hear the hollow rip sound of a tape roll opening, something sticky touching my back in four lines to make a big square.

I'm rolled to my back, which tears a gagging scream out of me, even though I'm trying like fuck to keep the sounds on the inside. Not that I can breathe to scream very loud, mind you.

Fuck, this sucks. I've taken some shots before, but this is bad.

There are different kinds of not being able to breathe, and they're all terrible in their own ways.

Getting the wind knocked out of you in a sparring match is level one. Sucks, but passes quickly.

Then there's being forced to hold your breath longer than you really can, and that's level two.

Actually drowning is level three.

That really fucking sucks. Zero out of ten, do not recommend.

Then there's taking a slug to the vest; that's level four—avoid at all costs. Horrible. Leaves terrible bruises at best, breaks ribs at worst. Negative ten out of ten.

Then, apparently, there's getting extra holes put in your chest by some rather inconsiderate arsewipes. Negative infinity out of ten. Really, really, *really* do try to avoid it. Take it from me.

Things are all dark and blurry, which doesn't bode

well for my future, but I see Bryn's face looking tweaked and upset, tears flowing.

"Oi, oi," I grit out, looking at her. "None o' that."

She hovers over me, a beautiful, brown-skinned angel. Her puppy brown eyes are terrified for me. "Don't talk, Rush. Save your breath."

"Fuck that," I gasp, as whoever is patching me up presses a sheet of transparent plasticky something to my chest over the unwanted holes. Tape covers the edges, and just like that, a seal is created, and I can draw a breath. I mean, I'm still shot thrice in the fucking lungs, so I'm not, like, fine, but at least that damned elephant has gone off my chest.

"Rush," Bryn whispers. "Fuck."

I grin at her. "Might be…a minute…before I can manage…a good fucking…love."

She laughs through her tears. "God, you're incorrigible."

"That's my daughter, asshole," A growly voice snarls in my ear—the owner of the voice is the one patching me up. Harris. "Don't piss me off while I'm saving your life, son."

I find Harris's eyes. "Am I gonna make it, doc?"

He rolls his eyes at me. "Probably. We've got a helo en route."

"The boy?"

"He's good. Thresh is with him."

"Bryn?"

She appears in my line of sight again. "I'm here, baby."

I wiggle my fingers at her—I can't quite make my

arm lift more than an inch or two. I guess that's understandable under the circumstances, but I don't like it when my limbs don't obey, the silly buggers.

I might be a bit loopy.

Her fingers fit with mine. "Hey. I'm here."

"Alright, love?"

She nods. "I'm fine. Not a scratch. You took them all, you hog."

I lock gazes with her, determined to say what's been percolating away in the dusty corners of my black, ugly, sinful heart for days now. "Bit of a…" I wince, struggling to breathe; I said I can breathe *better*, not *normally*. "Bit of a shit moment for this, but…" it takes the last of my courage and all of my fortitude. "I love you."

She laughs through tears, cupping my face with tender hands. "God, Rush. You're impossible. Only you would tell me you love me at a time like this."

"Just…in case."

"Hey, no. *No.* Don't even talk like that. You're gonna be fine."

"Not…feeling my best…at the moment." I grimace as a wave of pain rolls over me. "Want you to know. Calling you 'love'…it's not—it's not a Cockney thing… anymore."

"I know."

"Might be it…it never was." The sound of an approaching helo starts to drown out my words. "Never… been in love. So I'm only guessing, mind. But I'm…I'm fairly…certain."

She laughs, sniffling. "Shut up, Rush. Just…shut up. I love you, too."

Fuck me, that hurts to hear. A good hurt, but it fucking hurts.

I'm getting tired. Also, feeling a bit sloshy on the inside. Probably not a good thing.

"Rush?" Her voice is concerned.

"Say it again."

"I love you, Rush."

The helo is here, landing in the field. Helmeted air medics appear over me, a stretcher between them. I'm rolled so the stretcher can be wedged under me, which fucking hurts, but all I care about is Bryn.

Brown eyes search me. "Rush? You're okay."

"Eliza."

"What about her, baby?"

"If anything happens to me—"

Wrong thing to say—she gets angry. "You're not allowed to talk like that, Rush."

"I've got…three holes in my…my chest."

"We've got you, bro. You're less than fifteen minutes from a hospital by air." The voice is male, American, and decisive. He's not guessing. "You'll live."

"Fine, then." I let my eyes close. "Don't tell Eliza until after Disney."

"Rush—"

"Nah. She ain't ever had a vacation. Let her have fun."

There's a warm rush, then, or maybe a cold rush. A tingling. The pain fades, replaced by a drowsy euphoria.

"Ohhh, that's nice, that is," I murmur.

"Morphine, bud. The good stuff."

"Bryn?"

"Yeah, baby?"

"I'm sorry."

"For what?"

"What I did."

"I know."

"What is love…?" Not sure why I'm singing the fragment of the song, but I am.

Bryn laughs—god, I love her laugh.

Oh bugger, I think I'm passing out.

19

ELIZA

HE'S BEEN IN AND OUT OF SURGERY FOR TWO weeks, repairing his lungs, getting them to reinflate, getting him off supplemental oxygen. He's out of it, most of the time. Barely aware of his surroundings, exhausted, in perpetual pain.

Yet, when Richard and Evelyn arrive with Eliza, he somehow manages to gather himself together for his daughter.

If I wasn't in love with the man already, seeing him with his daughter would have done it. He uses the wired remote to lift his bed upright as the door opens—Eliza's voice can be heard from halfway down the hallway, singing an adorable little ditty about going to see her daddy.

I'm sitting on the far side of the bed with my hand resting on his thigh when the door swings open. A fireball of a child bursts in, a half-pint firecracker in a gauzy pink taffeta explosion of a princess dress, the train trailing behind her muddy and torn. She's got a pink wand in one hand with a massive blue plastic jewel in the center, which flashes with light every time she waves it. In her other hand is a stuffed rabbit with long floppy ears, one eye missing, and the other an old brass coat button. Her hair is as black as Rush's, but it's an inch of patchy new growth coming in after radiation treatment.

"...*Daaaaaa*ddy, Daddy, going to see my Daaaaaddy!" she sing-songs, bursting into the room with a dramatic flourish of her wand. "Tah...*DAH*! I'm here, Daddy!" *Dahhh-DEE!*

"C'mere, Lizzy-Lovey," Rush says, his voice breathless and soft and ragged. "I need at least eighty-seven squeezes and a hundred kisses."

Her wand lowers slowly to her side as she sees him in the big hospital bed, wires and tubes in a tangled snarl, looking haggard and weak and tired. "D-Daddy?"

He scoots over in the bed, each movement eliciting a wince and a groan he does his level best to hide. "C'mere, Lizzy-Bean. C'mere. Daddy's okay. I'm alright. Just come here."

She shuffles closer, her eyes—changeable hazel like his—wide and scared. "Grandmama and Grandpa said you got hurted."

He pats the space beside him. "I did get hurt, sweetheart, but I'm alright. I'm on the mend."

She approaches the edge of the bed, her eyes gone greenish the way his do—she glances at me, and I can see her deciding to figure out who I am later. She refocuses on Rush, hesitant and fearful—I imagine it has to be a hell of a shock to see her big, strong, invincible warrior daddy in this state.

"Are you sure you're going to be alright?" she asks.

He draws a breath, eyes closing, steadying himself. "Climb on up here with me, my little monkey." She climbs up in a swish and scrabble of taffeta and limbs, grabbing at Rush with accidentally careless hands. Fortunately, his injured arm is on my side, so he's able to pull her up, stifling a groan when she settles in with a child's restless thrashing, an elbow landing in his ribs.

"Oh, yeah," he groans. "There we are."

Eliza taps her wand here and there, gaze flicking to me with naked curiosity. "Who're you?"

I smile at her. "My name is Bryn."

She looks at Rush, then me again. "Are you one of Daddy's nurses?"

I look at Rush, too, for guidance. "Um, no. I'm... Your daddy and me are..."

Rush saves me. "Bryn and I have had an adventure together, Lizzy-Bean. We've fallen in love with each other just like in your stories, and we're going to be together happily ever after." He lets that sink in. "Whatcha think of that, then?"

I think a lot of it, myself, but I watch Eliza for her reaction.

She looks at me. It's a long, hard, thoughtful, searching look. "Are you going to be my new mum?"

I choke on my saliva, coughing as I try to collect myself. "I...um. Maybe first we could just sort of...start out as friends?"

"I think that's probably a good idea, don't you think

so, Daddy?" She looks at him. "I've had an adventure, too, you know. D'you want to hear all about it?"

"I absolutely want to hear every last detail, sweetheart. Tell me *every*thing."

"Well, it was lunch time, first off. Grandmama had made my favorite, cheese toasties with tomato soup. And then, from the middle of nowhere, the door broke open. Just…*SMASH!*" She whacks Rush in the face with her wand, continuing her riveting narration heedless of Rush's amused laughter as he rubs his offended nose. "Big ugly men just came into the house! One had a wart on his nose *exactly* like a witch. Do you think he was a witch, Daddy?"

"Seems likely," Rush answers, shoulders shaking. "And then what?"

"They pointed guns at Grandmama and Grandpa, big machine guns." She stage whispers, then. "I think they were *real guns*, Daddy. Don't you think so, too?"

He nods solemnly. "I do think that's likely, darling."

"Don't worry, no one got shooted. Not even grandpa. I thought maybe grandpa would fight them off with his spoon like a real hero, but then I thought that would be bad, because I love Grandpa and I'm not sure he could fight very well with just a spoon." She pauses, head cocked in thought. "Could you fight someone with a spoon, Daddy?"

Rush is trying *so* hard not to lose it. "Well, maybe." He nods. "Yeah, I reckon I could. Was it a big spoon like for soup, or one of those fiddly little guys for sugar?"

"It was just a little one."

"Hmmm. That's tricky. Spoons aren't my weapon

of choice." He kisses the top of her head. "I do think Grandpa made the right choice, though. One spoon against two big machine guns ain't the best odds, in my professional opinion. Discretion is the better part of valor, and all."

"And Grandpa isn't a spring chicken anymore, he says. I'm glad they didn't shoot anyone."

"Me too, darling."

Over by the door, Richard and Evelyn are stifling laughter as well—Richard is medium height, with thin off-blond hair and round glasses with thick lenses. He's got no fewer than three pens in the breast pocket of his short-sleeved button-down, which is tucked into pressed chinos. Evelyn is short and curvy, with curly brown hair and sharp, lively blue eyes.

"Well, what happened next?" Rush asks.

"The men put a sack over my head. It smelled very bad. Almost as bad as your gym bag but not as bad as your nasty farts." She waves her wand this way and that as she speaks, flicking it and tapping the railing, the wires, the beeping, pumping machines. "Then I was in a car for a *very* long time. It was very boring. There were lots of turnings and I was quite afraid, but not as afraid as when I had to get radiation the first time."

Rush blinks hard, fury clouding his features before he masters it. "You're a very brave girl."

"I know." She says it with the simplicity of a child's assurance. "They brought me to a hotel. It was quite manky, Daddy. I didn't like it at all. They put on the telly for me, but all the programs were in French. And then they got food, but that was shit as well."

"Eliza!" Rush admonishes. "What've I said about talking like me?"

"No swears until I'm thirteen or I've had my first period," she drones, annoyed.

"Rush!" Evelyn says. "You didn't tell her that, did you?"

"I did." He arches an eyebrow at Evelyn, daring her to argue.

"She's only six, Rush. She's not old enough to know about her period. And thirteen is *much* too young to be swearing."

Rush just laughs. "Ev, darling, kids understand much more than we think." He tickles her. "Don't you, bug?"

"A period is when girls become women and bleed everywhere," Eliza announces. "Colin, from my class before I got sick again, said his mum told him all about it." She looks at Rush. "Is that true?"

He nods, and then tips his head to the side. "Sort of. Not everywhere. But it…" he looks at me for help, bless the man.

I smile at the little girl. "You know, sweetheart, I think both your daddy *and* grandma are right. I think you don't need to worry about periods for a while yet. I didn't get mine till I was almost twelve, and my best friend Rin got hers at ten. So you've got a while before you need to worry about it. But you're also a very smart girl, I can tell already. So if you have questions, I'm sure your dad or your grandma would be happy to answer them."

"What about swears?" she asks.

I shrug. "Well, I think you should listen to your dad and do what he says." I lean over him, whispering conspiratorially. "But sometimes, you just gotta say a bad word."

"So if I really, *really* need to say a swear, I can? As long as I don't say them as much as Daddy does?"

"I mean, that sounds pretty fair to me." I look at Rush. "What do you think?"

He snorts. "I think we shouldn't negotiate with terrorists." He kisses her head again. "But yeah, I think that's fair. Once in a while, as long as it's not a habit." He glances at Evelyn. "What do you think, Grandma?"

She sighs, clearly unhappy with this turn of events. "I'm obviously outvoted on this one. But I suppose as long as you don't curse at school or at nurses or doctors, once in a great while wouldn't be the end of the world."

Eliza looks at me. "Do you kill bad guys like Daddy?"

My eyebrows go up. "Um. I…well, see…" Shit. How do you answer that? "Eliza, your daddy is a very special person. He chose to serve your country by fighting in the military. That means he's very, very brave. But your daddy wasn't just any old soldier—he was a very, very special kind of soldier. He fought against the baddest of the bad guys. And sometimes, yeah, he had to kill them. But he only did that to keep you and me and all the little boys and girls everywhere safe. Because a smart girl like you must know by now that there *are* bad men out there, huh? Like the guys who stole you from your grandma and grandpa."

She nods very seriously. "Mr. Nick and his friends

killed those bad men. It was very loud and very scary, but I could tell they were good guys."

"How could you tell that, Lizzy-Bean?" Rush asks.

"Well, bad men have bad eyes," she answers, as if it's the most obvious thing in the world. "The bad men who stole me had bad eyes. They didn't hurt me, but they still stole me away, and that's bad. But Mr. Nick, he broke in the door just like the bad men did, but his eyes were nice. He gave me a wink, like this." She turns to look at Rush and winks, very broadly and exaggeratedly. "And I knew he was a good guy and I wasn't afraid of him, even though his friends were great big giants. Mr. Thresh was so giant he had to duck under the door to fit inside the room! But do you know, he was very silly. He let me watch Bluey on his phone while we were on the helly-copter."

There's a long pause, and Eliza's face betrays the depths of her thoughts—Rush waits patiently for her to formulate her thoughts and get them out. "Daddy?"

"Yes, my beautiful, brave girl?" HIs eyes are hazy with emotion, his voice thick with it.

"When can you go home?"

"Well, I don't know exactly. When I got hurt, it made it hard for me to breathe." He taps the cannula in his nose. "That's what this is—it helps me breathe better while my lungs heal. So I have to stay here in hospital until my lungs are all better and I don't need this anymore. Unfortunately, that might be a while longer, yet."

She nods. "Can I sleep here with you, Daddy?"

He blinks hard. "I don't think so, darling. I'd love

nothing more in all the world than to snuggle you all night, because I've missed you so, so, so, so, so, so—"

Eliza giggles, clapping a tiny hand over his mouth. "Daddy! That's enough! You're too silly!"

He laughs, pretending to bite her fingers. "*So much.*" He nuzzles her cheek, sighing. "But. Grandma and Grandpa and you are going to stay in a very, very fancy hotel nearby. And you'll come see me every day, and you can order *anything* you want from the room service menu and grandma isn't allowed to say no, *even* to dessert for breakfast."

"RUSH!" Evelyn protests.

"Hush, dear," Richard murmurs.

"Could I have pancakes for dinner?" she asks.

"Absolutely. With *buckets* of syrup."

Another thoughtful pause. "When will we go back to England?"

Rush blows out a breath. "Well…" he looks up, as if the ceiling has answers, then back to her. "This is the hard part, darling."

She nods, looking down at her dress, tapping her knees with her wand. "I need a special treatment, but we haven't got the money for it." She looks him in the eyes, unflinching, braver than anyone I've ever met. "Am I going to die soon, Daddy?"

Rush's shoulders shake. His mouth opens, but nothing comes out. He clears his throat, sniffs hard, tries again. "N-no, sweetheart. No." He kisses her head yet again. "Mr. Nick has a friend, you see."

"Mr. Valentine!"

Rush's gaze snaps to hers with a puzzled frown. "You know him?"

"We met Mr. Valentine and Mrs. Kyrie in Disney, didn't we, Grandmama? They went on the rides with us, and Mr. Valentine didn't even yell or scream on any of the rides. And he told me he'd make sure I got all better as soon as possible, even if he had to buy all the hospitals in the whole world." She looks at Rush again. "Can he do that?"

"Do which, lovey?"

"Make me all better?"

"Well, no. He can't as he's not a doctor," Rush answers. "But he's something better, in a way—he's very, very, very wealthy. Which means he can pay for the treatment you need."

"But why would he do that?" she asks. "He doesn't even know us, hardly."

I answer this one. "Mr. Valentine is part of my family, honey. And he likes to help people. It's one of his most favorite things in the whole world, and he *especially* likes helping brave, strong, smart little girls like you."

She spends another moment thinking. "Will you have to go to work for him? The bad men who stole me away said you owed your boss money, so you had to work for him and that you were no better than them."

"Bloody mouthy bastards," Rush mutters. "The truth is…" he stops, looks at her, and starts again "I did have to go to work for a bad person, so I could get you the treatments you need, Eliza. That's a true thing a lot of people probably think I ought not to tell you.

But I think you can understand, can't you? I tried not to do bad things, but…"

I cut in. "Eliza, when you become a grown-up, things get very complicated. Sometimes it's not always very easy to know what's good and what's bad when you're a grown-up. And sometimes, good and bad get so tangled up that they're all one thing."

"So he had to do bad things for a good reason?" she asks.

I nod. "Yes."

"Like telling a fib, but only so you don't hurt someone's feelings?"

"Sort of, yes," I say.

She nods, her expression gravely serious. "Daddy, I don't want you to do any more bad things, not even for a good reason."

"I'm trying, sweetheart."

"If Mr. Valentine is going to help me get my special treatment, does that mean you can do work that's only good?"

I reach across him and rest my hand on hers. "Sweetheart, you have my promise that your daddy will be the best good guy there's ever been from now on."

Rush's look, when he meets my eyes, is skeptical.

Eliza holds my gaze for a long time and then nods. "Okay." She scrutinizes Rush's face for a moment and then scrambles off the bed. "It's time for you to rest, Daddy."

This gets a chorus of laughter from all of us.

Rush, still chuckling, snags her hand so she can't escape yet. "Oh? Is that so? Do you say so, Dr. Eliza?"

"I'm not a doctor, silly. I'm only a little girl. But I've been sick lots and I know sometimes when you're very sick, you need to rest. And I can tell from your eyes that you need to rest." She prods beneath her eyes. "You've got tired eyes, Daddy."

He sighs a laugh. "You might be right, Lizzy-Bean, you just might be right. But I never got my kisses and squeezes. That's what'll make me all better the fastest."

Lizzy lets out a hysterically adult-sounding sigh of long-suffering. "Oh, all right. But not too many. You need to save your energy. So only…" she taps her forehead with her wand. "Four kisses and four squeezes. You mustn't overdo it."

"Deal. Now get back up here and deliver my kisses and squeezes, you little negotiator, you." Rush hauls her up one-handed, hiding a wince of pain.

I'd expected him to shower her with playful kisses and faux-aggressive hugs, but he doesn't. Each kiss is delicate and soft and tender—one to her left cheek, one to her right, one to her forehead, and one to the tip of her chin. And each hug, in the same way, is savored. Gentle. He visibly cherishes each one.

I'm not crying, you're crying.

The last hug is the longest, ending with Eliza whispering in Rush's ear that she loves him the very most. Richard and Evelyn escort her out, then, and the sound of her voice chattering on fades into the distance.

Rush sags against the bed, exhaustion washing over him in a visible wave. His eyes, closed, are wet with tears.

"Rush," I whisper. "Don't."

He shakes his head. "She understands things she shouldn't have to. God, I'm a shit father."

My bark of laughter is one of utter disbelief, earning me a sharp look from Rush.

"What the fuck are you laughing about?" he demands, ready to be angry at me.

"Rush," I answer, taking his hands in mine. "Nothing could be further from the truth."

He frowns at me, clearly not believing me. "How you figure that?"

"Well…I have to admit, I was shocked to find out you had a daughter. And I…" I sigh. "I have to further admit that I assumed you'd be…"

He arches an eyebrow. "Out with it, then. I'd be what?"

"A deadbeat. Or, at least, absent."

"Well, I *have* been absent a lot."

I hold his eyes. "Rush, I was *so* wrong about you. It couldn't be any more obvious that you love that little girl with everything you are. You'd do anything for her. And she loves you just as much. She *sees* you, Rush. *I* see you."

Swallowing hard, he shakes his head, looks away. "She's my little girl. You seen her, aintcha? How could you *not* love her?"

"Rush, you're missing my point."

He locks eyes with me, his wary and hard. "What's your point, then?"

"The whole bad boy thing you've got going on? Underneath that, underneath the whole street kid, orphan, operator, badass thing, you're a sweetheart. You're kind. You're sweet. You're affectionate. You're full of love, Rush. You're fundamentally good. I just…I think you just don't see it. Because no one's ever told you."

He shakes his head. "I'm not."

It's my turn to cock an eyebrow at him. "Are you really gonna argue with me about this?"

"Bryn, did you forget how we met?"

"Of course not. But I'm capable of picking up on things called *nuance,* Rush. We've been over what happened, why you did what you did. And I've forgiven you, I understand, and I'm moving on. You need to do the same. You need to forgive yourself. For that—and for everything. You're a *great* father, you're a good man, and I'm in love with you."

He rubs his eyes with his hand. "Dry in here."

I laugh. "Yeah, that's it. Big, tough Rush doesn't get emotional."

"Glad you get it." He groans raggedly. "Fuck. I love you, Bryn. I do. I just…what if I…what I'm not what you think?"

"Got any more secrets?" I ask.

"Nah, I mean, nothing big. Nothing that would surprise you. Things I stole, times I was an insensitive prick to women I shagged, shit like that. But no more secrets."

"Then what's the issue? I'm a big girl, honey. I can decide for myself if you're what I think you are. And I've decided that I love you, I want to be with you, and that you're gonna work for my dad."

He glances at me at the last part. "Oh, I am, am I?"

"Yep."

"Okay. I like him. All of 'em." He rubs his face with his palm. "The boy, how is he?"

I sink into my seat. "Alive. Staying with Aunt Cuddy, Aunt Temple, and Mom in our compound in the Keys while Dad and the guys..." I trail off because I wasn't supposed to tell him this stuff.

Oops.

His gaze sharpens. "While your dad and the guys what, Bryn? What's happened?"

"Ahhh..."

"Bryn."

I wince at him. "I wasn't supposed to tell you. It's not a secret, you just need to rest, and we were worried you'd try to leave too soon."

"Bryn, tell me what's happened."

"Well, we can't get a hold of Cal and Killy."

"Shit."

"But they're on it."

He growls. "They got away, didn't they? Pugli and Mercado."

I sigh, nodding. "Unfortunately, yes."

"And your brother and Cal are missing."

"Along with, um, Story."

"Who's that?"

"Uncle Anselm and Aunt Selah's daughter. Well, she's Selah's daughter, but Anslem adopted her."

"And she's missing, too?" He thuds his head backward against the bed. "And I'm stuck here."

"But Rush, baby, Cal and Killy know how to take care of themselves. They both have the same training as I do. Story, too. Story maybe even more so than Cal, Killy, and me. And now it's not just dad and the uncles out there, it's the Broken Arrows, too."

"What about RMI?"

"Oh, well, they had another case come in, but, they're on call if we need them." I rest my hand on his thigh again. "So you just focus on getting better."

His eyes fix on my hand. "How much better do I need to get?"

I glance at the door, then at him. "Rush, not here."

"I can't think of any better medicine than you," he murmurs.

I sigh. "Trust me, I need some of your medicine just as bad. It's been a very long time since we were well and truly alone." I thread my fingers with his. "So your motivation to listen to the doctors is me, okay? Because I need you, but I won't risk your recovery."

He closes his eyes with a pissed-off groan. "It might be weeks yet before I'm released, Bryn. How'm I meant to survive all that time without you? My poor balls will explode."

I laugh. "Poor baby." I lean close and whisper in his ear. "If you're very, *very* good for the doctors, maybe I'll see what I can do to help you out."

He looks at me, eyes glinting with mischief. "Maybe we'll help each other out."

"Rush, you're on supplemental oxygen. Vigorous exercise is definitely a no-no."

He smirks. "Doin' a bit of wiggling with my fingers don't exactly count as vigorous exercise, I don't think."

My face heats—and my belly. And certain southern locales. "Rush, don't be ridiculous."

He pats the space next to him where Eliza had been. "Come here, love."

"Fine."

I round the foot of the bed to his other side, carefully moving the various cords and tubes and wires so I don't lay on, pinch, or dislodge anything, and then settle in cautiously against his side. I rest my cheek on his shoulder, careful to make sure I'm not putting pressure on his chest.

"Okay?" I ask.

He sighs happily. "Be better if you were naked and I was inside you, but this'll do for now, I guess."

I laugh. "I'd rather you be inside me, too, honey. But I'm not going anywhere. Get better and I promise you, we'll spend at least a week fucking like jackrabbits."

He doesn't respond as I'd expected. He kisses my forehead the way he did Eliza's—tenderly, lovingly. "Sweetheart, I'll do so much more than just fuck you." He puts his lips to my ear. "I'll make love to you until you can't take anymore. It'll be sweet and soft, and it'll be hard and fast, and everything in between."

"Promise?" I whisper.

"Promise."

20

LOVED, ACCEPTED, UNDERSTOOD, SEEN

It's the longest, slowest, most infuriating recovery of my life. I won't bore you with the details, but it very much sucked. Definitely don't go getting shot in the lungs. The doctors don't exactly use the word "miracle" in reference to the fact that I survived the damage done to me, but it was definitely on the more unlikely side of things. So I suppose I should be grateful to even be alive, let alone back on my feet. Yeah, I still have to drag a stupid oxygen cannister around on those stupid wheely guys, and the cord gets tangled on things, and it's all very annoying. But I've been assured that in time, with patience and hard work, I'll get off the oxygen. It'll take months more before I'm able to start the much longer road to returning to operational fitness, which is purely maddening.

Not being able to get out there and help the guys look for Killy, Cal, and Story is almost harder than the recovery. Especially because Pugli and Mercado are still out there, alive, unpunished, and perpetrating evil upon the world.

Since I can't get out there, I've convinced the doctors that I can leave the hospital, which is a win—I hate hospitals. Developments on the home front are afoot, as well. Richard and Evelyn have decided to sell their Southampton home; having it broken into the way it was cast an ugly shadow on it for them, and for Eliza. They all went back together while I was in hospital, and none of them could stay there. Even Eliza was shaken by it. And with my recovery slated to take months rather than weeks, and with my relationship with not just Bryn but her father and uncles growing by the day, it's been decided that Eliza and I will move onto the Harris compound in the Florida keys, which encompasses several islands, contains multiple individual residences, not to mention state-of-the-art medical, training, and fitness centers. Naturally, we'll be moving in with Bryn. Richard and Evelyn, after years of caring for Eliza, are taking some time out to travel the world. Little do they know, there will be A1S operatives shadowing them everywhere they go, just in case Pugli gets any funny ideas, and Valentine has taken to not-so-surreptitiously padding their bank account.

Which means Bryn, Eliza, and I have become our own little family. It doesn't do to think about it too closely or I'll start blubbing, as Eliza calls it, because I'm just so damned happy. I'm still wary of it—the happiness, that is. The peace I feel.

I'm accepted. I'm free. I'm loved; I love. In time,

I'll get back out into the field, running ops with A1S—firmly in the good guy camp once more.

For now, as frustrating as it may be to be physically limited, I'm content to savor this period of life. It's a transition. I'm letting go of the past. Putting aside the trauma of everything, the guilt.

Just…be happy. That's a hard thing to do, you know, especially if you've had to fight for everything your whole life.

Right now, for example, I'm watching the most beautiful sunrise I've ever seen.

Our new home is not large, but it's luxurious. Windows form walls on all three sides, which can be accordioned open to let the whole house get the fresh air coming off the water. Palm trees sway. Gulls and other sea birds cry and play. Water laps quietly in the channels on either side of us, and the open ocean spreads away in the distance.

Eliza had a sleepover with the women last night—a real girls night while I spent time learning some of what Lear does—he and his wife, Cuddy, have temporarily moved into the compound as well to provide additional security while the rest of the guys hunt down Pugli and work on locating the missing people.

Lear and I worked late into the night, tracking Killy and Cal's movements while Bryn and I were gallivanting about the globe—apparently, Pugli made plays against them not long after he realized who Bryn was, but either Pugli was successful in covering his tracks, or the boys have been successful at staying off-grid. Or a third option, but that brings us into the world of conjecture, and that's useless.

The point is, they've been AWOL for weeks. There've been clues here and there that they're still alive, but the hunt is on.

A sound brings me out of my thoughts—a crunch of feet in the sand.

A moment later, Bryn appears in the open doorway, the rising sun backlighting her. She's wrapped in a red, white, and pink floral knee-length kimono-type thing, her feet bare and dusted with wet sand. Her hair is loose and wild and windblown, her lovely, rich brown skin sun-kissed.

"Hey, you," I say, smiling at her. "How was the girls' night sleepover?"

She shrugs. "It was fun. Ren was there, too, of course, so we decided he could be an honorary girl for the night. He got his fingers and toes painted blue. He's a sweet kid." She leans against the doorframe, arms crossed over her chest, her gaze lingering on me—I'm in nothing but a pair of rather short shorts. "You?"

"I'll never be a hacker like Lear, but I'm a decent hand with simpler computer stuff."

"How are you feeling?"

"Sick of that fuckin' question," I growl. "Fine, mostly. Ready to get rid of *that* thing for good." I fling a hand at the oxygen canister. "I only need it now and then. It's an improvement."

She pushes off the frame and prowls toward me, gaze lingering hungrily on my chest, flicking to my bare shoulders, my abs, my arms. "Do you need the oxygen right now?"

"Not anymore." I pull the cannula out and toss it onto the canister, stop the flow, and move to push up out of the chair.

She reaches me first, pressing her hands onto my shoulders, pushing me back down onto the chair. "Ah-ah-ah," she scolds. "Stay where you are."

I relax into the oversized easy chair, letting her take over. "As you wish, my love."

She levers the footrest down. Braces her hands on the arms of the chair, nuzzling her nose and lips across my cheek, huffing a hot, teasing breath into my ear. "I've knotted this robe too tight," she breathes. "I need help untying it."

"Is that so?" I say, trailing my fingers up her thighs, lifting the hem of the robe as I go; I reach her hips, and discover she's not wearing any underwear.

"Get me naked, Rush," she whispers. "Now. I need you inside me."

A thousand responses, each dirtier than the last, rampage through my brain. My idiot tongue manages none of them. "God, please," I whisper, overcome by need, by desperation, by love.

I fumble at the tie of her robe—the little minx has barely knotted the thing at all. One tug and the knot comes apart, the edges of the robe draping open, revealing her nude, perfect body.

"God, Bryn, you're so fucking gorgeous." I ghost my hands over her shoulders, brush the robe off. It flutters to the floor in a pool, and the sun glistens off her lush brown skin, slivers and shines through her dense black curls. Her curves tease and tantalize, all trim hips and tight waist, strong thighs and heavy breasts. We never did find any time alone in the hospital, not even for any handsy sort of fun. Too many doctors and nurses coming and going, or Richard, Evelyn, and Eliza, or the A1S crew, or I was too fucking exhausted, honestly.

But now…

It's been fucking weeks since I've done more than chastely kiss her lips or cop a greedy feel as she curls up in the bed next to me.

I'm absolutely ravenous for her.

"You're pretty fine yourself, Mr. Bellamy." She pushes her hips between my thighs, rests her hands on my shoulders. "You should do stuff to me."

I grin up at her, letting my hands carve up the backs of her thighs, a groan escaping me as I fill my hands with the plump, taut perfection of her ass. "It's been so long I've forgotten what to do. You may have to teach me, Miss Harris."

She looms over me, hips pushed forward, back arched, chest high and proud, chin tucked to gaze down at me, hands in my hair. "Just keep touching me. Everywhere. Please, Rush."

Up her back, over her shoulders. Down her arms. Scoop the weight of her tits into my hands, pulse pounding at the glory of her body, my whole body thrumming with anticipation. With joy. With love.

"Like this?" I breathe, rolling my thumbs over her nipples.

She gasps. "Yes."

I lean forward and lift up, suckle her nipple into my mouth. "And that?"

"Perfect." Her fingers dimple my scalp, trail through my hair and down my nape. "Keep going."

I kiss her belly, her navel. Feather a finger down her seam—she's wet for me. Fuck, I need to taste her. "Turn around and bend over for me, Bryn."

"Rush, you—"

I cut her off. "I'm not an invalid, sweetheart. And if you think anything is going to stop me from tasting the sweet sugar of your tight little cunt, you're greatly mistaken. I've dreamed of the taste of you for weeks." I slip a finger inside her channel, coating my finger in her slick, wet essence. Withdraw my finger and pop it into my mouth. "Turn around. Bend over."

With a soft gasp at the loss of my finger inside her, Bryn obeys. Turns on a heel, watching me over her shoulder. Bends at the waist, feet wide apart, presenting her ass to me, her pussy open and begging, dripping desire. "Rush...please."

The only thing wrong with me is my lung capacity—I lose strength swiftly, still. Lose my breath. But my limbs function just fine. The hole in my arm is not much more than a scar, now. So it's not a hardship to move to my knees behind her. Her upside-down gaze locks on me between her legs. Her tits hang, swaying. I cup one, the other, just because. Shift closer. Trail my finger along her seam, teasing her.

She whimpers softly. "Rush, please. Don't tease me. It's been forever—I'm dying without you."

I can't bring myself to draw it out any longer. I

need her as much as she needs me—maybe more. Who knows? Who cares? We need each other, we need this.

So, I give it to her. I bury my face in her sweetness, groaning my delight at the taste of her. She cries out as my tongue slides inside her, shaking already. I palm her ass and devour her, then. No teasing, no playing around. Just eager, ravenous pleasure. I bring her to the edge of climax, and when she's there, I plunge my fingers inside her slick hot pussy and fuck her with them until she detonates, knees threatening to give out. She comes on a wild cry, and I take my fingers away—she mewls in protest, but I give her mouth instead, my lips suctioned around her thick little clit, tongue flicking. She comes again harder, and this time her knees do give out.

She collapses in front of me, dropping to her knees on the floor, panting. I bend over her, kiss her back, caress her ass. After a moment spent catching her breath, she turns.

Pushes me away. "Sit."

I slide up and back into the chair. She drags my shorts off and tosses them over a shoulder, a greedy grin lighting her face as she gathers my iron-hard cock in her hands. For a moment, she just toys with me, squeezing, twisting, rubbing the tip with a thumb—getting reacquainted, as it were.

"God, I love your cock," she whispers, nuzzling it affectionately.

"It loves you," I answer.

"Does it love this?" she asks, licking up the underside of it with the flat of her tongue.

"*Fuck* yes."

"How about this?" She wraps her lips around me, groaning softly as I fill her mouth—without preamble, she takes all of me, until her nose touches my belly.

"Ahh fuck, fuck, darling, yes. Yes. Fucking *love* that." I pull at her. "But that's not what I need."

She wipes at her mouth with the back of her wrist, and then crawls up onto the chair with me, straddling me. Her thighs wedge outside mine as she hovers over me, pressing me back into the chair, lining herself up against me.

"Rush?" she breathes.

"Yeah, Gorgeous?" I grip her ass, every part of me throbbing with anticipation of being inside her at long, long last.

"Say it." Her forehead touches mine. "Say it."

"I love you, Bryn Harris."

My tongue has barely touched the roof of my mouth to form the L sound before she sinks down onto me, a long, raw groan scraping out of her throat as I fill her. It's a long, delicious slide, my cock entering her to the hilt. Her ass meets my thighs, and her hands go to my face, clutching at me with desperation, shaking and shuddering as she lets herself stretch around me, panting quietly, each breath a soft whimper.

"Rush, I—"

I touch her lips. "Not yet, babe."

She looks at me in confusion. I just grin up at her, thrusting into her. Her eyes roll back in her head, and she claws her hands into my shoulders, lifting up, drawing me out through the stretched-thin lips of her pussy. Her mouth crashes against mine, and she slams down, hard. I grunt into her mouth, gasp as she smashes herself lower, grinding on me, taking me as deep as I can physically go. "RUSH!"

I nip her lower lip. "Not yet, babe."

I thrust.

She cries out, head tossed back, her whole body spasming. I dig a hand into her hair, tug her head back, kiss her throat. Fuck into her again, hard.

"Touch yourself, my love," I order.

Her fingers go immediately to her pussy, one hand spreading her folds apart, the other pressing circling fingers her to her clit. Her eyes roll back in her head, fluttering as another climax ripples through her.

"Open your eyes, Bryn," I say. "Watch us. Watch me fuck you."

Her eyes fly wide, fix on our union—she swipes at her clit with increasing speed as we watch my cock slide through her, fill her, withdraw glistening wetly, plunge back in.

"Rush," she whimpers. "I'm—oh god, oh god, I'm coming, Rush. Oh my fucking god I'm coming so hard."

"Now, Bryn. Now say it."

"Come with me, Rush. Come first. Come with me first."

That's all it takes—her wish is my command. I drive into her and let go, pulling her down onto me as I give in to my orgasm. "Bryn!" It's all I can manage, my breath gone, dizziness washing through as my release empties me utterly.

She leans forward, hunching over me with her hips flying, grinding, taking me and taking me and taking me, hands clawed into the back of my head as she comes around me. "I love you, Rush," she whispers as we come together in perfect synchronization. "Oh god, I love you. I love you so fucking much."

She rocks on me until I start to go soft, and then finally sits back on my thighs, brown eyes liquid with pleasure, hot with passion, delirious with love.

Which is when she notices that I'm…well, somewhat less than able to breathe properly.

"Ohmigod, Rush!" She leans over the side of the chair, snags the cannula, and fits it onto me, and then starts the flow. I groan in relief as the cool oxygen rushes into my system.

"Leave it on, next time, Macho Man," she says, caressing my cheek. She starts to move off me. "I must be crushing you."

I hold her in place. "You're perfect."

"Why didn't you say you couldn't breathe?"

"Felt too good to stop."

"Your lips were blue!"

"Worth it."

She laughs, shakes her head. "You're incorrigible. Next time, the cannula stays on."

"As you wish, my love."

We stay like that for a while, her on my lap in the chair, salt breeze fluttering her hair, my hands trailing over her silky brown skin, her lips pressing kisses to my shoulder, my throat, my cheek, my lips.

At some point, that turns to kissing. Kissing turns to making out. And then I'm hard and she's welcoming me inside her once again, and this time it's slow and soft, and there are no commands, just love made in the soft light of sunrise, her gasps and my growls a song without words.

Later, after we've showered, Cuddy and Kyrie bring Eliza and Ren over, and the kids play in the water.

It feels like a lifetime ago that I was fielding a call from Pugli and heading to Berlin.

Just goes to show you that your life can change in an instant. Take a job you know is wrong, and somehow, you end up here—loved, accepted, understood, seen.

Forgiven.

Changed.

Definitely changed.

A couple of days later, Bryn, Eliza, and I are lounging in the main house with Layla Harris—and I see where Bryn got a lot of her personality from, now—when Layla's phone rings.

"Nicky?" she answers, voice shaky—every call could be the call saying they've found them. She listens for a few moments, her expression unreadable. "Okay, got it. Love you too."

She hangs up, tosses the phone aside, rakes her fingers through her long, curly black hair, so much like Bryn's.

"Mom?" Bryn asks. "What is it? What'd he say?"

She looks at Bryn. "They found a car abandoned in a parking lot at an airport in Belgium. Lear was able to find security footage showing that Killy and Story were alive, together, and in that car as of forty-eight hours ago."

"Belgium?" Bryn asks. "And…Killian and Story are *together*? I thought Story was in Minnesota, doing her residency at Abbot?"

"Well, we know she disappeared around the same time as the boys, but whoever it was that took them covered their tracks well. Assuming the boys were taken, that is. If someone went after them, it wouldn't shock me if they went off-grid. I don't know. I just think that there's direct evidence that Killy is alive."

"And Cal?" Bryn asks.

She shakes her head. "Nothing yet. Nothing new, at least. We know he was still in Zermatt with Killy two and a half weeks ago. Which about when Story vanished."

"How are Anselm and Selah?" Bryn asks.

Layla shrugs. "Selah is out of her mind with worry. But Anselm is out there looking. Everyone is. And you have to remember, Story was raised by Anselm. She's no helpless little lamb."

This gets a laugh out of me. "No one in this great big group of nutters is a helpless little lamb," I say. "You'd think those assholes would learn."

Layla shrugs. "You'd think. But I have a feeling this is almost over. With our guys and those Broken Arrows involved, it's only a matter of time before both Pugli and Mercado are found and killed."

Bryn huffs. "Can't be soon enough." She glances at her mother. "Do you think Killy and Story are…?"

Layla snickers. "I mean, if you look at our track record, it'd be weird if they weren't."

"I guess you're right," Bryn says. "I just worry about Killian."

Layla sighs. "I do too, sweetie. But your brother has steel in him. More than I think you give him credit for. And if there's a beautiful girl to protect?"

Bryn chuckles. "Well, Story is certainly beautiful, that's for sure. She's just so *damned...regal*. I feel like a putzy commoner in the presence of a queen whenever we hang out."

Layla sighs again. "I know Killy can take care of himself. So can Cal. So can Story, for that matter. But he's my son. I can't help worrying."

"If he's anything like you, Bryn, or Harris, he'll be just fine," I say. "He'll come out on top."

EPILOGUE PART 1

GLAD IT'S YOU

My coffee has long since gone cold. That's not new, though—when I'm working, I often misplace my coffee, find it, and drink it lukewarm or cold. This coffee, however, is too cold even for me to drink. I push it away out of reach so I don't keep grabbing it as I finish paperwork.

The office is dead silent, except for the soft hiss of the A/C from the vents overhead; *office* is a bit of a misnomer, really; it's more of a broom closet with a desk and chair, but it's an oasis of calm and quiet, a place to get away from the bustle and noise and chaos of the ER.

I hate paperwork. I hate charting. I hate bullshit admin work. What I love is the medicine. The chaos. The rush. The challenge of injury or illness. Yes, the patients are people—I have an impeccable bedside manner, thank you very much. But really, deep down, it's the rush and the challenge that drive me.

I became an ER nurse because of Mom. She'd come home after a long shift and even though I could see the exhaustion in her eyes, she'd spend time with me. Talk to me. Watch my favorite movies with me. Make me food. Sometimes even before changing out of her scrubs.

And then along came Anselm—Papa. I was seven when I met him, that awful, terrifying night when the bad guys took Mom. But yet despite all that happened, Anselm kept me safe. I'm sure you've heard the stories by now, or read about them, or seen the various made-for-streaming film versions that crop up every now and then, some more accurate than others, so I won't bore you with the details. Suffice it to say, Mom, Anselm, and I became a family. Anselm came to live with us in Minneapolis. They never legally married, so my last name is still Binyamin, like Mom's. Not that I would've minded taking Selm's last name, See. Story See would have been a pretty damn cool name, honestly. Although, it's pronounced "Zay" instead of the American English "see".

As a father, Anselm was…is…loving, supportive, compassionate, firm, quiet. He never once raised his voice to me, not even when I, in a fit of irrational, teenage angst, stole Mom's car, went on a 100-mile joyride, ran out of gas on a deserted two-lane highway in the middle of absolutely nowhere, and had to be rescued. At three in the morning. When he'd just returned, quite literally mere hours before, from a three-day op with A1S during which he'd managed to sleep a grand total of forty-five minutes. He'd arrived at the car, filled it with fuel from a dented, rusty, ancient old red jerry can that probably saw action in WW2, wrapped me in a long, comforting hug, kissed my forehead, and said in a very quiet, incredibly soft, and gut-wrenchingly disappointed voice, "Do not do this again, please, *liebchen*."

And then he left. My punishment, the only consequence delivered for my reckless behavior by him or Mom, was that statement, those seven words. And the long, agonizing drive home alone in which to think about what I'd done, and the crushing disappointment in his voice.

That was my one act of teenage rebellion. I couldn't stomach the thought of disappointing my beloved Selm that way ever again.

He loves Mom fiercely but quietly, as is his way. I saw it day in and day out. The flipside was how Mom loved him—she defended his freedom to be himself with the same ferocity as he protected her and took care of her. He's a wild thing, my Selm, my father. A creature of shadows and darkness and the hunt. Houses, buildings, cities, streets, these things confine him, make him restless. He can only stomach civilization for a few weeks before he needs time in the wilderness to recharge. And Mom never, ever begrudged him that, even though I knew she missed him deeply when he was gone. His work, too, was dangerous. It kept him away for days at a time, during which we wouldn't hear from him at all. Unlike most children of men who do dangerous jobs, I was always intensely aware of the danger he was in every time he went on an op. How could I not be? I'd been through hell with him. I watched him end a man's life with a knife at seven years old, but of course, that was far less traumatizing than watching my biological parents get gunned down by a shooter in a mall at five years old.

My favorite memories of Anselm are of the times I got to go into the wilderness with him. He began taking me with him on his days-long treks when I was ten. I remember the first one with vivid clarity. It was April. There was still snow in places, but during the day, it still got warm enough to not need a jacket. He woke me up at five in the morning, made me pancakes, and let me drink a cup of coffee with him—heavily cut with chocolate milk, of course. He gave me a special backpack—a weathered, battered leather rucksack, well-oiled, older than my imagination could fathom. Only later would he tell me it was the same backpack his own father had given him as a boy. He showed me how to roll my clothes up into neat, tight packages. He gave me a brand new canteen, a six-inch fixed blade survival knife, a compass, and a Zippo lighter.

We got into his car and drove away in the lightening gray of dawn. He'd already discussed this with Mom, of course, not that that ever crossed my mind. If Anselm said let's go, I went, no questions asked. We drove and drove—north into Canada, west toward British Columbia. We parked at the end of a barely visible two-track path in the foothills, shouldered our packs, and walked into the mountains. We spent two weeks out there, just the two of us, with nothing more than our bags, knives, and canteens. He brought no food of any kind. In fact, the only concession he did allow was water purification tablets. He taught me how to survive with nothing but my wits, courage, and determination. He taught me orienteering, how to read a topographical map, how to make a fire, how to create shelter, how to find water and purify it, which plants I could eat and which would kill me, which would help with various ailments, which would soak up blood if I was to get cut, or since I'm a woman, deal with my periods when out in the wilderness. He taught me to stalk-hunt with a bow—and how to make one from nothing with only my knife. How to skin a carcass. How to defend myself if I'm attacked or threatened by a bear, wolf, coyote, mountain lion…or that most dangerous of predators, man. Yes, he taught me to fight with my bare hands and feet, with a knife, with a rifle, with a handgun. With a bow. With a spear.

By the time I was sixteen, I was a thoroughly competent outdoorswoman, capable of being left absolutely anywhere on the planet with nothing more than basic survival gear, and I could make it home. He also taught me how to survive if I'm left out there with nothing. And I have. He drove me out into the wilderness of Michigan's Upper Peninsula and left me hundreds of miles from anything with nothing more than the clothes on my back.

I loved every second of it.

To this day, I keep up those skills. Every couple months, I pack that leather bag and go exploring the way Anselm taught me. Just go. No destination, no purpose, just go and just be.

I'm finishing up the last bit of paperwork when my

pager goes off—there was an MVC on the 35, multiple casualties inbound.

Fuck it, I'll need the caffeine—I toss the cold, bitter coffee back in three swallows, chucking the empty cup in the small wire basket under the desk on my way out.

It's go time.

I hustle to the ER, arriving just as the first victims are wheeled in by the medics, and then I sink into the familiar flow of emergency medicine.

It's the only career I've ever even considered—other than out in the wilderness, the ER is where I'm most comfortable. My life has been shaped by trauma, defined by violence. It's just where I live. I move and breathe and exist in the chaos.

My current victim is a twenty-year-old female with an open femur break, multiple contusions and lacerations, and most concerning, free fluid in the belly from an internal injury. She's screaming in agony despite having received the max dose of fentanyl in the field, thrashing and howling. I FAST her belly and find the injury, but she's thrashing too wildly to be able to set her leg.

I grab her face with my bloody-gloved hands and fix her pain- and fear-maddened eyes. "Jen!" I shout. "Jen. Look at me. Look at me."

Her eyes find mine, panicking, frantic. "Jason—Jason—where's Jason? Jason!"

I scan the ER and see Tammy and Mario working on a young male with a massive piece of glass in his belly—I lock eyes with Mario, who gives me a shake of his head. Fuck.

I go back to Jen. "They're doing everything they can for Jason, but you need to stop moving. You can scream as loud as you want, but you have to hold still for me so I can set your leg."

She grits her teeth, nodding. Reaches blindly for someone's hand to hold as I line up at her foot and prepare to set her femur.

Kelly, the charge nurse, takes Jen's hands. "Squeeze my hands, honey. We've got you." She looks at me, nodding her head in a three-count.

In synch with her, I grab hold of Jen's leg, hold her frantic eyes. "Ready? On three. One…two…*THREE*." I pull her fractured leg straight away from her, and the jagged pink-white spur of bone slips back within the sheath of flesh and muscle. A bedside X-ray shows that it's correctly set and ready for ortho to cast it, but first, we have to get her to surgery to stop the internal bleeding.

I leave Kelly to arrange for Jen's surgery and take the next incoming patient—a sixty-year-old male with a closed skull fracture, GCS 6.

And so goes the shift—another two-car collision, a stab victim, several GSWs, an intentional opiate overdose. I lose a GSW victim—he'd simply lost too much blood, and we couldn't stem the bleeding in time, despite the field medic's heroic attempts en route.

By the end of my shift at eight the following morning, I've been on my feet without a break for sixteen hours, sans the forty-five minutes I spent in that broom closet doing paperwork.

I'm thoroughly exhausted and ready to get home,

shower, and crash. I trudge out of the ER on aching feet, my brain racing with things I could've, should've done differently. How I could've saved Gus, the GSW who died. I reach my car after what feels like an hour of walking, even though I only parked on the second level of the garage. Unlock the doors and slide behind the wheel. Let out a long sigh of relief—I absolutely love what I do, but it's exhausting, physically, mentally, and emotionally, especially these forty-eight or seventy-two hours on call shifts spent at the hospital, grabbing shut-eye when and where you can, living on old coffee and vending machine garbage.

It's a scent that catches my notice, first. Body odor and old cigarette smoke.

I don't smoke, and while I may smell like three-day-old ass at the moment, this is not my scent. Warning bells go off in my head, and I'm already reaching into my purse for my bear spray. Anselm drilled a lot of lessons into me over the years, but the one he impressed on me as being the most important was to trust my gut. If something *feels* off, believe yourself and act *immediately*. Never second-guess, never hesitate.

I don't.

I squirt the bear spray over my shoulder blindly, and I'm rewarded by a howl of masculine rage and pain. A heavy blow from a fist crashes into my temple, sending white sparks dancing across my vision. My sparring sessions with Anselm prove their worth, then, because I know how to take that punch and keep fighting despite the dizziness. I spray wildly into the rear seat; my attacker bats at my hand, knocking the bottle out of my grip. I lash out with my fist, then catch flesh and bone with a satisfying crunch, but it's not enough. I twist in the seat for a better angle, catch a glimpse of furious pale blue eyes and angular features, and then something sharp punctures the side of my neck. I still get off a good punch though, despite the blackness flooding my system, the weakness spreading through me.

I feel myself slumping. Drowsing, being dragged under.

"She fights like animal," I hear a heavily accented male voice say. "But she is out."

Not quite, fucker.

My phone is in the back pocket of my scrub bottoms. With the last of my strength, my sight fading, I work it out and get off a text to Anselm—911. I hear my phone hit the floor with a thump.

"Fuck," my attacker mutters.

I fight my left foot up, up, off the floor. Crush it down onto my phone's screen so he can't unsend it.

The darkness wins, then.

Consciousness returns in fragments, slowly. First, there's pain, a headache infinitely worse than my worst hangover: that time, Rin, Bryn, Cal, Killy, and I got wasted together on Cal's parents' yacht down in the Caribbean, the summer I finished med school. For a long while, I just languished in the sharp throbbing agony occupying my skull.

And then I become aware of thirst—cotton-mouth times a billion

The need to urinate, badly, is next.

I observe all this with clinical detachment and put together a theory: I've been drugged and have spent a long time unconscious.

Memory is next. Work—the MVC. Losing Gus—I remember the names of every patient I've ever lost; they're written in a pocket-sized Moleskine notebook I keep in my purse. What else do I remember? Finishing my shift. Going to my car. Blue eyes. Fighting. I sent a text to Selm. I can't relax, because I know I'll have to get myself out of this, but I also know that Anselm See will tear the Earth apart with his bare hands to bring me home safely. I just have to stay alive until then.

I do keep tabs on what's happening with everyone—the A1S world is its own small, insular community. We take care of our own. So I know that Bryn has been through hell, and I know Cal and Killy are AWOL and presumed kidnapped. Selm called me to tell me to keep watch and be prepared for anything, which is when I put that bear spray in my purse. Fat lot of good it did. My assumption is that I've been kidnapped by the same people who took Bryn, as retaliation of some sort. And, to be perfectly honest, I'm somewhat surprised it took this long for A1S enemies to come after me.

It's why I've kept up with my self-defense training, why I spend several hours a week at the range, keeping my weapons skills current.

I crack an eyelid, but there's nothing to see but darkness. There are other sensations to gain clues from, however. A subtle motion—side-to-side rocking, a dip, a lift. I'm on a boat. What else? I work my limbs: I'm not shackled or otherwise restrained. I'm clothed—in my scrubs, still. My Apple watch is still on the inside of my wrist, and I tap the screen to wake it up—the dim whitish glow illuminates a tiny patch of my surroundings; it's of little use, though, as it's a wifi-only model. Dull reddish metal behind me and underfoot. I tap a fingernail against the wall at my back, and it thunks hollowly. I'm in a container, then. The air is somewhat fresh, however, which means there must be a vent of some kind, somewhere.

"Who's there?" A male voice pierces the thick black silence. A familiar one, at that.

My heart pounds frantically, seared with hope and relief and worry and fear. "It's Story," I murmur, my throat on fire with thirst, my voice raspy.

I hear movement. "Where?"

I tap on the floor. "Here."

"Keep doing that. I'll find you."

I tap, tap, tap until the shuffling is near, and then I reach out. My hand finds rough denim. A hard thigh muscle. A firm abdomen covered by a thin T-shirt.

"Got you," he says, his hand finding mine. He chokes, then. "Story? Is that really you?"

"Killian?"

He laughs, a half-crazed bark of desperation. "Story. I hate that you're here, but I'm also glad it's you."

"You've been in here the whole time?" I ask.

"Yeah. They send in food and water once a day.

There's a bucket in the corner over there for using the bathroom." He moves my hand and points.

"Who is it? Who has us?"

"Fuck if I know." A pause. "Did they…they didn't hurt you? Or…or anything?"

"No, Killy. I mean, I fought, but no. A decent punch to the temple, but I'm fine. They didn't do…anything else. That I know of, at least. I'm dressed and nothing hurts."

"At least there's that." He squeezes my hand.

"They fucked up, though," I say.

"Oh? How?" he asks.

I grin into the blackness, squeezing his hand back. "They put *us* together. And they have *no idea* who they've kidnapped."

He laughs. "I've been biding my time. We're on a fucking giant ass boat in the middle of the ocean—we were in port somewhere in Europe when they put me in here, and we've been at sea ever since. They brought you aboard via helicopter—I heard it."

"How long ago was that?"

"Barely an hour."

"No indication as to what they want?"

"To fuck with our parents, I assume."

Silence.

"Story?"

"Yeah, Killy?"

"I'm really, really glad it's you. I hope you understand what I mean by that."

I laugh. "I do. I'm glad it's you, too."

I've always been fond of Killy. He's a few years

younger than me, but of all the A1S kids, he and I were always closest. Just friends, since we were somewhat raised together, but in the last few years I've become more and more aware of him as a male to whom I'm not actually related. He's seriously hot, dryly funny, competent, and kind. Cal has always been more like Uncle Val—quiet, reserved, watchful. Killy is a mix of his parents, whereas Bryn is her mother's spitfire, hell-on-wheels twin in every way. Killy has more of his father in him, a bit more cautious, a bit less reckless, a lot less hot-tempered. The funny thing is, Cal is the daredevil of the boys. Killy is always down to do whatever Cal does, but it's always Cal's idea. Killy just won't be left behind and he won't be the one to wimp out on the fun.

So now I'm locked in a container on a cargo ship in the middle of the ocean with Killian Harris.

No one knows where we are. People are gonna be looking, but in the immediate future, no one is coming to save us.

Something tells me this shit has just started to get interesting.

EPILOGUE PART 2

LA VÍBORA HAS COME FOR BLOOD

An irritated Sophia de Silva is a dangerous creature, indeed. In her current mood—seething with an icy, venomous, murderous rage—even I dare not breathe too loudly.

It has been forty-eight hours since we learned of Beatriz's murder, and Sophia's fury has not relented. No, if anything, it has only fermented, crystallized into a vengeful, bloodthirsty emotion so potent there is no single word for it in any language.

Hate, fury, rage, anger, these do not fully encapsulate the atomic violence radiating from her.

I fear no man, but right now, I am more than a little afraid of Sophia.

Our stolen car—a rattling, smelly, jouncing rustbucket with an anemic engine, no air conditioning, no radio, no suspension, and no muffler—wheezes as it struggles up the hill…if you can even call this slight incline a hill.

Sweating, Sophia reaches once more for the A/C controls, even though she's prodded, smacked, switched on and off, and verbally berated it in English, Portuguese, and Spanish countless times in the last sixteen hours.

Finally, with a wordless snarl of rage, she pulls out her Beretta and fires a single shot into the A/C controls.

"Sophia!" I snap, rubbing at my ringing right ear. "For fuck's sake!"

"There was no reason to leave my car behind, Lorenzo." She has her pistol out, still, and I'm worried that if I don't carefully consider each word I speak, she very well might just shoot me. "You could not have stolen a worse vehicle. I'd rather take a bus than spend another moment in this sweltering death trap."

"Your Mercedes, as excellent as it is, was far too conspicuous," I answer. "I'll trade us up at the next opportunity."

She only glares at me for a moment and then turns her gaze out the window. For a long time, she's silent, seething, plotting, scheming.

"She harmed no one," she says, eventually—her first words on the subject of poor, innocent, murdered Beatriz. "Her only crime was that of love."

"I know," I murmur. "At least we know Reninho is safe."

"Without his mother. What am I meant to say, Lorenzo? What am I meant to do? After I deal with Mercado, what then?" For a moment, I'm worried she's about to cry, which is something I am frightfully ill-equipped to deal with.

A crying Sophia is akin to…god, I don't even know. I can more easily imagine a cobra weeping as Sophia.

Not that she doesn't feel emotions—she's no psychopath or sociopath. She just keeps them very, very well hidden from the world. She deals with such strong emotions only when alone.

Once, she trusted me with her feelings. Now, however, our reunion is still too fresh for her to allow me so close to her most intimate self.

She really isn't Sophia anymore. Especially now. This is Inez, the cold, calculated, precise, emotionless killer, her current mood notwithstanding.

I see glimpses of my Sophia in there, though.

"We have to find him, Lorenzo," she whispers. "I will kill Mercado with my bare hands, or I'll die trying. Do you hear me? I swear it on Beatriz's immortal soul. I swear it on Santa Maria." There was a hint of her old accent in there—faint, but present.

"I know. We're hunting him, Sophia. We'll find him. We'll get him."

"Not fast enough."

"I know."

"Stop saying that!" she growls. "I know, I know. Find something else to say."

I say nothing—it's safest.

We crossed the border into Mexico hours ago. A contact in the NIC—Mexico's version of the CIA—placed Mercado somewhere in Central Mexico. This intel is rather thin, however, as it is based more on the movement of Mercado's entourage than his movements. Basically, it's a guess. But it's all we have to go on, so we are on our way to the coordinates my associate at the NIC gave me.

We still have a long way to go.

We have found ourselves in Fresnillo, in the Mexican state of Zacatecas. It's a silver mining town, but lately it has become something of a hub for organized crime. In other words, a perfect place for Mercado to hide in plain sight.

We're at a cafe in Fresnillo's Centro area, sipping sparkling water from sweating bottles. A fan lazily stirs the air overhead, and a bored waitress idly scrolls on her phone with a basket of silverware and a stack of paper napkins in front of her, which she ignores.

On the opposite side of the street is a trucking company's garage, which is our focus. In addition to the usual, normal traffic coming and going from the fenced-in lot, there's a steady influx of old pickups, battered SUVs, and the occasional rattling sedan. Each of these vehicles is packed with armed men. They arrive, park, the men disgorge, and then…nothing. It's very curious.

"What do you think they're doing?" I ask Sophia in Portuguese, rather than Spanish.

She shrugs. "Sucking each other's dicks, I don't

know. I don't care. I only care about ripping Rafael's spleen out of his body with my fucking fingers."

"At least thirty men have arrived in the last hour, by my count," I say, ignoring her outburst.

"Wonderful."

I sigh. "Sophia." She ignores me. "Inez."

This gets me a withering stare. "*What*, Lorenzo?"

"Even if he is in that building, with that many of his men, we can't do anything."

She reaches into the backpack at her feet and withdraws a frag grenade. "Sure, we can."

I reach across the table and push her hand down. "Jesus fucking *Christ*, Sophia," I snap in English. "Put that fucking thing away. Do you want to get us arrested? Because I've been in a Mexican prison. I do *not* recommend it."

She puts it away—slowly, laconically. She glances at me with idle curiosity. "You have? When? Why?"

"It is a long story. I was undercover and things… went sideways. I spent a month there before my people could get me out." I shake my head. "I really do not fancy another stay."

She nods, the topic already dismissed. When yet another Toyota pickup enters the yard and disgorges four more men with assault rifles, Sophia shakes her head, hissing a serpentine sound of irritated fury. "Fuck this. You sit here and watch if you like. I'm done playing fucking games." This is in English, as well.

"Sophia, wait," I say, grabbing her wrist.

Mistake.

Before I can so much as blink, there's a blur of silver and a snick of metal, and a butterfly knife has blossomed open, the blade resting at my throat, drawing a spot of blood.

She leans over the table, spitting her words in a savage whisper. "You are with me or you are against me. Do as you wish, Lorenzo. But do *not* think you can tell me what to fucking do."

"I'm not, Sophia. I just—"

She pockets the blade as swiftly as she produced it. "Stay here or come with me. I don't give a fuck. I'm going, and I'm getting answers."

"There must be nearly forty men in there, at minimum."

Her grin is downright barbaric. "Excellent. At least one of them will have information."

She snags her backpack and strides out of the cafe.

Fuck.

This is bad.

Sophia Bruna Santos de Silva on the warpath is a very, very, very bad thing for anyone in her blast radius. There is no rationality left in her. Only a thirst for death, havoc, vengeance, and blood.

As tempting as it is to sit here and watch the fireworks, I cannot do that. I love Sophia, and so, I must go.

But I don't like this.

At fucking all.

As it is, I'm nearly too late. By the time I toss some cash on the table for the meal we just finished and head for the car, she's already donned her vest, filled her pockets with magazines and grenades, and is marching with singular, determined focus in a beeline for the trucking lot.

Fuck, fuck, fuck.

Hurrying, now, I shrug into my own vest, clip my MP5 to the vest, add some mags and flashbangs—since it seems she's got us covered on the grenade territory—and jog after her.

CRACKCRACKCRACK!

She's in the lot, MP5 to her shoulder, peppering the windshield of a sedan as it enters the lot after her.

Red paints the interior, and the car lurches to a halt for a split second, and then the horn blares and the car bolts forward in an arc as the dead driver slumps forward against the wheel, foot burying the pedal. It smashes into a parked trailer in a shattering of glass, wedging beneath the trailer; if any of the occupants survived her shots, they're dead now.

There's shouting from inside the warehouse, an overlapping chorus of voices all yelling competing orders.

She's kicked the hornet's nest, it would seem.

I charge the MP5, reposition the spare mags for easier access, check my sidearm's positioning, and follow Sophia toward the warehouse.

There's no strategy to her attack. She marches up the rickety wooden steps leading to the loading platform, the shadows of the platform all but swallowing her trim, black-clad figure. I jog after her, but I'm a good twenty yards behind her.

She kicks in the door and fires a burst into the opening. There's a scream, and a barrage of gunfire, but as far as I can see, none of it comes even close to her.

She vanishes into the warehouse, then, and that's when all hell breaks loose.

La Víbora has come for blood.

ALSO BY
Jasinda Wilder

Visit me at my website: **www.jasindawilder.com**
Email me: **jasindawilder@gmail.com**

If you enjoyed this book, you can help others enjoy it as well by recommending it to friends and family, or by mentioning it in reading and discussion groups and online forums. You can also review it on the site from which you purchased it. But, whether you recommend it to anyone else or not, thank you *so much* for taking the time to read my book! Your support means the world to me!

My other titles:

Forbidden Fruit

Wild Ride: Biker Billionaire

Delilah's Diary

Big Girls Do It:
Big Girls Do It
Married
On Christmas
Pregnant
Rock Stars Do It
Big Love Abroad

The Falling Series:
Falling Into You
Falling Into Us
Falling Under
Falling Away
Falling for Colton
The Ever Trilogy:
Forever & Always
After Forever
Saving Forever

From the world of *Wounded*:
Wounded
Captured

From the world of *Stripped*:
Stripped
Trashed

From the world of *Alpha*:
Alpha
Beta
Omega
Harris: Alpha One Security Book 1
Thresh: Alpha One Security Book 2
Duke: Alpha One Security Book 3
Puck: Alpha One Security Book 4
Lear: Alpha One Security Book 5
Anselm: Alpha One Security Book 6
Sigma
Gamma

The Houri Legends:
Jack and Djinn
Djinn and Tonic

The Madame X Series:
Madame X
Exposed
Exiled

The Black Room (With Jade London)

The One Series
The Long Way Home
Where the Heart Is
There's No Place Like Home

Badd Brothers:
*Badd Motherf*cker*
Badd Ass
Badd to the Bone
Good Girl Gone Badd
Badd Luck
Badd Mojo
Big Badd Wolf
Badd Boy
Badd Kitty
Badd Business
Badd Medicine
Badd Daddy

Goode Girls:
For a Goode Time Call...
Not So Goode
Goode To Be Bad
A Real Goode Time
Goode Vibrations

Dad Bod Contracting:
Hammered
Drilled
Nailed
Screwed

Fifty States of Love:
Pregnant in Pennsylvania
Cowboy in Colorado
Married in Michigan
Christmas in Connecticut

Billionaire Baby Club:
Lizzy Goes Brains Over Braun
Autumn Rolls a Seven
Laurel's Bright Idea

Club Sin:
Rev
Kane
Chance
Silas
Saxon
Solomon

Blood Heir:
Blood Heir
Blood Bonds
Blood Reign
Blood Bonds

Three Rivers:
Into the Light

Standalone titles:
Yours
The Cabin
The Parent Trap
Wish Upon A Star
Big Hose

Non-Fiction titles:
You Can Do It
You Can Do It: Strength
You Can Do It: Fasting

Jack Wilder Titles:
The Missionary

JJ Wilder Titles:
Ark

To be informed of new releases, special offers, and other Jasinda news, sign up for Jasinda's email newsletter.

Printed in Dunstable, United Kingdom